EAGLES

Also by Ray Rosenbaum

FALCONS
HAWKS
CONDORS

EAGLES

Ray Rosenbaum

LYFORD
Books

The characters in this novel are fictitious. Any characters (except histori-
cal figures) resembling actual persons, living or dead, are purely coinci-
dental. The dialogue and specific incidents described in the novel are
products of the author's imagination and creativity. They should not be
construed as real.

Copyright © 1996 by Ray Rosenbaum

LYFORD Books
Published by Presidio Press
505 B San Marin Dr., Suite 300
Novato, CA 94945-1340

Library of Congress Cataloging-in-Publication Data

Rosenbaum, Ray, 1923–
  Eagles / Ray Rosenbaum.
      p.   cm.
  ISBN 0-89141-557-2 (hardcover)
  1.Korean War, 1950–1953—Fiction. 2. Air pilots—Korea—Fiction.
  I. Title
  PS3568.077E25   1996
  813'.54—dc20   95-49293
                                                          CIP

Printed in the United States of America

For my sister, Mabel

EAGLES

1

30 June 1948
50 Miles West of Wright Field, Dayton, Ohio

Major Ross Colyer yawned and retuned a commercial broadcast station on the ADF set. He glanced at the instrument panel clock—another hour to go. The F-51's big Rolls-Royce Merlin engine rumbled contentedly at its minimum-cruise power setting. Not exactly the kind of flight testing he'd bargained for, he thought ruefully—boring holes in the sky slow-timing a new engine. The rangy, blond pilot squirmed to a more comfortable position in the plane's single bucket seat and thought: Oh, well, you're back on active duty and flying fighters—quit bitching.

The light colonel at ops, Babcock, had brushed aside his questions about the F-80 when Ross reported in. "We have six ahead of you waiting for checkouts," the balding, heavyset officer told him. "Two of our Shooting Stars are out of commission for parts, and the others are all flying profiles." He scanned Ross's Form 5 and his manner brightened. "But hey, am I ever glad to see you. Look at that '51 time. Maintenance has been on my back all week for a pilot. They have two '51s just out of engine change, and all our Mustang pilots are over in Flight Test farting around with the F-82. I'll give you a checkout this afternoon—you can do your first maintenance test hop tomorrow morning."

The minute hand passed twelve, and Ross dutifully recorded coolant temperature, oil temperature and pressure, and a host of other instrument readings on the pad strapped to his right leg. He reversed course and mentally computed an arrival back over the field—get there in time to add war emergency power, hold for two minutes, record instrument readings, then land. That brief bit of activity would be his only respite during the boring ordeal.

After that, it would be a ride to the BOQ, shower, change, and go to the club for a couple of drinks and dinner. The routine held little more appeal than a future of test-hopping airplanes coming out of major overhaul.

"You'll get your F-80 squadron," Colonel Cipolla had told him back at Langley. "But not right away. First we're sending you to Wright Field to finish your engineering degree. They have the new jets there for operational suitability testing, and you'll not only get to fly them, you'll help write the handbook."

When? Ross wondered.

Thoughts of Janet intruded, and his jaw muscles tightened. Apparently nobody here had heard the wartime housing shortage was over. Married less than a month, and he was living in bachelors' quarters while his new bride stayed in D.C.

"Ross, I can't risk our beautiful marriage living in some walk-up room with a cockroach-infested bath down the hall," she'd said. "I'd be a bitch. Why don't I keep my job and stay here until you get a permanent assignment? We *can* use the money, you know."

Piss on it, he snarled to himself. Cipolla's new air force—exciting, adventurous—was little better than the way he remembered wartime life in the States. He threw the Mustang into a series of snap rolls—prohibited during a test hop—to vent his frustration.

His headset crackled. A VHF transmission overrode the smooth strains of Tommy Dorsey. "Albatross Three, this is Wright Tower, over."

Ross jerked with a guilty start. Christ, had they seen that unauthorized maneuver?

"This is Albatross Three, Tower, go ahead."

"The highway patrol just called base ops to report a possible aircraft crash, Albatross Three, approximately thirty miles south of the field on a bearing of one-three-five. Colonel Babcock asks that you overfly the area and investigate. Can do, over?"

"Roger, Tower. I'm about fifty miles west right now, changing course. I should be over the area in roughly fifteen minutes."

"Roger, understand, Albatross Three. The colonel asks that you make a preliminary report by radio, over."

Ross rolled into a turn, set nose-down trim, and let the Mustang settle into a shallow dive. Details of the emerald- and dun-colored checkerboard beneath him started to emerge. Dark green cornfields formed a geometric mosaic with black squares of fallow ground, all bisected by arrow-straight roads. He made a quick mental calculation: He'd been holding an airspeed of one hundred eighty miles per hour—fifteen minutes at three miles per minute equaled forty-five miles—should be in the vicinity. While scanning the horizon, a plume of dark-gray smoke spiraling lazily upward caught his eye. Ross nosed over and leveled at five hundred feet.

He'd overflown crash sites before. It was always a sobering experience, a grim reminder that men and machines are fallible. A routine flight through serene skies was transformed into a hell of flame, twisted metal, and lifeless flesh in a matter of seconds. Ross swallowed and repeated the pilot's ever pervasive question: Wonder if it's anyone I know?

The scar gouged into a field of knee-high corn indicated impact out of a vertical descent—it hadn't been a controlled touchdown. A crater, surrounded by scattered scraps of metal, still gave off tendrils of smoke.

Flying in a tight orbit, Ross watched a half-dozen figures examining the larger bits of debris. A bright-red fire truck was parked nearby, any need for its services apparently past. His stomach knotted at the sight of a long, black limousine unhurriedly picking its way across the field's recently tilled surface—the roof-mounted red lights dark.

He identified one of the pieces as most of the tail section of a relatively small, all-metal aircraft—not a civilian-owned light airplane in all probability. It had vaguely familiar lines. He keyed his mike. "Wright Tower, this is Albatross Three, over."

"This is Wright Tower, Albatross Three, go ahead."

"Roger, Tower. I'm over an airplane crash site south of the field. It looks to be a true auger-in; an all-metal job I'd guess to be a military fighter type. Rescue equipment is on the scene, including an ambulance. I see no sign of survivors, however, over."

"Roger, Albatross Three, copy all. Colonel Babcock advises you to terminate your test hop and report to him immediately upon landing, over."

Ross set his parachute pack on the gleaming, battleship-linoleum floor of base ops and tossed his helmet and gloves alongside. He turned to face Lieutenant Colonel Babcock and three other grim-faced officers. He shook his head.

"It's a total. Unless the pilot bailed out, he couldn't possibly have survived. The tail section—what was left of it—looked like it may have been a P-39—maybe a '63."

"I'm afraid you're right." Babcock stared at the floor. "Tower lost contact with an F-80—a ferry flight from Muroc—about an hour ago. He reported field in sight and started a penetration turn from twenty thousand. The '80's empennage resembles a P-39, all right."

A slim, sandy-haired major extended a hand. "I'm Major Hall, Colyer —flying safety officer. Did you by chance see a canopy close to the crash site?"

Ross shook the proffered hand. "No, the tail section was the biggest piece around. Of course, if the pilot jettisoned the canopy and bailed out, both would be miles away."

"Exactly." Hall turned to Babcock and said, "I've tried to tell those stubborn bastards, they simply *have* to redesign that canopy. We'll find it—I'll get a search under way as soon as I leave here. And when we do, I'll lay odds we'll find blood on it." He saw Ross's puzzled expression and added, "I take it you aren't familiar with the airplane?"

"Afraid not."

"Okay. They put a canopy on the bird that slides open on a track. We suspect that the rear end is sucked up first when you try to jettison the thing in flight—the front end dishes in and hits the pilot's head. You say there was an ambulance at the scene, but no sign it was responding to an emergency—odds are that the pilot didn't get out. This isn't the first time it's happened."

"Oh, for Christ's sake. That sounds like a simple thing to fix," Ross blurted. "Surely there's a way to keep from getting clipped. Hasn't anyone just taken one up and tried ducking low in the cockpit to see what happens when you hit the jettison handle?"

Babcock gave Ross a quizzical look. "Okay, Hall, you get to work on finding that canopy. Keep in touch with the sheriff's office in case anyone reports seeing a chute. You two"—he turned to the pair of captains standing in the background—"find a hangar where we can try to reassemble pieces of that bird. A waste of time, I imagine, but maybe we can find something. Colyer, can I see you in my office?"

The junior officers turned to leave. One, his dark complexion and rugged good looks hinting at Mediterranean ancestors, paused and said, "You got a lot to learn about test flying, Major. We don't need hot rocks trying to show how fearless they are. This is serious business—not a county-fair air show."

Ross gaped at the man's departing back, too astonished to respond. He shrugged and followed Babcock.

Babcock's "office" was one of a series of cubicles formed by plywood and glass partitions lining one wall of the base operations building. A neatly lettered placard alongside the doorless opening proclaimed it the domain of Lieutenant Colonel Babcock, Chief, Fighter Test Operations.

The unhappy-looking L/C dropped into a swivel chair behind his desk and motioned Ross toward the only other seat, a gray steel, straight-backed chair alongside the desk. Babcock rubbed his misshapen nose, twisted slightly to his left, and said, "Don't mind Captain Sears. He has a bad habit of speaking his mind, but he's a good pilot. He's chief test pilot for the '80 just now, and we're having problems. He didn't need this," the harassed-looking colonel added, seemingly to himself.

Ross nodded. "I gathered that. I can't wait to have a go at it myself."

Babcock didn't answer immediately. He regarded Ross with pursed lips, then said, "Colyer, right now there's a question in my mind that you'll become a regular member of the test flight."

"What? I thought that was the reason I was assigned here—to do some test flying before I'm assigned to a squadron."

"Assigned as squadron commander—yes, I know the plan. And I'm also acquainted with Colonel Cappy Cipolla; I know you're his protégé. Colyer, I'll be brutally frank: I don't like having people shoved down my throat. Now, I've looked at your records—two combat tours, Purple Heart, DSC, Silver Star, DFC. I'm impressed. Ordinarily, I'd fight to have someone with your qualifications in my outfit."

Ross frowned. "Sir, I'm not some kind of prima donna. I've done my share of dirty, unrewarding work. I flew with Colonel Cipolla during the war. He isn't the kind to do favors for those he doesn't think can hack the program. I'm not clear about what concerns you, but I'll pull my weight."

"Golden boys are always regarded with a jaundiced eye, Colyer. To be given command of a jet fighter squadron before you've even flown the plane—and after three years' inactive duty—well, that doesn't happen often. A lot of the boys in the F-80 program resent it. I'd give my left nut for the job, incidentally. Milt Sears wasn't all that tactful, but he speaks for a lot of us. This is not a grandstanding operation. It's slow, slogging work. It carries a measure of danger, but there are no heroes, no medals.

"Fixing that canopy problem, for example; that can take hours of painstaking investigation. It may even require building a model for wind tunnel tests—tedious engineering work. We don't know for certain that the canopy design is the culprit. You come along and say, 'Hell, I'm a hot pilot, I can handle that. Just let me go up and see what happens.'

"Well, the life of a test pilot and an expensive prototype airframe won't be placed at risk until we're damn sure we know ahead of time what will happen when you hit the panic button. We're doing damn nearly everything for the first time—these jets are a whole new breed of radically different airplanes. In other words, you shot off your mouth without knowing what the hell you were talking about."

Cheeks flaming, Ross responded, "Yes, sir. I guess I did."

Babcock continued as if Ross hadn't spoken. "Now you can do one of two things: You can go running back to your rabbi, or you can do it my way and go to work. You'll get your checkout in the '80 because I have orders to that effect, but we'll wait and see about test flying."

"It won't happen again, Colonel—talking out of turn, I mean. Where do I start to work?"

"After you clear the backlog of F-51 maintenance test hops, I'll put you with the F-82 project—the twin Mustang. After you learn the basics of flying engineering tests, I'll move you into jets, the YP-59 first. There's no plan to develop the Airacomet into an operational fighter, by the way. It's a test bed we use to tinker with things we don't know a lot about—like that goddamn canopy. In fact, that plane we just lost had a new, improved engine installed, which partially explains Sears's reaction to your remark.

"Like I said, we're in a whole new world with these jets, Colyer. Things happen at the altitudes they can reach and the speeds they develop that we don't understand. That's why I don't have time to pamper Cappy's fair-haired boy. You think it over tonight, and tell me tomorrow which way you plan to go, okay?"

"I don't have to think it over, Colonel. I came here to fly airplanes."

"Then we'll get along. See you around."

1 July 1948
Bolling Field,Washington, D.C.
The ground crewman, barely visible against the setting sun's red-orange glare, crossed his parking wands and moved to the Follow Me jeep with a lighted sign reading, WELCOME TO BOLLING FIELD on its rear. Ross braked the Mustang to a halt and moved the mixture control to idle-cutoff. He penciled entries into the Form 1, then stepped onto the wing. "I'll

RON," he called to the OD fatigue-clad airman. "Figure on a late Sunday afternoon departure. All I'll need is full tanks; there're no maintenance write-ups."

Ross reached back to extract his parachute, then leaped to the ground. Minutes later he trudged into base ops and tossed his flight plan onto the counter. He hefted a steel-sheathed attaché case and searched for the Pentagon warrant officer for whom it was destined—this Friday night transfer of classified documents being the official reason he could make weekend jaunts to see Janet.

The messenger was no place to be seen. Ross scowled and asked, "Any sign of the guy I'm supposed to deliver this thing to?"

"No, sir," the cigar-chewing sergeant replied. He prepared to close out Ross's flight plan and added, "The major's wife is waiting in the snack bar, though."

"Really?" Ross's face crinkled in a pleased grin. "This is an unexpected surprise. Wonder how she got here?"

"Dunno, sir, but I'll bet the courier you're looking for is just coming in the door."

Ross and the nattily uniformed warrant officer exchanged IDs, and the attaché case changed hands. Ross tucked the receipt into his wallet and hurried down the hallway to the dingy flight-line snack bar. He grinned as he saw that Janet's perfectly coifed mahogany-hued hair, fashionably tailored slacks, and well-filled white nylon blouse were the focus of a dozen sets of male eyes.

Janet leaped to her feet and strode, arms outstretched, toward Ross. "Hi, stranger," she said with throaty softness, after planting a resounding kiss on his sweat-streaked cheek. She traced marks left by his oxygen mask with a red-tipped forefinger and murmured, "God, are all weeks going to be this long?"

"They do get that way," Ross agreed. "What a great surprise to have you meet me. What's the occasion?"

Janet linked her arm through his and led him to a corner table. "It was Ed's idea." She stopped before a table where a distinguished-looking man lounged in a wire-backed café chair. "You remember Ed Adair, of course—from our wedding?"

"Sure." Ross extended his hand. "You're Janet's boss at International

News Service. Thanks for being so thoughtful; I wasn't looking forward to that cab ride across town this time of day."

Adair uncrossed his legs, clad in sharply creased gabardine slacks, and stood. Glancing at Ross's somewhat grimy paw, he hesitated only slightly before grasping it with a lazily drawled, "I'll confess to wanting to show off a new car, Ross. Just picked it up today. But I had to keep Janet after hours for a rush job. I knew she was pressed for time—one way to say thanks to a loyal employee. If you're ready, why don't we grab your bag and get under way."

"As soon as I toss my gear into a locker, I'm all set," Ross replied. "Having clean underwear and shaving gear at both ends simplifies things."

An annoyed look flickered briefly on Adair's lean, deeply suntanned features. He crossed to the cashier, dropped a pair of bills on the counter, then turned and led the way without waiting for change.

The new car was a dark-blue Buick convertible. Ross let out a low whistle. "Wow, some machine. How long did you have to stand in line for it?"

Adair waited until Ross had settled into the slightly cramped rear seat, then helped Janet into the front before replying. "INS has a way of circumventing things like long lists—car dealers like to see their name in print, you know."

Ross leaned back and regarded the man's aristocratic profile while Adair expertly tooled the car into late afternoon traffic across the Anacosta Bridge. The breeze rippling across his and Janet's hair didn't disturb so much as a strand in Adair's carefully barbered hair, he noticed. Good God, the guy uses some kind of pomade, crossed his mind. The way the man had neatly arranged the seating rankled, too. Now he saw him say something to Janet, an aside muttered half beneath his breath. Janet blushed slightly and said, "Ed . . ."

You know, Adair, you're something of a prick, Ross told himself. I could get to dislike you with very little effort.

Janet knelt in the front seat and turned to face Ross. "How's the job going?"

"Hectic," Ross replied. "Ten-hour days, and no letup in sight. I'm beat."

His wife reached back and squeezed his hand. "You need to get out and have some fun. I'll tell you more when we get home."

An hour later, Ross slumped on the apartment's living room sofa and crossed his ankles on the coffee table. Janet chattered incessantly as she deftly mixed a pitcher of martinis. ". . . And on Tuesday Ed gave me the job of interviewing the Italian ambassador's wife. I was scared to death, but he insisted. Ross, Ed says I'm a natural when it comes to dragging interesting stuff from reluctant interviewees. He says I have a great future in the news business, and—"

Ross accepted his chilled drink and interrupted his wife's animated discourse. "I'm dying to hear about your week, sweetheart, but could I have a hot shower first? I'll take this with me and work on it in the bathroom."

"Of course, darling. I'll mix another pitcher, change, and put together something for us to eat. Okay?"

Ross emerged from the bathroom wearing a towel knotted around his waist and carrying his empty martini glass. Janet sat at her dressing table wearing only a slip as she applied makeup. After pouring a fresh drink, he crossed to stand behind her and caress one bare shoulder. He grinned at Janet's reflection in the mirror. "I got a great idea," he purred. "Why don't we lie down, and I'll tell you all about it."

Janet's face assumed a stricken look. "Oh, Ross," she wailed, "we can't. Really. Oh, I'd like nothing better, believe me. But there just isn't *time*. I didn't get to tell you earlier, but we're due at a reception for a Romanian princess at seven. She's here in exile and has a simply astonishing story to tell. Ed wants me to meet her; plus, this is sort of my debut as an international journalist. It's the break I've worked for. Please, Ross. Can't we wait until we get home?"

Ross's ardor cooled as he regarded his wife's pleading expression. "Sure," he said. "Anything you say. I . . ." He turned and reentered the bathroom.

Janet sprang to her feet and padded after him. "Ross, you're angry," she said softly. "Please, don't be. Tonight is very important to me. Try to understand—please?"

"I said okay, Janet. I'm getting dressed."

"I—oh, well, I laid out your tux; it's a black tie affair. Cold cuts and cheese are on the counter; you'll probably want to eat before you dress— I bought a jar of that German mustard you like. Ed will pick us up at eight—you're a sweetheart to understand. I'll make it up to you, I promise." Janet brushed his cheek with her lips in passing and returned to her dressing table.

Ross regarded the La Maison Rouge's thinning ranks of patrons through slightly out-of-focus eyes. Ed Adair and Janet were using most of the postage stamp–size dance floor, swirling through intricate steps of a tango. He picked up his half-empty scotch and soda, grown flat and tepid, then set it down untasted. It was his what? Seventh? Eighth? He'd lost count.

He peered at the pinch-faced woman seated beside him. Her heavy makeup was starting to sag, and an expensive hairdo was beginning to sprout mousy blond strands. Her eyes looking blurred with drink and fatigue, she toyed with a sickening-looking pink concoction—some of which had already spilled on her frumpy, floral-patterned evening dress.

Look, Marsha—Ross felt tempted to say—your husband and my wife are having fun dancing. Why don't you and I go out to that new Buick in the parking lot and have a quickie? They'll never miss us. He chuckled out loud at the reaction he could expect and acknowledged that he was just a bit loaded.

Marsha responded to his outburst of laughter with a vacuous stare. He recovered and asked, "How about a fresh drink, Marsha? They tell me the party's on ol' INS tonight."

Ed and Janet's return prevented Marsha's response. "Hey, you two look like the end of the world's just around the corner," Adair observed. "You're missing out on a great little band, aren't they, Janet?" He beckoned a hovering waiter. "One more bottle of that prewar Monet, my good man. Where are the others?"

"The *others,* Ed," his wife snapped, "are long gone. "It's one-thirty. *I* have things to do tomorrow—unless, that is, *you* want to take Lucy to her ballet lessons and pour tea at the garden club luncheon."

Ross saw Adair quickly control an angry flush. "Ah, Marsha, my little homemaker," the man said with forced gaiety. "Look, dearest, this is Janet's big night. She scored with that snotty Balkan piece of phony royalty. INS has an exclusive! This party is for her: You aren't going to be a nag about things, are you?"

Janet had linked arms with Ross and cocked a quizzical eye at his rumpled countenance. Her radiant glow faded. "You've had a long day, haven't you, dear?" she said before Marsha could reply. "Ed, it *is* late. I can't thank you enough for throwing this impromptu bash, but I do think we should call it a night."

Ross fought to stay awake during the ride back to the apartment. Adair and his tight-lipped wife sat silently in front; Ross could detect anger close to the surface. I'm glad I'm not going to be around when those two get home, he thought.

Janet's elation was far from fading, however. She kicked her shoes off as Ross closed the front door, and headed for the tiny corner bar. "A nightcap?" she inquired. "Brandy? Scotch? We still have a bottle of cold champagne in the fridge."

"Janet, I'm out on my feet. I'm sorry, but I'm going to fold."

"Well, I'm *not*," Janet pouted. "This was a big night for me, and I'm not through celebrating."

Ross shed his tux jacket and stripped off the bow tie. He slumped on the sofa and said, "I'm glad for you, honey, really. It's just . . . well, can we talk about it in the morning?"

"About what?"

"My assignment, the future, and such."

Janet idly examined a chipped fingernail. "Is something wrong?"

"I don't know—yet. I may not get an F-80 squadron, Janet. My new boss hates my guts—he thinks I pulled strings to get the promise of a squadron. This guy, Babcock, has more than two hundred hours in the airplane and is bitter because he got passed over for the job. I have six months at AFIT to finish my degree, and I'll bet I don't have fifty hours of jet time by then—and for damn sure no test flying. I'll probably get a lousy fitness report and Cipolla may decide to give the job to him.

"And I *don't* like this goddamned weekend commuting—nor do I like the moves I saw Ed Adair putting on you tonight."

Janet sat silently. She tasted her drink, made a face, and set it down. "Yes, perhaps it would be best to talk about things in the morning," she murmured.

Ross stretched full length and cursed silently as his feet slid past the end of the apartment's standard-length bed. Janet lay curled in the crook of his right arm, her hair spread over his shoulder. She had drifted off after their brief, somehow perfunctory, coupling, but sleep evaded Ross despite his bone-aching fatigue.

Cipolla's pep talk, and his own reassurances to Janet notwithstanding, his return to active duty promised to be less exciting than he'd envisioned. A BOQ room at Wright, going back to a damned classroom, his checkout in jets relegated to the indefinite future, only seeing his wife on weekends—what a way to start a new career.

Ross eased from the bed and fumbled for his robe. He padded through the living room and stepped onto the apartment's little moon-drenched patio. Slumping into a redwood bench, he lit a cigarette and let the sounds of a city at sleep wash over him. The soothing sounds of night insects, rustling leaves, the distant rumble of traffic, and the scent of freshly watered lawns went unappreciated, however.

Were he and Janet expecting too much? he wondered. Colonel Ted Wilson, his old training squadron CO and mentor, had moved heaven and earth to get Ross back in uniform. He classed Senator Broderick Templeton's withdrawal of that political interest flag on Ross's master personnel records to be in the category of a miracle. He seemed to be saying: You're damned lucky, Colyer—stop complaining. Did he dare divulge the entire truth about the business with Senator Templeton to people like Cipolla and Colonel Ted? Lying to those who had done so much for him—even to his wife—was a bone in his throat. Janet already suspected that her ex-father-in-law's change of heart hadn't been voluntary. After all, it had been information she dug up that turned the trick; she just didn't know how it had been used.

Hank Wallace, the Central Intelligence Agency (CIA) operative who'd recruited Ross for undercover work during the time he'd been flying for the Israelis, once told him, "That feeling goes with the trade." He'd said that after Ross complained that spying on the man he worked for made him want to scrub his hands.

Ross stared into the warm summer night with unseeing eyes. A feeling that he hadn't heard the last of that deal he'd made with the shadowy intelligence agency wouldn't go away. Okay, so they *had* lived up to their promise. But talk about making a pact with the devil to get back on active duty . . .

The memory of jets streaking across the field that day at Fairfax Field intruded. He stood and squared his shoulders. No, damnit, he'd done the right thing. He was a military man through and through. Flying combat airplanes is what he did best. The price might prove high, but perhaps the gray man—introduced to him as director of the CIA—had been right.

During a brief, private award ceremony in his office, he'd said, "Reward for outstanding service to your country doesn't always come through reading about your exploits in the paper, Colyer."

2

5 July 1948
Wright Field

Ross stood beside and one step behind the slightly stooped, lanky figure of test branch chief Col. Luther Roberts as Col. "Cappy" Cipolla leaped off the wing of his personal, slicked-down Mustang. Ross forced a smile. After his problems with Babcock, a personal visit from Tactical Air Command's fighter chief had an ominous implication.

"Luke, Ross, good to see you," Cipolla growled. "After I change, I'd like to grab a cup of coffee, a sandwich, and gab a bit. Then"—his handsome Latin features spread into a wide grin—"I'd like to log some jet time. You got an '80 in commission, Luke?"

"'Fraid not, Colonel," Roberts replied, deadpan. "You can take one of the YP-59s, though."

Cipolla chuckled. "You lie in your goddamned teeth, Luke. You have a flyable Shooting Star—I checked before I left Langley. And you're *not* going to get me in that other miserable excuse for an airplane."

Their desultory banter continued in base ops while Cipolla changed from his flying suit. "Let's go to the O Club pool for lunch," Roberts suggested. "They serve a mean barbecue sandwich there, plus a cold beer for them what ain't gonna fly the afternoon period. We can talk while we eat and enjoy the scenery."

"Lead on." Cipolla transferred change and billfold to his khaki uniform pockets. "But since I can't have a beer, I'll kneecap the first bastard that orders one."

Halfway through the meal, Cipolla wiped barbecue sauce from his chin and barked, "Luke, what the hell's wrong with the '80? I'm told there won't be enough production to activate the 66th Squadron on schedule."

"Engines, mostly. We're still finding cracked turbine buckets after about twenty hours. Then, there's a pressurization and cockpit tempera-

14

ture control problem, fuel control fluctuation—it's a radically new bird, Colonel."

"What's the outlook?"

"Well, sir, General Oldham is meeting in Burbank with the Lockheed engineers this week. They promise delivery of twenty planes that meet our specs by October."

"Piss on the eggheads' estimates, Luke—they gonna make it?"

"Nope. And there's still the business with that fuselage tank mounted directly behind the pilot. The final report of Dick Bong's crash suggests that fuel from that tank somehow got sucked into the engine. I'm not about to sign off on operational feasibility until it's fixed."

"I see." Cipolla frowned. "The old man is dead set on entering a pair of Shooting Stars in the Bendix races. The navy is entering two North American Furies—you know how that sets with him."

"Don't I know. Lockheed will give him a couple that won't resemble production models, you can bet. You plan to fly one? Is that what brings you to the wild and wooly West?"

Cipolla grinned and put down his sandwich. "No comment. No, I did want to keep my jet currency up to date, but I also need to talk to Ross—and you—about something that's come up."

Ross felt his stomach muscles knot.

"It's gonna break today, but intelligence has been predicting it for two weeks or more. The Soviets have imposed a total blockade on goods entering Berlin from the West. They've been dicking around for weeks harassing supply convoys entering the Soviet zone, but on the twenty-fourth, they tore up about a hundred miles of railroad and announced 'technical problems.' They're making no effort to replace the track; it looks like they're going to shut the border down cold—indefinitely."

Both Ross and Roberts considered Cipolla's words while chewing on bites of their sandwiches.

"Jesus Christ!" Roberts blurted. "They can't get away with that kind of crap."

"Maybe not." Cipolla's tone was deceptively mild. "It remains to be seen—but it sure as hell looks like they're gonna *try*.

"We've been blindsided by that bunch. They were stealing our technology while we were still celebrating V-J Day. And already we're falling behind the bastards. They got hold of a B-29 that crash-landed in

Manchuria and are building a copy for long-range bombing. The British were working on a jet engine along with us—the Rolls-Royce Nene—and the Reds stole that damn thing, too. Now they're building a fighter around it."

"But, hell, sir, how can they be ahead of us if all they're doing is just *copying* our plans?" Ross protested.

"Numbers. Uncle Joe is pouring every ruble he can scrape together into airplanes, tanks, subs—we understand that practically no civilian goods are being produced over there."

"Why? Who the hell do they plan to whip?"

"The world, Ross. Read the intelligence briefs, but in short, *The Communist Manifesto* says that communism will only work when the entire world is converted."

"They're nuts."

"Maybe. But we can't sit back and pick our nose while they build a force we don't dare challenge."

"So what are we gonna to about this blockade?" Roberts shoved his plate away and cocked a questioning eyebrow. "If George Patton were alive, he'd be halfway to Berlin with an armored division by now."

"I understand the Joint Chiefs of Staff have two ops plans on the table, Luke. One: Do what you say old George would do. Two: Supply West Berlin by air—we have three air corridors across East Germany. That's what some Limey suggested—and General LeMay says we can do it. USAFE has about a hundred C-47s and a couple of C-54s—they moved eighty tons last Sunday. Just give him enough airframes to up that figure to the forty-five hundred needed for Berliners to survive. The smart money is betting that airlift will be our first effort. The Russians have five armored divisions parked just ten miles outside the city—and they're battle-hardened."

"Supply an entire damn city with an *airlift?*" Ross asked in awed tones. "Colonel, I was in the CBI and saw the ATC supply an *army* by air over the Hump, but a city the size of Berlin?"

"That's the plan. There're about two million souls, we guess, in the French, British, and American sectors. The Reds will feed those in the Russian sector, of course."

So why fly all the way down here to give us an intelligence briefing?

Ross asked himself. Suddenly he brightened. "Are you telling us that we're going over there with '51s to escort the transports across the Russian zone, Colonel?"

"Not exactly." Cipolla took time to light a cigar before he continued. "No, looks like I'll be going over as deputy commander of a provisional wing of C-47s. That is where you come in, Ross.

"The personnel guys have been searching records for anyone with multiengine time. To move the tonnage they're talking about, we'll have to throw every transport outfit—C-54 and C-47—into what we're calling 'Operation Vittles.' I told them to find me a field grade officer with multiengine combat time and command experience to be my chief pilot. Guess whose card popped out on top?"

Ross felt blood drain from his face. "Oh, no, Colonel Cipolla. Not me. Damnit, sir, I'm a fighter pilot now—"

"And the only guy who ever bested me in a dogfight," Cipolla interrupted dryly. "But with a combat tour in Europe flying the B-24, *beaucoup* hours of civilian DC-3 time with your air freight operation, a Hump veteran, *and* an outstanding squadron commander—you may as well start packing, Major. We expect the balloon to go up within twenty-four hours. When it does, your orders will be on the TWX. This is what it's all about, Ross. You'll get to finish your degree—you'll get that squadron, I promise you. But first things first. Agree?"

"Yes, sir." Ross signaled their waiter with his empty coffee cup. "Janet is—"

"Janet's going to be just fine, now. There's a program being worked up for wives with hardships imposed by having their husbands shipped out overnight."

"Yeah," Ross replied ". . . I know. Somehow, though, I don't think she'll be asking the air force for help." He stood and fumbled for his wallet. "Well, gentlemen, if you'll excuse me, I have a bird to put four hours on this afternoon. I'll start packing tonight." He was halfway across the parking lot before he remembered to put on his cap.

Alfred Rostock struggled to calm his frantic team of horses. They threatened to destroy not only the cultivator, but two rows of corn as well. He shook his fist in the direction of the setting sun where an airplane was rapidly disappearing. It had materialized seconds earlier, streaking barely fifty feet above the waving stalks of grain—its noise in passing a deafening, screaming thunder.

"Goldarn army fliers," he muttered. "What in tarnation would make one fly like that? He's gotta be crazy, madder 'en hell, or both."

8 July 1948
One Hundred Miles East of Gander, Newfoundland

Ross made a minute adjustment to synchronize the C-47's twin Pratt & Whitney engines and turned to accept a slip of paper from navigator Scotty Fenton. He glanced at the message and nodded to Cliff Worsham, his copilot. "Okay, you can tell Gander we're leaving their control zone."

"Will do Major," the rotund, sad-faced captain replied. He removed the mike from its hook and drawled, "Gander Radio, this is Candy One. Position report, over."

"Roger, Candy One. This is Gander Radio, go ahead."

"Candy One is one hundred miles east at four-three, nine thousand feet, IFR. Changing now to Oceanic Control, over."

"Roger, understand, Candy One. Cleared from this frequency. Have a good flight. Gander, out."

Ross handed the message form back to the navigator. "Give this to the radio operator and tell him to relay our position to air traffic control on HF. Also tell him to let me know when the other ships check in—and I'll want Reykjavik weather before we reach the point of no return."

He retrieved the weather map from his flight kit and held it for the navigator to see. "I figure you'll have about another half hour to get your last drift-meter reading. It appears we'll be in clouds after forty-five west."

"Okay." Scotty scanned the weather display. "You think we'll maybe be in the soup, or on top?"

"Forecast is for tops to only be around seven—but you never know. I'll give you enough time to get a sun line if I see the stuff building."

"Good enough," Scotty replied cheerfully. "Things looking good so far. The tailwind is holding, and we're right on flight plan."

Ross caged and reset the autopilot's gyro compass, then leaned his seat back. Turning to the copilot, he said, "Everything seems settled down, Cliff. You want me to take the first shift? You look like you could use some shut-eye."

"If you don't mind, Major. It was after midnight when we got all that crap loaded and tied down last night. What a fucking madhouse. Colonel Wise decided at the last minute they should put the extra ground power unit on the lead ship.

"Okay. Unload everything we'd just put on board. Nobody knows how much the friggin' GPU weighs. An hour getting that sorted out and computing a new weight-and-balance form. Then the transportation officer starts waving some regulation and yelling that we have to drain and purge the unit's fuel and oil systems for air shipment. 'For Christ's sake, Captain,' I tell him, 'we already got a fuselage tank that holds four hundred gallons of av gas. You worried about something blowing up maybe?'"

Ross chuckled. "Something tells me that was just a warm-up for what we're going to find at Rhine-Main. I spent all afternoon in the planning session. This idea of an independent provisional wing sounds good, but neither the Air Transport Command boys nor the troop carrier commanders are happy with it—they both fly by different books."

The weary, drawn-faced captain stowed his headset and unbuckled the seat belt. Before leaving his seat, he scowled and said, "They think they're gonna eventually move eight–ten thousand tons a day with Gooney Birds—they got granite between their ears. There just isn't enough airspace over Berlin to land and take off that many airplanes, even under VFR, which we won't have much of. We need four-engine stuff—C-54s, even the C-87s we used on the Hump."

Ross nodded. Cliff Worsham, the 901st Squadron's ops officer, knew his stuff; he'd been a pilot on the infamous Hump airlift in the China-Burma-India theater. Ross had occupied a ringside seat as a P-51 pilot and knew that only the best pilots had survived a full tour flying the awesome Himalayas.

"Well, I'll let you ops types sort that out," he said. "I'm going to have my hands full trying to qualify enough pilots to keep things moving. Now hit the sack; I'll see you in about four hours."

The radio operator reported via intercom that Candy Six was airborne, and all six ships of the advance echelon, strung out at fifteen-minute intervals, were accounted for. Ross extracted a sheaf of papers from his flight bag and tried to concentrate on the job that awaited him at Rhine-Main.

A sketch map showing the four occupied areas of a divided Germany displayed the Western powers' air routes across the Russian sector to Berlin. The three twenty-mile-wide corridors resembled an arrowhead. The northern barb originated just south of Lübeck; the central route, constituting the arrow's shaft, ran east from Hanover; the southern barb started at Frankfurt.

Ross shook his head. Say they could keep three hundred C-47s in commission, flying four sorties per day, each with a five-thousand-pound payload—three thousand tons, he calculated. Even if they got as many as fifty C-54s hauling ten thousand pounds, and the Brits managed to come up with a hundred or so airplanes, a whole bunch of Germans in the American, British, and French zones of Berlin were still going to go hungry—and cold if the operation dragged into winter.

He laid the chart aside and glowered at the sparkling blue expanse of North Atlantic stretching out of sight in all directions. How the *hell* had he gotten sucked into this job? Colonel Cipolla had given him a brief glimpse last evening over a quick dinner at the Langley Officers' Mess. The colonel and his wing headquarters staff were taking a C-54 to Rhine-Main immediately afterward.

The newly appointed deputy commander of the 7744th Air Transport Wing stabbed a fork in Ross's direction as he chewed a mouthful of steak. Cipolla swallowed and said, "Get that goddamn injured look off your face, Colyer. I know you're a fighter pilot—*I'm* a fighter pilot, for Christ's sake. So what are we doing hauling groceries? "Well, in your case it's easy: You're along for the ride because I handpicked you. Not only are you the best man to whip up a few hundred competent instrument pilots on short notice, but you're also my backup for the real reason *I'm* going."

The colonel checked to verify that other diners were out of earshot, then chuckled and refilled their wineglasses. "What I'm about to tell you is classified, of course—strictly need-to-know. General LeMay wanted me as a provisional wing deputy commander like he wanted a bad dose of clap. He told General O'Brien, DCS OPS, that I don't know shit about transport operations." Cipolla attacked his one-inch-thick sirloin with renewed vigor and gave Ross a wicked grin.

"Well, he's right," the dapper, flashing-eyed commander observed wryly. "But what I *do* know is combat flying, a little eventuality that seems to be overlooked in this wild scramble to put together an airlift. This business is more than just tweaking the Russian Bear's nose.

"That crowd is playing hardball. They need control of Berlin to weld their ring of occupied countries together." He stabbed the air with his fork again and added, "Anyone who thinks Stalin is just going to sit by with his thumb up his butt and let us make a joke out of their goddamn blockade believes in Santa Claus and the Tooth Fairy."

Ross realized that he'd become engrossed in the colonel's hard-boiled dissertation and only consumed a few bites of his dinner. He cut a piece of steak while he asked, "What do you think they might do? Surely the Soviets aren't dumb enough to start a shooting war."

"That's the question that keeps lights burning all night in the Pentagon and State Department. General Clay has been pounding the table and insisting that the army can escort an armed convoy right up to the Brandenburg Gate and face 'em down. Maybe he can, but what if just one nervous trigger finger twitches? You can bet your ass the Reds wouldn't back down—all hell will break loose, and the betting is that they're better prepared than we are. Plus, they're several thousand miles closer to the action.

"No, General Marshal thinks they'll watch the airlift effort, harass the hell out of us, and hope that when we fall flat of our ass, the Berliners will opt to accept Russian control rather than starve. Clay's been told to cool his heels while we gain some time."

"What if we *are* able to keep the city open?"

"Ah-hah." Cipolla's eyes gleamed. "That's when things just might get terse. The harassment has already started, you know. In April, a Russian Yak fighter was barrel-rolling around a British airliner in the corridor and sheared off a wingtip. Much of that shit, and we bring up the cavalry— that's us.

"Four more B-29 squadrons will be divided between Germany and England. The F-80 group at Selfridge Field is on its way to Fürstenfeldbruck right now. Frankly, these are scare tactics. The only thing that moving the heavies does is to pose a threat of dropping the big one on Russian soil in case of all-out war. The jets are impressive, but would only have about thirty minutes endurance over the corridors."

"Sounds like a job for the P-51."

"It is, but not yet. We're back to the basics now. I have an ops plan in my hip pocket to move the entire 14th Wing to Germany—all three Mustang squadrons. It's the only plane we have that can fly an extended eight- or nine-hour escort mission. The crews are sitting at home right now with their bags packed and can be in place within forty-eight hours.

"That's when you and I change hats. I take over my fighter wing, and you'll lead the first escort mission. In the meantime—when we're not hauling groceries—we'll both be scouting for airfields and the like, just in case."

Ross studied the table's centerpiece, a candle burning inside a little glass chimney, and turned it to let the wax melt more evenly. "Flak and fighters over Berlin," he observed softly, more to himself than to his dinner companion. "Well, it ain't like I haven't been down this road before."

Ross shook off his glumly pessimistic assessment of events as the intercom came to life. "Navigator to pilot. We're coming up on forty-five west, Major. What's it look like ahead?"

Resembling piles of giant cotton balls, the blinding-white cloudtops stretched out of sight toward the horizon. "The forecast for tops at seven thousand seems to be holding, Scotty," Ross replied. You should be so lucky."

"I lead a clean life, Major," the cocky, red-haired navigator quipped, "as opposed to my loutish friend on Candy Six. Just talked to him on the command set, and they're in the clouds at seven, picking up ice."

"Oh, shit," Ross replied. "Has his pilot requested a higher altitude?"

"Trying to, but they can't make voice contact. His RO is trying to raise ATC on CW. If they can't get out of the stuff, he thinks they may have to divert to Greenland for fuel."

"Oh, great. You ever been into Bluie West One?"

"Fortunately, no. I've seen the aerial photos, though. Looks nasty."

"It is that. You fly down a fjord with four-thousand-foot cliffs on both sides until you come to a particular one on your left. You turn down it and start your final approach—blind. There ain't no turning back at that point."

"Let's not do that, Major," Scotty pleaded fervently. "I'm a devout coward when it comes to flirting with mountains."

"Join the crowd; and just keep us on course," Ross replied with a chuckle. He replaced the mike and settled back. I can't wait until Scotty sees the final approach into Tempelhof, he thought. He'd seen pictures at Langley. Apartment buildings that seemed close enough to touch, unless you were still in the clouds following directions from Ground Control Approach radar.

He returned to his study of the air routes they would follow but couldn't concentrate. His brief phone conversation with Janet had been strained. She'd reacted to the news that he was on his way out of the country with a suspicious, "Are you sure you didn't volunteer, just to get in on the excitement?"

Women! he'd thought bitterly. Then she hadn't even acknowledged his admonition to contact the personnel officer at Bolling if she needed any help while he was gone. "I'll make out," she'd told him. "I've been on my own before."

She'd also rejected his offer to borrow money against the pending sale of Allied Air, Inc., the air freight outfit he'd operated before returning to active duty.

"Oh, really, Ross. Don't be foolish," was her response. "I can't up and walk off my job just to join you in Germany."

A picture of the handsome, arrogant Ed Adair flashed through his mind. He clamped his jaws and stared blankly at the paper he held. Even her response to his soft, "I love you, and I'll miss you like the devil," hadn't, to his way of thinking, sounded terribly distressed.

3

10 July 1948
Rhine-Main Airfield, West Germany

"Candy One, this is Frankfurt Approach Control. You are cleared to descend now to four thousand feet and proceed direct to the Frankfurt beacon for landing at Rhine-Main, runway two-one. Your approach time is one-four-zero-niner. Current Rhine-Main weather is seven hundred broken, visibility two miles in fog and drizzle. Winds light and variable; altimeter is two-niner-eight-eight. Report leaving present altitude and procedure turn outbound to Rhine-Main Tower on one-twenty-eight decimal five, over."

At Ross's nod, Cliff Worsham keyed his mike and acknowledged, "Roger, Frankfurt, Candy One—copy all. Leaving five thousand at zero-four and changing to tower frequency, over." Worsham squinted at his approach chart and said, "Damn. Is that guy serious about wanting us over that beacon at *exactly* zero-nine? I make us about fifteen miles out; that means increasing airspeed to at least one-eighty."

"According to the briefing officer at Aldershot, he means just that." Ross nodded toward the surrounding dirty gray mist and added, "Out there somewhere, there's a guy who's gonna be crossing that beacon five minutes ahead of us. There's another one five minutes behind. You better jolly well believe we're gonna see that ADF needle spin around at the stroke of zero-nine. After that, we'll be making our procedure turn for landing only about ten miles from the Russian zone. Ain't that cozy?" He rolled in nose-down trim and added power.

Exactly eleven minutes later Worsham called, "Field in sight, one o'clock. Gear down and locked, green lights. Standing by flaps."

Ross corrected his heading to line up for touchdown and watched the dreary scene emerge. His stomach muscles tightened as he made the transition from instruments to visual. Beyond the stretch of mist-haloed runway lights, shells of brick buildings—broken windows making them

24

resemble skulls of prehistoric square-headed monsters—bore mute testimony to Eighth Air Force bombardiers' skill. "Wonder if any of those buildings owe their fate to the old *Happy Hooker?*" he mused aloud. "The place looks different than it did from a B-24 at twenty thousand feet."

"I was thinking about that during the trip," Worsham said. "Wondering if you'd recognize any landmarks if we were VFR. Must be a spooky feeling."

"Yeah . . ." Ross agreed as he eased the C-47's main gear onto the rain-slick PSP runway. He let his words trail off as the tower advised, "Expedite your landing roll to the end of the runway, Candy One. You have traffic behind you on final approach. The Follow Me jeep will park you."

"Damn, this is gonna be like learning close-order drill in cadets," Worsham grumbled. "These guys mean business."

"They're moving a hundred airplanes, each one flying two–three sorties a day, with more planes on the way. You figure it out. I'd guess that the interval between landings and takeoffs will get cut even shorter when things get into high gear. Can your pilots hack that kind of precision instrument flying?"

"I been thinking about *that,* too," Worsham replied glumly. "Most of 'em can, but I have some who've been behind a desk for damn near three years—some just recalled from the standby reserve. There're gonna be some midairs, I'd say."

"That's what I'm supposed to prevent," Ross observed cryptically. "Without airframe time for training flights, the green beans are going to learn the hard way—by experience." He eased the plane to a stop and followed the ground controller's throat-slashing signal to cut engines.

Ross glimpsed at two six-by-six trucks backing toward the cargo door before the props stopped ticking over. An airman wearing a dripping poncho stuck his head inside the cockpit even before Worsham finished making Form 1 entries. "Any write-ups?"

"Nothing grounding," said Ross. "Number two engine has an oil leak, but the mechanic at Aldershot says it's minor."

"Good. Your crew still legal, Major?"

"Legal?" Ross asked. "What do you mean?"

"How much crew duty time have you logged today? Will a six-hour sortie put you over sixteen hours? We're supposed to have you fueled, loaded, and airborne for a sixteen-thirteen departure slot, if you're legal."

Ross opened his mouth to protest, then closed it. This outfit was on a wartime footing, he realized. You flew tired, hungry, and disgruntled as a matter of course. "We're legal," he said.

"Okay. Check in with wing ops—they're in a big tent on the other side of that hangar behind you. There's a twenty-four-hour mess in the hangar annex. You'll be flying as a crew of three—pilot, copilot, and engineer. You can turn your bags and personal stuff over to your navigator and radio operator to keep an eye on, if you like—or we can stow them in transient crew quarters."

"Right." Ross acknowledged. "You know there's a fuselage tank to remove, I guess."

"Yes, sir. They're disconnecting it right now. We'll have you ready on schedule. Show time at your airplane is fifteen minutes before start engines. Any questions?"

Ross and his already weary crew trudged toward where a circus-style tent sprawled across a former parking lot. "Well, so much for spending our first night drinking good German beer and frolicking with lissome *fräuleins,*" Worsham grouched.

"I don't know about the beer, but I don't think you'll find many 'lissome *fräuleins,*'" Ross said with a wry smile. "The ones that survived the war are still not getting enough to eat and living two families to a room. Besides, they're off-limits."

"Yeah, I know all about nonfraternization. I spent 1946 in Japan. It didn't work a hundred percent there, and I doubt like hell that it works any better here—biology has a way of getting crosswise with the regulations."

They entered the ops tent, where bedlam cut off further talk. A miasma of tobacco smoke, odor from rain-wet clothing, and fumes from coal-burning space heaters hovered over a swirl of fatigue- and flight-suit-clad figures. Handwritten placards identified functional islands, around which conversation was possible only by shouting. Administrative duties were carried out beneath the signs on trestle-style mess tables.

"My God, what a madhouse," Ross muttered. "Cliff, why don't you and I clear flight operations—I assume we'll get some sort of briefing for the Berlin run. The rest of you—why don't you go grab a bite to eat. Afterward, Clint"—he turned to the flight engineer—"you can go back to be sure the bird is ready to go. Be damned sure we have the right VHF crystals—I don't want to get caught up there without being able to talk to anyone. Scotty, you and Sparks try to line us up a place to sleep. I figure we'll be back shortly before midnight."

Flight Operations consisted of three tables positioned end to end alongside one wall. Chalk-scrawled entries reflecting current crew and aircraft status filled a row of hastily painted blackboards propped behind them. Ross and Cliff slid onto a bench seat across from a harassed-looking master sergeant. "Candy One closing our flight plan," Ross announced, sliding the rumpled form across the table's painted wooden surface.

A haggard, middle-aged NCO turned to scan the status board. "Candy One," he repeated half to himself. "Yeah, just in from the States. Major Colyer. Okay, you're due for a sixteen-thirteen takeoff, right?"

"That's what they tell me."

"It'll be the same bird, but your call sign will change. Let's see." The sergeant ran his finger down a smudged, typewritten list. "You're from the 901st Squadron, right?" Before Ross could respond, he added, "Your new call sign is Hobo Seven, Major. You can pick up your flight plan for Berlin and get your weather briefing from the dispatch desk—next table down."

"Gotcha. We're a new crew. Where do we go for a route briefing?"

"Oh. You'll get your corridor checkride from, ah"—he stopped to scan the status board—"Captain Gross. They'll point him out at flight dispatch. He'll brief you en route." The NCO snapped his fingers. "And, oh, yes. There's a note here that you're to report to General Cipolla before you leave."

Ross blinked in surprise. "*General* Cipolla?"

"That's right, sir. Promotion orders caught up with him yesterday. He's set up an office behind those file cabinets in the far corner."

"Well, I'll be triple damned," Ross said, grinning from ear to ear. "This will be a pleasure. Cliff, why don't you track down this Captain Gross and get a weather briefing while I check in with the boss."

Ross rapped his knuckles on one of the filing cabinets forming a barrier around the wing deputy commander's desk. Cipolla laid aside a two-page TWX he'd been glowering at.

Ross snapped to attention and saluted. "Sir! Major Colyer, Ross, reporting as ordered, sir!" he barked in a parade-ground voice.

"Knock that shit off, you clown," the neophyte one-star growled with a self-conscious grin. "If it wasn't for the pay raise, I'd have turned it down. By God, it makes me feel *old*."

"Why, you *are* old, sir," Ross responded with mock concern. "If they ever let you fly by yourself again, why, I'll be glad to carry your parachute to the plane for you. Seriously, congratulations."

"Thanks. How was the flight over?"

"Routine. Atkins limped into Reykjavik with number two feathered—it may be an engine change—but the other four are right behind me."

Cipolla grunted. "You got your work cut out, guy. We're getting outfits from all over, and they each have their own way of doing things. In themselves they're damn good, but we have trouble when we try to interfly planes and mix crew members. For example, the squadron commanders insist on maintaining unit integrity—wanted to fly into Berlin in formation, like they did during the war. The first run was damn near a disaster. A dozen planes arriving at Berlin simultaneously, no maneuvering room, well . . ." He shrugged.

"I can imagine. I flew over with the ops officer for the 901st. He's an old Hump pilot, and sharp. We came up with a few ideas."

"Good. We've been lucky just to have lost one plane so far. I want your impression of the setup at the other end before we start making too many changes; that's why you're not getting any crew rest. Look for ways to streamline the turnaround process. More sorties per bird, *not* a whole damn skyful of airplanes, is the answer. Don't worry about doing everything by the book—the books are going to have to be rewritten for this job. Now, I know you're pressed for time. I'll see you here in the morning."

"Yes, sir." Ross started to leave, then asked, "Er—General—about that business we discussed at dinner the other night. Anything happening I should know about?"

Cipolla regarded Ross at some length. "Hard to say. The politicos are optimistic—the brass is pessimistic. A lot will depend on how many groceries we can get into the city." With a mirthless smile he added, "Just like the war—only this time we're trying to win it with dried potatoes and Spam."

Ross spotted Worsham's battered, sweat-stained flight cap at the tent's far end. Cliff and a serious-faced captain stood in front of a planning map tacked to a piece of wallboard. They turned as Ross approached.

"Here's Major Colyer," the copilot announced. "Ross, this is our check pilot, Captain Gross. I have our canned flight plan and weather. Chuck was just showing me the corridor route."

Gross extended his hand with a friendly, "Hi, Major. Welcome to the circus. Understand I have the privilege of giving our new chief pilot a checkride—not to mention a squadron ops officer. They sure as hell didn't give you much time to get settled in."

Ross returned the captain's handshake and did a swift summing up. The man's craggy features and easygoing drawl would seem more at home in a Stetson and cowboy boots, he thought. "We got us a general who believes in hitting the ground running," he replied. "Can you fill us in over chow? My stomach feels like it has a wolf down there."

"Not a problem. Chow is one thing there's plenty of. We're working our asses off, sleeping cold and damp, and have the social life of a cloistered eunuch, but by God we eat good. C'mon."

Seated at a long, oilcloth-covered table inside the malodorous dining hall, Ross swallowed a mouthful of fried steak and asked Gross, "What's the crew situation in general?"

"Existing crews are okay—oh, we may have to waive the hundred-hour-per-month rule, but all squadrons are almost up to TO authorized strength. Crews for the planes coming out of mothballs in the States will be something else. We're trying to get as many copilots left-seat qualified as possible, but that means upgrading existing pilots to instructor pilot so they can check out copilots in the left seat on missions."

Ross grunted understanding and mopped up the last bit of gravy with a hard roll. "What happens to planes that wander outside the corridor?"

"Nothing so far, but then, we haven't had a pilot who's confessed to straying off course." Gross chuckled. "We know they have antiaircraft batteries, and the Russian fighter pilots fly with hot guns. I also know we *must* have had some violations. You only have reliable ADF tracking for about seventy miles outbound from Fulda beacon and maybe fifty miles inbound to Tempelhof. In between it's pure dead reckoning. The Brits use a better setup. They keep their planes dead on centerline with the Rebecca-Eureka system."

Ross glanced at his watch, shoved his empty tray back, and said, "Okay. I guess we'd best go back, file our flight plan, and leap off. The quick glimpse I had at the weather map shows the Berlin area to be in the clear. I hope so; I want to have some idea of what we're up against."

Gross stood and said, "Yeah, you should be able to get a good look;

this time of year it stays light until about twenty-one hundred." He laughed. "Sometimes I think it's better *not* to see that approach. Next time you come wheeling in, busting minimums on a rainy night, just thinking about what you can't see out there will increase the old pucker factor."

The trio worked their way through the noisy press of bodies to the dispatch table. Gross led them to an oversized clipboard to one side labeled, NOTICES TO AIRMEN. "*Always* check the NOTAM file," he advised. "Things change every hour, it seems." He turned to one yellow TWX, mounted separate from the others, and framed with red grease pencil. He gave a low whistle. "Those arrogant bastards," he grated. "Look at this: 'SMA'—that's the Soviet Military Administration—'announces that Soviet Air Force units will conduct a training exercise in both the south and west quadrants on ten and eleven July. Aircraft not participating in the exercise are advised to avoid flying below four thousand meters in the designated area.'"

"Can they *do* that, for Christ's sake?" Worsham asked.

"Just who the hell is going to stop 'em? Our people will file a protest— which they'll ignore. We'll fly through the warning area—they'll protest, which *we* will ignore." Gross shrugged. "It's a game—a war of nerves which they are very, very good at."

"I'd like to have just one flight of four Mustangs," Ross said, his eyes taking on an icy glint. "See how pucker-proof *their* assholes are."

"That's right, you are an old fighter jock, aren't you? Well, today, we'll just have to hope the crazy bastards keep out of our way. You ready?"

Ross made a quick walk-around as four GIs, wet with sweat and the persistent drizzle, lashed down the last of a stack of cartons labeled DEHYDRATED POTATOES—U.S. Army Quartermaster Corps. He grinned at Cliff. "Bet there's singing and dancing in the GI mess halls to see that stuff disappear."

"Yeah," Cliff said. "Hard to believe them folks in Berlin will be just as happy to *get* this load. During the Hump, we didn't mind risking our asses to haul bombs, but *dehydrated potatoes?*" He shook his head. "I dunno. . . ."

Their check pilot stood between the pilots' seats as Ross cranked up with Cliff reading him the before-takeoff checklist. While they waited for taxi-out clearance, Gross explained, "Now you gotta follow that flight plan without deviation—altitudes, times, and headings are all mandatory. You won't need to make position reports—the damn radio is cluttered enough as it is. You'll report 'Ops Normal' leaving the Fulda beacon, on course, and that's it until you cross Wedding beacon south of Berlin. There you slow to a hundred and forty and wait for landing instructions from GCA."

The laden C-47 seemed to shudder with distaste as it poked its nose into the gloomy murk after takeoff. Cliff, an E6B navigation computer in hand, followed their progress with tight-lipped concentration, calling off turning points as Ross nursed the laboring Gooney Bird to their assigned altitude of four thousand feet. "Okay, over Darmstadt at one-three, the heading for Aschaffenburg is zero-eight-three. After that, our ETA for the Fulda beacon is seventeen one-five."

Worsham's precise navigation placed them on course for Berlin from Fulda exactly on flight plan. Ross set up the autopilot and accepted a cup of coffee. Lumbering along through the opaque cloud mass gave you a false sense of security—of being invisible—he mused. The damn Reds down there were watching them on radar, you could bet. Like Gross had said, there hadn't been a reported corridor violation yet, but . . .

Thirty minutes later, the ADF needle, pointing behind them toward the Fulda beacon, commenced swinging erratically. "Out of range," Gross advised. "You're on your own through this part. Looks like we're getting some breaks in the clouds, however . . ." He stopped as the plane plunged into brilliant sunlight. "Hey," he continued, "you're living right. Let's see." He scanned the rolling, green terrain below. "There, see that town where the autobahn and double-track railroad cross? That's Dessau, and marks the exact center of the corridor. You're maybe a mile to the right of course—good job there, Cliff old boy."

Worsham grinned. "You got this route memorized? How many damn trips have you made along here?"

"During the past year, several," the soft-spoken Texan drawled. "And any time you can see the ground, you cross-check. Up to now, a violation of Soviet airspace got you a written reprimand, and maybe meant getting busted back to copilot. Now, who knows?"

Ross listened to the exchange, but was concentrating on a visual examination of what he still subconsciously considered enemy territory. He wouldn't have been surprised suddenly to see blue-white muzzle blasts of the hated German 88mm antiaircraft guns—a swarm of dots swirling out of the sun, spitting red tracers. He jerked to rigid attention as he spotted an airplane on a converging course from their right.

"Hey," he called. "Over there, ten o'clock level. We got company."

Gross leaned over Ross's shoulder and studied the distant aircraft. "Not one of ours," he muttered. "Could be one of their Il-4 twin-engine bombers, or a transport. The son of a bitch is on a collision course, whatever he's flying."

"Well, Cliff," said Ross, "jot down the exact time, position, our heading and altitude, and his heading. We'll write it up when we land. But," he added grimly, "with the legal business taken care of, I'm going to give that bastard a lesson about unauthorized flight inside a control zone. Set climb power, Cliff. Check pilot, you wanta go back and examine the cargo while I maybe do something you shouldn't know about?"

Gross nodded with feigned concern. "We sure wouldn't want anything to happen to those dried spuds back there. But I think I'll wait a bit. You have the right-of-way, and you're an old fighter pilot—I'd like to see what you can do with your speedy CF-47."

"Okay, grab hold of—"

Ross halted in midsentence as Worsham yelled, "Hold it! He's towing something—Christ, it looks like a sleeve target."

"I'll be damned," Gross muttered softly. "So that's what they meant by their NOTAM. 'Conducting training exercises,' my ass. They're practicing air-to-air gunnery *inside the fucking corridor*."

Ross watched distance between the two planes close swiftly. He was the first to see the two black specks materialize at nine o'clock and dart toward the tow plane. "Well, ol' buddy," he told Gross, "like you said, 'I got the right-of-way.' One small problem. I guess you remember the rest of that joke: 'Yeah, but the other guy's got a truck.' I do believe evasive action is called for." The crew watched with set expressions as a pair of ugly, stubby-nosed Yak fighters flashed past, wings spitting tracers at the sleeve target.

11 July 1948
Rhine-Main Airfield, West Germany
Ross accepted Cipolla's invitation to sit and settled gratefully onto a battered wooden chair beside the general's scrounged table-cum-desk. The

general stripped the cover from a fresh cigar and applied flame from a Zippo lighter. It was all done with great deliberation and without further comment. When the rolled, aromatic leaf was burning to his satisfaction, he leaned back and said, "You look kinda ragged around the edges this morning. Rough trip?"

"A long day. And the Reds aren't going to make it easy for us. Would you believe they were doing air-to-air gunnery practice in the middle of the goddamned corridor? Much more of that shit and I'm going to insist on a fighter escort—like you know who."

Cipolla answered with a noncommittal grunt, and Ross continued. "Thank God it was VFR at the other end—that approach is a bitch. For one thing, you skim across a graveyard just off the touchdown end that doesn't exactly inspire a warm, cuddly feeling. The guy that gave us the corridor check told us we maybe shouldn't have made our first landing during clear weather. He was right. Airplanes everywhere; the Brits going into Tegel and Gatow almost in Tempelhof's traffic pattern—it's downright scary. Captain Worsham and I talked on the way over about cutting the interval to about three minutes if we were ever to move the tonnage they're talking about. Now I dunno."

Cipolla nodded. "So happens, you were on target. I have the ops people working on that right now. But"—the general paused and scratched his chin—"flying isn't what I wanted to talk to you about."

"Oh? I thought that's why you gave me that hurry-up trip, to get a first-hand look, sir."

"That was yesterday." Cipolla's demeanor turned chilly. "Ross, I want to know what the hell you've been up to. I have a TWX here I don't understand, and I'm going to scream like a wounded wildcat until I have some answers."

Ross regarded his suddenly irate commander with a look of utter bewilderment. "Sir, I'm sorry, but I don't have the foggiest idea what you're talking about."

"Oh? Then I'll proceed to enlighten you. I'm talking about this." Cipolla unlocked a file drawer and extracted a buff-colored folder. Ross saw it contained a single sheet of paper and was stamped SECRET in red, block letters.

"Okay." The general removed the cigar from his mouth and bent a cold stare in Ross's direction. "I hold here a TWX from—never mind who—

that tells me to cut orders on you, detaching you from your present duties for performance of an as yet unspecified mission under operational control of an unspecified agency of the United States government—by direction of the president, no less. You will remain assigned to the 7744th for administrative purposes and will report back at completion of aforesaid mission."

Ross had never seen the normally unflappable Cipolla so angry. His voice trembled, and his face was suffused with an apoplectic hue. "Now, I want to know, chapter and verse, what the flaming hell is going on? I have an impossible job on my hands, a top priority contingency plan in my hip pocket, and I'm told—ever so casually—'By the way, you don't have your chief pilot anymore.'"

"Sir—I—I'm as much in the dark as you are. Believe me, I don't have a clue. Could it maybe have something to do with that ops plan you were telling me about?"

"Not a chance," Cipolla went on, his tone moderating slightly, "I believe you—it's just that . . . ah, to hell with it. You're to report immediately to a Lieutenant Colonel Pearson in USAFE headquarters."

Ross's driver skidded the jeep to a halt just short of a barber-pole barrier. "As far as I can go, sir," he said.

An air policeman in combat gear, and with a carbine slung from his shoulder, saluted and asked, "May I see your orders, sir?"

"Well, I don't have written orders," Ross replied. "I was told to report to a Lieutenant Colonel Pearson in USAFE headquarters."

"Yes, sir. May I see your ID?"

After being escorted inside the brooding, stone building that once housed Goering's finest, Ross was escorted past yet a second checkpoint. A neatly lettered sign on the door read SPECIAL OPERATIONS.

Lieutenant Colonel Pearson was a slender man whose sandy hair, thinning in the back, made him look older than the midthirties Ross guessed him to be. He waved Ross to a chair while speaking into the phone wedged between jaw and shoulder. He cradled the instrument and sighed. "This place is a madhouse. No one seems to know what the hell is going on, or what's going to happen next." He waved to his cluttered desktop. "Half of this stuff will be rescinded before I even get a chance to read it. But . . . you must be Major Colyer."

"Yes, sir. Here's my ID, but I don't have orders."

"That's okay. I have your records." He retrieved a folder from an overflowing file basket. "I guess you're wondering just what the hell you're doing here."

"A good guess, Colonel."

Pearson smiled briefly. "And not overjoyed, I imagine. Well, I'll give it to you as shortly and sweetly as I can. Special Operations is a catchall for jobs no one else wants. In this case, we've been told to get a German rocket scientist out of Berlin's Russian zone. The pipeline we've used before got cut when the Reds closed the border. The only way out now is by air."

"And you want me to bring him out on one of our supply runs."

"It isn't that simple, I'm afraid. You see, we can't get him into the Allied zone. He's holed up outside Berlin."

"Oh."

"See the problem? Someone is gonna have to pick him up from right under the Vopos' nose and get him to one of our bases in West Berlin.

"And that someone? Let me guess."

Pearson's face cracked again in a fleeting grin. "I do believe you've been eavesdropping. We figure that a light plane, at night, quick in, quick out, is the best bet. Our contact is nervous—scared silly—and won't even talk about smuggling the man into East Berlin and through a checkpoint."

"Why me, Colonel? Hell, I've only been in the theater two days."

"The Pentagon personnel types can move real fast when they have to. You were involved in a clandestine operation with the sneaky-Petes, and most important, you're qualified in the Norduyn Norseman. The Brits have one at Gatow they'll loan us, and we don't have a pilot in our records with recent time in one."

"You say the Brits have the airplane? Why not let one of their pilots do this little chore?"

"Not in the cards for this one. We consider this scientist *ours*. The British bring him out—*they* want him. Understand?"

"Not really, but I'll take your word for it. But does it have to be a Norseman? I know they have L-20s, Cubs, and the like there."

"The Norseman is the only one with enough range."

"Range? Just where the hell *is* this guy, that he's out of a Cub's radius of action?"

"I don't even know that myself. His control is in Berlin. You'll get your mission briefing from him."

"I just hope this guy is worth the effort."

"He is—according to the eggheads. They almost wet their pants when the overland route went down. Now, you can sit here and read what I know. Memorize your instructions; there'll be nothing in writing."

4

13 July 1948
Tempelhof Airfield

Ross keyed his mike and said, "Roger, Tempelhof GCA. Leaving four thousand feet for one-five hundred, turning now to heading one-four-zero. Before-landing checklist complete, over." He watched Worsham let Hobo Four settle into a five-hundred-foot-per-minute descent and roll onto the runway heading. The man had a deft touch that made the precision approach look easy.

The captain would make a good replacement as Cipolla's chief pilot, he decided. He returned his full attention to monitoring the approach to landing through rain-lashed darkness; the thought of four-story apartment buildings just off their left wing was a powerful incentive to stay alert.

"You're approaching minimum altitude, Hobo Four," the GCA operator droned. "You're on centerline, on glide path—you are now cleared to land. Wind is presently from one-eight-five degrees at one-niner, gusting to two-seven. Reported runway visibility is one mile in rain showers. You're drifting left now; correct two degrees right to one-four-six. You're passing through minimums; take over visually and land your aircraft. If runway is not in sight, execute missed approach, over."

Ross watched mist-shrouded runway lights emerge from the darkness and called, "Field in sight—eleven o'clock. Standing by landing lights and flaps."

"Roger," Cliff responded. "Let's have full flaps—lights on, and I'll need the windshield wipers."

Ross flipped switches with sure fingers and watched the field boundary pass underneath. Moments later, Worsham was wheeling the plane in a tight circle to park beneath Tempelhof's huge terminal overhang.

"Neatly done, m'lad," Ross stated as he flicked on cockpit lights and reached for the Form 1. "Have a smooth flight back, and good luck with your new job. You'll find the general to be a super guy to work for. If I ever get away from this place, we'll look up some of those 'lissome *fräuleins*' and put away some beer, okay?"

"Anytime, Ross." Worsham's face took on a speculative squint in the dim cockpit lighting. "I'd wish you luck in *your* new job, if I understood just what the hell it was. With all the 'liaison' types running around USAFE headquarters, it's hard to understand why the general picked the best pilot in the theater to send up here. Is there more to this than meets the eye?"

The pained expression Ross assumed wasn't entirely a facade. He *was* pissed off, damnit. "Cliff, this is just between the two of us, but I screwed up before we left the States—said the wrong thing at the wrong time. The old man has banished me to the Berlin end while the brass decides whether or not I'll face a board. I'm not all that worried, but at the same time . . ."

"It happens—just hope you come out with a whole skin. Anyway, it's been a real pleasure working with you, brief as it was. I'm in your corner, if ever I can . . . you know."

"I appreciate that vote of confidence—more than you know," Ross said gruffly. He eased from his seat and clapped Cliff's shoulder as he left the cockpit and entered the cargo compartment. The lieutenant who would replace him as copilot for the return trip had already pointed out Ross's B-4 bag and an unlabeled carton to one of the cargo handlers.

Well, the lies are starting, Ross thought as he watched his baggage being loaded onto a weapons carrier. Do you ever get used to it? Do you ever get to the point where you *believe* the disinformation you spread? Does it become instinctive to invent an untruth when there's no real reason to? I thought all that crap was behind me.

The exit interview with General Cipolla had done little to improve his frame of mind. "General, I have orders transferring me to Berlin as a member of the four-power Air Safety Board. That's all I can tell you, officially. There may be some strange stories coming back to you. All I can ask is that you trust me. I want that jet squadron, sir."

Cipolla's expression was bleak as he replied, "I do trust you, but I gotta level with you. The mission comes first; I'll not jeopardize it to cover your ass. Will you be available if we implement that ops order I discussed with you?"

Ross's anguish deepened. "I—I can't guarantee that, sir."

"I see. Then do what you must do. Do you recommend anyone for your replacement?"

Ross winced; the words sounded so damn final. "The job isn't supposed to take long, sir. But you know how that goes. . . . I'd suggest Captain Worsham for the chief pilot job here, General. As for the F-80 squadron, Colonel Babcock, back at Wright, is tops—and he's bitter that he wasn't selected over me."

"Well, we both have work to do." Cipolla shuffled papers that didn't need shuffling. "I'll go with your suggestion of Worsham as chief pilot, even if he isn't field grade. About the squadron, let's not borrow trouble." He stuck out his hand. "I've seen others go the route you're taking. It's a thankless job, but I know you'll do your best. Only time will tell whether it . . ." He let his voice trail off.

Ross shook the proffered hand, then stepped back and saluted. Worming his way through the noisy hubbub of the ops tent, he wondered what the general was about to say there at the end. He had a strong suspicion that the old man was about to tell him that forays into the spy business did little to enhance one's career as an operational commander.

Ross took his time transiting the terminal's main corridor next morning, following directions to the commandant's office. He couldn't help gawking at the sumptuous marble columns and vaulted ceiling. The building was huge, its floor plan an arc embracing a concrete block parking ramp beneath a four-story-high overhang. One of Hitler's many ostentatious showplaces, Tempelhof was a miniature city within the city of Berlin. Its three stories aboveground had, in better days, housed shops, restaurants, and spacious living quarters for the Luftwaffe personnel manning the fighter planes charged with defending the capital. Subterranean chambers had concealed a major Messerschmitt aircraft factory.

The few low-wattage bulbs permitted under Berlin's sharp curtailment of electricity reduced the formerly opulent main concourse to a dingy, gloomy cavern. Conversion to strictly utilitarian purposes hadn't completely obliterated the structure's former grandeur, however. Ross located the entrance to headquarters by joining the stream of uniformed figures scurrying in and out of a set of eight-foot double doors. A sentry checked his ID and pointed toward a waist-high counter supporting a sign reading, RECEPTION.

"I'm to report to Colonel Yates," Ross told the corporal who greeted him.

"Yes, sir. If you'll just sign in, I'll see where he might be—he ain't never in his office. Sarge," he called above the din of ringing telephones, banging file drawers, and voices of a dozen clerks talking at once, "you know where the major can find Colonel Yates?"

Without looking up from the clutter of his desk, an annoyed-looking staff sergeant yelled back, "Last I knew he was up in the tower. You might try there, but who knows?"

"Take them steps over in the corner, Major," the corporal advised. "The control tower's four flights up, on the roof. You'll have to walk, sir; elevator don't work since they cut back our electricity."

Ross paused to catch his breath on the fourth-floor landing. He faced a blank door with RESTRICTED AREA—AUTHORIZED PERSONNEL ONLY printed in six-inch block letters. A typed notice above a bell push advised visitors to ring for admission. He complied, and soon confronted a sharp-eyed NCO who asked, "Yes, sir?"

"Is Colonel Yates up here? I'm to report to him."

A swift scrutiny produced a cheerful, "C'mon in, Major. The colonel is right over there." He pointed toward a khaki-uniformed man seated atop a desk, coffee mug cupped in both hands, and wearing a morose expression on his craggy features.

Ross blinked as his eyes adjusted from the unlighted stairwell to blindingly bright surroundings. The sun, just emerged from low, scattered clouds, cast a warm glow through floor-to-ceiling glass panels, revealing a beehive of activity. A half-dozen GIs, bathed in swirling cigarette smoke and surrounded by Coke bottles, sat at consoles wearing headphones and staring hypnotically at a panel of radio controls. Most were speaking into pedestal microphones and shifting strips of paper in a specially designed air-traffic display board. A beefy master sergeant, chewing a dead cigar, roamed the enclosure, barking directions.

Colonel Yates watched Ross make his way around a table where four haggard, off-duty operators were taking a break. "'Morning, Major. What can I do for you?"

"Good morning, sir. I'm Ross Colyer, and I have orders to report to the commandant, Tempelhof Terminal." He extended the buff-colored envelope he'd removed from his briefcase.

Yates reached for the missive without removing his gaze from Ross's face as he added, "That's me, I guess." His eyebrows raised as he remarked, "*Sealed* orders yet—my, my, what bad news can you be bringing that I don't already have enough of?" He casually examined the envelope's contents and made a wry grimace. Ross caught a glimpse of the word SECRET stamped in red on the first page.

The colonel slid from the desk and said, "Guess we'd best go to my office to discuss this." He grinned and added, "I come up here to relax. It may seem chaotic to you, but it beats the mob scene down below. Besides, I feel like I'm in control of something up here; in my office I only seem to react to a never-ending parade of crises."

Ross followed the amiable commandant back down the stairs to a second-floor office. Yates waved aside a worried clerk, frantically waggling a sheaf of papers, with, "Later, Norton, later. I'm going to close my door—don't put through any calls until I finish, okay?" The colonel pointed Ross toward a baroque side chair and perched on the edge of a massive antique desk of gleaming dark wood.

Yates read the two-page document carefully while Ross surveyed the office's impressive decor. The colonel's German predecessor had had lavish tastes, he observed to himself—paneled walls, heavy, dark-blue draperies that framed windows overlooking the airfield, and a lush matching carpet. The colonel refolded the pages and tapped them absently on his thigh. "Do you know what's in here?" he asked.

"Generally, sir. I didn't read them."

"Okay," Yates said with a sigh, "the first thing I'm supposed to do is put you in the picture—the political picture, not the operational one.

"Your assignment to the Air Safety Center of the Allied Control Commission is a joke. The ACC hasn't functioned since the Soviets pulled out of it in March. The Air Safety Board still meets, ostensibly for the purpose of keeping our airplanes from running into each other. In actuality, no one pays the slightest bit of attention to their reports.

"The Reds still show up at the Kommandatura, the four-power administrative body, but already the city is divided into two zones for all practical purposes: Soviet and Allied. Their grand strategy seems to be one of starving the Berliners into asking us to leave. So far the Germans living in the Allied sectors are firm in their desire to have us stay—but they aren't *really* hungry yet, nor cold." Yates stroked his chin. "Can we sustain an operation to provide the fifteen hundred tons per day they need for just minimum subsistence? And this doesn't include the coal required to keep a trickle of electrical generating capability or heat this winter."

"General LeMay says we can," Ross said. "More planes—including three wings of C-54s—are on the way. B-29s and F-80s, too—for backup. Do the Russians show any signs of starting a shooting war if we stay? And what would be the Berliners' reaction if they thought they were going to be caught in the middle of another war?"

"Sixty-four-dollar questions," Yates mused. "The Russians aren't easy to second-guess. So, that's a quick and dirty rundown. Don Banks will give you details of the operation. He's with the security detachment here—that's a euphemism for cloak and dagger. They all wear civilian clothes, but who knows? Most are former OSS types. I'll send for him, but in the meantime why don't you find a place to live. If, as you say, this isn't apt to be a long stay, I suggest the transient BOQ right here in this building. There's a mess in the basement."

Ross's attempt to catch a quick nap was interrupted by three quick raps on the door. He swung his feet to the floor. "C'mon in," he called "it's unlocked."

"Major Colyer?" a man in a rumpled suit inquired.

"The one and only. What can I do for you?"

"Hi, I'm Don Banks. Colonel Yates said you might still be here. It seemed like a good place to talk. I can't take you into our area until we get your clearance processed."

"Be my guest. Take the chair, I'll use the cot. Sorry I can't offer a drink or a snack."

"I'll survive. So you're our pilot. I suppose you know some of what's up."

"Just that I'm to sneak a Norseman into someplace in Red territory, pick up one of your people, and bring him back here."

Banks chuckled. "You do have a succinct manner of stating things. I'm afraid there's just a wee bit more to it than that, however."

Ross sighed. "Somehow I thought there would be. I've dealt with your crowd before. What's the catch?"

"The first problem is getting things set up at the other end." Banks's round, pink face wore a disarming smile. "Our man—we'll call him

Max—is at a way station about a hundred miles south of here, near Leipzig. The plan was to move him by land to a chink in the Iron Curtain, and into West Germany. That route is closed; the network that ran it has been rolled up."

"Oh, great. Then we're starting from square one. Arranging a pickup point, times, signals—the whole bit."

"That's about it. The idea of flying him out was just recently hatched. We didn't have a pilot lined up, so not much has been done."

"Whoooo, boy. Okay, where do we start? I'll need to know the landing strip, the radar coverage down there, some way to communicate, things like that. Then I understand the Norseman is at Gatow. I'd like to take a look at it, fly it if possible."

"I'll get some people on working up a plan as soon as I get back to my office. Communications won't be easy. You see, we've been using the Gehlen operation, and everything has to be relayed."

"Gehlen?"

"Reinhardt Gehlen. You've not heard of him?"

"Afraid not."

"He was chief of intelligence for the German Army. He survived the war with his entire espionage network intact. He just went into business for himself, selling information to the highest bidder. We sort of have a— well, subcontract with him."

"That's peachy. How long is all this going to take?"

"We'll move as fast as humanly possible. Max has been missing from his job inside the Soviet Union for about two weeks now. The East Germans have been alerted and are going balls to the wall to intercept him. The people who are hiding him are nervous." Banks stood and stretched weary shoulder muscles. "I'll get your clearance okayed and give you a place to study maps and such by tomorrow morning. Okay?"

"And the airplane?"

"Uh, that can be touchy. Max was a team leader at Peenemünde. We're in a polite race with the British for rocket technology just now. We have no objection to sharing, but we'd like to look at the merchandise first, if you get my drift. Let us come up with a cover story about why we want to borrow the Norseman."

Banks squirmed to a more comfortable position and continued. "While you're waiting, be sure to follow through with your cover—the Air

Safety Center. The Russians have a man on the board, a General Pavel. An interesting guy, I hear.

"Now, the Reds always make a point of having an officer who is senior in rank to the Allied members of all boards, committees, and the like— it's easier to dominate proceedings that way. Major General Sergei Pavel is a good example. He's a hero of Stalingrad and wears the gold star Hero of the Soviet Union medal. He's definitely one of Stalin's favorites—and Uncle Joe isn't known for his fondness for his officer corps.

"The general is their figurehead on your relatively minor committee; he speaks fair English but pretends not to understand. He uses a translator who, incidentally, is listed as an air force major but is actually the Soviet mission's Communist Party watchdog. Try to get to know the general; you might pick up something useful about radar coverage from him."

Ross accepted the cup of coffee Colonel Yates offered and stirred in canned milk. The incessant roar of planes, a voice of cold, mechanized anger, filled the colonel's comfortable office. It reverberated in the bizarre stone ears of the hollow, broken houses; its throbbing thunder meaning one thing: The West was once more standing its ground and fighting back.

They stood at an open window and watched. Three battered C-47s squatted nose to tail, waiting to take off behind the one just flaring for landing. Lumbering ten-ton trucks were being loaded from two other planes, whose crews were wolfing down sandwiches and hot coffee from a Red Cross canteen truck. "It won't be enough," Yates muttered, half to himself. "Eighty tons yesterday—we need ten times that much."

Ross realized that this was the first sunny day in more than a week. The Berliners were forgetting their grim plight, and several hundred had traveled to Tempelhof Airport. Sitting amid the ruins surrounding the field, perched in trees and on fences, they watched the steady, reassuring stream of planes roaring out of the skies. "I can't help but wonder," he muttered, "how many of those same sets of eyes watched me five years ago while our formation of B-24s dumped a few tons of high explosives and incendiaries on their fair cities."

Yates's eyes crinkled at the corners. "It's a strange world we live in, all right.

"Okay, Don Banks asked me to introduce you to Wing Commander Ashcroft over at Gatow and invent a reason to borrow their Norseman." He smiled. "Don and his crowd get so wrapped up in their mysterious games that they forget how to do anything the simple way. I'll just go over and say, 'Ashy, old chap, we want to borrow one of your bloody airplanes for a couple of days. Don't ask questions, hear?'"

26 July 1948
Berlin

Ross felt his eyes growing heavy and snapped awake. The little meeting room was fusty with heat and the odor of infrequently bathed bodies. The Russian translator's droning discourse was a more potent sedative than any morphine derivative. He caught, ". . . and the commander, Soviet Military Commission, objects most strenuously to the arrogant disregard for . . ." and returned to a study of the other conferees.

Major Bruce Creighton, Royal Air Force, wore a dazed, vacuous expression on his ruddy features. Comdr. Guy Desmond, French Air Force—making no pretense of hiding his impatience—glanced at his watch and lit a small, black cigar. Only General Pavel, representing the Soviets, seemed interested in hearing his own words repeated in English.

Ross reran the Russian's file in his mind. Quite a guy, he mused. Veteran of the Spanish War, he commanded the VVS's 285th Fighter Air Division, whose Il-2 Shturmoviks took the brunt of the German advance on Stalingrad. Their backs to the wall, the bitter Russian winter both ally and enemy, the sturdy fighter-bombers flew around the clock against targets sometimes within ten miles of Stalingrad's city walls.

Pavel claimed one of his men invented the "ramming" attack. Out of ammo for his 23mm guns, the frustrated pilot deliberately flew into the tail of an attacking Dornier bomber, chopping it's tail assembly to shreds with his prop. The fighter was destroyed on landing, but it was a victory. Pavel's commendation for the Order of the Red Banner read in part, ". . . Colonel Pavel's inspired order not only led others to destroy large numbers of the enemy, the ramming tactic struck fear in the hearts of the Nazi pilots. . . ."

The Hero of the Soviet Union was awarded the newly promoted general for leading a most devastating attack on units of Hitler's Sixth Army dug in at Pitommik. Under cover of darkness, Pavel led the entire Six-teenth Air Army to the German's sole remaining airfield. Making their first pass at tree-top level, then returning to make up to six following passes, the Il-2s—dubbed "The Concrete Bomber" by the Germans—destroyed seventy transports.

Ross realized the meeting was being adjourned. Major Creighton, whose turn it was to act as recording secretary, was stuffing papers into his attaché case and mumbling, "Be it resolved that the matter of over-flights across Soviet-controlled airspace is tabled. A full report will be submitted by the Soviet representative at our next meeting. Copies of minutes will be provided all parties." The last was flung over his shoulder as he fled.

General Pavel remained hunched in his chair, pockmarked features unreadable. Ross stood, posing slightly to demonstrate the fit of his new, impeccably tailored uniform. He closed his hand-stitched leather brief-case with studied indifference. From the corner of one eye he caught Pavel casting him an envious glance.

The Soviet general growled something to his interpreter. The words were quickly translated: "The general notes that this is the major's first appearance at our gathering. You are recently arrived in Berlin?"

Ross favored Pavel with a languid nod of acknowledgment and said, "Just two weeks ago." He gave a slight shudder of distaste. "A dreary place, I must say. I've had the devil's own time finding decent accom-modations."

Again, the minion quickly translated, "You were successful, I gather?"

Ross gave a scornful laugh. "Somewhat. It seems that the widow of a deceased Nazi admiral is anxious to accommodate the sole source of her dehydrated potatoes and dried fish—happy that I would permit her to reserve two rooms for herself." He smirked. "There was, of course, another consideration." He rubbed his thumb and forefinger together.

Pavel's expression didn't change. He regarded Ross from beneath hooded lids and barked a guttural question that came out, "A temporary arrangement, I trust? I hardly think the chances of prolonged American presence here would require a long-term lease."

Ross shrugged. "Who knows? I adapt. One week—two years—I make the best of unpleasant surroundings. Now, if the general will excuse me?

He smiled broadly and strolled to the door, feeling the general's gimlet eyes boring into his departing back.

Ross emerged from the partially restored offices of a prewar clothing factory—commandeered by the occupying powers to house the Air Safety Center—into a steady drizzle. Cursing his failure to bring a raincoat, he trotted toward where, hopefully, a tram would arrive to take him back to Tempelhof.

5

Ross sipped his coffee, made a face, and shoved the mug to one side. "When was this damned stuff made? It tastes like it's been used to soak old flashlight batteries."

Don Banks rubbed bloodshot eyes and tossed his pencil onto the table's jumble of papers. "About the same time we sat down here—eighteen hundred or thereabouts."

Ross looked at his watch. "Good God, after midnight. Are we any closer to a go time?"

"Harv," Banks yelled at a figure slumped in front of the glowing dials of a Siemens radio transceiver, "you got anything?"

The man addressed as Harv removed his headset and shook his head. "They left Elmstadt at sixteen hundred and should have reached the lodge a couple hours ago. But Uncle says the whole area is crawling with Vopos. They may be holed up someplace. There's still time."

"Not much," Ross said. "If I can't get airborne within about an hour, we're gonna run out of dark. Stooging around with that crate after sunup is out. Besides, the damned weather forecast calls for early morning fog in the Frankfurt area. That Norseman is a great airplane, but I'll be VFR."

"We're running out of time, Ross, not hours, but days." Banks walked to the coffeepot, took one look at its black, brackish contents, and shuddered. "If the Vopos smell a pickup, they'll saturate the area and camp out on every place where a plane can land. The friendlies that Uncle has lined up to get Max from the lodge to the landing strip, light flares, and mount some kind of rearguard action, will vanish.

"They'll have to move Max yet again, and start all over. I'm surprised that they haven't been caught already—three weeks of playing hide-and-seek is close to being a miracle, and his baby-sitters are getting an advanced case of the jitters."

"Colonel Yates is getting upset as well," Ross said. "The British air ops officer is asking him when he can have his bloody airplane back. Plus, I'm—"

"Contact, Don." Banks and Ross turned to see Harv with the headset clamped to his ears. He was scribbling madly. "Stand by," he said shortly into the transmitter.

"Not good, Don," Harv advised. "They never reached the lodge—they spotted a reception party. Uncle says the group is hiding in a bombed-out railroad station. He thinks they can get Max to the airstrip, but it's a one-shot trip. If he isn't picked up, they're hanging out to dry come daylight. Unless we can confirm, they'll move him east yet tonight."

"East? They're already damned near out of the Norseman's range," Ross protested.

"Believe me, it's an emergency move," Banks said. The Reds are going all out to keep this guy away from the frontier. And just a reminder: A few more nights, and we won't have enough moonlight for you to find the strip."

"He must be a hot property to have the entire East German police force out." Ross scowled at the map spread before him. "Ask this Uncle if they can have him in place not later than oh-three-hundred, and to confirm the light signals."

"That was his one and only transmission. There's a direction finder truck in the area. I can send him messages, but he won't fire up his transmitter again."

Ross started folding up the map. "Tell him that I'll make one pass between oh-three-hundred and oh-three-fifteen. If I don't get an all clear, I'm gone."

"I can understand your problem, Ross," Banks said softly, "but before you decide to abort after one pass, there's something you should know— something that I had to hold back until the last minute. Max isn't just a rocket scientist—he was working on the Soviets' atomic bomb."

Ross, flashlight in hand, ran a quick exterior inspection. The Norduyn Norseman wasn't a pretty airplane—squat, fabric-covered fuselage, the

front end blunted by a single Pratt & Whitney radial engine. Fixed landing gear added yet another awkward-looking appendage. Slow, capable
of only 100 mph at cruise power, the Norseman carried an amazing two-
thousand-pound payload. It had become the favorite of Canadian "bush
pilots" from the very beginning and was perfect for the job ahead.

Ten minutes later, he watched the Tempelhof runway lights fade as he
swung onto a heading leading to the Americans' south corridor to Frankfurt. The Norseman's sturdy engine rumbled contentedly. He leveled off
at a thousand feet and leaned the mixture until he could barely see the
telltale blue exhaust flame. That beacon would be his worst enemy for
the entire flight.

Flashing red and green navigation lights of an inbound C-47 passed
overhead. He looked at them longingly—they'd be the last friendly lights
he'd see until crossing the Fulda beacon, inbound to Frankfurt. Reluctantly he reached up and turned off his own navigation lights—he'd be
leaving friendly airspace in fewer than five minutes.

To his left, the landscape appeared devoid of human life. Only an occasional single light relieved the dark void below a horizon just beginning
to expose a rising moon. One of the dim lights was moving toward him.
All right, he thought—that's the headlamp of a locomotive on the double-track railroad. Turning point coming up. He examined his flight plan,
marked the time, and rolled into a shallow turn.

Harv's briefing returned. "We don't know how good their radar coverage is like between here and Leipzig, Ross. Try to stay at about a thousand feet above the surface—that should keep you beneath any heavy
search radar. Plus, with a fabric-covered airplane you'll be hard to paint.
Don't get so low that your engine noise and exhaust flare are too noticeable, however.

"This zigzag course should throw off anyone trying to track you with
visual sightings. And remember, if you're forced down, eat the map,
whatever you do—it's digestible. The course line marked on it would
lead the Vopos straight to where Max is waiting for you."

The rising moon began revealing trees and buildings now, but the irreg-
ular smudges made by villages were without lights of any kind. The
blackout was not intentional, Ross knew—East Germany was still without adequate power-generating plants. A comforting sight, however, was
the gleam of twin, polished rails in the dim light; he was dead on course.

A cross-check of his watch and flight plan showed that a turn onto the first leg of his zigzag course was due. Reluctance to lose his "iron beam" was dispelled by a blue-white finger of light probing the darkness dead ahead. Damn! a searchlight—emanating from a dimly lighted rectangle of low-wattage bulbs. He'd blundered onto some type of military installation. His change in course from southeast to southwest would throw them off for a while, but not for long. Alarms would be sounding in every Vopo outpost within a hundred miles.

Instinct told Ross to climb above visual range and head straight for Leipzig—maybe thirty minutes away on a direct course. The thought of being tracked by radar, however, stayed his hand. Stick to the flight plan, he thought. Pass to the west of Leipzig, then double back, land, and be gone before they figure out what you've done. Without a visible landmark to guide him, he turned due south by dead reckoning.

Thirty minutes later, a scattered cluster of lights materialized to his left. It can only be the city of Leipzig, he thought with a sense of relief. The easy part is over. Now to find the rendezvous—an open field, three kilometers west of the city limits; pick up the all-clear signal—a row of blue flashlights flashing a series of dashes—land without lights; be sure that whoever it is waiting for you doesn't have mayhem in mind; then take off with your passenger—all without being seen. He took a deep breath.

A brief snatch of garbled speech in his headset sent a tingle up his spine. The one fragile link with Banks was an improvised recall arrangement. Theoretically, if the mission was scrubbed after takeoff, Harv could have Tempelhof Tower contact an airlift plane in the corridor and ask them to broadcast the code words "Rainy Day" on VHF emergency channel—that was the sole common frequency installed in the British Norseman's radio. It was a weak link indeed, as both Ross and the relay plane would be at extreme limits for reception.

The voice didn't repeat itself, and Ross turned to setting up a stealthy approach. Reduce rpm setting to 1700 and carry just enough manifold pressure to stay above stalling. Try to pick out the clearing by moonlight on his southbound leg, then do a 180-degree turn and line up with the blue flashlights or, hopefully, flarepots. He glimpsed a solitary white light pass beneath the left wing—it looked dim and had a faint halo. Oh, good Christ! Fog—not heavy, but could he see a *blue* flashlight? More importantly, could he see the ground well enough to land?

The plane drifted lower. Suddenly the moon, until now a friend, became his worst handicap. As Ross sank into the thin, misty haze, moonlight turned it to a milky opaqueness. He pounded a fist on his knee. So close, but a landing was out of the question. Loath to give up, he hesitated before turning onto the escape heading. As he started his turn, three quick bursts of incandescent light pierced the filmy obscuration.

There could be no other answer, he decided; someone down there knew his dilemma and had risked capture to send a signal, probably car lights. Ross recalled Banks's words about Max ". . . he was working on the Soviets' atomic bomb." He rolled into a steep turn, seeking the point where he'd glimpsed the light.

Ghosting through the eerie, filtered moonlight, Ross took up a south heading. The engine noise was barely discernible; he crossed what he judged to be the field's south boundary and punched the dash-mounted clock's stopwatch button. It had been a long time since he'd used this primitive low-visibility approach maneuver. Hold the outbound heading for one minute; turn right forty-five degrees, hold that heading for one minute; make a standard, single-needle-width turn to the left, and roll out on the runway heading. Properly flown, the plane would now be exactly on the reciprocal of its outbound course.

It was time to descend. Without a recent altimeter setting, this part could be dicey. Ross lowered landing flaps and peered into the murk. One minute had passed since rolling out on the approach heading—how long could he wait before adding power and aborting the landing? He clenched his teeth and forced himself to continue his glide.

A tiny, orange flicker of flame at his eleven-o'clock position—he'd done it! He turned left and saw a second flare. Line up the flarepots, let her settle until the individual flares merged and you were very close to the ground. Slower, slower—the beginning shudder of a stall—lower the nose a hair. Then he felt the controls grow mushy and the Norseman fall out from beneath him. A tooth-rattling jar, and the gear was bouncing along the unpaved surface.

Ross could hardly control his elation. Grinning into the darkness, he noted that among other things, the clock read exactly 0315—an on-time landing, by God! He let the plane roll to the last flarepot and turned for an immediate takeoff in the opposite direction. Now, where the hell is my passenger? he wondered. His answer came in the form of a fist pounding on the cockpit door.

"You must go quickly," a disembodied voice, speaking passable English, advised as Ross opened the door. "The Polizei are only minutes away. Our watchers say they heard your motor as you flew overhead."

"That's fine with me. Where's my passenger?"

"Beside me. Is the passenger door unlocked?"

"Right. Get him aboard and strapped in." Ross heard activity in the passenger compartment behind him.

"*Ja.* Go when you hear the door close. And I have a message from your control. By radio only moments ago you are directed to return to Berlin—all fields in Frankfurt area report zero visibility."

Before Ross could recover from his dismay, he heard both doors slam. Oh, well, he'd sort things out after they got the hell out of this trap. He ran a quick cockpit check: flaps up, mixture full rich, prop control to high rpm, temperatures in the green. He crammed the throttle forward and yelled over his shoulder, "All set back there, Max? Here we go."

The response did little to improve Ross's composure. "*Bitte? Ich spreche kleine Englisch.*" He concentrated on holding a heading by the gyrocompass—scurrying figures had extinguished the flarepots even as he'd rolled to a stop after landing.

"So, you can imagine how I felt." Ross pushed his empty plate—no scrap of the scarce fresh eggs and ham remaining—to one side and reached for his coffee mug. "Looking forward to a trip through enemy territory without a flight plan; sneaking into Tempelhof between airlift takeoffs and landings while observing radio silence; Russian twenty- and forty-millimeter AA guns all over; and with a goddamned passenger who doesn't speak English."

Banks, his face almost as drawn and haggard as Ross's, nodded. "That was one helluva stunt you pulled off, Ross. Harv says he doesn't know another pilot who could have done it. If it's any consolation, your CO will have a letter of commendation in a matter of days. It'll be weasel-worded to where no one will know exactly how critical to national security this mission was, but the signature will raise eyebrows, I guarantee."

"Glad to have been of service, sir. We scouts strive to please," Ross quipped. "Now, I'm gonna grab twelve hours' sleep, then catch a hop back to the job I came over here to do."

"Uh—get your sleep first, but you might not be leaving just right away."

"What?"

"Max. He's—well, being a problem. When we started talking about going back to the States and debriefing, he refused to talk to any of us. Says that you're the only man he trusts—you made a lifetime buddy there."

"Oh, m'God. Don, I know nothing about debriefing techniques. Hell, I don't even speak his language."

"All we ask is that you hang around and vouch for the rest of us—reassure him, you know. Get him started talking."

"I'm too tired to argue now, Don, but you're going to have another 'problem' on your hands if this takes more than a day or two."

3 August 1948
Berlin

Ross's sleep-fogged brain finally identified the strident clanging sound as coming from a telephone. He glanced at his watch as he stumbled through the darkness to silence the offending instrument—the timepiece's luminous dial read ten minutes after 2:00 A.M. "'Lo, Major Colyer here," he croaked.

"Major, this is Captain Lewis at the Tempelhof Command Post. Ah, sir, we have a Russian officer here who insists on talking with you. Can you possibly come down?"

Ross pondered the request while he cleared his sleep-drugged brain. His first elation at hearing the phone vanished; he'd assumed it was a pre-departure alert to return to Frankfurt. "A Russian officer? He wants to see *me?* This time of night?"

"Yes, sir. Says he knows you."

"I'm confused. What's his name?"

"His interpreter, who says he's a Major Keivetsky—or some such name—claims the prisoner serves on the Air Safety Board with you, a Major General Pavel."

Ross snapped instantly awake. "Sergei Pavel? You say he's a *prisoner?* What the hell is he supposed to have done?"

"He's charged with exceeding the speed limit and resisting arrest, sir. He is highly intoxicated and being difficult about matters, I might add."

"Holy shit." Ross's mind raced. A Soviet general resisting arrest—on a traffic violation, of all the stupid things? He could see diplomatic implications. His first inclination was to duck, but how could he? Then he remembered the Russian's airy dismissal of the matter of conducting training exercises with hot guns in the air corridors. Could this be an opportunity to . . . ?

"Give me time to dress," Ross said. "pour some black coffee into the general, and I'll get there as soon as I can." He hung up and grinned into the darkness. Difficult? I'll just bet that arrogant son of a bitch is being "difficult," he thought. Now, what the hell am I supposed to do?

On impulse, Ross shaved and donned a freshly pressed uniform. Pavel would be a bit worse for wear—the clean-shaven, neatly dressed member of a confrontation always held a psychological advantage. How should he play this heaven-sent opportunity to befriend the pugnacious Russian? He paused in the act of knotting his tie—befriend, hell. These people respected sheer, brute demonstrations of power. Privately, Pavel would sneer at the weakling who kowtowed to someone he had at a disadvantage.

A half hour later, Ross strolled into the provost marshal's cubicle. "Morning, Colonel," he greeted the bleary-eyed L/C. "I understand you have an angry Russian on your hands."

"Do I ever," the man replied. "Jesus Christ, why did this have to happen on my shift? Those goddamned Russkies are over here 'most every night hitting the western hot spots. Then they roar around town raising hell until one of our patrols chases them home. But this bastard? Oh, no. He has to make a big deal out of it. I'll be up to my ass in paperwork for a month."

"Maybe I can help."

"You can?"

"Is there any problem releasing him?"

"Naw. We almost never write these things up. Nothing ever comes of it. Only reason we brought him in is because he refused to pull over and stop. Now he refuses to accept a citation."

"Okay. I think I can get him to drop the whole business. Just go along, okay?"

Ross strode into the security facility's brightly lighted interrogation room, his features set in stern displeasure. General Pavel crouched in the room's only comfortable chair behind a plain wooden table, regarding the world with a ferocious scowl. A ferret-faced man Ross recognized as the general's interpreter sprang to his feet.

"Major Colyer. The general demands that you correct this outrageous mistake. He is being illegally detained and treated in a disgraceful manner—an insult to a senior officer of an occupying power."

Ross ignored the little major's shouted protest and nodded at the military policeman standing by the door at rigid attention. "'Evening—or I guess it's morning now, Sergeant. You can leave us if you will." He pulled a straight-backed chair to the table and straddled the chair backward, facing the glowering Pavel above its painted headpiece. Ross appeared to be deep in thought as he removed a pack of cigarettes from his pocket and took his time lighting one. He tossed the nearly full container onto the table and blew smoke in the general's direction. "Looks like you kinda crapped in your mess kit, General," he said casually.

Major Keivetsky bounced from his chair. A fine spray of spittle accompanied his shrill, "There will be no discussion of the trumped-up charges. The general demands to be returned to the Soviet sector. You have no jurisdiction over members of the Soviet military forces."

"Will you sit down and shut up, Major?" Ross said wearily. "I spoke with the provost marshal just now. He says your car was being driven erratically at speeds in excess of a hundred kilometers per hour. When two armored patrol cars formed a roadblock, the driver attempted to evade them by driving onto the sidewalk. It required a display of automatic weapons to get the general to dismount from his vehicle. You well know that the traffic ordinances reflect laws agreed upon by the entire Kommandatura, and they apply equally to all." He turned back to face General Pavel and said, "We need to talk about this a bit, I think."

Keivetsky was on his feet once more. "The general speaks no English. You will address your remarks through me," he snapped.

Ross sighed deeply. "Major, you're a real pain in the ass, you know that? Since you won't keep your mouth shut, you'll have to leave. As for English, I happen to know the general *does* understand the language—at least the kind I intend to use. Now, out!—before I have the sergeant throw you out."

Pavel's bloodshot eyes seemed to flicker briefly with a glint of amusement, Ross thought as the indignant major stalked out the door. He continued. "Okay, the provost marshal is wondering just how to write up his report, General. Maybe we can help him." He nudged the pack of cigarettes across the table.

"Report?" the beefy Russian rasped. "A harmless escapade after an your blond looks, American, I'd swear I was dealing with a Lebanese rug merchant. But you are obviously a master at the American game of poker. I learned it from one of your pilots during the war—from the state of Texas, I recall. I believe you hold aces, Major. The air force will be instructed tomorrow to conduct their training exercises elsewhere."

Ross hoped his weak feeling of relief didn't show as he stood and extended his hand. "A deal," he said briefly. "I'll instruct the provost to escort you to the Soviet checkpoint." He forced a smile as the general enveloped his extended hand in a viselike grip.

"And Major," Ross stopped halfway to the door and turned.

"Yes, General?"

"I've been thinking of giving a small party for members of the Air Safety Board. I believe our supply of food and drink is somewhat more adequate than yours, and young ladies are always happy to attend one of my soirees. Could you favor us with your presence—say, Friday next?"

"Duty permitting, I'd be happy to, General." Now, why in the hell did I do that? Ross asked himself as he strode out the door.

Don Banks added a swirl to the geometric shape he was doodling and chuckled. "That's the goddamnedest thing I ever heard of. General Pavel getting himself arrested for drunken driving."

"*And* resisting arrest," Ross added.

"Yeah. Can't forget that. That was some pretty quick thinking on your part. Do you believe he'll actually stop that corridor harassment?"

"You know, I have a hunch he will. He's a funny guy. Hard as nails, but something tells me he'll keep his word. I suspect he saw something I didn't, though."

"Damn right he did. Stalin doesn't like the military—the air force in particular. He purges general officers like he changes shirts. And your sending that worm Keivetsky out of the room was a stroke of luck for him. The good major is the Soviet Political Administration's watchdog—they assign one to every major commander. It'll be interesting to see what happens. Are you going to show up at the party he mentioned?"

"No, I plan to be long gone, just as soon as my orders come through."

"Hmmm." Banks scratched his jaw, a reflective light in his eyes. "Ross, I think we'd like for you to attend that party. We don't have a single source inside the Soviet Military Government's inner circle."

evening of entertainment. Hardly a matter worthy of an endless exchange of paperwork."

Ross shrugged. "*I'm* inclined to agree. My God, copies will have to be sent everywhere—to our headquarters in Rhine-Main—even to the Kremlin, perhaps. I hardly believe your political bosses will enjoy reading what your interpreter will include in his report, either. It doesn't seem a good time for an awkward, shall we say, misunderstanding."

Pavel appeared totally sober as he bent a suspicious glare toward Ross. He reached for the open pack of cigarettes, extracted one, then tucked the cellophane-wrapped package into an inside pocket.

Ross produced a lighter and applied flame; then, with a wintery smile, held out his hand. Pavel scowled, grew red in the face, but tossed the pack onto the table. "What is the alternative to this annoying inconvenience?" he asked reluctantly.

Ross leaned forward until his nose was only inches from the angry general's. Ignoring the smell of stale vodka, garlic, and tobacco on the man's breath, he hissed, "Get your fucking fighter planes out of our air corridors."

Pavel's eyes bulged, his barrel chest swelled—Ross thought the man might explode. His gaze never wavering, Ross added, "Think hard, General, think real hard."

"This is preposterous," the furious Russian spluttered. "Do you think I fear, er, sanctions for a petty traffic violation?"

"If not, you'd better," Ross responded. "This is *not* a petty traffic violation, General Pavel, and you know it. We're talking about a serious diplomatic incident—a most embarrassing one for the Soviet government. This is the only reason you asked for me—you could use a friend. Need I say more?"

Pavel's pockmarked jowls quivered. His voice trembled. "Do you expect me to submit to blackmail?"

Ross spread his hands. "This is something you have the authority to arrange—a friendly favor in return for another friendly favor. No one is hurt, everyone benefits."

Pavel's expression became shrewd and calculating. Seconds ticked by. Ross maintained his air of cold determination. Finally the Russian's fleshy lips split in a broad smile. He chuckled; the chuckle became a rumbling belly laugh; his huge frame shook with mirth. "Were it not for

"Oh, come on, Don. I hung around to pamper Max for you, but doing your cloak-and-dagger work? No, thanks. Besides, what could I accomplish? I don't speak either Russian or German."

"For one thing, we'd like the names of some of the Germans who are collaborating with the Reds—and they all speak English."

Ross glared. "Only if my orders back to Rhine-Main don't come through first. And why do I have this feeling that they're going to get delayed, lost, whatever?"

7 August 1948
Berlin

Ross nibbled a canapé and sipped from a stemmed glass of chilled Rhine wine. "Yes," he drawled to the tuxedo-clad man facing him, "it's abominable, I agree. I fear that before winter ends, the Gruenwald will be completely stripped of those lovely trees. Did they survive the war in vain?"

Tiring of efforts to speak and act like a fop, Ross made a question mark with his eyebrows then turned to scan the softly lit dining room. A portable generator issued comforting mutters in the background, but candles in overhead crystal chandeliers provided the major source of light. They cast seductive flickers over the bare shoulders and satin-lapeled dinner jackets of the dozen guests gathered around the buffet, laden with contents of unmarked cartons delivered by a Soviet truck that afternoon. Fifty feet away, he knew, sunken-cheeked figures, bundled in rags against the nighttime chill, fought rats to salvage scraps of garbage.

He nodded to where General Sergei Pavel stood—his heavy jowls flushed with drink and one meaty hand resting unobtrusively on a svelte brunette's hip. "Unless, of course," Ross added, "our friends to the east relax this stupid blockade. But," he added with a smirk, "trees will grow back. In the meantime, our young lovelies here must be kept warm; otherwise they might migrate."

His companion's pale, skeletonlike features reflected no trace of appreciation for Ross's sally. Transparent eyelids closed slowly over pale blue eyes. "Barbarians," he stated flatly in barely accented English. "I don't understand Giesele's receiving these animals socially."

Ross grinned cheerfully. "I gather our hostess is a survivor, Herr Von Klug. What if, for example, we Americans decide to withdraw? Has not that eventuality crossed your own mind?"

The stiff-necked Prussian's aristocratic nose elevated slightly; his lips formed a thin line. "Berliners have a record of perseverance, Major. Even in the dark days under the iron hand of that upstart Austrian paperhanger, we maintained our dignity."

"So I understand," Ross replied with forced gravity. Dignity indeed, he snorted to himself. Don Banks's watch list had a rundown on the coldly correct Von Klug. It included details of his lucrative contract to furnish the oven-tenders of Belsen a superior blend of lethal Cyclon B gas.

What a gathering, he thought. Rendezvousing at General Pavel's mistress's palatial town house to wolf down astonishing quantities of scarce gourmet food and alcoholic beverages as if it were an everyday occurrence. Behind their facade of social propriety lay the souls of jackals. Pavel might well be a dangerous barbarian—Von Klug's sneering description—but one with a soldier's sense of honor. A firing squad?— yes, without hesitation. A knife in the back or poison gas wasn't his way of dealing with opposition.

Ross murmured an inane excuse and strolled to where Pavel regaled a circle of coldly polite guests in crude, heavily accented English. Giesele, wearing a look of tolerant amusement, stood at his side, sipping champagne. Their eyes met briefly.

Now there's a number, Ross thought. The perfect Aryan. Long blond hair, creamy complexion, and a pampered figure that he suspected was older than it looked. How had she, and most of the other women here, survived the war? As playthings of the Nazi hierarchy, no doubt. Changing allegiance came naturally.

Pavel, resembling a friendly St. Bernard in formal dress, black tie slightly askew, turned to greet Ross. "Ah, my good comrade, the rich and powerful American major," he boomed. "Are you enjoying our little gathering?"

Ross adroitly parried the man's intended friendly buss on both cheeks and replied, I had no idea that life in the Soviet Army was so pleasant."

The genial Soviet wagged a sausagelike forefinger before Ross's nose. "You believe all Russians are ignorant peasants, eh? Why else do you think we fought across a thousand miles of frozen wasteland to reach this mecca of decadent luxury?" His huge frame shook with laughter. "To the victor belongs the spoils, eh?"

Ross grinned. It was impossible to dislike the old bastard, he thought.

Ruthless leader of a hundred thousand bloodthirsty descendants of Genghis Khan, the general was a giant among men. He couldn't resist a sly riposte to Pavel's reference to being a "victor," however.

"Very true, General. But when the spoils grow bitter, we'll be happy to provide you a means of returning home with our magnificent air transport fleet."

Pavel's florid features hardened abruptly. "Do not press your luck, American. A good poker player checks his hole card carefully—bluffing with only a deuce in the hole can prove disastrous."

The Russian's sharp comeback reminded Ross that he was dealing with a hard and powerful man, his jovial veneer notwithstanding. He resisted an urge to goad the Russian further in hopes that anger might provoke an indiscreet disclosure but settled for a light, "But the times a well-played bluff works makes the game exciting, don't you agree?"

Pavel quickly regained his good humor, and the conversation turned to a discussion of the superior qualities of pâté made from the livers of genuine Strasbourg geese.

12 August 1948
Berlin

"Well, it looks as if our pipeline into the Russian military government dried up before we could use it." Banks regarded Ross over the half-glasses he wore for reading. "A shame. Just that one party gave us three new names, and it sounded like you were getting on famously with the general."

"What happened?"

"Sergei got reassigned. Supposedly to command an air division somewhere in the South."

"I'll be damned. You said, 'supposedly.' Is there something more?"

"N-o-o-o, but it makes one wonder if he did get off scot-free after that incident you fixed for him. But he must not be too deep in the doghouse. They let him bring his mistress, that Giesele, with him."

"What? They let him bring a *German* into the Soviet Union?"

"Turns out she isn't German. Her papers state she's Polish—a refugee. Anyway, it looks as if you're without a job here. Wanta go back to Rhine-Main?"

"I'd say it's about time."

Banks extended a hand. "Pick your time; I have your orders here. I can't tell you how much I enjoyed working with you, and that commendation should be on your general's desk right now."

Ross zipped his B-4 bag closed and stood at the window. Two C-47s were taxiing out for takeoff. Three others were being unloaded; the roar of engines went on unabated around the clock. He felt relaxed for the first time since arriving in Berlin—it was going to be good getting back.

6

Muroc Airfield, California

Kyle Wilson stood at rigid parade rest, billed cap set squarely atop short, curly black hair, his summer class A uniform crisply emphasizing a trim, five-foot-ten figure. He was positioned at the left end of the front row, having been briefed earlier that the speaker, General Yost, would present him with the Commandant's Trophy as top graduate. The stirring notes of "The Stars and Stripes Forever" sent faint shivers of pride coursing down his spine. A red-faced adjutant bawled, "Offizurs, '*ten-hut!*" Eighty pairs of heels clicked together as one.

An officer, wearing a single star on his shoulder epaulets, strode briskly to the microphone atop the reviewing stand. Kyle looked again to where his parents occupied seats of honor, immediately behind the wing commander. His dad looked as distinguished as ever. After four years behind a Pentagon desk, his body was still trim and athletic. The new eagles he sported prompted a warm glow in the young pilot's chest. Even from this distance he could detect his mother's pleased smile—the white flash of a tissue—damn, she was crying.

"Gentlemen, you are to be congratulated—*congratulated—congratulated*," echoed off the surrounding buildings. Kyle's mind wandered. The trite words meant little more than the ones spoken at high school, then VMI, then graduation from pilot training. These pompous old farts believed that they could instill dedication to duty, high morale, and pride in wearing wings on an air force uniform with speeches. Bullshit. *They'd* had a war in which to prove themselves; well, there wasn't any war now. You had to make your mark by being a better pilot than any of them had thought of being, and he was. It's what *you* felt deep inside that counted. And you got that feeling by what *you* did—what other pilots said about your skill and conduct.

Dad could have maybe been as good, but that heart attack back in '42 had cheated him out of a flying career. Well, I don't see anyone else in this class I can't outstrip, he thought. I'll be the youngest general in the air force—maybe the youngest chief of staff. Dad will be proud of me.

But a twinge of guilt marred the perfect morning. He dreaded telling Dad—and Mom—about Judy. Not to mention that he'd be starting his career with the handicap of a 104th Article of War on his record. Silly bitch—no, he'd been to blame. He should never have let her talk him into anything so stupid.

Judy Conklin was base commander Col. Webb Conklin's daughter—nineteen, nubile, and a nutcase. She'd been visiting her parents while on summer break from UCLA. They'd dated, clandestinely. Colonel Conklin forbade her to date student officers.

Forbidding Judy to do anything was tantamount to telling a kid to stay out of the cookie jar. So when Kyle told her he couldn't see her the following night because he was scheduled for a night cross-county, she demanded that he smuggle her aboard. Kyle hesitated. The F-80 students were prohibited from flying the new jet aircraft at night, so mandatory night time was logged in the two-seat training version of prop-driven F-51s. Judy's teasing, "Maybe we can figure a way to do it in a two-place fighter trainer at ten thousand feet—get written up in *Famous First Facts*," was irresistible.

Two weeks later, a dough-faced light colonel in the judge advocate's office regarded Kyle with an expression resembling a worried basset hound. "This is what's called an Article 32 investigation, Lieutenant Wilson. Do you understand what that means?"

"Yes, sir, I believe I do. You are to decide if I've done something that's a court-martial offense."

"That's right. Do you want an attorney present during these proceedings?"

"No, sir."

"Very well. It's alleged that you permitted an unauthorized female civilian to accompany you in a military aircraft. Did you do that?"

"Yes, sir."

If possible, the JAG officer—the name on his desk read, A. C. DUNCAN, LT. COL. USAF—assumed an even more mournful demeanor. "Lieutenant Wilson, you are being a royal pain in the ass. Of all the, quote, 'unauthorized female civilians' available, why, in Christ's name, did you have to pick *the base commander's daughter?*"

"I guess I wasn't thinking straight, sir. She's a very attractive girl. When she asked, I just couldn't say no." Kyle's words were direct quotes from Lt. Mack Tyson's briefing session. Mack, reputed to have taken prelaw, was in constant demand as legal advisor for student officers finding themselves in tight situations.

"Look," he'd told Kyle, "you're entitled to demand a court-martial. Now, not Colonel Conklin, not the general, but *nobody* wants that. Y'know why? Number one: You're the shining star of the F-80 class; they get egg on their faces if you get ripped. Number two: Judy would have to testify. Now you better believe Papa is passing bullets about *that* possibility.

"So you just sit there, with your bare, innocent, all-American face hanging out and say, 'I done it, and I'm real sorry'—that's as long as they don't try to fuck you over. You can expect to get an Article 104 and have a written reprimand put in your 201 file—the same punishment you get for getting caught in town out of uniform.

"If they start making noises about anything stiffer, you just put on an injured look and say something like, 'Gee, sir, that sounds pretty serious. I guess I'd better ask for a defense lawyer and take my chances with a court-martial.'"

Colonel Duncan cleared his throat. "This is a most grave offense, Lieutenant—do you realize that?"

"Yes, sir."

"I'll have to recommend a court-martial to the convening authority—unless, that is, you can provide me with some *strong* mitigating circumstances." The legal officer assumed an almost pleading look.

"I'm sorry, sir. I can only hope that the court will understand it was an impulsive act—we're very much in love. Do you think it would help if we were to get married?"

"Harumph. Hardly the time to be thinking of that," Duncan said. "In view of your sterling record as a pilot and an officer up to now, however, perhaps a plea of guilty to a lesser charge—say, failing to file a complete passenger list—could result in something less severe in the way of disciplinary action."

Kyle feigned a worried frown. "I'm not sure I understand, sir. What *is* the penalty for failing to file a passenger list with my flight plan?"

"A written reprimand," Duncan replied promptly, "to be withdrawn after one year of exemplary duty."

"Well, sir, I don't want to put everybody out by having to go through with a court-martial; maybe it would be best to handle it this way."

"You had better believe it is," Duncan said with grim emphasis. "I'll so recommend to the convening authority. But," he added, "Colonel Conklin must agree with this, and I'll tell you, he's extremely upset."

"I can understand that he is." Kyle's features reflected deep concern. "Should I offer him an apology?"

"Better than that, Lieutenant." For the first time Duncan's thin, blood-less lips spread in a wolfish grin. "I do believe he would consider your volunteering for two weeks' duty as permanent officer of the day a better expression of your remorse."

Kyle returned to reality with a jerk. The adjutant was crying, "Offizu-urrs, attention to orders. Second Lieutenant Kyle Wilson, front *and* center . . . *harch!*"

31 August 1948
Patoosie, West Virginia

Kyle turned off the big Indian Scout's ignition and let the bike rest on its kickstand. He let out a resigned sigh and dismounted. Bathed in rosy light from the police car's baleful red orb, he reached for his wallet.

Behind him, the Mercury's front door swung ⌐pen—it displayed a gold star circled by the words PATOOSIE POLICE DEPARTMENT—to dis-charge a slightly built, nattily uniformed officer. The man—Kyle judged him to be in his early twenties—settled a billed uniform cap squarely on his head and strode through the deepening dusk to where Kyle waited. "Evenin'," he drawled. "Could I see yo'ah driver's license, please?"

Kyle extracted his Virginia driver's permit and handed it over without speaking.

The youthful, bantam-size minion of the law held the wallet-size card in light cast by the cruiser's headlights while he examined Kyle's vital statistics. Mumbling aloud to himself, he read, "Height: five feet, ten inches." He looked up briefly, then continued. "Weight: one-seventy. Okay. Hair: black." He regarded Wilson's curly, jet black mop and nod-ded. "Year of birth: 1926—could be."

His sallow features tightened. "This gives your address as Alexandria, Virginia. Yo'ah bike, it has a California license. This yo'ah vehicle?"

"Yes, sir. You see, I was stationed at Muroc Air Field in California. It's a state that doesn't require servicemen to obtain a new driver's license," Kyle explained. "Alexandria is my home of record—my parents' address."

"I see. Yo'ah AWOL, boy?"

Kyle winced at being called "boy" by someone he suspected was younger than he, but replied, "No, sir. I'm on travel time. My new station is Wright Field, up by Dayton. My orders are in my saddlebags."

"That so? Well, I clocked you doin' forty-two in a thirty-five-mile zone. I gotta issue you a summons for speeding."

Kyle's suntanned features formed a wry grimace. "Hey, look, officer. I was just following traffic ahead of me—two cars passed me, in fact. And seven miles an hour—do you stop *everyone* driving seven miles over the posted limit?"

"Everybody we catch. Now, yo'ah lucky. Squire Kemp is usually in his office until eight or nine. We can go down there right now and get yo'ah court appearance ovah with. Otherwise I'd have to take you to the station and make you post bond." He tucked Kyle's driver's license in a shirt pocket and added, "If you'll just fall in behind me, I'll lead the way."

Muttering frustrated epithets, consigning Patoosie officialdom to horrible fates, Kyle halted behind the official Mercury in front of a modest, ageing cottage. A floodlit sign on the unkempt lawn announced, JUSTICE OF THE PEACE. Below, in letters only slightly smaller, it read, CHIHUAHUAS FOR SALE.

Kyle followed his escort up creaking, weathered board steps into a lean-to screened porch. The sloped roof retained much of the day's ninety-degree heat and smelled of dog urine. "If you'll just have a seat, I'll see if the squire can see you," the officious young cop told Kyle. "He 'pears to have a customer right now."

The disgusted traffic violator sank onto a battered metal porch-glider. Ignoring protesting squeaks, he selected a cushion free from protruding springs and glumly contemplated the gathering darkness. Faint voices, overlaid by shrill canine yelps, reached him through the open doorway. Kyle heard, "Now, Miz Archer, that bitch was in good health when I sold her. I don't know *why* she dropped a stillborn litter, but I can't refund your money; you know that."

"You mean you *ain't gonna*," a shrill, waspish female voice responded.

"Very well, Oscar Kemp, I'll see to it that everyone within a hundred miles of Patoosie knows you sold me a barren dog. You haven't heard the last of this, either." The last words were flung over the shoulder of a bird-like figure that stormed out the porch's screen door.

Kyle was still grinning to himself when his arresting officer announced, "Okay, you can come in now."

It was not a propitious time for fair, evenhanded justice, Kyle decided. The seated figure, his shirt button-straining paunch concealing his belt buckle, wore a dark scowl on sagging, unshaven jowls. He threw an irritated glare at the posturing uniformed officer and growled, "Well, Kenny, whatcha got?"

"A forty-two in a thirty-five zone, Squire. And he's riding a motorcycle," Kenny added with a knowing leer.

The disgruntled magistrate scanned the yellow citation and Kyle's driver's license with a cursory glance. "What brings you to this neck of the woods, son?"

"I'm in the air force, your honor. I'm on my way to Wright Field—permanent change of station."

"Hmmmf," the fleshy man responded. "You in such an all-fired hurry, you got to endanger folks' life and limb by roaring through Main Street like you was goin' to a fire?"

Kyle bit back the retort which sprang to his lips—to the effect that forty-two miles per hour, a mile outside a fleabitten burg's single street crossing, didn't seem to pose much danger to the town's 372 advertised citizens. He replied, "I guess I was just concentrating on avoiding the heavy traffic, your honor. I'm sorry."

The JP's deep-set piggish eyes regarded Kyle's bland expression with suspicion. Apparently satisfied that the youngster wasn't being sarcastic, he asked, "What's your job in the air force?"

"I'm a pilot, your honor. I'll be flying a new jet fighter at Wright."

Kyle realized he'd made a mistake even before he finished speaking. The JP's eyes bulged, his jaw actually dropped. "Airplanes? You fly *airplanes*? Jets—them ones without propellers?"

"Yes, your honor," Kyle replied, with only a trace of a sigh.

"Well, I'll have you to know we don't hold with speed-crazy hoodlums racing through the streets of Patoosie. Nosiree. You can tell your hell-raisin' pals that, too—just stay out of *this* town. Fine'll be twenty-two dollars—dollar a mile over the speed limit, and fifteen dollars costs. Pay Wilma in the kitchen on your way out."

Kenny followed Kyle to the street. He regarded the gleaming Indian with open envy. "Give anything to own one of them," he murmured. "What'll she do?"

"I really don't know," Kyle lied cagily. "Faster than I want to go, I expect."

"Bet anything she'll do a hunnert," Kenny mused. "I been after the chief ever since the war to buy one. Sure as hell no speeder gonna outrun me then."

"I'm sure you're right," Kyle replied. "That four-thirty-five, overhead-cam V-twin really boots her along." He checked the straps holding his B-4 bag on the rear luggage rack and added, "Well, I best be going, I got a long night's ride ahead of me. I have to report in tomorrow."

Kenny refused to be dismissed so easily. "You mean you're gonna ride all night?"

Kyle chuckled. "So right. I came all the way from D.C. last night. Too damn hot to ride this thing during the day."

"Yeah, you got it made, ain't 'cha? Money, good looks, an air force officer—you get to see the world, have all the fun. And you get to fly airplanes. Man alive, I'd like to be in your shoes. I ain't never done nothin'. Been to Chicago once't. M'brother Jack, he got into the aviation cadet program, but he washed out. Got killed on a place called Omaha Beach. I tried to enlist. Flat feet, they told me.

"Guess I'm stuck in this asshole of creation. And, I gotta say this, I only pulled you over because you pissed me off. I'm settin' there in the heat all day, watchin' people roll past in their fancy cars. Then you come cruisin' by—another rich, snotty show-off, I tells myself: I'll teach him. Well, turns out you ain't. You're really sort of a nice guy. I'm sorry."

Kyle regarded the suddenly woebegone figure with new insight. He stuck out a hand. "Can't say I blame you," he said gruffly. "No hard feelings on my part. You ever get to Dayton, Ohio, give me a call; we'll have a beer and chase some girls." He shoved the 450-pound motorcycle off its parking stand and swung into the saddle. The engine roared to life with one thrust of the starter pedal. He threw a friendly wave and a grin over his shoulder.

Other than a pair of mangy stray dogs, Patoosie's Main Street was devoid of life as Kyle eased out of town, the throttle barely past idle. He waited until he was beyond the town's one oasis of social activity, a cinderblock building with a flickering neon sign advertising Budweiser Beer, to upshift and unleash the Indian's impatient power plant.

Sheesh, he muttered to himself. What a dump—I feel sorry for that cop. He's right, he'll never break out of the rut he's in. Have I, like he said, "got it made"? Kyle goosed the throttle to roar around a lumbering cattle truck and resumed his introspection.

What would I do in his situation? he wondered. Hell, I'd do *something*—hold up the bank, run away to South America; I don't know. Okay, I had an easy life. Dad was able to send me to a good college. Mom always saw I had pocket money—money Dad didn't always know about. She bought me this bike for graduation. But, by God, I did my part. Graduated with honors from VMI—again, I was top of my class at advanced fighter school—that got me the choice assignment to jets and test-pilots school. Even after that business with Judy, and that 104th that pissed Dad off so—I'm gonna make it.

But would I have been able to do all that if I'd been brought up in a two-bedroom shack on the edge of a town like Patoosie? Dad pumping gas until he was too old? Mom taking in washing and ironing? A pitcher pump in the kitchen and a privy out back?—barely making it through high school with a "C" average? I just dunno.

Traffic was thinning now. Kyle crouched behind the skimpy windscreen and watched the dimly lit speedometer needle creep past eighty. Damn! He loved this machine. It was the next best thing to flying. The blacktopped surface of U.S. 35 jerked crazily in the narrow beam of his headlight, but he felt totally in control. And he was going to fly the fastest airplane in the world. The first light of a rising moon revealed his mouth spread in a savage grin.

A cluster of feeble streetlights and a sign, HAWKENSVILLE, POP 783, prompted a deceleration, the barking exhaust replaced by a contented cackle as he rolled the handgrip throttle—one speeding ticket is enough, he thought.

The open highway beckoned once more. He resumed speed and turned his thoughts to the job ahead. Test-flying jets. Could he hack the stringent requirements for a test pilot? He could have asked for a different assignment—top grads had their pick. Why hadn't he? Raised eyebrows

from his classmates? Veiled sneers in the mess? Maybe. But his dad—
who learned to fly in fabric-covered biplanes when just taking to the air
was an adventure—wouldn't have understood either. His lips set in a
determined line. He'd make the grade—damned if he would ever do *anything* his dad couldn't brag about to his cronies in the Pentagon.

A somnolent milk cow stopped chewing her cud and turned startled eyes toward that thundering apparition ripping the moonlit silence
asunder.

7

Ross felt the C-54's landing gear thump down and lock. The cabin steward came back to advise General Cipolla that they were on final approach. The general nodded, stuffed papers into his briefcase, and tightened his seat belt. These were the only clues that landing was imminent. Dirty gray mist swirled outside the rain-smeared windows, making it hard even to see the wingtips.

Helluva homecoming, Ross thought. I had enough of this kind of weather in Berlin. His memory of the past three months was an unending blur of too much coffee and Spam sandwiches, too little sleep, and rain. How about a little sunshine to greet the returning heroes? His outlook brightened as he thought of Janet, no doubt pacing the waiting room and chain-smoking cigarettes. Wonder how she spent last night while we sat there in Bermuda waiting for Langley weather to improve? He chuckled to himself; Janet didn't suffer delays and disappointments gracefully. He'd make it up to her tonight, though.

Then what? he wondered. Would he have a few days' leave before returning to Wright Field? General Cipolla had been vague about how the now unassigned members of the provisional wing would be sorted out. But he'd been emphatic about Ross's future remaining unchanged—welcome news.

The engine note dwindled to a muted rumble and Ross heard the flaps whine into their full down position. He glanced outside; the terrain was still obscured. Damn, he muttered to himself. We're almost at minimums. . . . He froze as he heard the four Pratt & Whitneys surge to a deep-throated roar. The airframe shuddered, and he felt the nose lift.

Okay, a go-around, he thought, and relaxed somewhat. I was right, we were at minimums and didn't break out. Damn, now we'll end up at our alternate, and Janet will be left standing in the rain.

Something isn't right, he sensed. The plane's shuddering assumed the sickening, mushy feel of a stall—he glimpsed expressions of tight-lipped concern on other faces. A jolt threw Ross sideways. The crash alarm set up its raucous, nerve-shattering clamor. His unspoken, Oh, m'God, we're going in, was confirmed by a benign bump, followed by the ear-piercing shriek of metal on concrete.

With landing gear retracted, the jouncing, strident movement seemed to go on forever. The airplane fuselage slowly rotated until Ross could see that they were sliding sideways, still on the runway. A cold fist clutched his heart as he saw an orange glow following their progress. Visions of wartime B-24s, returning home with battle damage, flashed before him—sliding gear-up, trailing sparks from their bellies before bursting into balls of flame and smoke. He grabbed a GI blanket folded on the seat beside him—an involuntary, reflexive action—and buried his face in the harsh, woolly fabric.

He felt their deceptively gentle motion cease and raised his head. Pandemonium filled the cabin as passengers leaped to their feet and rushed for exits. The ominous reddish-orange glow intensified as flames engulfed the now-stationary airplane's port wing. The thought that the tanks might blow at any moment raced through his mind. He saw the cabin steward run to a cabin emergency exit and twist the locking handle. "No!" Ross heard himself shout. "Not that one—go forward!"

His warning, drowned out in the bedlam, came too late. The cabin steward, wearing buck sergeant's stripes on his uniform, was following standard crash-landing drill. He wrenched the exit door open, even as Ross yelled an effort to stop him. Air pressure differential sucked a solid shaft of flame inside the cabin.

Ross threw the blanket he still held over the screaming man and dragged him toward the cockpit. A calm but tight-faced flight engineer helped him join the stream of crew and passengers scrambling from the forward entrance. His struggling burden made him stumble against a jagged piece of metal, jerking the protective blanket from his grasp.

Outside, in blessedly fresh air, the survivors formed a confused gaggle in front of the mangled number three engine. "Get the hell away from here," Ross tried to shout. No sound resulted, only a lance of chest pain—a red mist blurred his vision. His last coherent thought was an amazed, "I'm gonna pass out, for Christ's sake."

16 November 1948
Walter Reed Army Hospital, Washington, D.C.

The noise sounded familiar, but try as he might, Ross couldn't identify it. There it was again. A faint, sighing wheeze—almost, but not quite, like an F-51's oxygen autoregulator. It was irritating. He wasn't in an airplane, of that he was reasonably sure. Besides, it was dark—there should be instrument lights. He tried to raise his arm and discovered something was tied to it. That's funny, he thought. Then it no longer made any difference; he'd take a short nap—figure it out later.

Pain roused him. A dull throbbing, but he had to do something to make it go away. He opened his eyes. The stygian absence of light remained. What the hell? It was his left hand that hurt, but when he tried to lift it to see what was wrong, he couldn't—it was tied to what seemed to be a damn board. Awareness returned with a rush. He was in a helluva shape, he realized. Blind, hurt, tied up—he had to get help. A harsh rattle was the only sound he could muster.

"Ross? Are you awake, darling?"

It was Janet. He made another unsuccessful effort to speak. A warm hand engulfed his own right one.

"Oh, you poor darling," she continued. "If you understand, squeeze my hand, okay?"

Ross complied, prompting her to say, "Oh, that's wonderful! There was an accident, Ross, and you were hurt. You're in the hospital.

"I know you must be miserable. There's a bandage over your eyes, so you won't be able to see for a time. You have an IV needle in this arm, and your left one is immobilized to protect your hand—it was hurt in the accident. It sounds terrible, I know, but the doctors say you'll be fine. I've rung for the nurse. When she gets here, we'll see if we can make you more comfortable. I'd give you a big kiss, but there's just a little-bitty hole cut in the bandage over your face."

Ross remembered the accident now. The fire, the noise—a thousand questions flooded his brain. He shook his head in angry frustration. Why couldn't he talk? The squeak of rubber soles on polished tile and the swishing rustle of clothing announced a new presence.

"Well, good morning, handsome," a strange but cheerful voice announced. "I won't ask how you're feeling; you might hit me."

Ross felt cool fingers on his wrist as she continued, "I'll just check you over a bit. Can you hold this thermometer beneath your tongue? Nod your head if it's okay. It is? Fine. We'll get this over with before the doctor comes; he's on his way. Do you have a lot of pain anyplace?"

Ross nodded and moved his left arm.

"Your hand? I'm not surprised; it took a bit of a beating. Well, we'll give you something for that as soon as the doctor has seen you. I'll take this thing out of your mouth now. I expect it feels like a desert, but we won't try giving you water just yet. Janet, you can give him a piece of ice to suck on—that should help some."

The doctor, smelling of carbolic soap and aftershave lotion, talked as he probed and flexed Ross's extremities. "We're treating you for a number of things—mostly minor, but painful, I know. You have second-degree burns on the skin that was exposed, including the eyes. We don't believe there's any permanent damage there, but we'll watch 'em real close. The bandages can probably come off tomorrow, but we'll keep the room dim.

"You inhaled some smoke and superheated air, so your throat and lungs are going to hurt some, but again, it doesn't look like any permanent damage. We have you in an oxygen tent until you can breathe normally, and we'll keep that IV in until your body fluids are back to normal. Now, your left hand is both burned and deeply lacerated. It's going to require a good while to heal, but other than that, we should have you up and out of here in fairly short order."

Ross felt his good hand enveloped by warm fingers—Janet's, he knew. A drop of warm liquid splashed onto his bare arm. Don't cry, damnit! he wanted to say. He couldn't, and felt tears form in his own eyes. The doctor was saying, ". . . I know you're feeling woozy just now, I gave you some sedation so you can get some rest. But I have a one-star general down the hall raising hell because I won't let him see you. I'll come in tomorrow morning, take a look at those eyes, maybe take away this oxygen tent, and let him in, if you're up to it." He chuckled at Ross's vigorous nod.

Janet had never looked more desirable, Ross told himself the next morning. Blurred vision and dim lighting notwithstanding, the sight of her wan, drawn features and trim but fashionably attired figure moved him deeply. He didn't shift his gaze from her as the white-smocked doctor—he'd introduced himself as Jacoby—unh-hunhed and clucked approving noises while he unwound Ross's facial bandages. He probed his patient's eyes with a tiny flashlight beam, then stepped back, his face wreathed by a pleased smile.

Ross waited for a verdict. Funny, he thought, the angels of mercy he'd visualized from their voices and demeanor had resembled Betty Grable and Robert Montgomery. In the flesh, Jacoby was short, fat, and bald. Nurse Tyson was late middle-age and had a mustache.

"Excellent," the doctor enthused. "With some drops I'll give you and dark glasses you'll wear for a few days, the peepers will be good as new. Now, I'd like to let that ill-tempered general see you, if you agree."

Ross managed a weak, "Yeah."

General Cipolla—wearing a drab blue-gray hospital-issue robe, Ross noted with surprise—strode into the room with a manner resembling MacArthur's return to the Philippines. "About goddamn time," he growled as he surveyed Ross's recumbent figure.

"Hi, Janet," he added. "You've had a rough time as well, haven't you, gal?" Without giving Janet time to respond, he continued, "This place gives me the willies. They treating *you* okay?"

"Good," he said as Ross nodded. "Don't try to talk. Just wanted to drop in and say hi before I get sprung. They kept me here for 'observation' even though I told 'em there wasn't anything wrong with me. Idiots," he snorted. "Have they told you anything about what happened?"

Ross shook his head.

"Thought as much. Okay, it was a 'bad show,' as the Brits are prone to say. The crew of a transient C-45 got confused and pulled onto the active just as we were crossing the fence. Our pilot damn near cleared 'em, but number three prop caught the C-45's crew compartment—just enough to throw us out of control."

Janet stooped to catch Ross's harsh whisper and translated, "He wants to know about survivors."

Cipolla scowled. "The C-45 crew probably never knew what hit 'em. Four of our guys are in here with you. Three are out of danger, but the cabin steward, the kid you pulled to safety, is still under intensive care with burns. "And you"—he cocked a speculative look at Ross—"other than looking like you'd been in the oven too long, don't look too bad off. I understand that hand is your most serious injury."

Janet spoke from her chair by the bedside. "The doctor seemed certain that his eyes and lungs will heal without permanent damage," she advised.

"Good, that's great news," Cipolla said, nodding his head. "Well, I gotta keep moving. I hate to think of the stuff piled up at my office."

The general stood silently for a moment, then added gruffly, "You saved some lives, guy—this sorry old ass included, if that's any consolation. Slamming that exit door closed is all that prevented Langley Field's most spectacular cook-out of the year.

"Sergeant Billings's wife—he's the cabin steward—won't leave the building until she sees you, incidentally. There'll be some other wives and mothers slobbering all over you as well, I predict. In fact, I think your ever-loving spouse intends to play smacky-mouth as soon as I leave. So I'll get out of your hair, for the present. Hang tough, now." Cipolla stalked from the room with all the military bearing his felt-slippered feet could manage.

Ross crooked a summoning finger toward Janet and brushed her quivering mouth with cracked, dry lips. "Get out of here. Go home and get some sleep," he whispered. "I'll be okay. I love you."

Ross fought off drug-induced oblivion and tried to arrange jumbled thoughts after Janet made her reluctant departure. Details of the accident were a tantalizing blur, like something that happened to someone else a long time ago. That open exit door, for example: for the life of him he couldn't recall closing it. Okay, he asked himself muzzily, did you dodge the bullet again? It would seem that way, but he replayed Cipolla's conversation. The one thing he'd been listening closely for hadn't been mentioned. What would happen after Ross was discharged from the hospital?

30 November 1948
Washington, D.C.
Ross watched a trench-coated woman struggle through slanting sleet and wet snow toward a bus stop. The view from their apartment window would depress even Fibber McGee, he grumbled to himself. Cooped up in this four-room jail while Janet went to work was bad enough, even when he could get outside and walk. He'd memorized every street within

a three mile radius during the past two weeks. Sick in Quarters, his orders read—amen to that!

He kneaded the sponge gripped in his left hand—the physical therapist said it would help keep the fingers from healing stiff. It sure as hell better, he muttered. I don't know how much more of this I can take. Damn doctors. Once you get in their clutches, it's like trying to escape from quicksand.

"No smoking, Ross," the bald-headed Jacoby had admonished. "That lung tissue is still healing." Janet magnanimously agreed to quit as well, as a support measure. I'll bet anything she still smokes at the office, he snarled inwardly.

And it was, "Lay off the booze, Ross. You know how eyes get bloodshot from drinking? We sure don't want that to happen. Oh, maybe one martini before dinner, but no more." Just as well, he had to concede. In this frame of mind I'd be a complete lush by now.

He glanced at his watch and scowled—only five minutes had passed since he last checked. Another whole hour before he could take a cab to Walter Reed for a checkup. He simply *had* to be upgraded to Duty Not Including Flying. Cipolla told him during one of Ross's incessant phone calls that he could at least go back to Wright Field and work on his degree in DNIF status.

Ross bent a suspicious glare at the white-smocked flight surgeon seated behind an OD steel desk. After two hours of being poked, peered at—and into, giving up body fluids, and the like, it was summing-up time. Instinct told him the verdict wasn't going to be DNIF; the bastard wore a shifty, evasive look as he shuffled through Ross's file. Finally he leaned back in his chair and favored his patient with a broad smile.

Oh, oh, Ross thought. Here it comes. That's his phony, bedside look.

"Well, Major, you're recovering nicely. Better than we'd hoped for, actually."

Major? Ross felt his gut contract. Until now it had been a jovial "Ross."

"The X rays show that little shadow on your left lung has cleared; eye exam shows nothing abnormal; and those burns are healing smooth—no scars to mar your handsome looks, ha, ha."

"How about the hand?" So that's it, he thought. My damn hand. . . .

"Well, we have a little problem there," the doctor replied in unctuous tones.

We? Ross fumed inwardly. What's with this "we" shit? *I'm* the one with stiff fingers.

"Here, I'll show you on this X ray." Ross regarded the gray and black filmstrip with unseeing eyes as the surgeon continued. "This is scar tissue forming at the wrist between the tendons that control your ring and index fingers. It can, in some cases, prevent full articulation of the phalanges."

"You mean I won't be able to bend those two fingers."

"That's an extreme prognosis, but it's one we can't rule out."

"That's my throttle hand, Doc."

"Yes. But don't get overly concerned. Surgery in these situations has an extremely high success rate. And it may not come to that. We'll watch the healing process very carefully for, oh, the next six to eight weeks. If impairment still exists, a decision will be made then regarding feasibility of restorative surgery.

"Now, I'm classifying you as DNIF. I understand you're slotted into the AFIT program to finish your engineering degree. Do that while you heal. I know Art Wilmack at the Wright Field base hospital. He's chief of surgery there, and one of the best. You'll get the finest of care."

Ross sprang to his feet and placed his face only inches from the flight surgeon's. "This isn't just a goddamned hand you're talking about, Doc. This is my *life!* I'm a pilot, remember? It's all I know; it's all I want to know."

"Not everyone in the air force is a pilot, Ross. You're on your way to becoming an engineer. My God, the guided-missile program is begging for scientists. Radar and communications, armament—the career opportunities are endless."

Ross stood erect and drew a deep breath. *"Well fuck your opportunities."* Before the shaken medical officer could recover, Ross spun on his heel and marched out the door.

Janet was in the kitchenette rattling cooking utensils when Ross returned home. "Oh, hi there," she called gaily. "How'd it go?"

Ross wordlessly slammed the brown paper bag he carried onto the kitchen table.

Janet took one look at her husband's expression and said, "Oh, dear. Bad news?"

"Not good, that's for damn sure."

Janet peered at the paper sack's contents—a fifth of Johnnie Walker Scotch and two packs of Camel cigarettes. "My goodness. Did the doctor say—"

"The doctor said I'm gonna be a goddamned cripple, that's what the doctor said."

Janet covered her stricken features with both hands. "Oh, no," she whispered. "Whatever. . . ?"

"My hand." Ross waved the offending, half-healed member beneath her nose. "The one I use to move the throttle, operate the gear and flaps, gun switches, just a few things like that. It's broke, for good. I fly two combat tours, walk out of the Burma jungle, take a hit from a Jap Zero, tangle with a Spitfire while flying a mongrel Messerschmitt half-breed killer, and it takes a goddamn *passenger* plane to give me a permanent disability. I quit."

"Ross, Ross. You aren't making sense. Come over here, sit down, and tell me everything the doctor said."

"After I mix a drink—and have a cigarette."

"Stop it! You're acting like it's the end of the world. Things *can't* be as bad as you think. Tell me."

After taking seats on the sofa, Janet propped her chin in cupped hands and listened intently while Ross recited details of his checkup.

Ross's unimpassioned discourse wound to a dispirited ending. Janet took his good right hand in hers and said, "But it isn't definite. There seems to be a very good chance that you'll regain its full use."

"It'll never happen. They'll just screw around, holding out hope, then say, 'We did our best, old man. Rotten luck, you know.' To hell with it. I'll get out and get a desk job of some kind. Or I can go back to Detroit where I know Big Mike will give me my old bartender job back. Hell, you can wait tables there while I pour rotgut booze for the factory workers. We'll have a ball."

Janet's eyes blazed. "Ross Colyer, in all the time I've known you, *never* have I heard you use the word 'quit.' You can—and have—done everything you've ever put your mind to. This situation is no different. You can't even think about not having full use of that hand again. And if you resign and go to Detroit, you'll go alone."

Ross sat erect and gave her a look of disbelief.

"I mean it. I love you dearly, I always will. But I will not sleep in the same bed with a quitter. Now, the therapist told you to go from the sponge to a tennis ball when you felt you were ready. It's in your dresser drawer. Get it, and start squeezing while I fix dinner."

Janet stalked to the kitchen, jerked the bottle of Johnnie Walker from the bag, and emptied it down the sink. The two packs of Camels were consigned to the garbage can. She kept her eyes averted all the while— Ross didn't need tears at this point.

8

15 December 1948
Wright Field

Kyle lounged against a maintenance stand and listened to the man from engineering outline their flight profile. His attention kept wandering, however, as he eyed the awkward-looking aircraft parked in the hangar's doorway. Christ, he grumbled to himself, what have they *done* to my Mustang? The twin P-51 fuselages, joined at inner wing panels like Siamese twins, resembled somebody's taxi accident.

"This F-82, gentlemen, is different than the B and C models in several respects," the white-smocked man explained.

Don't tell me! Kyle thought, glancing sideways at the bored lieutenant introduced as, not his copilot, but his radar observer, whatever that meant.

The engineer—his name tag read BARTOK—removed and polished thick-lensed, rimless glasses as he warmed to his briefing. "First, we've gone back to the Allison V-17-12 engine. Counter-rotating, four-bladed Aeroproducts props give you a much more stable craft by eliminating engine torque. They're full-feathering, by the way, since you're now flying a twin-engine job."

Kyle's disposition remained sour. I can see myself tangling with another fighter—*any* damn fighter—in that job, he thought. Half-a-county turning radius, I'll bet—probably climbs like a sick chicken and can't outrun a Piper Cub. Am I ever going to get back in an F-80? Lieutenant Colonel Babcock had immediately relegated him to duties as a utility pilot when he checked in. "Next jet flight-test class will start in November, Lieutenant Wilson. Till then, since you're F-51-qualified, you can help out over at the F-82 project." He was still here.

Kyle turned as a shadow crossed the sunlit rectangle beside him. Babcock gave a casual wave and said, "Don't mind me, folks. I haven't had a good look at this configuration myself."

The civilian engineer frowned at being interrupted and continued. "The real reason we have this bird for suitability testing, however, is this." He walked to a cigar-shaped protuberance suspended beneath the center wing panel. Roughly three feet in diameter, the cylinder extended just beyond the prop arc. Bartok slapped its gleaming surface and continued with, "The optional armament package of eight fifty-calibers, or the cameras used on the photo-recce version, is replaced with this radar pod."

Kyle straightened from his slouch. "*Radar?* You mean like . . . ?"

"Exactly." The man responded in a testy voice. "Radar. The same kind you see over there in that GCA trailer. Except, instead of providing information for a ground-controlled approach for landing, you use it to locate other airplanes—enemy airplanes.

"The dish antenna is located in the nose behind this plastic fairing. That's why it extends past the propeller arc, to give it a clear sweep. The screen is located in the right-hand cockpit. This is not a fighter plane, gentlemen, in the context you probably are accustomed to using."

You can say that again, Kyle thought. Just what the hell are you supposed to do if you *find* an enemy airplane? Hope he flies into a mountain while he's doubled up laughing?

As if in reply to Kyle's unspoken sarcasm, Bartok added, "This is a gun platform, nothing more. You close on your target from the rear, select your armament, and let the radar-coupled fire-control system do the rest."

Kyle's eyes narrowed. "Are you saying that you may never even *see* what you're shooting at?"

Bartok favored the skeptical pilot with a smug smile. "Precisely." He nodded toward the other flight-suited figure. "Lieutenant Orkin has flown a number of intercepts at Eglin Field. He's up here to continue that phase of weapons system development concurrently with our performance test program."

Kyle cocked a quizzical eyebrow at the saturnine Orkin—the man wore navigator's wings, he noticed. "Is this for real?" he asked.

The lieutenant's features split in a brief grin. "Have I made blind intercepts with this rig, you're asking? The answer is yes. Can I do it every time? The answer is no. The system is far from being debugged. That's partially why I'm here. So far, tests have been carried out under near ideal conditions in a modified B-25. You'll be putting the hardware under stress, high-speed dives, high-G pull-ups, and at altitudes the old Mitchell can't reach. What's that going to do to the electronic gear?"

Babcock smiled as he watched Kyle's reaction. "You don't appear overwhelmed, Wilson," he said. "I think you'll be pleasantly surprised. I've flown the 'B' model; it's a good, honest airplane. You give up some performance—rate of climb on takeoff is only about a thousand feet per minute, service ceiling is only thirty thousand. But with the added weight and extra power she's actually rated faster than the 'D' model Mustang by twenty to thirty miles an hour."

Bartok expressed mild irritation by tapping on the radar pod with his pencil. He cleared his throat and continued, "The improved SCR-720C radar will give you a twenty-degree search cone and acquisition of bomber-size targets at up to thirty miles. A new feature—an AN/APS-13 tail-warning radar—actuates an alarm when an enemy comes within four thousand feet.

"The pilot has the same range of equipment you'll find on an airliner: instrument landing system, VHF navigation radio, even an autopilot. Yes, Lieutenant Wilson? You have a question?"

"Yeah," Kyle responded. "You say this radar thing can see maybe *thirty* miles. How do we even get that close?"

"Land-based heavy radar, with height-finder equipment, will vector you within acquisition range," Bartok replied without hesitation.

"And then?"

"The fire-control officer in the right cockpit will provide range and azimuth for you to close with the target."

"I see. Then at the right time, he's gonna say 'shoot.' And up there in the dark, rain pouring down, I'm gonna let fly with my trusty fifty-calibers, and boom—splash one Russian."

Orkin chuckled. "That's pretty much the scenario, Wilson. By the time the system is operational, however, we hope to have the guns coupled to the fire-control system. You won't even have to squeeze the trigger."

"That's downright scary." Kyle frowned. "What if, instead of being a Russian, this is some poor slob flying a TWA airliner—wandering around lost?"

Bartok's dark scowl betrayed his displeasure. "We're digressing," he said sharply. "For now, we're concerned with flying profiles to determine the effect this pod has on performance: best climb speed, a stall and spin series, high-speed turns, the usual. For your information, however, procedures are being developed to identify friendly or hostile aircraft— exactly how is still highly classified."

Kyle shook his head. "Okay, okay," he said resignedly. "I guess I'd better get this checkout ride under way. You going along, Orkin? Watch me circle and bounce?"

"You just acquired a new wife, Kyle," the grinning RO replied. "From now on, I'm along for everything, maybe even Saturday night dates."

19 December 1948
Wright Field

Kyle released the parking brake of what he was calling his double-breasted Mustang, and swung in behind the Follow Me jeep. Even the rotating beacon atop the control tower, probing the rain-swept darkness with a ghostly finger, seemed to be saying, Go back to bed, you idiot. This is no night for flying.

Kyle fervently agreed, Babcock's cheerful greeting over the phone that afternoon notwithstanding. "Kyle, good news," he'd enthused. "The metro types say we'll have icing above eighteen thousand tonight. The bomber boys are launching a B-29 for you to attack so we can maybe get that square marked 'icing effects on intercept capabilities' colored in. Briefing's at eighteen hundred hours."

"Well goody, goody," Kyle had responded sourly. "I'm not sure I want to be around when you have *bad* news to pass on." Then, everyone was so damned cheerful at briefing. "We really lucked out," the bouncy, red-faced weather officer announced. "Good moderate rime icing without too much turbulence—it looks perfect." Even Orkin, the dumb-ass, had chimed in with, "Wow, we never had this opportunity in Florida."

Nobody thought to ask the pilot what he thought about the situation, Kyle grumbled to himself. That one time over Kansas when he noticed a line of frost forming on the Mustang wings leading edges had prompted a near-panicked call to flight service for a lower altitude.

He'd listened to the older heads arguing the merits of anti-icing equipment on fighters. "Nope, no place for that crap on a fighter," a grizzled major observed. "You take a hit in a wingboot, and the thing tears loose and screws up your lift. Alcohol tanks for the prop? Forget it—just another fire potential."

"Well, I don't know," his drinking companion objected. "A pursuit plane, okay—you can get up or down out of the stuff. But this all-weather business is different. If that bomber's chugging along right in the middle of the crap—well, hell, you gonna be there, too."

"Don't see that it matters much one way or the other," a bored captain offered. "You cover the nose of that radar pod with ice—you don't see nothin', I'm bettin'. You put deicers on the prop, and you're gonna throw chunks of ice right through that thin skin—the son-of-a-bitchin' pod is settin' there only a couple of feet away. If that happens, you ain't gonna have no radar anyway."

Kyle wished the confident-talking major was here, and keyed his mike. "Wright Tower, this is Bluejay Seven, ready for takeoff, over."

"Roger, Bluejay Seven. You're cleared into position on runway two-one—hold for release. After takeoff climb on runway heading to three thousand feet and contact Pinetree on tactical frequency, over."

Kyle read back the clearance and taxied onto the runway. He lined up with the double row of mist-haloed runway lights and switched to intercom. "All set for takeoff over there, Gus?"

"Roger, roger, pilot," Orkin responded from the right cockpit. "All lights are green and the radar's on standby." Kyle scanned his own instrument panel, thinking: This guy is okay. Didn't believe I'd get along too well with him at first. A navigator in the right seat—it just didn't sound right. But he knows his stuff. Not only that, he likes motorcycles—hope he buys that Harley he's been dickering for. The young pilot's musing was interrupted by, "Bluejay Seven is cleared for takeoff, over." He shoved the throttles forward and concentrated on making a flawless night-weather takeoff.

"It's no use, Kyle, we may as well go home." After two hours of futile attempts to pick up their target, Orkin's voice sagged with frustrated dejection. "The thing works great down at sixteen, but as soon as we climb back to eighteen thousand and start picking up ice, I get nothing but a screen full of snow."

Kyle sighed, reduced power, and rolled into a descending turn. He keyed the mike and called, "Pinetree, this is Bluejay Seven. No joy. We're breaking off and returning to sixteen, below the freezing level, over."

"This is Pinetree, Bluejay Seven. Do you wish to terminate the project, over?"

"Unless you can bring the bogey down to sixteen, I think we may as well. We had a target this time until we climbed back up to eighteen. We assume the problem to be ice on the radar pod in front of the antenna, over."

"Understand, Bluejay Seven. Be advised the command post duty officer unable to divert the target from its flight-planned route. Turn to heading zero-two-five for vectors to Dayton radio range. Expect a GCA into Wright Field. Maintain sixteen thousand feet. The project is terminated at twenty-two-one-four hours, over."

"Roger, Pinetree, copy all," Kyle droned. He switched to intercom. "You copy, Gus?"

"Yeah, I heard," the RO responded. "Shit. We had it made. Radar vectors were right on the button. The set was working perfectly. Well, the whiz kids in engineering will be busy tomorrow. They gotta figure some way to keep that nose cone over the antenna ice-free."

"There's another thing as well," Kyle came back. "This bird isn't any happier than I am chasing around with a load of ice. We weren't in the stuff more than fifteen minutes on any of the three passes, and there's no way I could have gotten recommended closure speed. She was struggling to maintain two-fifty."

"I noticed that—" Gus's comment was interrupted by a VHF transmission.

"Bluejay Seven, this is Pinetree, over."

"This is Bluejay Seven. Go ahead, Pinetree."

"This is the command post duty officer, Bluejay. What is your remaining fuel situation, over?"

"Uh . . ." Kyle scanned the fuel gauges and continued, "a good four hours at cruise setting, Pinetree."

"Roger, understand. We have an emergency in progress. Wright Field ops has authorized a departure from your briefed mission to provide assistance if you agree, over."

"Go ahead, Pinetree. What's the problem?"

"Air traffic control reports a civilian plane lost near your present position. The pilot reports loss of all navigational radios. They request our assistance, over."

"Well"—Kyle peered outside his canopy where the red, port-side navigation light was barely visible—"I can try. What is it you want me to do?"

"We're getting a skin paint on an unidentified aircraft at ten thousand feet that's near the lost plane's last reported position. The target is outside our VHF transmission range. Request you attempt to contact the pilot on emergency frequency. The call sign is Nan Three-Three-Two-Eight. Please call back this frequency and advise, over."

"Roger, Pinetree. Switching to frequency one-thirty-five-decimal-zero, over." He punched channel D on his radio panel. "Nan Three-Three-Two-Eight, this is Bluejay Seven on emergency channel. Do you read? over."

Kyle waited for what seemed an eternity. Then a hesitant voice said, "Hello, Bluejay, this is Three-Three-Two-Eight, over."

"Roger, roger, Three-Three-Two-Eight. Read you loud and clear. I understand you have a problem, over."

"Yes—yes. My radios won't work. I don't know where I am. I'm in solid clouds, and my last weather report gives cloud bases below a thousand feet in the entire Midwest. I don't dare try letting down blind!" The words came back in a shrill rush.

"Okay, okay," Kyle replied soothingly. "We'll work out something. Now, give me your type aircraft, number of people on board, and your fuel remaining. I'm in touch with a military radar station, and between us, we'll get you on the ground—no sweat. Why don't you start flying a triangle using left-hand turns with two-minute legs. The radar station will need to have positive ident before they start giving directions, over."

"Oh, thank God," Kyle heard. "I'm flying a Beechcraft Eighteen; there are five people on board—one a baby—and I have perhaps an hour's fuel remaining. I'm turning to a southwest heading now and will fly two-minute legs. Please hurry."

"Stand by, Three-Three-Two-Eight," Kyle called cheerfully. "I'll contact radar and get instructions for you." He switched channels but sat silently assessing the situation. One: the airplane—a civilian version of the C-45. Twin-engine, all metal, carried seven or eight passengers. Two: the fuel situation. The thing cruised at about a hundred and fifty or sixty. According to the weather briefing he'd received, there wasn't a VFR field within reach. Three: the pilot sounded close to panic. Maybe it was just a poor radio set, but the guy's voice came across like a scared kid's.

He switched frequencies. "Pinetree, this is Bluejay Seven, over."

"Go ahead."

"I'm in contact with the civilian plane. It don't look good. He's down to an hour's fuel and no radio navigation aids. He's flying a left-hand triangle for ident. I suggest letting me relay vectors to Wright Field with a GCA handoff, over."

A pause, then, "Bluejay Seven, Pinetree here. There's a problem with that. The unidentified target just dropped off our scope. It may be Nan Three-Three-Two-Eight beyond our search range, then it may be a plane that landed."

Kyle pulled his oxygen mask free and wiped sweat from his face. Damnit! "Okay, Pinetree, what do you suggest?"

Following a long pause, he heard, "Bluejay, this is Pinetree. Advise the Beechcraft to turn to a heading of three-two-zero and climb to twelve thousand feet. Maybe we can reacquire the target, over."

Kyle made swift calculations, then said, "Pinetree, that's taking the plane *away* from Wright. He's already low on fuel. What do you have in mind if you *do* reacquire, over?"

"Do you have a better plan?" Pinetree's voice was testy.

"Stand by, Pinetree." Kyle switched to intercom. "Gus, just how good are you with that gizmo? Think you can locate a small plane without vectors?"

"Get him within a twenty-degree azimuth, on our altitude, and thirty miles—yeah, I can paint him," Gus replied promptly.

"Okay, get set. We're going to have a go at it," said Kyle. He flipped the VHF to TRANSMIT. "Three-Three-Two-Eight, this is your old buddy Bluejay. Do you read me, over?"

"R-roger, Bluejay. This is Beech Three-Three-Two-Eight."

"Okay. Here's what we're gonna do. I'm flying a plane equipped with radar. If you'll take up a heading of one-three-five, maintain ten thousand feet, and an airspeed of one-fifty, I'll pull in behind you, pick you up on my radar, then give you directions to Wright Field. Once there, I'll hand you off to the GCA and let them talk you down. Understand, over?"

"I'm not sure, Bluejay. A GCA?"

"Right. Stands for ground-controlled approach. Once they have you on their scope, they can give you directions right down to the runway. It's neat. Now, my name is Kyle. We're going to be talking quite a bit, so it'll be easier to use first names. What's yours?"

"Terry." Kyle thought he detected a measure of relief in the pilot's voice."

"All right, Terry. You just relax, now. I'll be off this frequency a few minutes, but we'll get you down." Kyle swiped sweat from his forehead with his sleeve and called, "Pinetree, this is Bluejay. If you'll give me vectors toward Three-Three-Two-Eight's last position, I'm going to descend to ten thousand and try an intercept. Then I'll steer him to Wright for a GCA, over."

"Roger, understand, Bluejay. Take up a heading of three-zero-zero. I estimate the target's present position is roughly fifty miles on a bearing of three-zero-zero from you. Stand by for a turn onto a tail attack position. I'm in touch with air traffic control and will clear all altitudes below ten thousand. And—good luck, Bluejay. You got guts, over."

Yeah, Kyle thought, more guts than brains. Refusing even to consider the odds against success, he snapped, "Okay, Gus. Can you do it?"

"Do I have a choice?" Orkin replied in a laconic drawl. Kyle grinned into the darkness, suddenly relaxed by Gus's unflustered response. "Oh, I suppose you do," he responded. "You can admit you're a big fake—don't have the faintest idea of what the hell you're doing. Go home and tell everyone your Rube Goldberg rig is worthless. In fact, I'll bet you a beer that you can't locate that plane."

Orkin managed to transmit an indignant snort. "Bullshit, flyboy. If you can follow instructions without spinning in, we'll find it—even if I have to climb out there on that radar pod and peer into the night like an Indian scout. Let's go—and I'll have a Schlitz."

Kyle sobered and said, "Okay. You work Pinetree for vectors and relay instructions. I'll call Dayton Approach and get things set up on that end while I hold that pilot's hand. This is going to be dicey, even if we find the guy." He switched to the VHF emergency frequency. "Hi, Terry. This is Kyle. We're moving into position—should pick you up shortly," he announced with forced cheerfulness. "Everything copacetic on your end?"

"Roger. I'm holding your heading, airspeed, and altitude. How far from Dayton are we? I'm down to less than an hour's fuel, over."

Kyle bit his lip. "Should be plenty, but keep her leaned out, just in case. I—" He stopped short as Gus's voice on intercom said, "Turn right, now, to a heading of one-two-zero. Pinetree estimates us to be forty miles behind the target. Hold two-hundred-fifty indicated—we should acquire the target in about one-five minutes."

"Turning to one-two-zero, Gus. What's our ETA for Wright, by the way?"

"About forty minutes from now," the RO replied after a brief pause.

"Shit. Look, this guy's down to less than an hour's fuel. This is cutting it pretty fine. He's never done a GCA; it might take more than one pass. What say I add some power, say, to three hundred indicated?"

"Wel-l-l, okay—we don't want to overshoot, you know."

"We don't want him to run out of gas either. Keep me posted." Kyle shoved the throttles forward and felt his stomach churn. Christ—what have I done? he asked himself. The full import of his impulsive decision settled on his shoulders like a hundred-pound weight. Five people—one an infant—blundering around in the dark like a blind hog in an outhouse. Shit! If they crashed, as they probably would, it would be his fault.

He tore his eyes from the creeping instrument-panel clock and pressed the mike switch. No, he thought, releasing his grip, I can't lie to the pilot, and I don't have anything encouraging to say. C'mon Gus, damnit—say something!

As if in answer to his impassioned plea, he heard, "RO to pilot. Turn left, ten degrees." Then, unable to conceal his excitement, he added, "I may have something, Kyle! Fuzzy, but it's a moving target—thirty miles, now dead on our nose."

Kyle turned to the new course. He discovered his jaws were clenched, his leather flying gauntlets wet with sweat. He forced himself to relax, resisting the urge to key the mike and start talking, to Terry, to Gus, to Pinetree, *anyone*. He slumped with relief as Gus said, "I think we got our man, Kyle. Have the pilot make a ninety left for ident."

Kyle forced a casual, "Hi, Terry. Think we gotcha, but turn left ninety degrees for positive identification, over."

"Roger, turning to heading zero-three-zero, Kyle," followed quickly by, "what is our position from the field, over?"

"Approximately thirty minutes northwest, Terry—" Gus's yelp interrupted. "That's him. Positive contact, pilot. Pinetree advises Dayton radio range is seven-zero miles on heading of one-eight-zero, I have it tuned and identified on number-one ADF. We're closing fast, though. Suggest you slow down."

Grinning from ear to ear, Kyle said, "Sorry for the interruption, Terry. We're locked on seventy miles north of the field. Turn to one-eight-zero, reduce power to seventeen-hundred rpm and start a gradual descent. Let your airspeed build to about one-eighty so I don't overrun you." Kyle pulled his own throttles to idle, lowered half flaps, and keyed the intercom.

"Okay, hotshot, I owe you a beer. That pilot owes you a whole case—great work. Now I've lowered half flaps, but I'll still have to do some S-turns to stay behind him."

"Okay, but keep them shallow—don't lose him now, for Christs sake. Range is seven miles and still closing."

Fifteen suspense-laden minutes later, Kyle uttered a wild yell as he heard, "Nan Three-Three-Two-Eight, this is Wright GCA. I have you in positive radar contact ten miles north of the field. You are cleared to descend to two thousand feet. Wright Field altimeter setting, two-niner-decimal-six-four. Current weather is seven hundred overcast with light rain; winds light and variable. Turn now to heading two-one-five for a left base leg to runway one-three. Expect turn onto final approach in three minutes. Perform your before-landing checklist now. You are cleared to land. You need not acknowledge my instructions after entering final descent, over. Break break, Bluejay Seven, hold southeast of the Dayton radio range at four thousand feet. You will be number two to land, over."

Kyle felt the tailwheel touch down and breathed deeply, letting the plane rumble toward the runway's far end. His headset came to life as he peered through swirling fog and rain searching for the Follow Me jeep's friendly yellow beacon. "I have you down at two-seven, Bluejay Seven," the operator droned. "Colonel Babcock requests you to report to base ops before proceeding to mission debriefing, over."

Too drained to express himself, Kyle confined his congratulations to Gus to a slap on the shoulder as they trudged toward base operations. He was rewarded by a weary, "About that beer, cowboy . . ."

A dozen chattering people milled about in the space in front of the flight dispatcher's counter. Kyle spotted a chaplain and two white-uniformed medics. Colonel Babcock strode toward Kyle and Gus, hand extended and a wide grin on his lumpy features. "Good show, fellows," he growled. "You had some sweaty palms down here, I can tell you."

"I really can't believe it myself," Kyle confessed. "Just keep your eye on ol' Gus, here. He's got powers that got people burned at the stake a few years back."

Babcock chuckled. "Won't hold you up long, but the folks in that Beechcraft wanted to say howdy—the pilot especially." He led the exhausted crew to a group dressed in civilian clothes and seated to one side. "Kyle, I'd like you to meet Terri Vincent—she was at the controls up there. Miss Vincent, Lieutenants Wilson and Orkin, your knights in shining armor."

A slim, tousle-haired blonde stood. Kyle gaped as the wan-faced young woman extended her hand and said, "I've never been much for heroes, but you two qualify. I just can't express my thanks."

Kyle took the proffered hand in hands suddenly nerveless, his eyes roving over the well-filled tan, whipcord slacks and matching military-cut shirt. "Why—why, you're a *woman*."

9

4 July 1949
Syracuse, New York

Ross lounged in welcome shade cast by the parked C-47's wing, his back propped against a main landing gear. Beside him, Capt. Doug Curtiss hunkered far enough toward the wingtip to peer through a muggy heat haze toward the horizon. Across the airfield, the blare of a brass band mingled with sounds of a happy, noisy crowd filling temporary bleachers. Widely publicized, the air show had struck a patriotic Fourth of July chord, but most had turned out to see the new jet-powered F-80 fighters perform, he knew.

"It'll be a goddamned miracle if Seven-Seven-Three makes it back to Wright with that balky fuel control," Curtiss muttered. "In fact, I wouldn't be surprised to see only three birds make their low pass instead of four."

"You're a worrywart, Doug. Kyle Wilson knows damn near as much about that J-Thirty-three engine as you do. He isn't going to do something stupid."

"I know he's a friend of yours, Ross, but he's too goddamn cocky for my way of thinking."

Ross smiled tolerantly. Curtiss had just been rewarded with an assignment to the F-80 flight test program for outstanding work as an aircraft maintenance officer. He was a perfectionist and a worrier. He was also decidedly unhandsome. Ross had overheard someone say, "No other word for it, Doug is just as plain ugly as the south end of a mule going north."

Crude but true, Ross thought. The guy's ears protruded like fenders on a Model A Ford, his nose was too big for his narrow visage, as was his lantern jaw, and he regarded the world through a perpetual squint. A product of the Pennsylvania coal-mining region, Doug had the heart and generosity of a saint, however. He and Ross had been assigned as "buddies" for the F-80 class beginning on Monday next.

Even the dourest cynic would be hard-pressed to disrupt Ross's euphoria today. He flexed his left hand, a habit formed over the past six months. The fact that everything still worked always reassured his subconscious. His thoughts drifted back.

Things had looked pretty damn dark for a time. Had not Janet goaded him into dogged effort, he'd have thrown in the towel—more than once. He saw Curtiss stand and stroll away from the overhanging wing.

"Four of 'em by God," the taciturn maintenance officer advised with grudging admiration.

Ross joined him in time to spot four dots low in the sky that swiftly became recognizable as airplanes. He heard the P. A. system rasp, "Ladies and gentlemen, approaching from your right—" Before the M. C. could complete his announcement, four sleek F-80s flashed across the field, barely fifty feet above the runway. The spectators oohed and aahed—the fact that noise of the formation's passage hadn't been detected until they were over the airfield's boundary was impressive.

"They got those engines wound up to a hundred percent and riding the machmeter's red line," Doug grumbled. "Goddamnit, they can make a flyby without overstressing."

Ross waited until the formation split in four directions and climbed out of sight doing vertical barrel rolls—his hands itched to get into the cockpit. "That's why we're along with a Gooney Bird full of spare parts, and a mechanical wizard like you, Doug," he observed mildly. "The folks are entitled to see the best we got."

Ross stood to one side as the four pilots mingled with Chamber of Commerce bigwigs and members of the press the next morning. Behind them the sleek F-80s were being groomed for departure. A chain-link fence surrounding the parking ramp held back a solid wall of spectators anxious to get a close-up look at the air force's latest, and the world's hottest, fighter plane.

He would have given much to be one of them—not for egotistical reasons, but just for the sheer thrill of being part of the action. No, the fact he was even on the scene was sufficient reward. Returned to full flying status only two weeks ago, he'd jumped at the opportunity to fly the old Gooney Bird. He and Doug provided support of the ever-increasing demand for public appearances of the speedy Shooting Stars—it was ample compensation. His time for basking in a star role would come, but it didn't seem as important as it once did.

Word that surgery on the injured hand was necessary to restore full move-ment had hit him hard. He had no faith in the process. The flight surgeon left him with no option, however, and Janet had stayed up most of one night coping with his funk. Then the long weeks of waiting. How he maintained a passing grade average, he'd never know.

Again it was Janet. She'd taken a leave of absence from her job with INS to be with him during the protracted convalescence. The shabby two-room apartment was depressing, the snail-like healing process was depressing, and hearing others describe their exploits in the air was even more de-pressing.

The flight surgeon withdrew his no-drinking stipulation, but Ross dis-covered that alcohol offered no escape. He plodded from one day to the next, finalizing plans in his mind for a future that didn't include flying. Janet had bawled like a baby the day Doc Wilmack announced, "Well, Ross, you've goofed off long enough. I'm restoring you to full flying sta-tus; get back to earning your pay." It was then he realized that Janet's or-deal had been almost as bad as his own.

Doug strolled back from where he'd had his head in one of the birds' nose compartment. They watched the pilots shake hands with their ad-miring group and climb into their cockpits. The ground power unit's en-gine barked to life, and Kyle gave the thumbs-in signal for a crew chief to insert the electrical power cord. Moments later, Kyle scrambled from his cockpit, and trotted to the plane parked next to his. That pilot dismounted, and the pair strode over to peer into the tailpipe of Kyle's ship.

"Now what the fuck's wrong?" Doug started forward.

Ross grasped the alarmed man's elbow and said, "Hold it. Your services aren't required."

"What? What the hell do you mean? If Wilson's got a problem, then I—"

Ross grinned and interrupted with, "Believe me you aren't needed for what's about to happen. Just stay put—hell, you may even learn some-thing."

Spluttering in protest, Doug stood and watched as Kyle and his buddy mouthed indistinguishable words and gesticulated wildly. Finally Kyle returned to his cockpit while the second pilot raced to his own airplane, returning seconds later with a rolled-up newspaper.

Kyle leaned out and made a circling motion with his forefinger. His buddy withdrew a Zippo lighter from his flight suit, applied flame to the paper, and thrust it behind the plane's tailpipe. The tailpipe promptly disgorged a lance of orange flame—they could hear the jet engine's turbines whining to full rpm.

Curtiss stood slack-jawed then said, "What in Christ's name is going on? You can't start that engine by—"

Ross slapped Doug's shoulder and bent double with laughter. "You saw it," he gasped. "How can you doubt it? I told you that you'd maybe learn something."

Doug's face turned crimson as he realized he'd fallen for a hoax. "That smart-ass Wilson. Shit. What're people going to think? That we're a bunch of goddamned clowns? And you knew he was going to do that—why didn't you tell me?"

"People are going to think that they were entertained," said Ross. "They got a kick out of watching the show; I got *my* kick watching your face. Okay, I filed the flight plan. As soon as they get that starter unit loaded, we're ready to go. It's your turn to fly left seat."

21 July 1949
Dayton Municipal Park

Janet spread a red-checked cloth on the picnic table while Betsy Curtiss unpacked a picnic hamper. A stone's toss behind her, Janet could hear Ross and Doug arguing the relative distances of their horseshoes from a steel peg. How peaceful and bucolic can it get? she wondered. The corners of her mouth twitched as she visualized Ed Adair's reaction to a beer-and-hotdog outing—pitching horseshoes, yet. Ed's idea of an outdoor social event ran toward catered meals—with a selection of three wines—beneath a screen-mesh-enclosed circus tent pitched on a manicured lawn.

"Here's Ross's cake," Betsy announced, lifting the cover from a cake plate. "German chocolate with burnt-sugar icing, the kind you said he likes."

Janet leaned forward and examined Betsy's handiwork—a graduate's cap outlined in white pastry icing above a miniature slide rule with CON-

GRATULATIONS spelled out around the cake's edge. She chuckled. "Perfect. I really appreciate your doing this. We have trouble just scrambling eggs in that shoebox we call home; baking a cake would be a guaranteed disaster. And I'm glad I didn't follow my first idea of a big sit-down dinner at the club to celebrate the occasion. This is so much nicer."

Her petite, elfin-faced companion grinned. "It is fun, isn't it? Doug and I haven't been on a picnic since we've been here. You don't do a lot of entertaining in company-grade quarters either. God knows we're lucky to have base housing. Doug's assignment as permanent party was a fluke actually, but they *aren't* exactly palatial. Heaven help us if I ever get pregnant."

Janet cast an amused glance at Betsy's slim hips and the flat tummy visible beneath her halter top. "Never happen," she announced firmly. "There isn't enough room down there."

The staccato cackling of a decelerating motorcycle engine interrupted their laughter. Janet looked toward the parking lot. "There're Kyle and Terri. I hope he brought ice like he was supposed to. Speaking of ice, why don't we open a cold beer? Why should we slave away preparing a feast for those oafish louts without a bit of R&R of our own?"

Kyle called from a dozen paces away, "Hey, what's this? The women slurping up beer when they're supposed to be providing food. Do you have permission from your lords and masters?"

"Until our so-called lords and masters deign to light a fire, there ain't gonna *be* anything but beer to sustain you, wise guy," Janet replied laughingly. "Hi, you two, you're late."

Terri Vincent, her tousled blonde cap barely reaching Kyle's shoulder, gave a derisive hoot. "Adonis here may be able to do feats of skill and daring with an airplane, but he can't get back and return a high lob for sour apples. I waxed him, six-four, two-six, seven-five, but it took a while."

Betsy cocked an appreciative eye at Terri's sun-bronzed legs extending from brief tennis shorts and her close-fitting jersey top. "Maybe he has trouble concentrating," she observed dryly.

Ross and Doug joined the gathering during the ensuing hilarity. "I'll never know how this guy ever earned a degree—a degree in *engineering,* of all things," Doug grumbled. "He doesn't even know how to do simple measurements."

Kyle held up a hand. "Ross, I can't account for it, but Terri says she hasn't met you. So, this is the gal I've told you about. Terri, this is the man who once saved my father's life."

Ross shook Terri's slim, brown hand. "Now I understand why he keeps you out of sight. You *can* do much better than him, you know."

Terri's eyes crinkled at the corners. "Kyle's told me a great deal about you, Major Colyer, I'm so happy to get to meet you. And don't get any wrong ideas. I'm still considering offers—and I just *love* men with six-figure incomes."

Ross and Doug lit the charcoal, and only slightly burned the hotdogs—arguing hotly all the while—before proudly announcing it was time to eat. The group filled paper plates and took places at the long trestle table. Janet seated herself at one end and listened to the male banter turn to airplanes. It is, after all, our lives, she thought. A gathering of bankers, plumbers, or insurance salesmen would be no different.

Kyle, younger but with more accumulated jet time than Doug and Ross combined, held his own in the spirited discussion. Ross, with extensive combat time, and Doug, the admitted mechanical genius, kept the conversation interesting. Janet noticed that Doug's former animosity toward the younger Kyle was absent.

"Muroc lost another one on takeoff yesterday," Kyle announced. "Engine blew up right after liftoff. That J-33 engine—I just don't know. The word in test group is that someway, raw fuel is getting past the regulator. They think maybe the float valve in the fuselage tank sticks. This lets fuel pumped from the wing and tip tanks go straight into the air intakes. As of today, we're taking off just on the fuselage tank, with the others switched off."

"Damn," Ross observed, "those two hundred gallons aren't going to last long at takeoff and climb power."

"Yeah, you can't go to sleep, gotta turn on the tip tanks right away."

"I don't think that's the problem," Doug interjected.

"No?"

"Nope. Back when Major Bong's ship blew up on takeoff, nobody wanted to point to a famous wartime ace and call it pilot error. But the word circulated by crew chiefs through the NCO clubs says that Bong didn't check the filler cap on his fuselage tank."

Ross swallowed a bite of his sandwich, then asked, "What does that do? I know the instructor pilots pound that into you, but hell, if it's that important, why isn't on the checklist?"

"Good question. If you look at the setup behind the cockpit, you'll see that the engine air intakes aren't a foot away from that tank. Before you get enough airspeed to create ram air flow, those spring-loaded flapper doors behind the cockpit provide air to the engine. What happens when you have a loose cap? Well, when those doors close after you reach flying speed, the engine sucks unmetered fuel past the loose cap, and blooie."

"We got a helluva lot to learn about these birds," Doug added into the thoughtful silence that followed. "Why can't we have a heating and cooling system that works? Why can't we design fittings for the nose armament doors that won't let them blow off? How do you keep the windshield from icing up? Fix a canopy that will slice your head off if you don't duck when you jettison it? We've known about these things for four–five years, and they're still around."

"And how about a fuel system that won't feed in an inverted position?" Ross added. "Whoever heard of a fighter plane you couldn't fly upside down?"

Kyle nodded. "You know what I think?" When no one responded, he forged ahead with, "I think they've given up on the '80. Guess what I saw yesterday over in Hangar A-4?" Again his question went unanswered. "We have two North American F-86s."

"Yeah?" Doug and Ross responded in unison.

"Yeah. Wait until you see it. The wings sweep back, and it has a different engine, an axial-flow General Electric J-47. It's already been flown faster than mach one! I'll bet the '80 isn't around six months after we get that job on line. That's my next airplane, guys."

Doug surveyed the empty plates, then stood. "Okay, everyone, listen up. We're here to congratulate Ross, who just added another scalp to his belt. Let's drink to a guy who is not only one of the finest pilots in the business, but one that can now read and write. If you have anything to say, Colyer, be quick so we can cut Betsy's fancy cake."

Janet watched Ross blush slightly. He stood and looked straight at her. "It's said that behind every successful man stands a good woman," he said slowly. "I'm here to tell you that for the past few months I've not only had a good woman behind me, but one *damn* good woman. Thanks, my dear."

Tears spilled from Janet's eyes as she bobbed her head in appreciation to raised bottles of beer and a chorus of "Hear, hears."

The men headed back to the horseshoe pits. Terri thrust a bundle of used plates and napkins into the trash barrel and seated herself on the picnic bench. "Tell me, Betsy, was it a really tough decision? I mean, do you have to give up *everything* you dreamed of doing to be a good wife? While Kyle and I aren't serious; he's fun to be around, handsome as hell, and he makes me feel good about myself. But I was wondering just the other day: Terri, what if he said, 'I'm being reassigned to Alaska. Will you come with me as my wife?'

"I—I am fond of him, I have to confess. But *Alaska?* Give up my flying job? My apartment? My independence? I want to be the first woman airline pilot. Pop's trying to get me into a school in Oklahoma City to get my air transport rating—I'd be the only woman they've accepted. Must these decisions be so goddamned hard?"

Janet opened fresh beers for all of them and sat beside Terri. "Times are changing, Terri. In 1942, when I married BT, my first husband, the question of what to do didn't exist. I'd never given a thought to making my own life, doing the things I wished, living wherever, and, yes, with whomever I liked.

"Then I found myself alone. I was terrified that day I left my folks' home and headed for a job in Seattle. But I did it, and as I grew good at my work, I enjoyed that freedom." She chuckled.

"But when Ross asked me to marry him, I didn't think twice. Oh, I had some misgivings—things got a bit strained when I stayed with my job in D.C. instead of joining him here. Then he was in that plane crash. He almost gave up when he thought he'd never fly again.

"I didn't know what to do! I'd always admired his strength, his ability— he was invincible in my eyes. I couldn't believe he wanted to quit without trying. So I nagged, I even threatened to leave him. Well, when he said what he did just now, it all came together. I think he was trying to tell me that we're now partners.

"I guess what I'm trying to say is: Mostly we want to prove to ourselves that we *can* do something worthwhile. Once we do that, then we can look at being 'just a wife,' having kids, and providing support to our men without feeling we're inferior or less than an equal partner. Am I making any sense?"

"A great deal of it," Betsy said softly. "You asked if these decisions had to be so hard, Terri. They do. You've heard the old adage 'There's no such thing as a free lunch'? Well, everything worthwhile extracts a price."

Janet stood and uttered a shaky laugh. "Well," she said, "this conversation certainly got serious. This is a party, remember? Why don't you two go harass the gladiators? After I go to the potty, I'll join you there."

The long walk to the rest rooms gave Janet a chance to collect her thoughts. That was quite a speech, she told herself. Whatever brought it on? More than that, do I really believe everything I said? I'd planned to tell Ross tonight that I called Ed Adair last week—told him you no longer needed me and I was coming back to work next week. Is this what I want? Damn Betsy Curtiss. And damn Terri Vincent. Why did she have to ask that question?

5 August 1949
Tashkent, USSR

Yuri Pavel, lieutenant, Soviet Air Forces, stifled a yawn and added a pair of obscenely oversized breasts to the nude girl sketched on the margin of his notebook. The classroom was stifling hot, and he surreptitiously wiped a trickle of sweat from beneath his uniform tunic's linen collar-liner. A swift glance at the other forty-odd pilot officers revealed equally marked indifference to their instructor's impassioned message. Turning to a blank page, he started outlining a radically streamlined airplane. Concern regarding the outcome of his request for assignment to the new jet fighters overshadowed any serious consideration of the political commissar's strident tirade.

A shouted statement penetrated his musings and caught his interest. ". . . aircraft, so advanced in technology that no nation—even the vaunted United States—dare put up a challenge . . ." Yuri returned to his previous borderline somnolency. The daily lecture on Communist Party doctrine represented a low point in the academy's curriculum. Taught by officers of the Air Force Political Administration, wearing the gold epaulets of an aviator, none had ever been at the controls. What did this fool know about airplane technology?

Yuri was very much aware that he and his classmates formed a small, select group. Appointment to the accelerated jet fighter program from distinguished graduates of the Armavir Higher Aviation Academy removed them from the rigors of life endured by the proletariat. In addition, Yuri's father, Maj. Gen. Sergei Pavel, emerged from the battle for Stalingrad a hero. His son thus enjoyed all privileges extended to immediate family members of famous army officers.

Neither was he unaware of his handsomely arranged, almost Caucasian, features—without the Mongolian influence evident on his father's side. When abroad in the city, he pretended casual indifference to covetous scrutiny of his tailored uniform and aviator badge. The admiring glances and respect shown by public servants, even senior party members, had come to be taken for granted, however. Good looks, a repertoire of witty conversation, and unlimited access to the family dacha combined to assure Yuri of a most satisfactory social life as well. He never lacked for companions, especially the female variety.

Despite the good life he led, the dashing young officer was determined to be a credit to his father's image as a leader. Not only graduation from the nation's most prestigious military academy, but also earning that coveted assignment to the jet-engined MiG-15 remained uppermost in his mind. He scowled. An examination would follow today's discourse, he knew. Some notes were in order. Not all would survive the rigorous training regimen, and political reliability was an essential element.

He wrote today's topic across the top of a blank page. "The Party's Posture With Regard To Our Eastern Frontier." Beneath that he scribbled, "Concern with USA designs on Japan—springboard for Western invasion of Asia?"

So who cares? Yuri asked himself. *Give* that miserably cold, barren part of the world to the stupid imperialists. He took time to sketch a caricature of the red-faced, perspiring speaker in the cockpit of his futuristically designed airplane. His neighbor, an equally bored young flight officer, grinned as he glanced at the drawing of a rat. The rodent had prominent beady eyes behind steel-rimmed glasses; a long nose that ended with feral buck teeth; and long, antennalike whiskers.

Pay attention, Yuri admonished himself. In quick succession he jotted, "Essential to establish military presence—not only Sakhalin and the Kuril Islands, but the Korean peninsula as well. Link with People's Republic of China—create pincers around Japan." He embellished the words with a crab claw. "Drive Westerners from South Korea. Equip North Korean People's Army? Foment takeover?" Quickly he added: "A politically dead enemy is the only safe enemy." He smiled inwardly. *That* catchphrase would earn him a passing grade in itself. Once again, his attention wandered.

A scrap of notepaper slid before him returned Yuri to the mundane present. His neighbor Anatoli had scrawled, "The dacha this weekend, as usual?"

.

Yuri frowned. Partially concealing the query with his notebook, he wrote, "???—Papa returns from Berlin with companion—*female*. Perhaps *he* will use dacha for party????" He turned it so Anatoli could read his words and shrugged.

Yuri sensed other people were present as soon as he closed the door to the family apartment. Fragrant cigar smoke signaled his father's, the general's, return. His sensitive olfactory faculties detected another scent he recognized instantly, but not one he associated with his father: perfume. Marya's. His current paramour had been here two days ago, her dark eyes sparkling as Yuri loaded her down with delicacies from the academy's Voyentorg.

"Not for your exclusive pleasure, my sweet," he'd admonished. "Papa returns any day now. I wouldn't want to see his loutish friends devour my hard-won hoard. We'll save until . . ." Marya purred with anticipation as he caressed her ivory-skinned neck.

No, Yuri decided. This isn't one of the scents I've given darling Marya. He slung his carryall crammed with manuals and textbooks onto the vestibule table and proceeded into the spacious apartment's living room. He paused in the open doorway and regarded its sole occupant with cool appraisal. A looker, was his first reaction—Papa always exercised good taste when it came to women. Even his mother had had the figure and grace of a ballerina.

The blonde woman was seated at a corner table, writing. She'd stand tall, he observed, past his shoulder. Lush curves outlined by her Western-style skirt and blouse prompted a stirring in his groin. He knew instinctively she was older than she appeared—one of the "older women" he and his friends pretended to find unattractive, but . . . Without entering the room, he said, "Hello, I don't believe we've met."

"I believe not," the woman drawled. She laid down her pen and added, "I'm Giesele. You must be Yuri, Sergei's son—correct?"

Yuri donned his most winning smile and replied, "I have that distinction. And you must be the, ah—refugee? mentioned in his letter."

Giesele uttered a throaty chuckle. Switching to English, she said, "I'm sorry, but we've almost exhausted my Russian vocabulary. Do you speak the English? *Sprechen sie deutsch?*"

"Some English," Yuri replied haltingly. "It's a required subject at the academy, but I have small opportunity to practice it. No German, I fear."

"Then we must learn together," said Giesele. "One evening we speak nothing but Russian, the next English. Agreed?"

Was there a suggestive overtone there? Yuri wondered. "I look forward to many such evenings," he replied boldly. "May I come in?"

"Of course," Giesele responded laughingly. "It is, after all, your home."

"Papa's," Yuri corrected her. "I mostly live in the barracks."

"But entertain here, yes?" Giesele teased with an arch look. "Certain traces remain."

Yuri ignored the innuendo. "Will you live here then?"

Giesele hesitated. "I believe that is your father's plan. Perhaps you should discuss it with him."

"Of course. Is he not here?"

"He should return any minute. He had business with—" Sound of the entrance door opening interrupted her. "In fact, I believe he's here now," she finished.

Sergei Pavel entered the room with a rush. Embracing Yuri and kissing him on both cheeks, he roared, "Ah, Yuri Sergeievich, more handsome than ever. The life of a military scholar agrees with you, no?" He held Yuri by both shoulders at arm's length. "Let me look at you. I've been away too long."

Giesele stood, folded her writing portfolio, and said, "If you will excuse me, I'll leave you two to get reacquainted."

"No, no, nothing of the sort," Sergei scolded. "I assume you've met Giesele, Yuri?"

"Just this minute, Papa. I had no idea that the refugee you mentioned was such a breathtakingly beautiful creature. I'm still trying to recover."

Sergei's big frame shook with uninhibited mirth. "Still the silver-tongued young rascal, I see." He wagged an admonishing finger at Giesele. "Take care that Yuri's flattery doesn't turn your head, my dear. The mothers of Moscow's finest examples of young womanhood grow uneasy when this lad is about—those of them who don't secretly lust for him themselves." The general roared with laughter.

Giesele smiled and patted Sergei's cheek in passing. "Never fear, my brave, handsome benefactor. I recognize the source of Yuri's winning ways. Please, I'll leave you now and rejoin you for an aperitif before dinner."

Yuri followed Giesele's swaying hips with frank admiration as she glided from the room. "I congratulate you, Papa. Duty in Berlin must have been enjoyable."

Sergei strode to the cellarette and removed two crystal glasses. "The city is a pesthole," he grumbled as he poured vodka. "Politics, vice, and subversion are more valued than military strategy. My reassignment to a front-line fighter-bomber division was welcome news." He handed Yuri one of the brimming containers and dropped his jovial banter. "To a long and distinguished career," he said with his glass raised.

Yuri joined his father in tossing back the fiery liquid in one swallow. "I promise not to disappoint you, Papa. My only wish is to be your equal."

"I'll accept nothing less," Sergei responded gruffly and reached for the vodka bottle. "Now, you no doubt wonder about Giesele."

"A lovely and gracious lady," Yuri murmured.

Sergei snorted. "Don't try to flimflam your old father. You're dying to know what part she plays in my life. I'll set your mind at rest. Giesele is a Russian refugee. Daughter of a monarchist, she was taken from the country when only a child. That fact, however, is for only us to know. Upon my recommendation, the party has granted her citizenship. I plan to marry her—next week, to be exact. There will be no ceremony."

This time it was Yuri who poured drinks. "My sincerest congratulations and best wishes, then," he said, lifting his glass.

Sergei bent a suspicious glare in his son's direction. "Your mother. You feel I'm showing a lack of respect? Letting my glands dictate a foolish absence of propriety?"

Yuri laughed. "Your private life is your own, Papa. Giesele will never occupy the same place in my heart that Mother claims, but that will not alter my relationship with your new bride. I like her as a person already."

Sergei showed obvious relief with a brief sigh. "You're being most sensible about the situation. I'd feared—"

"That I'd create a scene?" Yuri smiled broadly. "I'm not a child any longer, Papa. I'll move my spare wardrobe from here, of course. My quarters at the barracks are most adequate."

The general expressed displeasure with an extended lower lip. "You will do what you feel you must, of course. Giesele has already told me she wishes you will still consider this apartment your home."

"I'll explain it to her—thank her for her consideration. But it wouldn't be comfortable, and you know it."

"Possibly," Sergei replied briefly. "As for this evening, I'd planned for the three of us to celebrate with dinner at the Metropole and get better acquainted. Unfortunately, we're invited to an evening with Marshal Yokolov. I can't refuse. There is a matter of ah—well, some importance to discuss. My adversaries have been busy during my absence. Certain rumors and allegations must be put to rest. The marshal is supportive of my position and has the secretary-general's ear. I trust you understand. You will face many similar situations during your career." He gave Yuri a bleak smile.

"Of course I do," Yuri assured his distressed parent. "Papa . . ." He hesitated, then went on. "I'd planned to discuss this with you at the first opportunity, but I want very much to fly the new jet fighters. Only a few of our class will be selected. Do you suppose—"

"That I could put in a good word for you with Air Marshal Yokolov?" Sergei finished for him. "I will, of course, though it pains me that you choose interceptors over the fighter-bombers. Shturmoviks defeated our German enemies, not pursuit planes."

Yuri smiled. "You must, one day, observe the jet-powered MiG in action. I'd hate to be in a tank with one attacking me. I'll be forever grateful if you can help arrange the assignment. Oh," he added as an apparently casual afterthought, "the dacha. Will you have need of it this weekend? I'd like a day or two of solitary study to prepare for final examinations."

Sergei dismissed the request with a perfunctory grunt of consent. Yuri crossed to the liquor supply as the door closed behind his father. He selected scotch whisky this time and strolled to a window overlooking the tranquil expanse of Gorki Park. He regarded the view with unseeing eyes as he savored the smoky, single-malt liquor.

Contrary to what he'd told Sergei, he had deep reservations about his stepmother-to-be. There'd been no mistaking her subtly worded expression of interest in creating something other than a mother-son relationship. Was she a slut? Or was the exchange a calculated thing? To what purpose? His lips formed a grim smile. Our Giesele doesn't strike me as being a cheap flirt, he mused. Watch your step, sweetheart; if you betray my father's love and trust, disgrace him in any way, I'll ruin you.

10

Lieutenant Colonel Babcock hiked his butt onto the plane's wing and grinned at Ross. "Okay, hotshot, you made me eat my words of a few months ago. I'll concede that you're one of the best airplane drivers we've had through here. The Form 8 Kent wrote after your F-80 checkride was so gushy it made me want to throw up. I gotta remind you, though, that dogfighting is *not* one of the required maneuvers for a checkride. Anyway, welcome to the test group."

Ross moved to a minuscule strip of shade and squinted toward where Babcock was outlined against the blazing midwestern sun. He returned the colonel's smile. "Already I'm suspicious. I get handed a two-inch-thick manual some egghead has titled, *The Mark-IV Emergency Egress System.* Memorize it, I'm told. Then I'm fitted for the new plastic 'Brain Bucket.' 'It can withstand an impact of forty pounds per square inch,' the man says.

"Next, I'm led out here, where I find one of the brand-new TF-80 two-place trainers. Right away I notice the rear half of its canopy is missing. 'Gadzooks!' I exclaim. 'What can all this mean?'"

Babcock chuckled. "Like I said, 'Welcome to the test group.' You got your very own project right off the bat—if you want it."

"I have a choice?"

"Sure. I don't ask anyone to take on something they don't think is workable. The bang seat is controversial as hell. For example, Bob Hoover—one of the best test pilots in the business—won't touch it. But you're better equipped experiencewise than any pilot I have. You've bailed out in a combat situation, you've shown that you have above-average judgment, and," his grin returned, "I like you."

"Well, thanks a whole bunch, Colonel. Why is it I don't feel overwhelmed with gratitude? Seriously, I'm flattered. I'll do you a good job."

"I know you will. This escape system—or something like it—is a must if we're ever to fly routinely at supersonic speeds. We're losing pilots who try to leave a crippled bird by climbing over the side. We're losing others who think they can ride 'er in for a belly landing like the old Jug and Mustang. Do you have any questions after reading the book?"

"A few. Number one: You mention the need for a way to leave the ship at supersonic speeds. Four hundred mph is the record for successful ejection so far. What happens to the old body at, say, even six hundred? Two: The guys making these jumps are highly skilled test pilots. They do a lot of things that take trained reflexes. What happens to the poor slob who gets in trouble on his first flight in a new plane?

"Number three—a big question in my mind: A parachute comes down pretty damn slow, relatively speaking. Assume you go out at thirty-five or even forty thousand feet. It's fifty below and you can expect to survive about twenty seconds without oxygen at those altitudes. How now, brown cow?"

"Well, I'll try to answer those in reverse order. These are engineers' projections, by the way, not personal knowledge. The high-altitude bailout. They say the pilot has to free-fall to at least fourteen thousand before opening the chute. They're designing a built-in barometer to yank the rip cord automatically at about that altitude."

Babcock smiled at Ross's skeptical look and went on. "Training is the answer to your second question—that and more automation. The goal is a single trigger squeeze—blow the canopy, fire the seat, separate pilot and seat, then automatically deploy the chute. A long ways to go, there, so a training program to instill some confidence in the device is a top priority; but more about that later.

"Last, they've ejected dummies at up to six hundred mph with no discernible threat to life. The only thing they've done is add a visor to the newest helmets to protect your face from the wind blast. Satisfied?"

"Marginally," Ross replied with a wry grin. "Okay, where do I start?"

"Why, at the place you like best," Babcock said with an innocent expression. "The training program. Look, you're a combat ace; you've been there. The kids will listen to the old, grizzled veteran."

"Damnit, Colonel! You've conned me. You want me to be a *training* officer?"

"Simmer down, Ross. You'll be project officer, but bear in mind anything you do will be wasted effort unless the guys have some faith in your product. As of now, this is your airplane. You'll be given test profiles, and you'll write up the results. A veteran jumper is already assigned to you, but you'll also fire some dummies with instrumentation."

Ross paced the length of the wing in front of Babcock. Pausing in front of the seated flight test chief's dangling legs, he said, "I'm in charge?"

"I don't see anyone standing behind you."

"When can you get me into jump school?"

"Now, just a damn minute—"

"*Am* I in charge of the project?" Ross insisted.

"Yes, damnit, but we have a dozen qualified jumpers. This *is* a test program, remember? The unexpected *can* happen."

"Colonel, both of us have been in classes where some jerk was telling us what to do in case of . . . things he'd never actually done himself. I'll always remember my dad telling my six-year-old cousin what to do if caught out in the path of a tornado. He told the kid, 'If you can't find shelter, lie down in a ditch—the storm will pass right over you.' My cousin gave him a fishy look and asked, 'Anyone ever tried that, Uncle Bob?'

"And that's exactly what I'm talking about. When this 'grizzled old veteran' tells a bunch of slick-cheeked youngsters that this gadget really works, he wants to have an answer for, 'What's it *feel* like when you eject, Major?'"

Babcock glared at Ross for a moment, then snapped, "Have your ass out here at oh-seven-thirty tomorrow."

Ross heard Janet answer the long-distance operator and thumbed quarters into the pay phone. "Hi, Red-on-the-Head," he called gaily. "Whatcha up to?"

"Ross. What a lovely surprise! A few minutes later and you'd have caught me with a headful of shampoo lather. What prompted you to call on a Wednesday night?"

"Some good news I just had to share with you."

"Really? I can't wait. What's happened?"

"I've been assigned to the test group. I have my very own project."

"Oh, how wonderful. What will you be doing?"

"I'm in charge of running tests on a new ejection seat."

"I don't really understand, but I'm happy for you. You'll have to explain it to me this weekend."

"Count on it. But Janet, I had another reason for calling."

"Oh?"

"Yeah. You see, this assignment will be a permanent change of station instead of TDY. We'll be eligible for base housing."

"I see."

"So, hon, I know we talked this all out when you decided to go back to D.C., but . . . well, I was wondering . . ."

"If I would resign from INS and join you? I know I agreed to when you got your squadron, but Dayton? How long would we be there?"

"That's something else we need to discuss. This is important work—it's exciting. I—I'm having second thoughts about a squadron."

"Ross! I can't believe what I'm hearing."

"Well, this hit me pretty sudden. It'll take some time to think about it."

"I would think so." Janet chuckled. "You big ape, I know what you're thinking: Without a war going on, what does a fighter pilot *do?* I heard you ask that, remember?"

"Now, it isn't that at all—"

"We'll talk about it this weekend. I miss ya." Janet made a kissing noise into the transmitter and cradled the handset.

Okay, kiddo, she thought, you have three days to make up your mind. Am I a Betsy, or am I a Terri? Do I eat those noble-sounding words I spouted that day at the picnic?

15 August 1949
Tashkent Military Academy

"Lieutenant Pavel—Yuri Pavel?" the orderly inquired.

"Yes."

"A message from the commandant's office, Comrade Lieutenant. You are to report there immediately."

Yuri scowled. "Is that all? Is there no reason given?"

"No, sir."

"Very well. Thank you." Yuri reentered his room and retrieved his best uniform from its rack. What have I done now? he wondered. A pre-emptive summons to the commandant's office did not bode well. He pondered past sins as he quick-marched to the ugly pile of stone where the dreaded administrative staff lurked.

Yuri presented himself to an elderly white-haired woman who held forth behind a table just inside the main entrance. She examined Yuri's identification card with a nearsighted squint, and checked it against a list at her left elbow.

"You're to report to Colonel Gundorov, on the second floor," she stated indifferently. The building's second floor housed the personnel office, Yuri recalled. He relaxed somewhat. Had he been directed to the *third* floor, well, that was call for alarm. A summons to a senior political officer invariably meant trouble.

Colonel Gundorov was a pleasant surprise. Displaying blue infantry flashes on his uniform, he was of small stature, totally bald, and had blue eyes that twinkled when he addressed Yuri. "It seems that you're to have a change of scenery, Comrade Lieutenant."

He chuckled at Yuri's surprised look. "I'm to examine you for suitablilty before a final decision is made, but I'm confident you're our man." He tapped an open file folder in front of him. "Are you conversant with any languages other than English?"

Yuri realized the man had asked the question in English. Startled, he thought swiftly. What was going on here? Political–reliability was closely associated with undue interest in Western culture—he'd best tread cautiously. No point in trying to deny he had studied the language; it was included in the file Gundorov held. "English was a required subject in my secondary school, Comrade Colonel. I not only speak it poorly, but have no other language."

Gundorov cocked his head. "You handle the tongue quite well, contrary to your opinion. Your father is Major General Pavel. Did you perhaps have an English governess?"

Yuri's response was automatic. He'd had too many examinations by political officers to fall for this one. Admission to being raised by a *servant* was tantamount to suicide. "Oh, no, sir. Papa would never condone such a decadent Western custom."

"I see. You have applied for assignment to jet fighters. Why?" The colonel had switched back to Russian.

Very much cognizant of the infantry flashes Gundorov wore, Yuri chose his words carefully. "My father commanded an air division at Stalingrad. Although he didn't hold a commission in the air force, he flew with our army in Spain. It is his belief that our air force must overcome the temporary superiority demonstrated by English and American planes during the Great Patriotic War. I, of course, will serve willingly in any capacity the party deems necessary."

Gundorov chuckled. "Spoken like the outstanding student your file describes. Unwittingly, perhaps, you have just shown an aptitude for the field you're being considered for."

"I—I'm not sure I understand, Comrade Colonel."

"I'll explain more in a moment. I assume your father has also told you that the air force is presently a suspect arm of the military? Since the infamous 1937 mutiny in Manchuria, Generalissimo Stalin considers them unreliable—your father is one of the very few who escaped the wholesale dismissal of air force generals. Even today, promotion of flying officers is almost nonexistent."

"I believe my generation can dispel those misgivings, Comrade Colonel."

Gundorov grunted. "Just possibly. Anyway, to your immediate future. Have you heard of the Military-Diplomatic College of the General Staff of the Workers' and Peasants' Red Army?"

"No, sir."

"Not surprising; they don't enjoy public inquiries. Briefly, the school provides foreign-language training for military staff destined for assignment to our various embassies abroad—hence my comment regarding your carefully phrased replies to my questions, they were pure diplomat talk."

"But—but, sir. My flying—"

"Never fear. You'll continue your flying career. Any assignments outside the country are never of long duration." The colonel's voice grew brisk and businesslike. "You will pick up your orders here tomorrow morning and proceed to the college's admissions office in Moscow. There you will be tested and assigned to a department. I can't tell you more, only that we receive quotas from time to time to provide candidates.

"I do know the testing, both academic and political, is exhaustive. Anyone not meeting the highest standards of either is returned to his unit. Be advised that the commandant takes great pride in the fact that no candidate endorsed by him has been rejected. Don't count on completing your training here in that unfortunate eventuality."

Yuri scarcely heard the last of the colonel's admonishments. Moscow!

His wildest dreams were realized. Tashkent Military Academy was considered a choice station, being only thirty kilometers from Moscow, but socially it was the hinterlands. Only the precious weekend liberty granted fourth-form students made conditions bearable. But actually living in what he considered Mecca—his mind raced—such a prestigious institution undoubtedly had a liberal off-post pass policy. Don't look for *me* to come back! he wanted to shout.

A more sober assessment set in the following morning as Yuri trudged toward the train station. Last night was a blur. Anatoli had produced a clandestine liter of vodka upon Yuri's return to barracks. Others appeared, as did more vodka, when the news spread. After falling into bed long after midnight, Yuri was barely able to throw his belongings into a duffel bag and sign out in time to make the early morning train.

What was in store for him? His alcohol-fogged brain wrestled with the question. Until now he'd been steadfast in his vow to become a jet pilot and emulate his father's enviable military career. The colonel had blithely assured him that this was still very much in the cards, but . . . The whole thing smacked of that shadowy world of political intrigue. Assignment to a foreign country—to do what? To spy, cold reasoning told him—certainly not to fly jet fighters. Would he become one of those secretive, furtive-eyed characters who lurked in doorways and wore leather coats?

Yuri shook off the depressing thought. He had made this walk to the station many times, but always with an evening of excitement in mind. Now he took a closer look at the district he traversed.

Four years after that riotous night following the German capitulation, the village outside the gates appeared, if possible, more wretched than during the war. Already, at this early hour, drab, vacant-faced citizens stood lined up in front of stores with empty window displays. Ragged children followed each other in endless succession, gathering up anything with potential value as fuel or sustenance. Yuri shuddered and increased his pace. There would be a samovar of scalding tea aboard the train.

In Yuri's opinion, the Military-Diplomatic College of the General Staff of the Workers' and Peasants' Red Army looked less like an institution of higher learning than it did a factory for making shoes. Facing a narrow street, Filin Allee, the three-story structure squatted like something a

child would design with wooden blocks. It boasted a stuccoed exterior—
the mustard-yellow paint chipped and peeling—relieved only by rows of
geometrically exact windows that were in need of washing.

Yuri tried the door handle—the only new feature on the worn and
scratched panel. It turned without resistance, and he eased inside. Is there
no guard here? he wondered. A background of muttered conversation filtered down a narrow passage. Treading the splintered floorboards cautiously, he sought the building's sole evidence of life.

"Das machen est schön. Das mann est hasslich. Est tu . . ." Yuri halted
in his tracks. The people just inside the open doorway were speaking
German! Well, of course, you idiot, he scolded himself. This is, after all,
a language school. He stood at the threshold and asked, "Hello. Excuse
me, but I'm looking for someone to report to. This *is* the College of the
General Staff—"

A pale-complexioned man of indeterminate age cut Yuri off with an
imperious wave. "We don't speak Russian in this department. Go to the
receptionist on the next floor up."

Yuri glared but held his tongue. Don't get off on the wrong foot here,
he thought. So the bastard was asking for a clip on the jaw—you can't
afford to get tossed out before you even get started. He retraced his steps
and trudged up open stairs opening off the vacant entry hall.

The stairway exited into a sizable room, bare of furnishings except for
benches along two walls and a large, square table in the center. A dozen
figures lounged on the benches; two sat cross-legged on broad win-
dowsills, studying the street scene below. All wore uniforms. Yuri recognized flashes from infantry, artillery, and armored units. Five wore navy
uniforms. He concealed his surprise at finding that four of the group were
women.

"Come in," a nattily attired lieutenant of the infantry greeted Yuri.
"You'll be after Anna Petrovna, here, for your interview. I'd invite you to
join me at the canteen in the basement for tea, but I'm due next. Anna
will hold your place in the line if you want to go on your own, however.
Won't you Anna, dear?"

A heavyset woman seated beside the speaker shot a venomous look at
the lieutenant. She tugged her green uniform skirt lower over beefy
thighs and muttered a sullen, "Speak for yourself, comrade. I'm not a
reception clerk."

The lieutenant loosed a peal of laughter. "See the kind of jolly comrades you'll be working with, Lieutenant . . ." He stopped and extended a hand. "I'm sorry, I'm Pietre Tichhof. And you?"

"Yuri Pavel."

"Ah, yes, I'm very pleased to make your acquaintance, Yuri Pavel. As I was saying, we promise to be a happy group. Anna, here, and I've just met, and already we're fast friends. Right, Anna? Say hello to Yuri Pavel. Perhaps you'll be in the same division with this handsome fellow."

Anna's doughy features expressed nothing but disgusted scorn. "You are a piece of dog shit, Lieutenant."

Tichhof's hilarious response was broken off by the appearance of a middle-aged lieutenant colonel who appeared in one of the four doorways opening off the large meeting room. "Lieutenant Pietre Tichhof?" he called.

Yuri slid onto the bench alongside the disgruntled female—a captain in the artillery, he noted—and said, "You seem to find Lieutenant Tichhof objectionable."

Anna stared straight ahead without acknowledging Yuri's attempt to strike up a conversation. Finally she said, "The slug pretends to be the illegitimate son of Marie Nicolau, of Romania. Illegitimate he may be, but I doubt he knows his father, or mother either, for that matter." She half turned and added, "You are air force. What are you doing here?"

"Why—why," Yuri replied, "I was ordered here from Tashkent Military Academy. I have no idea, actually, what I'm here for except, to learn a language."

"Who is your sponsor?" Her eyes squinted with suspicion.

"No one—that I know of. Colonel Gundorov, at the academy, endorsed my nomination; I didn't really apply. I only want to fly the new jet fighters. I'm already a pilot third class in prop airplanes."

Anna snorted. "Nonsense. No one is considered for entry here without a high-ranking sponsor. Mine is General Bessonov. I was a battery commander in his division at Stalingrad; later, his aide. What languages do you speak?"

"Other than Russian, fair English."

The response promoted another snort. "You'll never be accepted. Only one language and no sponsor. Besides, political reliability constitutes sixty percent of your score—the air force is not a favorite of the generalissimo's. You are the only one here wearing gold flashings, you'll notice. I speak six: Farsi, Uzbek, Latin, English, and German—in addition to an understanding of Romanian. I'll probably be placed on staff here."

"I would think so," Yuri observed with raised eyebrows. He looked again at the ribbons spread across her ample bosom—Red Banner Award, the Order of Lenin, a gold watch presented only by a representative of the generalissimo himself; an artillery battery commander at Stalingrad. This girl was one tough nut.

A woman in civilian dress appeared at noon and shrilly announced that a meal would be served in the basement canteen. "For this meal only," she announced in disapproving tones, "food ration points are not required for candidates."

The afternoon dragged for Yuri. He had little inclination to pursue the dialogue he'd struck up with Anna, and even less to become involved in some of the dialectic arguments others of the diverse group seemed to delight in. At a few minutes before sixteen hundred, Anna was summoned. His named was called from an opposing doorway minutes later.

A slender man with light blue cavalry tabs summoned Yuri with an impatient gesture. He was already seated behind a massive oak desk when Yuri advanced and saluted.

"Have a seat, Comrade Lieutenant," the man said without bothering to return the salute. "I'm Colonel Volkov. Have a seat," he repeated absently. Volkov rubbed his balding pate and with twinkling, pale-blue eyes set in a sly, foxy face scanned the documents Yuri had passed him.

"Ah, an aviator," he exclaimed. "We don't get many aviators, and seldom give them a warm welcome. A boisterous, disruptive bunch, generally speaking. What's your view of a future career?"

"As the interests of the state require," Yuri replied without the slightest hesitation.

"Exactly so. At least you've had some competent political instructors. Why have you chosen to take up foreign languages, after your graduation from the air academy?"

"I consider mastery of foreign languages to be essential to a flying officer's career," Yuri lied.

The colonel's twinkling eyes took on a merry cast. "You'll do well on the political examinations," he said. "You decided no such thing— you were nominated by my old comrade Colonel Gundorov. I have faith in his judgement, by the way and will dispense with the customary examinations. Do you know what kind of educational establishment this is?"

"Uh, Colonel Gundorov wasn't very explicit in his description, Comrade Colonel."

"Of course not. Very well, are you aware that anyone who graduates from this school is obligated to give life service in the military? You can throw away your civilian possessions. Do you wish to apply for release before we go further?"

Yuri gulped. "I wasn't aware, no, sir. But I've always intended to follow in my father's footsteps."

Volkov chuckled. "And you have no wish to return to the reception the academy at Tashkent gives rejected nominees, eh? Well, now, to business. We have more English linguists than we need. I'm assigning you to an exceptionally important department, the Eastern Faculty. You'll learn Chinese. It's a difficult regimen—starts at the fourth level. You'll be rewarded with unlimited off-campus passes, however—provided you can find time." Volkov uttered a mirthless chuckle.

Yuri gaped. "Ch—Chinese?" he stammered. "Sir, isn't there something else for me? The language has thousands of 'chops' to memorize. It is said that fully literate natives of the country know less than half of them. And the tongue—it is totally without . . ." He let his voice tail off as Volkov's twinkling eyes turned icy.

"You have a choice, Yuri Sergeievich. If you refuse, it will be so noted in your file."

Yuri looked up, surprised that the colonel had addressed him by his patronymic. He swallowed and responded with, "I am proud to be accepted by the college, Comrade Colonel. *I will finish at the top of my class,*" he added with a defiant glare. Later he would sort out how his father's name had become a factor in his life. "My adversaries have been busy during my absence," he recalled Papa saying.

Yuri departed the examination room with a dazed expression, looking very much like a disappointed lover. He spotted Anna sitting alone on her bench, a vacuous expression on her plump, tanned features. Apparently theirs had been the last two examinations of the day. He wandered over.

"I see your interview didn't last long either. Do you have your assignment?"

Eyes straight ahead, Anna replied, "I was rejected."

"*What?*" Yuri sat uninvited beside her. "With your qualifications—"

"I no longer have a sponsor," she replied without letting him finish.

"But—but, I thought—"

"General Bessonov was arrested yesterday. He is presently held in Lubyanka Prison—charged with sabotage. An NKVD investigation of his service record revealed that he had failed to 'vigorously engage the enemy at Stalingrad, resulting in unnecessary losses of brave Soviet soldiers.' The examiner told me. I'm being returned to my division."

Anna faced Yuri with brimming eyes. "*I was there!* We burned out the barrels of four of our guns, then engaged the enemy hand-to-hand to keep them from overrunning our gun emplacement. General Bessonov was also there, a pistol in each hand."

Yuri reached to take one of her moist, plump hands in his. "Surely, *someone* who knows the truth will intervene."

Anna barked a bitter laugh. "Intervene? With the NKVD? By tomorrow night he will have had a secret trial and been executed—that's what happened to his former comrades."

"So you're being returned to your unit. What then?"

"If I'm linked to the general as a collaborator, probably a prison camp in Siberia. If I'm lucky, nothing more than being stripped of my rank and decorations, then sent to a labor battalion—also in Siberia."

"It's—it's—"

"Unbelievable? You must have led a soft life to date, Yuri Pavel. Were you accepted?"

"Yes, if you can call it that. I'm scheduled to study *Chinese,* of all things. There's no way out of it, that I can see."

They sat silently, each wrapped in gloomy introspection. "Look, Anna"—Yuri retrieved the hand he'd relinquished— "I was going to call Papa to tell him the outcome of my interview. He has a dacha on the river. We both have unrestricted passes for forty-eight hours. One last taste of the good life. We'll drink vodka and champagne, eat smoked salmon and oysters, and spend two days and nights in bed."

Anna jerked back and regarded Yuri with shocked amazement. *"What?"* she asked in a strangled voice.

"You heard me. Both of our good worlds just came apart. Two days and nights neither of us will forget."

Tears ran unchecked down Anna's pudgy cheeks. "You're a handsome man, Yuri Pavel. I'm fat and ugly. Why . . . ? You're just . . ." She removed her hand and stood. "I'll collect my kit and meet you in front," she announced firmly.

11

Ross rechecked the backpack chute's release pins, snapped their cover in place, and heaved it into the TF-80's rear cockpit. He turned to Lieutenant Colonel Babcock and the two Martin-Baker tech reps, identified by logos on their white coveralls. "I'm ready," he said. "Let's get airborne."

Babcock climbed onto the wing and watched the two factory reps help Ross hook up. "M'God, you look like something from outer space. And just think, we're supposed to fly an airplane in that get up. I'm going to strap in up front before we melt in these goddamn insulated flying suits."

"Okay, Major," said the sandy-haired engineer. "Let's run through the procedure one more time— I'll be quick. You'll punch out at thirty thousand feet with an airspeed of point-eight mach. Remember, your cockpit won't be pressurized. The weatherman says the temp will be about minus forty, so don't be taking off your gloves, and be ready for the change in breathing pattern at that altitude.

"I've pulled the pins to the explosive charges,"—he showed Ross two six-inch steel pins with red tags attached—"so the seat's hot as of right now. Just before you go, switch your oxygen mask hose to the nipple on this bottle clipped to your harness. Yank the green knob to start the flow. Pull your helmet visor full down and tuck your feet close to the seat mounting—there's a tendency for your legs to fly up during ejection.

"Pull the left armrest up; that arms the ejection system and will blow the canopy in an actual situation. Sit with your back straight, look directly ahead, and pull the right armrest up. You'll get a solid boot in the ass from those thirty-seven-millimeter charges—but not too bad, actually—and all of a sudden you're a bird.

"As soon as you're outside, a drogue chute attached to the seat will deploy. It will slow you to about eighty miles an hour and pull the seat away when the automatic lapbelt release actuates. If none of this happens by the count of ten, pull this ring, then this one, for manual separation.

"We want to test the automatic chute deployment device today. If you can start making out details of houses and cars on the ground, it probably didn't work, so pull the manual rip cord D-ring. That's it; from there on down it'll be just like your practice jumps."

Ross reached for the bulky "hard-hat" crash helmet and slipped it over his head while the tech rep adjusted the shoulder harness and lap belt. After securing his oxygen mask and checking the oxygen-flow regulator, Ross pressed the intercom switch. "Predeparture check complete, Colonel. Intercom check."

"Roger, loud and clear. Starting engine," Babcock responded.

The J-33 engine behind Ross whined to life as he tried to find a comfortable position. Sit back and enjoy the ride, let someone else do the flying for a change, he thought, giving a jaunty wave to Doug Curtiss parked alongside. Doug and Kyle had insisted on flying chase today. He heard Babcock read back Tower's clearance, then felt the brakes release. Kyle and Doug fell in trail, and the mission was under way.

It wasn't until Ross saw the altimeter wind through five thousand feet that he was able to relax completely. Test dummies ejected below five thousand had a distressingly high damage rate. He grinned as the slipstream shrieked past his open rear cockpit. Just like the old Stearman trainer, he thought. Already he appreciated the insulated suit and gloves as the outside air-temperature gauge slipped rapidly below the zero degree Centigrade mark.

Ross heard Babcock on the VHF set. "Pinetree, this is Speedball One with a flight of three. Mission number is Fox Seven-One-One. Climbing through angels ten on heading zero-two-zero, squawking code three, over."

"Roger, Speedball. We have you in radar contact. Squawk Ident for positive identification."

"Squawking Ident, Pinetree."

"Roger. You are cleared to continue on present heading, climb to angels three-zero. Drop-zone weather is reported to be twelve hundred scattered, winds from one-four-zero at five knots. Call reaching flight-level three-zero, over."

Babcock acknowledged and switched to intercom. "Looks like a go weather wise, Ross. How are things back there?"

"Noisy as hell for one thing, Colonel. And I know how little kids must feel after Mama bundles them up to play in the snow. Christ, I can't move with all the stupid straps, wires, and hoses hanging on me."

Babcock chuckled. "Well, you won't have that problem much longer. ETA over the drop zone is in ten minutes. I'll go to the north end of the range and do a one-eighty. Watch for the orange smoke flare on that leg—that's your landing zone. Once established on a one-eight-zero axis, I'll give you a three minute warning and a one-minute countdown. Copy?"

"Roger, copy all," said Ross. He watched the altimeter settle on a reading of thirty thousand feet. By straining, he could catch a comforting glimpse of their chase planes a thousand feet below and spread to either side. Habit led him to scan the instrument panel.

Babcock added power, and Ross watched the machmeter edge past 0.7. He gulped and tried to visualize what it was going to be like getting shot into a five-hundred-mile-per-hour wind at minus forty degrees Centigrade. Suddenly he detected a low rumbling from the rear. It disappeared. Was he imagining things? He shot a glance at the tailpipe temperature gauge. Was it just in the process of moving back to seven hundred degrees? Had he missed a surge above maximum?

You're letting this thing get to you, Ross thought. Concentrate on making a last-minute equipment check. There was no mistaking the noise this time. A sustained throaty rumbling—a slight vibration—he saw the engine rpm fluctuate and TPT edge above seven hundred. He squeezed the mike button. "We may have a problem, Colonel. You see that rpm and TPT fluctuation?"

"Roger. Goddamned fuel control's acting up. I'm turning on the emergency fuel pump—oh, shit, my fire warning light just came on! You have one, too?"

Ross's confirmation that his light was indeed giving a steady red warning was blocked by, "Speedball One, this is Three—you got an engine fire, Colonel!"

Babcock never completed his acknowledgement. The rumble Ross had detected earlier turned into a shuddering clatter. He could hear sounds like Coke bottles being opened as debris was thrown through the fuselage skin behind him. "Engine's breaking up, Colonel!" he called over the intercom. "Jettison your canopy and go. I'll hold 'er straight and level while you go over the side."

"Negative," Babcock grated. "Finish your mission. Punch out *now!* That's an order. I'll try to nurse her down to a lower altitude."

Conditioned to follow orders without question during an emergency, Ross yanked his helmet visor down, cursed as he fumbled to change his oxygen mask hose, and lifted the left armrest. Grasping for the right armrest, he felt himself thrown violently sideways. The horizon spun crazily. Goddamn engine parts cut a control cable, flashed through his mind. Straining against face-sagging G forces, he managed to jerk the armrest upward.

Ross's last clear memory was the "boot in the ass" the tech rep had described, as the explosive charges drove his seat clear of the cockpit. A disorganized jumble of impressions followed. He was turning over and over—the silence after the noise he'd endured in the open cockpit was a welcome surprise. He had trouble breathing, the emergency bottle was spewing a solid stream of oxygen into his lungs—he saw his legs flailing and was helpless to stop them. He suddenly stabilized and realized the seat's drogue chute had deployed.

Recovering a measure of awareness, Ross looked around. He could see nothing but a blur of landscape below; he was still oscillating, face down. How long did it take the automatic seat harness release to work? To hell with it, he couldn't wait. He found the control with fumbling, gloved fingers and yanked. He started tumbling again as soon as he felt seat separation.

The urge to pull the main chute's rip cord and stop the gut-tearing rotation was nearly overpowering. No, damnit! He had to fight to keep his hands away from the D-ring. You're still at altitude. You'll freeze, plus your true airspeed up here will still be enough to pop panels in the canopy.

Spread-eagling his arms and legs, Ross was surprised that the instructor had been right: The unsettling head-over-heels motion stopped. The ground seemed a long way beneath his free-falling body—funny, he didn't have a sensation of falling. Watch for details, he admonished himself. If this barometer gadget doesn't work, you'll have less than a minute to jerk the rip cord. There. Damnit, that's a highway—those things are cars. Pull now?

A silver shape fluttering earthward distracted him. Good God, the plane! It was plunging toward the ground in a series of rolling turns, totally out of control. A breathtaking tug on his chute harness interrupted Ross's search for Colonel Babcock's parachute canopy.

3 October 1949
Wright Field

Ross glanced at his notes. It was an unconscious effort to put off the most difficult part of his testimony, he knew. After a pause, he looked at each of the solemn faces of the accident investigation board's seven members and said, "The G forces were quite high. I could barely get my hand on the right armrest to actuate the ejection charge. It is my considered opinion that Colonel Babcock could never have made a normal exit. The glimpse I had of the plane during descent showed it wound up in an uncontrollable inverted spin."

Colonel Luther Roberts, serving as board president, cleared his throat. "We appreciate your testimony, Ross. Inspection of the wreckage pretty well confirms your observations. Now, our report will contain both findings as to cause, and recommendation for action to prevent future accidents of this nature. Do you have anything to add to that portion?"

"I do, sir. Perhaps it's personal bias"—he gave the colonel a wry smile—"but that seat saved my life. I strongly recommend that the program to equip all fighter aircraft with ejection seats be accelerated."

Roberts returned Ross's smile. "Quite understandable, and I assure you that the board will endorse your recommendation. Is there anything else you'd care to comment on?"

Ross closed his notebook and contemplated its blank cover for a moment. "Yes, sir," he replied slowly, "Lieutenant Colonel Babcock had an opportunity to jettison the canopy and attempt a normal bailout. I'm sure that I could have held the plane steady enough for him to do so. He refused my suggestion and *ordered* me to eject. I remember his exact words. He said: 'Finish your mission.'

"I don't know what the highest award the air force has for placing duty above personal safety, but I'd like to see the colonel recommended for it. His was the act of a brave, a very brave, man."

Colonel Roberts nodded. "Consider it done, Major. Again, thanks for your cooperation. You're excused."

Ross stood outside the hearing room, deep in thought. You've lost buddies before, he told himself. Why does Babcock's death stick in your mind so? Because the others died in combat, damnit! The enemy, an enemy you could see, was responsible. This one seems so—well— unnecessary. Should I have refused to follow the colonel's order?

A voice in the outer office penetrated his introspection. "Major Colyer, sir, I have a message for you," a sergeant was saying.

"Oh—oh, I'm sorry. What is it?"

"General Cipolla called, sir. He asks that you and Mrs. Colyer join him for lunch at the Officers' Club."

Ross saw Janet wave to him from across the club dining room's crowded interior. He made his way between tables and kissed her cheek before reaching for General Cipolla's outstretched hand. "It's certainly good to see you, sir. What brings you to Wright Field? Still caging jet time?"

"I never pass up the chance, you know that. I have other business today, but it can wait until after lunch. In the meantime, your charming wife is giving me a rundown on your recent exploits. Take a seat and tell me how the accident investigation turned out."

"A depressing business, General," Ross said as he unfolded his napkin. "The engine turbine failed, and parts of it severed two main control cables. Colonel Babcock never had a chance—well, actually, he did. I should have ignored his order to eject first."

"That's bull—'scuse me, Janet—that's nonsense, Ross and you know it. Your wife told me that you're blaming yourself. By God, I'd have put you up for court-martial if you'd disobeyed a direct order. Now, I don't want to hear any more of that kind of talk. I *do* want to know how the seat worked."

"Flawlessly," said Ross. "Even better than expected, because we were out of control, pulling maybe five or six Gs when I ejected. I didn't have time to prepare myself and did a bunch of things wrong. Sir, I'm going to pound on all of the desks between here and the Pentagon until I see that seat installed in every jet plane the air force owns."

Cipolla grunted. "I don't think you'll find much opposition. The navy is going all out, too, but typical swabbie thinking, they insist their way is best."

The trio took time to order, then the general resumed. "Only thing is, I don't think you'll have much time to go around pounding on desks."

"What?"

Cipolla's lips stretched in a wide smile. "That's what I said. You heard me say I had other business here today? Well, I wanted to tell you this in person—orders are being cut right now to activate the 66th Squadron on 15 November. One Major Ross Colyer will be its first commanding officer."

Ross felt his jaw drop. "So—so soon?" he stammered. "I thought—had hoped—maybe sometime next year. . . ."

"Nope. The so-called Cold War is hotting up. Procurement is being accelerated. You'll have a dozen spanking-new F-80s by the year's end."

Ross met Janet's sparkling glance and impulsively leaned over and kissed her. "You knew!" he accused the laughing redhead.

"Fifteen minutes ago," she said. "The general had to explain why he was asking both of us to lunch."

"Oh?"

"That's right, Ross," Cipolla interjected. "You see, I take great interest in my squadron commanders; that includes their wives. I've seen too many potentially good commanders get so involved in domestic problems that they couldn't keep their eye on the squadron."

"You don't have to worry about this one," Ross answered shortly. He covered Janet's free hand with his own. "I may not have stayed around after I hurt my hand, if not for her. Additionally, she quit a career as a top flight journalist to be with me here."

"So I understand. I thought it was worth a trip to discuss, however. You see, your first base isn't exactly a garden spot. I wanted to be damn sure you both knew what you're in for."

"Oh, no," Ross groaned. "Don't tell me it's some hellhole just outside Miami—or maybe Honolulu."

"Nothing that bad," Cipolla replied with mock seriousness. "A place with more sunshine than either of those. Hanson Field. It's about a hundred miles southeast of Reno, Nevada—good, healthy desert climate."

"I never heard of it."

"It's there. A wartime P-39 base. It's an ideal place for your mission: bombing and gunnery ranges just outside your back door, no urban areas nearby to bitch about the noise and so forth. But a dependent heaven it ain't. The family quarters are—well, you know how temporary bases were thrown up during the war. And it's important that Janet be there with you. There'll be young wives that are going to need some help adjusting."

Ross observed that Janet's smile was a bit stiff as she said, "I'm an army brat, General Cipolla. I'll cope. By coincidence, I signed a contract to write a novel before I left D.C. This will be a wonderful opportunity to work without distractions."

"Glad to hear that," Cipolla enthused. "Now, Ross, you'll have orders to report to Hanson not later than 1 November with an advance cadre. If you have anyone in mind you'd like for key jobs, I'll do my best."

Ross sipped coffee while he considered the wing commander's offer. Finally he said, "There's a Captain Doug Curtiss in the test group—he's a magician with the '80's cranky innards. I'd like to have him as my aircraft maintenance officer, if he'll take the job."

Ross and Janet watched with somber expressions as Cipolla departed the club's dining room. "Well," Ross said at last, "I have my squadron. I'm sorry, and I'll not blame you if you balk. I have a pretty good job right here."

Janet's shoulders shook with silent laughter, but the smile she gave Ross was weak. "I remember once telling you I wouldn't sleep with a quitter. Damned if I'll give you a chance to turn that statement around. Do they open the bar here at lunchtime?"

1 January 1950
Hanson Air Base, Nevada
Ross tried to ignore the dull throb behind his eyes and match Janet's cheerful demeanor. Damn champagne, he grumbled to himself, when will I ever learn to stick to scotch and water? He winced as Janet nudged him forward to keep their place in the serpentine of mostly hung-over officers and wives shuffling toward the receiving line. Everyone agreed that the

traditional New Year's Day reception was a pain in the ass. Why did they continue the anachronistic custom, especially in this backwater of all backwaters?

Hanson Air Base indeed—a gross exaggeration to designate the huddle of sand-scoured prefab buildings and pair of cracked blacktop runways an "air base." Empty desert stretched in all directions as far as the eye could see, although some folks claimed they could see Reno, a hundred miles away, on days when the dust wasn't too bad.

The 4814th Air Base Squadron served a grand total of seven hundred men, women, and kids assigned to two units: the 66th Fighter Squadron, and the B-25-equipped 28th Tow Target Detachment. They have receptions for the sole purpose of punishing those who attend New Year's Eve parties, Ross decided.

Three couples ahead of them waited to exchange inane, mumbled greetings with the base commander, Lieutenant Colonel Krug, and his wife. Scanning the officers' club's drab interior, Ross did a mental roll call. Every goddamned one of the 66th's sixteen officers had better show, he thought grimly. Anyone who doesn't will think hell is a picnic. He'd accounted for all but one, 2d Lt. Dudley Murphy, when it was their turn at the receiving line.

Lieutenant Colonel Walter Krug had let his athletic build go to pot. Too many months behind a desk after spending the war years playing football on the crack Headquarters Eastern Flying Training Command team had turned muscle to flab. A rated pilot, he cked out his qualification for flight pay by spending eight hours a month in the base-flight Gooney Bird—always with an instructor pilot in the other seat. After their first meeting, Ross had relegated the man to the category he reserved for prize pricks.

Krug peered at Ross through eyes still faintly bloodshot. Ross drew a measure of satisfaction from the colonel's appearance, his normally florid face flushed with an obvious hangover. I hope you're suffering more than I am, he wanted to say. From the corner of an eye he saw Mrs. Krug unobtrusively try to tug her girdle in place around ample thighs as she cooed, "Janet, darling. You look absolutely divine, as always. *How* on earth do you manage, out here in the desert, always to appear so chic?"

Janet leaned closer toward the frumpily dressed woman. Ross heard her whisper, "Sears and Roebuck catalog—my secret weapon."

Ross allowed himself an inward chuckle. Liar, fake, he had a devilish urge to say. That little beige linen number, with matching shoes, long kid gloves, and cloche set you back a half month's pay before you left D.C. Instead he shook Krug's sweaty hand and said, "Happy New Year, Colonel. It promises to be a good one."

The obviously miserable base commander squinted at Ross and muttered, "Your pilots damn near wrecked this place last night, Colyer. My first sergeant is drawing up a statement of charges for damaged and broken government property. I suggest you use a firmer hand with that bunch."

Ross winced. He'd wisely left the club before things had gotten rowdy. His administrative officer, Lieutenant Kraft, had briefed him early this morning, however. One of the older pilots, stationed in England during the war, had described a favorite game played in an RAF mess he'd visited—run obliquely toward a wall and see who can leave the highest set of footprints on its surface without falling.

Not that they hadn't reason to celebrate last night. The last pair of factory-new F-80s were delivered that afternoon. The 66th had its full complement of men and machines now, and the status board in Capt. "Ace" Aldershot's operations office carried eight pilots in the "Combat Ready" column.

General Cipolla's words during a visit just before Christmas had given everyone a boost. Scowling, cigar clamped in the corner of his mouth, he'd growled, "I don't know how this bunch of goddamn misfits managed to do it, but you're already top squadron in the wing." With that he'd broken into laughter and ordered everyone to the club bar.

Ross and Janet joined Doug and Betsy Curtiss in a group huddled around the punch bowl. "I hope you people feel better than I do," Ross grumbled. "And if that punch is made with champagne, I pass."

Doug's homely features spread into a grin. "The other bowl is made with canned grapefruit juice—choose your poison. I figured I'd better try it; I'm leaving as soon as I can get away. A crew volunteered to work today pulling acceptance inspections on the two new birds. That's the good news. The bad news is that an ops immediate TWX is on your desk grounding all F-80s with the Mark V ejection seat—that's ours."

"What?"

"Major accident at Eglin Field, Florida, yesterday. The ejection seat cooked off on takeoff roll. The pilot was killed—blew the poor bastard right through the canopy. Anyway, an emergency tech order is on the wire to tear down and inspect the system prior to the next flight."

"Damn. Among grounding for TO compliance to fix engine problems, structural failures, and the like, we're getting just about a fifty percent in-commission rate. How about the T-33s? They grounded as well?"

"Nope. They have the old seat installed."

Ross swiveled his head, searching the room, "Okay, where the hell is Ace Aldershot?" He spotted the ops officer still waiting to go through the receiving line. Ross made an urgent summoning motion, whereupon the bored-appearing captain grinned and broke ranks.

"Ace, Doug just got an ops immediately grounding the F-80s—god-damn ejection seat. We can still use both T-Birds, though. Soon's you can get out of here, set up instrument-training flights for the newer pilots. Have the CQ alert the instructor pilots and an early morning class while they can still have legal time in crew rest."

Aldershot nodded. "Will do." He grinned mischievously and added, "I can go right now."

"Oh, no, you don't. You go through that goddamn line. You can bet that Krug has someone taking names. Which reminds me: Where the hell is that screw-off Murphy?"

"Well, Major—you see, Dudley has a problem."

"I goddamn well know he has a problem," Ross shot back. "But what-ever it is, it isn't half as big as the one he's gonna have if I don't see his Irish mug in that line before it breaks up."

"Oh, I'm sure you will," Aldershot quickly replied. "Dudley couldn't find the black bow tie for his formal dress uniform. His roommate, Lip-pert, was over here first in line. Right now he's on his way to let Dudley borrow the tie."

"Oh, for Christ's sake." Ross raised his hands in supplication. "Well, I'll be talking to him anyway about last night. *Who* the hell came up with the idea of doing that RAF stunt of running up the wall?"

Aldershot turned red and averted his eyes. "You'll find out sooner or later," he mumbled. "I guess it was me, sir."

Ross didn't answer, just glared and turned to where Janet, Doug, and Betsy stood. "I'll have a glass of that punch," he growled.

Betsy's eyes sparkled with amusement. "We're having some people over for a light supper later. Would Papa Bear like to bring Goldilocks and join us?"

"You have a smart mouth for such a little girl," Ross retorted with a conciliatory grin. He glanced at Janet, who nodded. "Yeah, we'll be there, but can't stay long. Tomorrow is shaping up to be a real lulu. In fact, if you're finished with your drink, Janet, I need to go by the office for awhile yet this afternoon."

12

15 January 1950
Resick Airfield, Georgia, USSR
Yuri Pavel applied brakes and let the MiG-15 rock to a stop. He hummed contentedly—the bright Georgian winter sunshine poured through the canopy and raised the cockpit temperature to summertime levels. Outside, a uniformed mechanic stationed at the runway's takeoff end made an awkward attempt to salute. Yuri smiled behind his oxygen mask and gravely acknowledged the young conscript's signal that his required check for leaks and loose equipment was complete.

Life is good, he thought. Black Sea winters contrasted sharply to those on the frigid, icebound steppes outside Moscow. And he was flying the finest airplane in the world—Comrades Mikoyan and Gurevich's sleek and deadly MiG-15. Yes, he was a proud and happy man.

Even the featureless terrain surrounding the base failed to dampen his high spirits. Resick Airfield had been hastily constructed on reclaimed swampland. Its two runways, constructed of concrete blocks laid over crushed rock, stretched toward the open sea and the NATO bastion of Turkey—forbidden airspace. Not because of any danger to planes and pilots, but because of the opportunity for a disgruntled officer to defect with one of the Motherland's closely guarded, secret airplanes, none but senior, politically reliable pilots flew solo this close to Western borders.

The young pilot turned his attention to the before-takeoff checklist. Magnetic compass showing runway heading and swinging freely; canopy, closed and locked; all warning lights showing green or dark; fuel gauge reading 1250 liters, the proper load for a one-hour sortie; the 2725-kg.-thrust V-2 engine, an improved version of the British-made Rolls-Royce Nene, whined softly behind him. He would only pull the charging handles for the two 23mm and the devastating 37mm nose-mounted cannon when over the firing range.

Yuri mentally reviewed that day's mission. He and his wingman were to fly thirty minutes high-altitude formation, switching leads, then descend to one hundred meters above the overwater gunnery range.

He glanced impatiently into his rearview mirror, where his wingman, Vladimir, should be sitting off his right wing. The man always seemed to be plagued with equipment malfunctions. Yuri wished he could be assigned a different partner; not only was he a weak pilot, but his political thinking was suspect as well.

Vladimir's assignment to jet fighters was a direct Central Committee appointment. His father was a high-ranking member of the socially elite *nomenklatura,* and one would think that Vlad would be a dedicated party member.

But when Yuri had entered his partner's room unannounced the previous week, the shortwave radio was turned on. Its volume was low, but Yuri heard the announcer saying, ". . . Sons of Czechoslovakia, resist the harsh rule of dictator Stalin by every means at hand. Your priests and church leaders languish in prison—your legal president has been dismissed by the invaders. . . ."

Vladimir looked startled. "Radio, uh, Free Europe," he stammered. "I was hoping to find some Western jazz. I—I like to listen on occasion, don't you?"

"Listening to Western radio programs is forbidden, Vlad," Yuri replied with a frown. "The KGB will have you dismissed—not only from the jet program, but from the air force as well. Their Otsobii Otdel has ears everywhere."

"I know, Yuri. But I can count on you not to report me, can't I? Here, Mama sent along some East German salami—try some."

Yuri had shamelessly accepted a portion of the rich, spicy meat and a chunk of black bread. The incident bothered him, though. Why would the Western agitators incite rebellion in a country that the Red Army saved from the sadistic Nazis? They should be grateful! And why would Vlad, a pampered son of the party elite, be listening to their treasonous lies so intently?

Now he spotted Vlad's plane swinging onto the taxi strip—too fast, he thought—and moving into position off his right wing. Yuri pushed the incident to the back of his mind and called the control tower for takeoff clearance. Completing another successful sortie toward the magic number, six hundred, was uppermost in his thoughts. His immediate goal was to qualify as a pilot third class before Papa arrived at the spa in Batumi for a brief vacation.

27 January 1950
Batumi, Georgia, USSR
Yuri stepped from the bus and accepted his carryall from the husky girl handing down luggage from the roof-mounted rack. He breathed deeply of the warm, jasmine-scented air. Georgians were lucky people, he decided. Street vendors offered real meat kabobs, citrus fruit, flowers, and a wide selection of handcrafted items.

At the air base, there were some who muttered—out of earshot of snooping Otsobists—that it was because most land here was worked by individual owners, noncollectivized. He shrugged. Whatever the cause, he hoped his assignment to Resick was a long one. The months of twelve-hour days in the language school in Moscow were already becoming a bad dream, despite the frequent weekends with Marya.

The bus driver gave Yuri directions to the Hotel Karpovich, a sprawling arrangement of cabins flanking the opulent beach resort reserved for high-ranking guests. Papa and Giesele had arrived two days ago and were expecting him. Yuri, a lowly lieutenant, would stay at the hostel set aside for military vacationers. But tonight, Papa had promised a royal reception for his son.

The effusive General Pavel was as good as his word. Yuri ate and drank until he was uncomfortable. Sergei stopped talking only long enough to dance with Giesele and for brief answers to his questions to Yuri: "Do they treat you well? Is the MiG as good as they say? Do you have girlfriends? Have you been asked to join the party? Why are you only a pilot third class?—why not a first class?"

Giesele, dressed in a dark-blue sheath of shimmering fabric, cut low to provide interesting glimpses of her full breasts, drew admiring and envious stares. Sergei reveled in showing her off on the dance floor. Yuri danced with her only once, uncomfortable at the easy manner in which their bodies fit together. He was certain he detected a hint of mockery in her gaze when he reseated her at their table.

Sergei's overindulgence took its toll, and by midnight he was slurring his words and nodding in his chair. At last he struggled to his feet and solemnly announced he would retire for the evening. "Shumthing I ate ishn't agreeing with me," he muttered. "Yuri, shee that Giesele enjoys herself." Yuri regarded his parent's retreating back and gave Giesele a questioning glance.

She shrugged. "The indomitable Sergei will brook no assisting hand. I will follow shortly, to be certain he's safely in bed, but he will be, never fear. Your father is an amazing man."

Suddenly Yuri felt closed in by the noisy, smoky dining room. "It's a beautiful night out," he ventured. "Would you join me for a nightcap on the terrace?"

Giesele regarded the handsome young pilot with a quizzical gaze. "I'd love to," she said finally. "Would you bring my wrap?"

Yuri ordered white wine for both of them and found a secluded table overlooking barely visible wavelets lapping on the beach. Giesele thanked him, then added, "Actually, I'd planned to have a private talk with you during our visit, Yuri. This is perfect."

"Oh?"

"Yes. I have a feeling you don't approve of Sergei's selection of a second wife. We saw so little of you in Moscow. Is it something I've said or done? Or do you find me a poor comparison to your mother? I'd like very much for us to be friends."

Yuri gulped, taken aback at her boldness. "Why—why, no, of course I don't; I mean, I *do* approve of you. . . ."

"I believe I'm what you would refer to as 'an older woman,' Yuri. As such, I'm not without experience in reading men's minds." Yuri detected her faint smile in the gloom as she sipped from her glass and waited.

"I don't understand you," Yuri blurted. "Why did you leave the West and come to Moscow with my father? You appear much younger than he, and you're totally different. You—you are cool, sophisticated, cynical, always in control. Papa rushes through life enjoying things as they come—a rough soldier, more accustomed to a field mess than a drawing room."

"You're very observant, other than your estimate of my age. I find your assessment of me—while less flattering than I'd like, perhaps—surprisingly accurate. But is it impossible for people with different personalities to share affection?"

"You're making fun of me—I can tell by your tone of voice."

"Oh-ho," said Giesele. "You *do* have misgivings. Have you mentioned this to your father?"

"No, no, of course not. What Papa does is none of my business."

"But it is—your business, that is," Giesele said. "Because, you see, I need your trust before I ask for your help."

"Help?"

"Yes. Both your father and I may need your help."

"My *father?*"

"Does it surprise you to learn that the man isn't without a chink in his armor? That he can be hurt, ruined, even?"

"By what? I can't imagine what you're talking about. Papa was awarded the Hero of the Soviet Union medal by the generalissimo himself. He was given a position of great importance in Berlin, then reassigned to command an air division in a most sensitive area. What possible help could *I* give him?"

Giesele held up her empty glass. "Another perhaps? This may take some time to tell." Yuri summoned a waiter and faced his now serious, hard-spoken stepmother.

"Sergei is threatened by your political system, Yuri. Wait"—she held up a restraining hand as she saw him about to protest—"hear me out, please. Because it's essential that you believe me, I must ensure your trust. I'll start by telling you why I stayed in West Berlin."

"I was born a Russian. I was fourteen when my Aunt Olga fled Saint Petersburg, taking me with her. The revolutionaries were systematically searching out, and either killing or throwing into prison, anyone of royal descent. I won't dwell on our journey west; I don't recall much of it, in fact. We had no money, no papers, and walked to the Polish border.

"I survived the war years in ways I'd rather not share. Your father is the first man who didn't treat me like a common prostitute. He—he gave me back a measure of self-respect."

"I—I don't know what to say," Yuri muttered.

"What you *say* matters little," Giesele responded. "It's what you may be able to *do* that's important. In hopes of gaining your trust, I've told you details I've never related to anyone besides Sergei. I would offer to go to bed with you if I thought it would make a difference. Don't look shocked; I know the thought has occurred to you. It wouldn't change your thinking, however. You have Sergei's ethical beliefs; officers don't sleep with other officers' wives, especially their father's. But will you help, risk your life if necessary, to save your father's career, possibly his life?"

"Of course! But I must know more."

"And you will believe what I tell you without question?"

"If my father trusts you, I respect his judgement."

Giesele chuckled and lit an American cigarette. "Not the most positive answer on earth, but one I accept. Very well. Sergei is *not* getting command of his air division, incidentally."

"What? I thought—"

"That it was all arranged? No, it's part of what I'm explaining. When Sergei commanded his VVS regiment during the siege of Stalingrad, he made an enemy. His regiment had its back to the wall—literally. He issued orders that *all* ranks arm themselves and take up defensive positions. "His civilian political officer—who wore the uniform of a captain—refused. Your father drove him to a gun pit at pistol point. The man's name was Valentin Novotny. Since that day, Novotny has risen in rank until he is now a deputy director in the NKVD. He has never forgotten his vow to destroy Sergei."

Yuri gave a derisive snort. "Impossible. The NKVD has no authority within the armed forces. It is a law—*enforcement* agency. Papa has broken no laws."

Giesele sighed. "Yuri, your love affair with airplanes has blinded you to reality. Earlier you asked what threatened your father. The answer is, your political system; it's corrupt—from top to bottom."

Once again she held up a restraining hand as Yuri started to speak. "Spare me. Novotny *can* destroy Sergei—simply by poisoning Josef Stalin's sick mind. Yes, I said sick. It's common knowledge in Kremlin circles that the man is terminally ill. Already the jackals are fighting over the remains."

The memory of Anna Petrovna's shattered life—her general, also a Hero of the Soviet Union, purged—halted Yuri's automatic rejection of Giesele's statement. He had always privately believed that while punishment was harsh in many cases, it was probably deserved. But *Papa?*

Her voice a low monotone, Giesele continued, "Sergei used identity documents I obtained in Berlin to obtain permission for me to become a Russian citizen and marry him—documents that concealed my orgins. Bluntly stated, the documents were false.

Novotny, with his sixth sense for deception, is digging. I—I learn from sources in the West that certain offices are being broken into, certain records searched. The NKVD is extremely patient and thorough; in the end, they will expose me as an illegal immigrant. I believe you can see the position that places Sergei in."

Yuri felt a chill clutch his insides. "He can explain everything. He didn't know the documents were false. Who can fault him?"

"Ah, but he *did* know," Geisele replied sadly. "But whether he did or did not know will be immaterial when he is charged by the NKVD. The fact that he brought me to the USSR and vouched for me will be enough for a finding of guilty."

Yuri stood and paced the now empty terrace. "Then it's your fault," he said bitterly. "You charmed him, seduced him, tricked him. . . ."

"It didn't happen as you think, but I accept a measure of blame. What has been done can't be undone, however. Put your feelings aside and face the fact that your father needs your help."

"I don't see what I can possibly do—"

"Then I will tell you," Giesele finished for him. "The day may soon come when Sergei must disappear. You are in a position to arrange that."

"Disappear?"

"Yes. I can provide names in the West who will grant him political asylum and a new life. You must provide the means for him to escape to Turkey from one of the ports along the Black Sea."

"My father *defect?* To the imperialists? He would never do that, never!"

"That will be for him to decide. If he chooses to do so, will you help?"

"I—I . . ." Yuri covered the length of the terrace with quick, angry strides. "I would be in disgrace as well," he said finally. "My commission, my flying—I would lose everything if Papa . . . The sentence for just being a defector's close relative is five years."

"Which is more important?"

"I took an oath—swore to defend the Motherland with my life." Yuri faced Giesele with a savage glare.

"We aren't speaking of the Motherland, Yuri," Giesele corrected him gently. "You're defending a group of corrupt, greedy men—a power-mad dictator. You render a service to Russia by helping defeat them."

"That's what *you* say. I don't believe you."

"Yes, that's precisely what I say, and I've done everything I know how to do to make you believe me."

"Does Papa know about this?"

"He is very much aware of the problem. He doesn't know of my plans for his escape—yet. Like you, he refuses to believe it could ever come to that. He believes that Air Marshal Yokolov will intercede for him. He rejects any suggestion that Yokolov himself may fall victim to one of Stalin's irrational rages."

"I have no idea what to do."

"Start with this." Giesele reached into her gold lamé evening bag and withdrew a cigarette lighter—the type sold in the base *Voyentorg*. "Sealed inside is an uncut diamond worth several thousand rubles. It will make many, if not all, things possible," she added dryly.

"People will wonder why I have it," Yuri said with a frown. "I don't smoke."

"Then, Yuri Sergeievich, I suggest you start."

1 February 1950
Nellis Air Force Base, Nevada

Ross toyed with his portion of stringy roast beef and decided to wait for dessert. You'd think an officers' club the size of this one at Nellis, where a host of generals was assigned, could offer better fare—at banquets especially, he thought. Janet, seated beside him, observed his scowl and gave her husband an admonishing poke in the ribs.

Please let the speeches be short, Ross implored silently. General Cipolla's would be brief, as were his comments at today's parade; they could count on that. Probably no more than, "The 14th Wing is happy to be here, and we'll do our best to be good neighbors."

Movement of the 14th's headquarters from Langley to Nellis had set off some grumbling, Ross knew. Base housing waits increased as senior officers took places ahead of their juniors—the new headquarters building was considered more desirable than the older office buildings constructed during the war; moves were never easy.

Should they drive back to Hanson yet tonight? he wondered. He'd like to if this affair broke up by ten o'clock. Janet had objected when he mentioned the possibility before dinner. "Ross, we haven't been off that desert since before Christmas. Please, let's spend the night—maybe drive into Reno and make a real party of it."

Just taking off two days to come to the ceremony had been irksome enough, he thought. A hundred things left undone as the squadron raced through his mind. He was mentally forming an argument for Janet when a waiter tapped him on the shoulder.

"Telephone call for you, Major. The caller says it's important."

Ross slipped from his chair and followed the man to a phone booth alongside the men's room. Picking up the dangling receiver, he said, "This is Major Colyer."

"Major, this is Ace. Sorry to interrupt your dinner, but we lost an airplane this evening."

"Oh, Christ. Who and how?"

"Lieutenant Murphy. He punched out—his last transmission was garbled, but the tower operator heard him say something about 'breaking up.' I've alerted the county sheriff, and they're putting search crews in the area. Our own AP's should be heading out any minute, and a couple of the tow-target guys are preflighting a B-25."

"Good work, Ace." Ross hesitated and added, "Look, have someone come after me in a T-Bird. Go to my locker and grab my flying gear, okay?"

Ross hung up the receiver and sat reviewing the situation. Damn. It was the second major accident this month. Two weeks ago, it had been Captain Woods—an armament compartment door ripped off in flight. Woods had ejected safely, but he and Doug Curtiss almost came to blows. Doug accused him of not closing the Zeus fasteners securely after inspection.

Ross sighed. The days when the '80 was considered a plane still under development were past. Squadron commanders got fired for accidents, cause and blame notwithstanding.

General and Mrs. Cipolla were seated at the head table. The general's questioning look spared Ross the embarrassment of a trip to the front. He nodded, and Cipolla excused himself to join Ross in the hallway.

"Problems?" he asked.

"Yes, sir. We lost another plane. Information is sketchy as yet, but the pilot is supposed to have used the words 'breaking up' before ejecting. We have search crews out. I'm headed back now. I'll phone you with a preliminary sit-rep as soon as I know anything."

Cipolla scowled. "Goddamnit, Ross, what's going on down there? Two in two weeks is more than coincidence."

"The first one was unavoidable, sir," Ross protested. We were submitting Unsatisfactory Reports on those armament door fasteners back when I was at Wright Field. Lockheed must have a stack of URs a foot high by now. I agree it looks bad, but this one could be most anything. We'll dig out the answer, though."

"Well, I think I can guarantee you'll have some help. When I call TAC headquarters, I'm betting they'll have a team down there tomorrow."

"We'll work with them, sir. I want to find out what's wrong as badly as anyone else. And I'll put Doug Curtiss up against any man they can produce at TAC or Lockheed."

"I know that." Cipolla slapped Ross's shoulder and added, "Don't let it get you down, but we've been getting this 'radically new airplane—gotta expect accidents' crap too long. I'm beginning to think we may have a fleet of hangar queens on our hands. If this accident turns out to be another engineering flaw, well, I'm gonna restrict the bird to about three hundred knots in straight and level flight until Lockheed can get its act together."

"It's a good airplane, sir. We'll work it out. Well, I have a T-Bird on the way. I'll collect Janet and take her to the transient quarters. She can drive back tomorrow."

"Aah, don't break up her evening. Maria and I will look after her, see she gets home safe and sound."

"I'd surely appreciate that, sir. This is the first time we've had a chance to get off base together for awhile, and she was looking forward to this evening. She won't be real happy about me running off."

Janet forced a smile as Maria Cipolla stopped at her table. "Hi, Janet," the matronly blonde said in greeting. "May I join you? Cappy tells me your man done gone and deserted you. I'm glad for an excuse to get away from that bunch of stuffy old farts up there, so why don't we enjoy ourselves. What are you drinking?"

"Oh, Maria, this is so nice of you. If I weren't so worried about Lieutenant Murphy, I'd strangle that husband of mine."

Maria chuckled as she allowed a waiter to seat her. "Being married to a flyboy has its down times, doesn't it? But overall, they ain't a bad bunch. Ross is one of the finest, and Cappy thinks highly of him. Is it pretty rough out there amongst the rattlesnakes and scorpions?"

"As you say, air force life has its down times, but really, it could be worse: They could stop making suntan oil and Jergen's Lotion. Ross is doing what he wants to do most, so I'm happy for him. We have a good squadron. Not much in the way of social life, but we won't be in the desert forever."

"A commendable attitude," Maria commented dryly. "I recall that I was a real bitch when Cappy dragged me off to Eagle Pass, Texas, during the war. How are the quarters at Hanson?"

Janet felt herself relaxing and laughed as she accepted her just-delivered drink. "With a little fixing up you could make them merely awful. Some of the girls have added curtains, slipcovers, and such—Betsy Curtiss has done wonders with theirs. I just don't have the touch, I guess."

"The days must get pretty long."

"It's surprising how fast time goes. Most of the wives are young and having a hard time adapting; I spend as much time giving advice as I do keeping house. Also, I'm trying to work on a novel. A publisher in D.C. offered a contract before I left INS, but it's going slowly."

"How interesting." Maria sighed. "I wanted to be a fashion designer when we were first married. I had a degree, and a flair for the business— if I do say so myself." She chuckled and continued, "But Cappy kept me pregnant for the first three years. That pretty well took care of my career planning."

"I see that happening with some of the squadron wives," Janet said thoughtfully. "You know, talking to some of those girls is the hardest part of being a commander's wife. They think I know everything—damnit, they make me feel old. God, was I ever that young and naive? I ask myself."

"It goes with being a CO's wife, I'm afraid. Oh, there's someone you should meet. . . ." Maria waved at a middle-aged man dressed in civilian clothes walking past. "Craig, could you come here a minute? I think you would enjoy talking with this young lady."

Janet saw the man turn and regard them, his suntanned features creased into a lazy smile. She was reminded of the pictures in magazine ads of successful businessmen who proclaimed the merits of aftershave lotion and expensive whiskey. She heard Maria say, "Craig Montgomery, I'd like you to meet Janet Colyer. Can you join us for a drink?"

"I'd be honored," the man said. "Why, may I ask, are two lovely ladies sitting alone?"

"Janet's husband had to leave—an emergency. He's commander of an F-80 squadron down at Hanson Field. I'm a refugee from that stuffy group up front."

"I see." Montgomery flagged a passing waiter and ordered drinks. "And, Mrs. Colyer, how are you enjoying your life in the desert?"

"I'm sure there are worse places," Jane responded laughingly. "Hopefully I'll never see them."

"Janet, Craig's in an interesting business," Maria interjected. "He's starting a new television-broadcasting station in San Francisco—down here to see about doing a feature on jet fighter planes."

"Really?" Janet's eyebrows rose. "How terribly exciting. Television! I was just telling my husband last week how I wished we could receive the signals at our base."

"I predict that day isn't as far off as a lot of people believe." Montgomery sampled his drink. "The technology is progressing by leaps and bounds. The problem now is finding people to fill a whole new range of job skills—"

Maria interrupted. "I'm sorry, but I'm getting distress signals from Cappy." She stood and added, "The reason I asked you to meet Janet, Craig, is because she's a writer. I thought you might have something in common. Now I have to run. See you all later."

Janet looked around the empty tables and realized that she and Craig were the club bar's two remaining customers. "Oh, m'God, it's after midnight," she cried. "Wherever has time gone?"

"It did zip right along," Craig observed. "May I offer you a lift to your quarters?"

"No, Ross left the car. I'll be fine, thanks."

"Very well. About the business we discussed, what do you think?"

"Oh, Craig. I—I just don't know. It's exciting, I'm overwhelmed, but I have so many things to consider. My husband needs me—oh, I don't actually help him with his job, but he is so busy that he doesn't have time to keep house. He'd have to move into the BOQ, and he hates that. Can I think about it—talk it over with Ross?"

"Of course. I know it's a big decision. But television is the communication medium of the future, including news. On the spot, live, right into your living room while it's happening. I like your ideas about developing the news angle, and your INS background is perfect."

"Ooh, I'd love to, but—"

"I'm not rushing you. But can you at least take over writing the script for this feature on the new jet air force? You could do a lot of it at home and not have to spend more than a day or two up here, plus maybe another couple at the studio in San Francisco."

Janet's jaw took on a determined set. "I'll call you at your hotel tomorrow night."

13

Ross ushered General Cipolla into his office and indicated chairs grouped around a wooden table situated in the modest room's far end. The grim-faced wing commander tossed his briefcase onto the table and sank into one of the government-issue wooden chairs. "You sure aren't extravagant when it comes to interior decorating," he observed sourly.

Ross surveyed the spartan surroundings. Other than an arrangement of strictly GI furniture, the only decoration was an American flag standing in the corner, and a framed, color photograph of the Lockheed Shooting Star on one cream-colored beaverboard. He chuckled. "I try to spend as little time here as possible. Coffee? Coke?" He slid an ashtray toward the general as he saw him reach for a cigar.

"A Coke, I think. I've had enough of your mess-hall coffee for a while, thank you. You should shoot that cook."

Ross, still smiling, asked the clerk outside to bring two cold drinks. After the corporal had slid a beaded bottle before each of them and closed the door behind him, Ross released a resigned sigh and broached the topic uppermost in his mind.

"It was pilot error, no question. Murphy had the makings of a great fighter pilot: aggressive, good eyes, and all the right instincts. Just a case of too much confidence and not enough experience."

Cipolla waited until his cigar was burning to his satisfaction before responding. "Had?" he inquired through a cloud of blue smoke.

"I don't imagine a Flying Evaluation Board will deal kindly with him. The best he can hope for is just to loose his fighter pilot MOS. The only thing that will maybe keep him on flying status is the way he handled things after he got himself in trouble; that, and the straightforward

146

account of what happened. He didn't try to lie his way out, and that impressed the board members I talked with later."

The general uttered a noncommittal grunt, then said, "I'm told the boy is a bit of a fuckup. That true?"

Where in hell does this man get his information? Ross wondered. Nothing misses his attention. He had dinner with Colonel Krug; I guess he must have gotten an earful there. Aloud, Ross said, "He's a cocky young fighter pilot, General. Probably no better—no worse—than you and I at his stage. At least he was dogfighting at twenty thousand instead of making head-on passes while brushing the tops of cactus." Ross gave the general a bold, direct look.

Cipolla shook with silent mirth. "You'll never let me forget that, will you? By God, I'll take you on again, any time. No man waxes my ass and gets away with rubbing my nose in it. But another time. What will be your recommendation?"

"Send him back to Muroc for refresher training and bust him back a hundred files on the promotion list," Ross replied without hesitation.

"We'll see," Cipolla said after a thoughtful nod. He examined a loose button on his uniform shirt and asked, "Now, what do you suggest I do with a squadron commander who has two major accidents within two weeks of each other?"

Ross drank from his Coke bottle and formed a wry grin. "I guess it'd be asking too much to suggest another cluster for my Air Medal. Is it pink-slip time?"

"Is that what you're expecting?"

"There's plenty of precedent, I'm afraid."

"Well, you're wrong. The team found your flying-training and aircraft-maintenance records to be clean as a hound's tooth and no basis for supervisory error. They made no recommendations for corrective action. So now, *I* got a problem."

"Sir?"

"Yeah. Lockheed has a contract to produce a 'C' model of the '80 with a bigger engine, a fifty-four thousand-pound thrust Allison J-33-A. Plus, an all-weather version of the '80 with an afterburner and radar-controlled fire-control system. The air staff isn't enthusiastic; they say Lockheed has too many basic engineering flaws in the birds they've already built.

"Thinking at the Pentagon is that the North American F-86 Sabrejet is a far superior interceptor. Republic has an F-84 undergoing suitability tests at Wright they say is a better fighter-bomber than the '80. I'm supposed to make a recommendation regarding the Shooting Star based on the 14th Wing's experience. See my problem?"

"Recommendation?"

"In a nutshell, do we halt production on the '80?"

Ross propped his elbow on the table, cupped his jaw in one hand, and stared at the scarred, yellow-oak tabletop. The silence dragged on. Cipolla puffed his cigar with quick, impatient drags.

"I can see your dilemma," Ross said at last. "It's hard to defend an airplane with the '80's record so far, but it's in the inventory, and the only combat capability we have right now."

"So?" Cipolla pressed.

"We're training for the wrong mission, General. As an interceptor, the plane is already obsolete. But, sir, I think we have a close-support fighter-bomber here that can be more effective than any prop job, including my old Mustang."

Cipolla snorted. "No way. Not enough range at low altitude; it isn't stressed for heavy wing loads, like bombs and rockets; it's equipped with fifty-caliber guns instead of cannons; requires too much runway and ground support for forward bases—no, the Jugs and '51s will be our first-line close support airplanes for a long time to come."

Ross placed clenched fists on the tabletop and leaned forward as he said, "Sir, the '80 is a more rugged airplane than most people think. I flew it at Wright Field and saw it come through some pretty rough treatment. Send me a good factory rep and let me fly some ground-support profiles. Both Doug Curtiss and I are qualified test pilots—let's try some low-level stuff. The results may surprise you."

"It would never sell at headquarters, Ross—or at the Armament Test Center at Eglin. Right now, the brass is more concerned with explaining our losses to Congress than with *extending* the risk factor. *If* we can bring this accident rate down—well, we'll see.

"In the meantime, I'm due on the carpet at TAC headquarters Monday morning. This latest crash came at a bad time. The best I can hope for is to get the 14th Wing designated a demonstration unit for ninety days to study the problem. In the meantime I'm slapping a three-hundred-mph and five-G limitation on the bird. We, and *you* especially, can't afford another major accident where structural or mechanical failure is a factor."

Ross concealed his bitter disappointment. "Yes, sir."

"Okay, new subject. Maria tells me that this television guy from San Francisco, Montgomery, wants Janet to do the script for a film on jet fighters."

Ross's lips formed a thin line. He could do without further discussion of *that* little matter after the quarrel he'd had with Janet. "Yes, sir, I believe he did."

"Is she going to do it?"

"Uh, I—I don't know for certain—we've talked about it," Ross hedged.

"Well, TAC ops is nervous as hell about the project. There isn't a damn thing they can do except offer full cooperation—no one is *about* to give an impression that the jets aren't the final solution. Here's what I'd like to do: Ask Janet to go ahead. We'll arrange to shoot most of the footage down here—desert base—tough and hard—real he-man stuff. I'll have Bob Kinney, wing public information officer, here to hold your hand, but I'm looking to *you* to keep this thing under control. Any problem with that?"

"No problem, sir."

"Great." Cipolla stood. "There's more than a little riding on the 66th these next three months. I know I can count on you."

Ross sat staring at the arid landscape outside his window for several minutes following the general's departure. "Shit, I almost wish he'd fired me instead," he muttered to the empty office.

Janet's eyes glinted dangerously in the purple evening dusk. "Ross, I *do* want to do the script, but I can't cover for General Cipolla, or you. To begin with, I'll just be a scriptwriter—there'll be a director, probably Craig Montgomery, who will arrange all the action."

Ross set his drink down and leaned across the little patio table separating them. "I'm not asking you to *cover* for us, Janet. But, for Christ's sake, let me see what you're writing before you submit it. There are some things that the airplane does better than others; I'd like you to emphasize those. There can't, simply *can't,* be an accident during the project."

"I've never submitted my material for censorship to anyone," Janet flared, "including you. You'll get a professional job. How Craig and the station handle the material is up to them, though."

"Well, I'll tell you how 'Craig and the station' will handle this project," Ross shot back. "Certain aspects of the F-80's performance are still classified. If, by God, they want a film to show the general public, *they* will submit to censorship. You can save yourself some embarrassment, and maybe grief, by letting me guide you."

Janet leaned back in her redwood deck chair and considered Ross's rebuke. "You still have your back up because I wanted to take that full-time job with the TV station. Okay, after thinking about it, I can see it wasn't a good idea.

"And I can read between the lines. You only suggested I go ahead with the movie script because General Cipolla wants a tame writer. That really burns me, but again, I'll concede. As soon as I meet with Craig and the wing public information officer, I'll let you see my notes and rough draft. Satisfied?"

Ross refilled their glasses from a pitcher of rum punch before answering. "No, I didn't want you to go running off to San Francisco," he said softly. "It was a selfish motive, I freely admit. I love you, Janet, and I want you near me. I'm sorry. I'm fully aware this assignment to Hanson is an ordeal for you. If you want to go back to the media business, we'll work things out; I know how badly you want that job."

Janet blinked and gave Ross a startled look. "I don't know what to say—I—I . . ." She took a reflective sip from her drink, and added, "I love you very much for saying that, Ross Colyer, but let's discuss the subject another time, okay? Just now, let's talk about what's worrying you. You've had that little squinchy look around the eyes that you always get when you're upset. Is it this last accident?"

"Sort of. Lieutenant Murphy doesn't deserve a suspension, but I'm not sure an FEB will agree—that bothers me. But it's all part of something bigger. General Cipolla told me they're thinking of phasing out the F-80—too many accidents. In addition, the 66th will probably have a new commander if there's another accident."

"Ross! Oh, no. After everything you've put into this job—top squadron in the wing, how could anyone—"

"It's the game we play, sweetheart. There's no room at the top for second best. Then, if what I have in mind backfires, well . . ." He took a long pull from his drink and laughed. "Come to think of it, maybe you'd better take that high-paying job. You may be the only one in the family to have a paycheck."

1 March 1950
Hanson Air Base

Ross, still wearing a sweaty flight suit after flying an afternoon training ride, leaned back in his chair and regarded Doug and Ace over his Coke bottle. "Well, we're gonna have the best damn bunch of instrument pilots in the wing if Cipolla keeps this restriction up," he said. "Either of you have anything new and startling to report?"

"The guys are starting to bitch about the situation," Ace responded. "Do you think wing is gonna keep this three-hundred-miles and five Gs thing up for the entire three-month demo project?"

"No clue," said Ross. "But"—his voice took on a pseudopomposity— "the reason I've called you all together this warm, sunshiny, spring afternoon is to make an important announcement."

"Janet's pregnant," Doug quipped with a broad grin.

Ross chuckled. "Whatever you do, don't tell her. She still thinks you find babies in old hollow stumps. No, this is something I've thought up that could get me fired. It needs to be done, however. I'll outline it, and if either of you don't want to be involved—okay. I'll cover for you all the way, but unauthorized stuff has a way of rubbing off on innocent bystanders."

"Unauthorized stuff?" Ace asked.

"Highly unauthorized. You see, some generals at air force headquarters have decided the '80 is a mistake—too many engineering flaws. They want to stop production and phase it out of the inventory—replace it with '86s for intercept work and the F-84 as a fighter-bomber."

"We've all heard the rumor. Is it true?"

"Not yet. General Cipolla got a ninety-day stay of execution while the 14th Wing serves as a guinea pig. It was the best deal he could make. If we can avoid a major accident by keeping away from the upper end of the performance envelope, they may give Lockheed the go-ahead for the 'C' model."

Ace uttered a derisive snort. "Oh, shit, Major. Telling a bunch of pilots to fly low and slow to avoid accidents is like playing poker with scared money. It won't work. Already, I see 'em landing long and hot, flying sloppy patterns, loose formation—this is the *quickest* route to a bunch of broken airplanes."

"That's your job, Ace." Ross's voice was flat and cold. *"Don't let that happen.* In the meantime, here's the playbook. The brass has always been afraid of the '80. It's an unknown quantity, they think it's fragile. I know a damn sight different, and so do you, Doug. We did things with that bird at Wright that would have made even the designers turn pale. Chuck Yeager—before he went into the F-86 program—won't admit to this day some of the stunts he did with the airplane.

"But is isn't a high-speed fighter-interceptor. What it is, is the best damn close support airplane I've ever flown. The word from headquarters is: Not enough range at low level, wings won't support heavy ordinance, requires too much hard-surfaced runway for advance tactical bases, and the systems are too sophisticated for front-line echelon maintenance. I'm gonna prove otherwise."

Ace and Doug regarded Ross with confused expressions. "To start with," said Ross, "when you see the Form 1 entry I made on tail number Two-Forty-Four today, you'll see I wrote up a hard landing, Doug. A *real* hard landing. I'd say it's going to take a factory teardown and inspection to clear it for unrestricted flight."

"Holy Christ, Major," Doug muttered. "That's gonna take a ream of paperwork and weeks—even months—to arrange. You sure the landing was *that* hard?"

"Believe me, it was a tooth-loosener."

"Okay, sir, but—"

Ross interrupted with, "Until you're satisfied, the airplane will only be flown by instructor pilots with more than a hundred hours' IP time. Here's a memo to that effect." He reached into a desk drawer, extracted two sheets of paper, and slid them toward the bewildered-looking pair.

Ace frowned. "But there's only me, you, and Doug, here with that much IP time."

"Exactly. Now, Doug, do you know a Lockheed factory tech rep you can talk with off the record?"

"Well, yeah. Hack Morris—he's up at Nellis, assigned to wing maintenance. I've always been able to pick his brain without going through channels."

"Great. Here's what I'm planning to do. Set up a field maintenance tent on the dry lake. We'll put number Two-Forty-Four out there and start doing some experimenting. I want to hang the equivalent of two hundred fifty gallons of fuel in wingtip tanks, two thousand pounds of bombs, and a couple of rocket pods on that bird, then see if we can get it off the ground. Find out from your pal Morris where we can best add bomb and rocket points—if there are any places where the wing might have to be beefed up—you know."

Ace sat in stunned silence. Doug's face spread in a wide grin. "Now we're talking," he said. "I agree with you, that airplane is one tough bird. Aside from the system problems, fuel leaking from the fuselage tank, those damned armament doors, the heating and air conditioning, and the like, it's a workhorse. But," he scowled and added, "how do you plan to keep this from being common knowledge? Wing is going to have a foaming fit and fall down in it when they find out what we're doing."

"First off," Ross said, "select only crew chiefs you can trust not to gossip. Our cover will be this film they want to shoot down here. We'll give them a good show—simulate a deployment to a desert location. Our extra tent and maintenance support will go unnoticed. The camera crew is going to be so damn miserable they won't want to see anything, and this PIO from wing isn't on flying status.

"Now, I'll give you written orders for everything. Here's an open-ended work order to modify number Two-Forty-Four, Doug. If we do prang the bird, we'll always have this hard-landing write-up to fall back on."

"In other words, if the shit hits the fan, you're the guy facing upwind," Ace observed.

"That's right. You two are just following orders—written orders."

Doug and Ace looked at each other, nodded, then proceeded to tear the memos they held into four strips. Doug tossed the scraps into Ross's waste can. "When can I have my TDY orders for Nellis?"

14

27 March 1950

Resick Air Field, Georgia USSR

Lieutenant Vladimir Orsini asked, "Why did the American imperialists invade Burma, Indonesia, and the Philippines?"

Yuri's forehead wrinkled as he considered the question. "To keep their promise to England and the Netherlands to protect their colonies."

Vladimir threw the red-covered book he'd been reading aloud from, to the desk. "Yuri, honestly. Did you learn nothing at Tashkent regarding world politics? The corrupt American monopolists wanted the *oil* supplies in Southeast Asia—oil rightfully belonging to the people."

Yuri winced and reached for the bottle of vodka. He sloshed a generous measure in both their glasses and said, "Of course, I remember now. I guess it's been too long since academy."

"Could it be that your mind was filled with the thought of those nurses living only four blocks away? The black-market vodka that you excelled at smuggling into the barracks? Yuri, you'll meet the oral examination board for admission into the party in one week. With answers such as the one you just gave me, well, you'll disgrace the entire air force. You're a pilot second class now and an instructor. But promotion, I guarantee you, won't come until you become a Communist Party member."

"I know that, Vlad, and I'm trying, honestly. And I really appreciate you taking the time to tutor me. It's just, well, I have a lot on my mind lately."

"Oh? Care to tell me?"

"Just family stuff—my father remarried, you know."

Vlad showed immediate interest. "No, I didn't. I don't know your father personally, of course, only by reputation. He's one of the few generals not found guilty of deviationism during the Great Patriotic War. A favorite of Generalissimo Stalin, it is said. Aren't they getting along?"

Yuri, surprised at his wingman's knowledge of Papa's background, uttered a lame, "I'm probably imagining things. Sorry to have bothered you with trifling personal problems. All right, I'm ready to get back to work. Ask me another question."

"No, Yuri Sergeievich, personal problems are never trifling where the party is concerned. Have you discussed them with Colonel Shvatsov? Perhaps some self-criticism would clear your mind."

"Oh, really, Vlad. It's nothing like that, I—I, well, find myself physically attracted to the woman—she's quite a looker."

Vladimir laughed. "Yuri, you are impossible. Your pecker is going to be your downfall yet—your *stepmother,* of all people."

Yuri laughed, a self-conscious chuckle. Secretly, he was relieved that the suddenly sharp-eyed Vlad had abandoned his searching questions. Discuss plans to help his father defect with the political commissar indeed! The meeting wasn't taking the direction he'd planned—not at all.

The time he'd walked in to find Vlad listening to Radio Free Europe stuck in Yuri's mind. Was the man a secret dissenter? If so, could he possibly be of help in arranging a contact with a boat captain on the docks? Weeks had passed since his conversation with Giesele, and Yuri had despaired of making a safe overture. Perhaps Vlad was putting on a front, trying to establish his loyal party member image. He'd try one more time.

"Speaking of the party, Vlad," Yuri said casually, "what do you suppose would cause a staunch, apparently dedicated commissar like Petlyakov, to defect?" Details of the high-ranking Petlyakov's arrest had been the main topic of discussion at Saturday morning's political discussion. The fact that the man had been removed from a boat already under way from its berth at nearby Odessa had prompted a senior party official from Moscow to conduct the session. Yuri had elicited favorable nods by standing and denouncing local law enforcement officials for permitting a situation to exist that led to the attempted escape.

Vladimir scowled and said, "Revisionist thinking is a disease. It breeds on ignorance of Marxist-Leninist teaching."

"But how would one go about arranging an escape? Is there a secret underground organization? Are the fishing-boat captains so corrupt that they break the law for money? Are foreign spies among us? Right here at Resick, for example?"

"All of those are possibilities. Western propaganda is a constant source of misleading, treasonous poison as well."

"Like Radio Free Europe?" Yuri gave Vlad a direct stare.

Vladimir's features took on an angry flush. "You're speaking of the time you found me listening to the radio," he shot back. "Don't get any wrong ideas. A part of my official duties involves monitoring those broadcasts."

"Official duties? Vlad, don't tell me you're a 'door knocker'?"

Vladimir's flush deepened. The allegation that he was one of the Otsobists who knocked on political officers' doors late at night to report his fellow officers' indiscretions appeared to be especially upsetting. "You'd best forget that incident," he snapped.

My God, the man *is* a member of the Otsobii Otdel, Yuri thought. And to think of what I was about to ask him! He felt a stab of panic. That time he found Vlad listening to the clandestine radio, *he hadn't reported it.* Was that, right now, a black mark in his file, just waiting to be used against him, like at the interview for party membership? And those stumbling, fallacious responses he'd given to Vlad's questions during tutoring—he'd been trying to lead the man into exposing an element of disloyalty, a source of help in arranging Papa's flight to the West. The magnitude of his error caused telltale sweat stains in his armpits.

But no. What if the man was bluffing? he wondered. What if Vlad himself was the one terrified of exposure? Should he denounce his wingman at the next political discussion as a means of self-protection? No, it was too late—why hadn't he reported the incident immediately? Vlad was regarding him with a suspicious glint in his eye. He must make one last effort to determine the man's true allegiance.

"I had forgotten it, Vlad," he countered. "I was prepared to denounce you, frankly. Then I thought, Vlad is the man I trust to guard my back in combat—can I not trust him in other respects as well? Perhaps I *should* go to Colonel Shvatsov and submit to a session of self-criticism. I can't go to the admissions committee with this on my mind. And, since your monitoring was done in an official capacity, it can do no harm."

Yuri saw his tutor's gaze waver, then drop. That's it! he exulted silently. Vlad is a counterrevolutionary. I have him cornered.

The crafty scion of a veteran *nomenklatura* member didn't surrender easily. "Yuri, I find your obsession with the Petlyakov affair interesting," he said. "I also find your frequent poring over maps of the Black Sea coastlines—both our own and that of Turkey's—to be puzzling. Could it be that you are plotting a defection of your own?"

Yuri blinked in spite of himself. *He,* Yuri Pavel, suspected of treasonous flight? He recovered and replied, "An amusing speculation, Vlad.
I wouldn't have the first idea of how to go about such a thing."

Vlad made a point of examining the walls and ceiling of his room.
"And if I could answer your questions about how the Petlyakov escape
was arranged?" he whispered.

The two young men's eyes locked. Understanding was implicit, albeit
unspoken.

"Well, we natter about inconsequential things," Vlad announced
briskly. "Back to work. Why is the myth of Christianity a harmful influence in a Communist society?"

The failed Petlyakov escape episode was two weeks old—during
which neither Yuri nor Vlad had broached the subject—when the base at
Resick was thrown into turmoil. An excited Colonel Shvatsov announced
at the regular Saturday political discussion that a marshal of the army
would visit the MiG-15 unit. The marshall wished to fly as a passenger in
one of the two-place trainer versions—it would be his first flight in a jet.
The cause of the colonel's agitation was an additional stipulation: Marshal Yokolov would personally select the pilot after reviewing training
records following his arrival.

The room buzzed with forbidden conversations. Who would be the
lucky pilot? Yuri scarcely heard Colonel Shvatsov roar, "Silence! I will
ground the next man I see talking."

Yokolov. Papa's friend in the Kremlin—Yuri's head spun at the implications. Would the marshal seek him out? Announce publicly that Yuri
was a family friend? Even, perhaps, select him as his pilot for the demonstration ride? Would that be good for his future with the squadron? Or, an
uneasy thought surfaced, would it focus attention on him if and when
Papa fled the country? Yuri left the meeting room after dismissal oblivious to the excited chatter around him.

Yuri rolled his eyes to one side as the squadron marched smartly past
the reviewing stand the following week. The marshal looked smaller than
he remembered. And older, he thought, if his quick glimpse at a distance
was sufficient to judge. After confiding his dilemma with Vlad, he'd
decided to leave the issue of his father's relationship with the marshal up

to the marshal himself. First of all, the man might not recognize Yuri, and give him some curt rebuff, a humiliation. Secondly, butt-kisser Colonel Shvatsov could well see the connection as something reflecting favorably on *him*. Even more terrifying was the thought of being dragged before the high-ranking officer by a fawning political commissar.

The more experienced pilots lounged around headquarters following the parade. Word had been passed that Marshal Yokolov would meet before the evening meal with the man he'd selected. Yuri debated returning to his quarters, where a bottle of vodka was concealed, then was drawn into a discussion he couldn't gracefully avoid. His heart sank as promptly at 1600 hours, an orderly appeared on the steps and asked, "Is Lieutenant Pavel here?"

Yuri stood at rigid attention beside the nose of a gleaming, hand-polished MiG-15 the following morning. Ground crewmen likewise snapped to attention as the base commander's spotless Ziv sedan delivered Marshal Yokolov planeside. An aide and two majors from base headquarters helped the diminutive figure don a helmet and parachute. The marshal returned Yuri's salute and rasped, "Good morning, Lieutenant Pavel. I trust you've been briefed?"

"Yes, sir. We will climb to seven thousand meters and observe the limits of the local flying area, under positive radar contact at all times."

"That's as I understand it," the marshal replied with a hint of a smile. "We can't have the old man flying around just any old way, now, can we?"

Yuri dropped his salute and climbed into his cockpit. He felt much better after the brief meeting yesterday. Yokolov had given no hint of recognition. "Lieutenant Pavel, I note that your superior piloting skills are further enhanced by recent admission to the party. I look forward to our little flight tomorrow morning. By the way, I once served with a General Pavel. Are you related?"

"Yes, sir. General Pavel is my father."

"Really, now. An excellent officer. I'm sure he has taught you well." He gazed over Yuri's shoulder with hooded unseeing eyes. Yuri realized the audience was at an end, and there would be no embarrassing aftermath.

Yuri used extreme care during engine start, taxi out, and takeoff, double-checking each checklist item. He watched the marshal in the rearview mirror, alert for any sign of distress.

They were leveling at their assigned altitude when he heard on the intercom, "All right, Yuri. Make doubly sure your radio transmitter is turned off. We must talk."

The startled pilot did as ordered and responded, "The radio transmitter is secured, sir."

"Very well. Now, I've grown to hate airplanes. Don't exceed thirty degrees of bank, and spare me any demonstrations of your fighter-pilot skills. I'll be brief and to the point. It saddens me to tell you that your father is, as of this morning, under close house arrest."

"What?" Yuri's startled cry was accompanied by an involuntary jerk on the control stick. The sensitive little plane leaped violently. "Sorry, Comrade Marshal, but—but I don't understand. What is he accused of?"

"We may never know. The NKVD seldom makes public announcements in situations like this. At any rate, what they write on the charge sheet usually has little to do with what actually transpires. The case may not—probably won't—ever be tried in a public court. Technically he isn't in prison, just confined to quarters pending the outcome of their investigation, which will never be finished."

Yuri concentrated on holding the plane straight and level; the horizon was a mere blur. "Can't something be done?" he asked. "Papa was awarded the Hero of the Soviet Union medal by Generalissimo Stalin himself. Surely if he were approached—"

"The arrest was ordered by Stalin personally, as was the edict stripping Sergei of his rank, awards, and decorations," Yokolov interrupted.

Yuri felt numb, too confused to speak.

"The political winds are swirling just now. Until I sort out what's in store for Sergei, it's best if you're as far removed from the scene as possible. I have orders with me reassigning you to the Far East—China, in fact."

"China, Comrade Marshal?"

"Yes, we have a request from the People's Army of China to provide instructor pilots. The General Staff has agreed to send twelve. You'll be briefed in detail by your squadron commander."

"China," Yuri said. This time it was a statement instead of a question.

"Yes, from a standpoint of timing, this may appear to be fortuitous, but I assure you that your assignment to the foreign-language school to study Chinese was no accident. It was part of a plan—a far-reaching plan. The Politburo's oversight reaches deep into all our lives. More than that, I can't tell you, but if I am to be of any assistance to Sergei and to you, I must not appear interested."

Yuri's jumbled thoughts spewed questions faster than he could organize and voice them. "My stepmother?" emerged without conscious effort.

"Giesele has disappeared. I assume she's in Lubyanka Prison, undergoing interrogation."

My God! Yuri thought. What will she tell them? If the NKVD methods are as effective as rumored . . . Papa knows nothing of her scheme for him to defect, but I . . . Will China be *far* enough? A sliver of comfort materialized—Giesele was tough. If anyone could thwart the specialists inside Lubyanka, she was a good bet. Had I acted more quickly and decisively, could I have arranged for Papa's escape? Is it still possible? Why must I face this terrible decision? Betray my country to save my father's life?

"I'm ready to return to the base, Yuri," Yokolov said.

"Yes, Comrade Marshal. Immediately."

"And Yuri, don't feel your father did anything dishonorable to warrant this. He is a fine officer."

He illegally brought Giesele, an enemy of the Soviet Union, into our country, Yuri raged inwardly.

"One more thing," the marshal said. "Don't entertain ideas of helping Sergei escape his confinement. It would be doomed to fail, and the composition of those in power can change overnight in our country. Trust me. The situation may be resolved as suddenly as it developed."

"Yes, Comrade Marshal. With your permission, I'll turn the radio transmitter on to request landing clearance."

This is all some horrible mistake, Yuri thought as he prepared the plane for descent and landing. The party *can't* be responsible. It's that NKVD agent, Novotny, Giesele told me about, a personal vendetta. If the generalissimo only knew the truth. That's the solution. I was right in questioning that woman's scheme for Papa's escape, he'd have been disgraced. I'll distinguish myself by exemplary performance of duty in China. When I'm recalled to Moscow to accept an award, I'll request a personal interview with Comrade Stalin.

Yuri's mind was fully made up by the time he brought the MiG in for a perfect touchdown. Be a more dedicated party member; strive for a leadership position. Become the very best pilot in the entire Red Air Force; volunteer for the most demanding, hazardous missions—abandon his frivolous indulgence in vodka and immoral women. Papa would be restored to his former prestigious status because of his, Yuri's, exemplary service to the Motherland. He had been wrong to consider placing Papa's personal safety ahead of party loyalty.

15

11 April 1950
Indian Springs Dry Lake, Nevada
Ross drank deeply from a cup of tepid water and squinted across the limitless expanse of baked alkali. He decided to shed his flight gear and join the others' near-naked state. Even in shade of the tarp stretched overhead, 110-degree heat reflected from the blinding-white lakebed was building to an intolerable level. By noon, tools would become too hot to handle—fatigue, induced by dehydration, would induce mistakes. The men would spend the afternooon sprawled on cots inside the big barracks tent, only partially cooled by whirring three-foot fans.

F-80 number 244 squatted in the center of the oasis of shade. Born to slice gracefully through rarefied atmosphere, to Ross she looked resentful that her aluminum bowels were exposed to reveal a maze of multi-colored electrical wires and control cables. He returned the aluminum cup to its hook and strolled to where Doug Curtiss pored over a stack of blueprints.

The darkly tanned maintenance officer straightened and rubbed kinks from his bare back. "It's looking good, Ross," he said. "These prints Hack Morris smuggled to me show that station fourteen on the main spar was designed with a safety factor of eight. That means instead of one five-hundred-pound bomb, it was designed—and static-tested—for two thousand pounders at two Gs."

A wolfish grin expressed Ross's delight. "All *right,*" he enthused. What are we up to now?"

"Well,"—Doug picked up a sliderule and made rapid calculations—"it works out that a gross takeoff weight of eighteen thousand, instead of fourteen thousand, is still within design limits. That gives you a full load of eighteen hundred rounds of fifty-caliber ammo, close to a thousand gallons of fuel—instead of seven-fifty—four, one-thousand-pound bombs, plus twenty-four, two-point-five folding-fin rockets."

162

"Jesus Christ," Ross breathed. "I knew she was rugged, but that kind of a load is unbelievable. Are you sure?"

"Hell, no, I'm not sure." Doug glared at his CO. "That's using a lot of untested extrapolation—that's the fancy name for guesswork. Somebody's gotta try it."

"That's me. I'm your man."

Doug threw a sour look at Ross. "Maybe. I'm gonna be the judge of that."

"Just a minute. Are you maybe forgetting who's the boss around here?"

"Ross"—Doug shuffled his stack of blueprints—"We're off the reservation out here. Your ass is flapping in the breeze so high that the buzzards are saluting it when they fly by. This ain't your ordinary boss-slave arrangement. I'm a better engineer than you are, and you know it. I'll call the shots, okay?"

Ross scowled and opened his mouth to speak; then he chuckled. "Betchya a beer you're wrong."

"You're on—boss. Now." Doug led Ross to where a pair of mechanics, stripped to their skivvy shorts, were riveting a section of aircraft skin into halves of a drop tank. "We're gonna test the extra weight at the wingtips first," he continued. "When they finish, we'll put fifteen hundred pounds of sand—these riveted seams won't contain liquid—in them and try to take off. We'll have to drop them before landing of course, but at least we'll know that the wings won't come off—or, hell, I don't know, maybe they will. See why I'm not eager to have someone else risk his ass on my guesswork?"

Ross held up both hands, palms outward. "Okay, okay, I surrender. I'll go along with you—up to a point. But you know, and I know, that what you're doing isn't 'guesswork.' Don't think for one damn minute that I'm gonna sit on the sidelines and let you hog all the glory." He grinned. "Now, what do you figure the takeoff speed's gonna be?"

"At seventeen grand?" Doug shrugged. "Something more than the hundred and thirty that's in the charts for fourteen thousand pounds. And here we may run into something I read about the B-47 test program. There's a thing called 'maximum tire rotation.' You spin a wheel fast enough and the tire starts throwing off chunks of rubber—centrifugal force. They know that speed on a B-47 wheel, but there're no test data on the smaller F-80 landing gear. Once again, by extrapolation, I figure we're safe up to a hundred and fifty."

"Wow." Ross's eyes grew round. "Okay, when do you plan to try a takeoff with the heavier drop tanks?"

"Tomorrow morning. We'll have these tanks hung by the time we stand down for afternoon break, and fill them tonight after the sand cools. The camera ship leaps off at about oh-five-thirty. I figure to go shortly after they're out of sight."

"I don't think I'll go back tonight." Ross stroked his chin. "I'll call Ace on the radio and tell him to hold down the fort—I gotta see this." The pair donned outer clothing and started the hundred-yard trek to the main camp.

Ross and Doug hurried through furnacelike heat past the film crew's camera ship—a modified B-25—and four of the squadron's F-80s. All had their Plexiglas canopies covered against the blazing desert sun, and dust plugs in air intake and tailpipe openings. They entered the relatively cooler mess tent to find a half-dozen idle crew members passing time with a desultory poker game.

Craig Montgomery and Bob Kinney, the wing PIO, abandoned their kibitzing post and wandered toward the new arrivals. "Hi, Ross—Doug," Montgomery greeted them. "How's the overhaul job coming along?"

Ross shrugged. "What started to be a simulated maintenance prop for your film has turned into a major headache. I doubt we'll have Two-Forty-Four back in commission in time for you to use it. How'd the shooting go this morning?"

"Fantastic!" Kinney interjected. "Those guys"—he nodded toward the poker game—"can make their airplanes do everything but waltz." He chuckled. "Cliff's cameraman—the pale-faced one sitting by himself over there—is still wondering what happened. He was strapped into the backseat of one of the TF-80s, shooting action over the pilot's shoulder."

"Yeah," Montgomery added before Ross could comment, "we were just talking. Two to three more mornings like this one and I believe we'll have all the action stuff we need in the can."

"Ah, now,"—Ross crossed to a cooler filled with lemonade and drew a glassful—"don't hurry off. This is a picnic. My guys are asking to stay out here for at least two more weeks—sort of a vacation, you know."

"Major, you lie through your teeth," Kinney responded good humoredly. "I'm beginning to think you dreamed up this dammed 'simulated forward operating base' as a sick joke."

Montgomery slapped the PIO's shoulder and laughed. "I don't know what your motive might have been, Colyer, but we're getting some eye-popping footage. And I saw the rushes last night on the scene your wife set up for a jet pilot's family. Those gals were terrific.

"I'll tell you Ross, this project is exceeding all my most optimistic expectations—I've already slotted it for an hour instead of thirty minutes. You'll be hearing from your bosses—and I don't mean just General Cipolla—when this airs. I guarantee it's gonna be picked up by every TV station in the country."

Ross grinned inwardly, thinking, I may be hearing from my bosses, all right, but not to pin a medal on me.

"A lot of the credit has to go to your wife, and her name will be a single credit line, by the way, If you weren't so big and mean-looking, I'd hug and kiss her."

"Thanks, Craig." Ross glanced at Doug. "I'm sort of sorry to see you making such rapid progress. Hate to see your guys leave; this thing has given all of us a shot in the arm. But I was serious about not closing down. Even if you pull out early, we'll have to leave a crew out here to finish that overhaul job."

Ross and Doug strolled toward the sleeping area. Other than the faint sounds of conversation from the mess tent and the subdued rumble of the diesel generator, the desert was locked in absolute silence. Ross stopped and swept the star-filled sky with an appreciative gaze. "You know this place is kinda spectacular, you gotta admit that," he said.

"Yeah, if it wasn't for the rattlesnakes and scorpions looking for a warm place to spend the night, plus other assorted creepy, crawling, biting, stinging creatures, I'd be tempted to bring my sleeping bag out here."

"Whatta you think about tomorrow morning? Is it gonna work?"

"I'm betting my ass on it," Doug joked. "But a lot of things we haven't thought of can happen. Little problems, insignificant in themselves, can stack up. We may be screwing up the airflow with this much stuff hanging under the wings, for example. We'll just have to add things gradually and see what happens."

"I almost wish I hadn't thought up the crazy idea," Ross mused aloud. "Of course, it still isn't too late to call it off."

"In a way, it is." Doug's teeth flashed in the starlight. "We gotta find out which of us owes the other a beer."

* * *

The desert sunrise washed the departing fighters with a rosy glow as they streaked skyward. Ross sat in the only emergency vehicle Colonel Krug would let him bring to the dry lake; a weapons carrier with a foam tank mounted in its bed. He reached forward and punched channel "B" on the dash-mounted VHF set. "Doug?" he called.

"Saddled up and standing by, Ross."

"Okay. Light 'er off. The field's all yours."

He watched four mechanics roll number 244 from beneath the protecting canvas sunshade. A puff of black smoke from the tailpipe marked engine start. Ross unslung binoculars and watched Doug taxi to the preselected takeoff point. The oversized tip tanks gave the plane an ungainly look, but, watching closely, he couldn't detect any alarming wing flex. The real test would come during takeoff roll. The dry lakebed wasn't as smooth as it looked. Would the uneven surface set up a sort of harmonic bouncing by the heavily loaded wingtips? Positive and negative G forces could build rapidly if that happened—had they underestimated that factor?

"Rolling," he heard Doug call.

Ross glued his glasses on the port tank as the screaming J-33 engine's two-hundred-mph jet blast threw a storm of white alkali particles behind. The F-80 lumbered into motion. Fifty knots, Ross guessed—some visible wing flex, but no more than usual.

Doug was accelerating rapidly now, and Ross switched his attention to the first orange flag planted five thousand feet from the takeoff marker. He saw the nose rotate smoothly to takeoff attitude and breathed easier—most of the weight was now off the main gear, forces would shift to lift produced by the wings. Wonder what his airspeed is? Ross asked himself.

Seconds later, he saw daylight between the main gear and runway, and stifled an impulse to yell. As best he could estimate, lift off had come right at the five-thousand-foot marker; the damned tip tanks hadn't seemed to add more than a couple hundred feet to takeoff roll. What a bird!

Thirty minutes later, Ross trotted to where Doug was removing his helmet, unhandsome features wearing a wide grin. Even before the engine had moaned to a halt, he yelled to Ross, "Piece of cake! Could hardly tell a bit of difference."

Ross jumped onto the wing and started helping Doug unhook his gear. "What were you indicating at liftoff?"

"Would you believe one-thirty-two, maybe three? Apparently stretching the tank didn't add enough drag even to mention."

Doug drank a cup of cold lemonade in two gulps and paced the tarp-covered work area in excited, bouncy steps. "No separation problems with the drop tanks," he babbled. Hell, I was still getting a thousand-feet-per-minute climb at thirty thousand—I was tempted to land with the things still on—wish there was some way to jettison that sand and save fabricating a new tank every time—while we're doing that, I'll run a lashup electrical rocket and bomb release. . . ."

He saw Ross's amused smile and let his words trail off. "Okay, so I'm fired up. We're gonna make this bird over into one helluva ground support plane." He turned to face the huddle of grinning mechanics. "You did great work, guys. Now while two of you get busy making new drop tanks, the others can start hanging two of those empty, thousand-pound bomb-casings." He stopped to join Ross in watching a C-47 turn on base leg and enter his landing approach.

"Well, looks like we have company," Ross said. "I suppose I'd better get the jeep and go meet whoever it is."

Minutes later, Ross parked in shade cast by the Gooney Bird's wing and leaned on a fender while he waited for the crew to deplane. The crew chief hopped out the rear door and affixed aluminum boarding steps. He was followed by a flight-suit-clad man wearing a silver oak leaf on his flight cap.

Ross stood, saluted, and said, "'Morning, sir. Welcome to the desert. What can I do for you?"

The colonel joined Ross in the shaded area. "I'm looking for a Major Colyer. Would that be you?"

"That's correct, sir."

Oh, shit, Ross thought. Some headquarters type out to get his mug on film. Montgomery's gonna love this. "I assume you're here to have a look at the movie filming. They're airborne just now—should be landing shortly. Shall we go to the mess tent and have something cold to drink?"

"No, I don't think that's necessary," the colonel drawled. "I'm Lieutenant Colonel Riggs—14th Wing IG. I'm not here in connection with the movie project. We hear that you're having some, er, maintenance problems with one of your F-80s—tail number four-seven-two-four-four. I'd almost bet that's it parked beneath that shelter over there. Could I have a look at it?"

14 April 1950
Nellis Air Force Base

Ross stood at rigid attention before General Cipolla's desk; the general lounged behind its polished oak surface, his olive-hued features wearing a look of pained tolerance. "Sit down, for Christ's sake, and get that whipped-dog expression off your face."

"Yes, sir."

"Ross, would you tell me just exactly what the fuck you've been up to?"

"You're talking about the airplane, I assume, sir."

"You're goddamned right I'm 'talking about the airplane', Cipolla roared. "Or is there some other stupid stunt you've pulled that should cause me to jerk you away from your squadron on an hour's notice?"

"No, sir. Well, it's sort of like this, General. After that talk we had about replacing the F-80, stopping production and such, I just *had* to try to prove it's a more rugged airplane than everyone seems to think."

"All by yourself. Never mind that the best engineering brains in the industry have set certain limits on the plane's performance—you know better. Never mind that we have a little operation back at Wright Field to do that sort of thing—you're smarter than they are. That's your thinking?"

"It was a dumb thing to do, sir. I accept full responsibility for the incident."

"Oh, I agree with that 'full responsibility' bit," Cipolla shot back. "I'd already reached that conclusion, without your help."

"It seemed that everyone's mind was made up, sir. I couldn't see that there was anything to lose by making one last effort to save the airplane."

"Just your ass, that's all. Now, Riggs tell me you were getting ready to hang a bigger drop tank and enough ordinance to turn the F-80 into another battleship *Missouri*. Is that right?"

"Well, sir, more or less. We've already made one flight with the equivalent of two-hundred-fifty gallon drop tanks."

"*What?*" You flew that plane with—what, maybe *fifteen hundred pounds* hanging on the wingtips?"

"Yes, sir."

"I don't believe it. I—I . . ." Cipolla bounced to his feet and strode to a window. He silently contemplated the landscape, then asked, over his shoulder, "How'd she handle?"

"Perfectly, sir. Doug says he could hardly tell any difference."

"And you planned to add two one-thousand-pound bombs *and* bigger rocket pods on her?"

"Yes, sir. The factory shop drawings—"

"*Factory* shop drawings?"

"Yes, sir."

"I won't even ask. Go ahead."

"They show that a max gross takeoff weight of eighteen thousand pounds is well within design limits."

Cipolla slumped into his chair. "Ross, I assume you know that, as convening authority, I wouldn't even be talking to you if there was any idea of a court-martial."

"I did wonder about that, yes, sir."

"Not that you don't deserve one, but something else has come up. I'm going to cobble up some sort of ops order authorizing something or other—confirming verbal orders, commanding officer—to cover your ass, but you're on notice, hear? Knock that kind of shit off!"

"Yes, sir. May I ask the general a question?"

"I don't see any kind of a gag on your mouth."

"How did Colonel Riggs know we were doing some, ah, informal test work?"

"You gotta snitch in your outfit, Ross. One of the mechanics. Don't worry about it, he won't be there long. But we have more serious things to discuss."

"Yes, sir."

"We've known all along that the Soviets were going all out to build an atomic bomb. Well, last September an intelligence-gathering detachment in Alaska found traces of radioactivity in their rainwater samples."

Ross looked blank.

"The radioactivity had to originate in Siberia—in other words, the bastards were able to explode an atomic device."

"Oh, m'God."

"Yeah. Since that time they've developed a bomb—very similar to our Fat Man—that can be dropped from an airplane."

"The B-29 they got hold of and copied." Ross nodded thoughtfully.

"Right. They call it a TU-4. Launched on a polar route, it can reach the United States."

"I'd heard that—not the A-bomb bit—but *Time* carried an article on the new radar sites being built by Air Defense Command."

Right again, but the radar sites aren't much good without fighters to direct."

"I believe I see where this conversation is headed," Ross said.

"We're activating some Air National Guard squadrons with Mustangs, but USAF wants the first team to suit up. The 66th will relocate to McChord Field, Washington, on TDY until Air Defense Command can get their own jet interceptors."

"When?"

Immediately. You can sign for the classified ops plan when you leave. I want you to go home and brief your troops—a classified briefing, of course. Dependents can only be told that the unit is on a deployment exercise. Have your supply section get priority requisitions submitted for any shortages in your wartime Table of Organization and Equipment. The flying restriction is lifted as of today, so get your crews as close to combat-ready as possible.

"You'll be attached to an air division up there commanded by one Lionel B. Truesdale, a BG with a short fuse. Try to stay out of trouble, hear?"

"You think this may be for real, General?"

"You were at Pearl Harbor, Ross. You remember ever hearing that question before?"

Janet poured dressing over a single salad, then checked the sizzling pork chop. "Finish your drink, dear." Dinner, such as it is, in five minutes."

"I'm ready," Ross drained his martini and struggled to his feet. "Thanks for whipping something up on short notice—I could have grabbed a bite at the club."

"You're out on your feet." Janet slid food onto a tray and asked, "You want to eat on the patio?"

"Great. You want to bring a cup of coffee or after-dinner drink and join me. I'm not long for this wide-awake world."

"Try to keep me away. I can't wait to hear what was so urgent that you had to rush off to Nellis without even having time to change clothes."

Ross cut into his chop. "The entire story is classified, but I must give you some parts of it—I need your help."

"Oh?"

"I sure do. Look, the 66th is being sent to McChord on TDY—don't ask questions, please. Dependents will have the option of staying here in base housing or being moved to their home of record. The news will set off a real storm of conjecture, rumors, and indecision—mainly because they can't be told details.

Ross heard Janet draw a quick, deep breath. "Oh, no," she murmured. "Is it serious, like war or something?"

"It isn't a training exercise." Ross chose his words carefully. "Now, I *don't* think most of the wives, the younger ones especially, will give a second thought to getting the hell away from this place. But if they ask you, and they will, casually suggest they go home—this thing could drag out."

"Then it *is* a threat of war." Janet studied the star-filled night sky. "I don't guess you can give me a hint as to where?"

"You know I can't. And Janet . . ."

"Yes."

"Is Craig Montgomery's offer of that job in San Francisco still open?"

"As far as I know, yes."

"I suggest you take it."

"Somehow, I find that statement more disturbing than anything else you've told me." Janet gathered Ross's empty dishes and added, "I love you more than I can say for putting my interests up front when I know you must have a thousand things on your mind. Unless, or until, all the girls leave, I'll stick around. Some of them need a mother hen. We seem to spend more time living apart than salmon," she observed laughingly. "They at least know they'll get together and mate every spring."

"You're a trooper, Janet, and *I* love *you* for it." Ross chuckled. "Now, while it's still officially spring, I'm going to bed."

Janet paused on her way to the kitchen and rubbed Ross's shoulder with a shorts-clad hip. "Does that mean I have to swim upstream?"

16

The alarm Klaxon's metallic bray reverberated through the sparsely furnished ready room. Ross tossed his paperback novel to the scarred coffee table and leaped to his feet. He saw Ace Aldershot do likewise, and they raced through the doorway toward the pair of F-80s, already plugged into starting units. The 66th pilots had learned after their first practice scramble that one didn't stroll, didn't trot, or otherwise dawdle after the warning horn sounded.

Brigadier General Truesdale had provided guidance in terms easy to understand. He'd arrived outside operations the morning following Ross's statement that his pilots and planes were operational. Stepping from his staff car, he'd said, "Morning, Major. Let's see how long it takes you to get your alert birds airborne." He'd crossed to the Klaxon's manual switch and pressed its red button.

Twenty minutes later, Ross watched with a measure of pride as the last of the four aircraft standing alert taxied toward the runway. Truesdale had paused in the act of returning to his sedan and said, "When your crews can do that in five minutes, give me a call. I'll come back and we'll talk."

Ross's cheeks still burned when he recalled that caustic evaluation. He and Ace had driven their pilots like galley slaves. By week's end, he was able to show the acerbic wing commander that each of his twelve pilots could measure up. He and Ace still took their turn standing alert, however—an ongoing learning process. This air defense mission was different. He scrambled into the already preflighted and cocked F-80's cockpit and donned his helmet while the crew chief helped him strap in. His watch showed that three minutes had elapsed when he pressed the starter switch.

Turning onto the main taxiway, Ross thumbed the mike button.

"McChord Tower, this is Blaze One on a hot scramble; flight of two, over." Seeing Ace fall into trail, he ran a swift scan of the instrument panel and closed the canopy.

"Blaze One is cleared for immediate takeoff," he heard the tower operator drone. "Climb to ten thousand feet of a heading of three-zero-zero and contact Flashlight on tactical frequency. Report reaching ten thousand and leaving tower frequency, over."

The flight broke into bright sunlight above Seattle's ever-present layer of haze and mist. Ross punched the VHF channel selector and called, "Flashlight, this is Blaze One, flight of two, climbing to ten thousand, over."

"Roger, Blaze One, this is Flashlight. Squawk ident, over."

"Blaze One, squawking ident."

"Roger, have you in positive radar contact. We have an unidentified aircraft, bearing three-one-zero degrees from your present position, altitude devils eight, range one hundred twenty miles. Stand by for vectors to intercept, over."

Ross acknowledged and rechecked to see that his eight fifty-caliber guns were armed. Foolish? he wondered. Looking for attacking bombers over Canada? A week of intensive briefings had proved sobering. A sneak attack *wasn't* some paranoid general's dream. Pearl Harbor was a grim reminder. Even now, a dozen Russian TU-4s could be sweeping toward the Canadian–U.S. border. Their strategically placed atomic bombs could eliminate 70 percent of American production capacity! Unbelievable, until you saw the analysis.

"Turn right, heading three-two-zero to place you parallel to bogey's inbound course," Ross heard Flashlight advise. "Expect visual contact in one–five minutes." He shook his head. This was something. To be able to spot airplanes two hundred miles away and direct an interceptor to within a matter of yards was spooky.

Ross glanced at his map. The target was off airways, and over water, it appeared. Probably another joe blundering around either way off course or without a flight plan. Civilian pilots just couldn't get used to the fact that *all* aircraft approaching from the north had to be identified, if not by flight plan, then by a visual intercept. He glanced across at Ace, off his right wing, and saw him give a thumbs up that he was copying Flashlight's instructions.

A speck, just below the horizon, caught Ross's attention. Flashlight's terse, "Bogey is at your one-o'clock position, Blaze One. Atmospheric conditions permitting, you should acquire visually at this time," followed almost immediately.

Ross felt his gut tighten. Decision time. The response to his questions during the brief training sessions—What are the rules of engagement? When do we shoot?—left him uneasy. Glib assurance that "The radar site maintains an open line to the division command post, the pilot will receive instructions after identifying the bogey," disregarded a lot of possibilities. If positive identification was left to the pilot, any decision reached on the ground was nothing more than guesswork.

"During World War II, the Germans rebuilt some crashed B-17s. They'd join our formations and unload," he'd insisted. "What's to keep the Reds from putting USAF markings on a TU-4?" The scenario had been dismissed as too unlikely to consider seriously. He shrugged and pressed the mike button.

"Unidentified aircraft one hundred miles north of Seattle at twelve thousand feet, be advised you have entered restricted airspace. If you have transponder equipment, place the transmitter in the ident position. Also identify yourself on all radio emergency frequencies and provide point of departure and destination, over."

The interval between them was closing rapidly. The plane was a four-engine type resembling a C-54. Ross waited two minutes and repeated his message. After no response was forthcoming, he switched channels. "Flashlight, this is Blaze One. I have visual contact with a four-engine aircraft that appears to be a transport, probably a DC-4. Unable to contact on emergency frequency. Please advise."

"You are authorized to close to a five-hundred-foot interval, Blaze One. Relay all identifing numbers and markings, over."

"Roger, Flashlight, I'm . . ." Ross blinked in disbelief. "Flashlight, the aircraft has just entered a steep turn to the west and descending—I'm in pursuit!"

"Stand by, Blaze One—stand by." The controller's voice crackled with tension.

"He's headed for a cloudbank about ten miles west, Flashlight. Shall I intercept? Repeat: Shall I intercept?"

"Stand by, Blaze One. I repeat: Stand by. Maintain surveillance, but do not take any action to endanger the aircraft."

"Understand, Flashlight—I'm standing by and maintaining visual contact. Please confirm that we are within the Air Defense Identification Zone—according to my dead reckoning, he's going to be over international waters in about five minutes."

"Be advised that we have lost radar contact with the aircraft, Blaze One, and division command post has terminated the mission. Return to base and submit a report of intercept by Flash precedence."

Ross saw the blue staff car pull away from operations before he had even finished his engine shutdown. It was General Truesdale's car, he was certain, but its tag displaying the single white star was covered. A wide-eyed crew chief helped him unhook and asked, "What the hell happened? This place has gone apeshit."

"Damned if I know." Ross grinned. "That's what's so funny—I don't think anyone else knows either." He stopped as the staff car pulled alongside.

"Colyer? Aldershot? Hop in. The old man wants an immediate rundown—before you file your incident report." After Ross and Ace had seated themselves, the officer Ross recognized as Colonel Sebastian, wing director of ops, asked, "All right, just what the hell happened back there?"

Ross retrieved his notebook from a knee pocket and answered, "Blaze One and Two scrambled at oh-two-forty-two Zulu, and contacted Flashlight Control at oh-two-forty-seven. I was advised—"

"Oh, shit. I don't want a travelogue. What the hell *happened?*"

"Well, sir, short and sweet, we were vectored to intercept a four-engine airplane about a hundred and twenty miles northwest. After we couldn't raise him on emergency channel, Flashlight directed us to close and make a visual identification. All of the sudden he hauled ass and headed for the cover of a cloudbank. Flashlight terminated the mission and sent us home."

"The GCI controller says you wanted to shoot him down. Is that right?"

"Well, sir, I don't recall using those words, but he was acting in a hostile manner; he was within the ADIZ—I think a burst across his nose might have changed his mind about escaping."

"Jesus Christ. You cowboys from World War II have a lot to learn. We aren't at war—you can't just go shooting down everyone who violates the civil air regs."

Ross felt blood rush to his face. General Cipolla's parting admonition came to mind: "Try to stay out of trouble, hear?"

"No, sir, I guess we can't." He saw a look of astonishment cross Ace's angry features.

20 June 1950
Kweilin Air Base, People's Republic of China

"To me it's absolute nonsense," Yuri said. "Captain Liu Shan was one of the best Yak-9 pilots in the squadron—a flight leader with more than five hundred sorties. Discipline, yes, of course. But to strip him of all rank and ratings? No one could have salvaged that landing—a lesser skilled pilot wouldn't even have walked away from the accident scene. So he blew a tire on landing? One that was worn to the cords to begin with. If they must punish someone, find the corrupt commissar who wouldn't authorize replacement of the tire."

Major Malozenov rubbed the stubble of brown hair covering his scalp and scowled. "Watch your comments regarding the CPA political officers, Yuri Sergeievich. They take the loss of scarce equipment most seriously. Men—even highly skilled officers such as Liu Shan—are expendable. A private is executed for losing his rifle. Do not protest. It is their army, and we are, after all, here at their invitation."

Yuri snorted. "Here at their invitation, my sick ox. We are here because their chairman went to Moscow and begged for help in liberating the island of Taiwan. Because of that visit, I'm here in this miserable place flying obsolete propeller planes—instead of being a pilot first class in jet fighters and stationed at a base where it never snows. And please don't think I was comparing you to that moronic Lin, their *zampolit.*"

Malozenov shot Yuri a sharp glance from deep-set, piggish eyes. "Major Lin has already filed a report blaming Liu Shan's accident on poor instruction technique."

"Is that right?" At the last minute Yuri desisted from expressing his opinion of Major Lin's knowledge of airplanes. Chinese political officers, like those in the USSR, wore air force uniforms but only flew as passengers.

"You come very close to expressing deviationism at times, Yuri Sergeievich," Malozenov continued. "Take care; remember the price your father pays for that crime."

"My father is innocent of *any* crime, Comrade Major." Yuri strode to the edge of the small, covered porch sheltering the entrance to their hostel. Without turning, he added, "When the investigation is finished, he will be exonerated and restored to his rightful status." He gazed at the foreign landscape, unwilling to expose his smoldering rage to the stolid political officer.

"If you insist, Comrade Lieutenant; if you insist. But the investigation you speak of has dragged on for several weeks. It might be well for you to denounce him now and spare yourself the consequences if he is found guilty. The party will most certainly expel you as politically unreliable if that happens. I will document testimony of your denouncement and self-criticism. And it will be much more convincing if done now instead of after the fact."

Yuri ceased grinding his teeth and forced himself to adopt a more conciliatory attitude. "I apologize for my outburst, Comrade Major. I don't question the *party's* judgment, but I have reason to believe my father is falsely accused by enemies inside the NKVD. Actually, I hope for a trial before judges who will ferret out the truth."

Keep this fat fool on your side, Yuri admonished himself. He is your only source of official information from Moscow. While he was undoubtedly banished to this remote outpost because of laziness, ineptitude, and drunkenness—and can't, in all probability, be of help—he can certainly stir up mischief if he takes a dislike to you.

Malozenov's fleshy jowls jiggled a nodded acceptance of Yuri's apology. "Such can't be discounted," he observed carefully. "Power such as theirs breeds an arrogant disregard for the welfare of the people. Marx himself cautioned against this."

Yuri smiled inwardly. The Air Force Political Administration had as much reason to fear the NKVD as did the military—one of his fellow instructors had already been enlisted by Malozenov to watch for evidence of an undercover NKVD informer in their ranks. But as for himself, he would continue to be the major's trusted confidant, despite his contempt for the man. Only last week he had filled in for Malozenov at the Saturday morning political discussion—the major being the worse for wear after an all-night session imbibing lethal Chinese "whiskey."

Daily, Yuri repeated his vow: Advance in the party by word and deed. Become the best pilot in the Soviet air force; do that by whatever means. Prepare for that day when you will be listened to with respect as you plead your father's case.

He yearned for news from home, but Marshal Yokolov had cautioned him, "You will be virtually incommunicado in China, Yuri. Your very presence there cannot be officially acknowledged. Mail will be forwarded from a central address in Moscow, however. Do you have someone, not family, who could be expected to correspond with you?"

"Marya," Yuri replied after some thought. "We were, well—"

"Lovers," Yokolov finished for him. "Perfect. I met the girl at your father's home, remember? Expect a letter from her once a month—closely censored, of course. If she writes of such things as attending the ballet, youth rallies, and the like, you'll know that things are well. If she injects a note of sadness, disappointment, or unhappiness, be aware that problems are surfacing for your father. If a two-month period passes without a letter, or if the words 'bright blue babushka' are included, prepare for the worst."

Yuri's dark thoughts were interrupted by sound reverberating through the compound of the huge gong used to announce an airfield emergency. Yuri stood. "Damn. I suppose I'd best go to operations. Thankfully, I have no students aloft this afternoon. But the accident yesterday has everyone jittery. Nothing would surprise me."

An excited Major Lin met Yuri at the door to operations. "Comrade Pavel! Cadet Wu Yung is overdue for landing."

Yuri eyed the slender, dapper-uniformed Chinese with distaste. A pencil-line mustache gave him a resemblance to the caricatures of Chinese bandits Tass used to display. "Ah, so," Yuri said. "Does he speak on the radio?"

"No, the fool probably forgot to turn it on. What will you do?"

Yuri ignored Lin's question and turned to the worried operations officer standing nearby. "What is his mission?"

"Fly northwest sector at three thousand meters and practice fighting maneuvers with Cadet Chang Shiu."

"Have you spoken with Cadet Chang on the radio?"

"We have, Comrade Lieutenant. He is unable to see the plane flown by Wu Yung."

"How much fuel does Wu Yung have remaining?"

"Enough for one more hour only."

"I see. Prepare a plane for me while I change into flying gear. Perhaps his radio has failed because of defective parts"—he shot Lin a venomous look—"and he can't find the field. I'll search the local flying area."

Yuri ran the starting checklist for the familiar Yak-9 fighter and called the tower for takeoff clearance. Actually, he thought, an opportunity to fly a sortie without a student to nurture was a welcome change. This older, slower aircraft he'd flown during his own training was less demanding than the swift, somewhat temperamental MiG. It gave the pilot time to enjoy the experience.

Climbing to three thousand meters, Yuri selected several channels on his radio and attempted to raise the wayward student. He gave up and tried to decide what the fledgling pilot would do after discovering that his radio was inoperative. At this altitude he was about a ABOVE deck of scattered cumulus clouds. Wu would go underneath, Yuri decided to hunt for the river or some landmark he can recognize. The mounds!

Yuri rolled into a diving turn and headed for the southeast sector, where the flat plain was dotted with huge, smooth mounds of solid granite. Centuries of ceaseless wind had eroded loose soil to expose the stone monuments, some reaching a hundred meters in height. Visible for miles, they would be an invaluable beacon for a lost pilot.

As he scanned the sky from a lazy orbit, his thoughts drifted to last night's news broadcast from Radio Peking. The Chinese people were being prepared for the forthcoming invasion of Taiwan. In strident tones, the announcer had condemned the United States' imperialistic policies toward Asia. "They attempt to bribe the weaker governments of Japan, Korea, and Taiwan into joining their unholy cabal!" he'd screamed. "The People's Republic of China's only response must be to restore territorial sovereignty—liberate Taiwan and Tibet!"

The Chinese Air Force's role in the rapidly approaching conflict didn't seem clear. No movement orders had been issued to place the fighter-bombers closer to the coast. In fact, the Chinese students were blissfully unaware that they were preparing for imminent combat.

The entire Chinese Air Force was woefully unprepared to engage in hostilities, Yuri suspected. Cadet Wu Yung was a good example. The young man had more than three hundred sorties in his logbook, yet he still couldn't find his way home from the local flying area. Proficiency in gunnery and delivery of bombs and rockets was laughable. It was unlikely that they could even *find* the island called Formosa, much less inflict significant damage.

The entire invasion plan remained cloaked in official silence. Major Malozenov had parried a question in this regard with, "Appropriate plans exist to deal with any contingency. You will be informed at the proper time."

More important, Yuri wondered, What role would the Russian instructor pilots play? The prospect of leading an air strike was both exciting and chilling. Properly executed, and assuming a CPA victory, praise by the general staff could be the beginning of his march to recognition. What resistance would they meet? It would seem reasonable to assume that the Americans were supplying arms to the renegade government. Airplanes? Not likely—not yet, at least. But the imperialist warmongers had the world's most powerful navy, including aircraft carriers. And the Bomb. Would they dare risk incurring the wrath of China's friends by using it?

Yuri returned to a glum assessment of his situation. That he was considered the de facto leader of the detachment of instructors and mechanics gave him little satisfaction. He accepted the distinction without protest solely because of his vow to gain recognition. Only he and two other instructors spoke passable Chinese. The others, Malozenov included, could barely make themselves understood. Ironically, English evolved as the language of choice for the Russian instructors and their students.

It did provide him an advantage, he conceded. He was expected to monitor radio broadcasts closely and relay important news to the others. He'd developed a habit of being somewhat selective with regard to what he told the political officer. Exactly why, he wasn't sure, but certain scraps of information he'd picked up during late-night broadcasts from a station on Taiwan were disturbing. An invasion of the little island could prove difficult.

A speck flitting across the distant terrain caught Yuri's eye. He turned toward it and increased his airspeed. Moments later, he identified it as a

Yak-9 fighter plane. He drew alongside and checked its markings: He'd found the lost Wu Yung.

Yuri parked next to Wu's aircraft and raced to be first to reach the shaken student. "What went wrong?" he snapped.

Wu Yung shook his head. "No electric power."

Yuri scanned the cockpit. The generator switch was in the OFF position. He reached across the cockpit and jerked the radio master control knob from its shaft. He pressed the broken part in Yung's hand and hissed, "Listen to me: This broke and came off in your hand when you tried to change frequencies. A defective part—Major Lin will have your head otherwise. Understand?"

Comprehension dawned in the young cadet's wide eyes. He nodded just as Major Lin's vehicle skidded to a stop beside the left wing.

17

Janet shifted to a more comfortable position in the padded theater-type seat. A half-dozen shadowy figures surrounded her in KSTV's darkened viewing studio; all eyes were focused on the wall-mounted television monitor. THE JET AIR FORCE—America's Guardian of Peace, flashed on the screen to a background of the air force's familiar, "Off we go . . ." The leader was followed by A FEATURE PRESENTATION OF THE BAY AREA'S LEADING TELEVISION STATION—KSTV.

"Your name will be on the next screen of credits," Craig Montgomery murmured at her left elbow.

Janet placed a steno pad on her knee and replied, "Why am I so damn nervous? I wish I could watch the reaction on the other's faces."

Craig chuckled. "Relax. Everyone who's previewed the film gives it four stars. Production is very impressed with your ideas for reformatting the news broadcasts, by the way—as is Don Simpson, who'll be doing the narration."

A flight of F-80s filled the screen then, and conversation ceased. Background music was replaced by the whining roar of jet engines. Janet glimpsed an usher whispering in Montgomery's ear. Craig picked up a handset cradled on the seatback in front of him and snapped, "Kill it and switch to monitor two."

The mutters behind them—"What's going . . . ?" "Hey! What the hell . . ."—ceased as the screen displaying the air force feature went dark and an adjacent one sprang to life. Don Simpson's handsome features filled the flickering rectangle; he was saying, ". . . interrupt our regular programming to bring you this news bulletin. I've just been handed a dispatch from Reuters International News stating that early this morning, units of the South Korean Army launched an attack across their border

182

with North Korea on the Ongjin peninsula. Fierce fighting is reported, and forces of the North Korean People's Army are said to be pressing a determined counterattack. Stay tuned . . ."

Montgomery sprang to his feet. "Okay, show's over. Let's get to our desks and try to find out what's going on. Janet, get with your old friends at INS. JoJo, head for the navy base. I'll try to raise someone at the Korean embassy. Why do big stories have to break on Sunday? Let's hit it!"

1602 Hours, 25 June 1950
McChord Air Force Base

"Roger, Flashlight; a good run. Request vectors to McChord VOR for pancake, over." Ross stretched aching shoulder muscles and checked the formation tucked into a fingertip formation behind him. He'd been driving his pilots to the limit learning to operate routinely in Seattle weather. An abrupt change from the desert, and chronic fog and low ceilings had given the newer pilots a problem. But they were getting pretty damn good, he thought. Maybe, with summer coming on, I can relax the training schedule a bit.

"Understand, Blaze One. Exercise terminated at oh-three-one-one Zulu. Turn right to heading zero-eight-zero for McChord VOR. ATC has cleared Blaze Flight to descend to and maintain four thousand. Contact McChord approach control on one-one-eight decimal five for approach clearance. Report leaving this frequency."

Ross acknowledged and gave directions for the flight to prepare for a weather penetration. He extended speed brakes and nosed over into swirling murk. As the altimeter unwound past ten thousand, he changed frequencies and said, "McChord Approach, this is Blaze Flight, fifty miles west, descending through ten for four thousand, over."

"Roger, Blaze Flight. You're cleared for VOR approach to runway three-one. McChord weather is two thousand broken, seven miles' visibility with haze and fog, winds light and variable. Altimeter two-niner-decimal-eight-niner—descend to three thousand and report procedure turn inbound, over."

Ross read back his clearance, then returned back to Flashlight Control. Before he could make his position report, he saw red OFF flags drop across his VOR direction indicator. "Flashlight, Blaze One here. I have indication of a navigation radio malfunction. Please confirm my position as fifty west of McChord on the zero-eight-zero radial, over."

"Blaze One, this is Flashlight. Be advised that you've dropped below our radar coverage. If you're experiencing an emergency, climb to ten thousand on a heading of two-seven-zero, squawking ident for reacquisition, over."

Ross blinked. What the hell, he thought. Before he could react, the OFF flags disappeared. "Disregard my last transmission, Flashlight. I'm continuing approach under McChord control, over."

Ross led his three wingmen into operations and tossed his clearance onto the counter. "Blaze Flight, down," he told the clerk. Turning to the others, he said, "Okay, guys, you're stood down until oh-eight-hundred. It was a good flight all the way." He returned their pleased grins and entered the corridor leading to the ADC command post.

"Sorry, Major, the command post is a restricted area. Do you have a green ID badge?" Ross drew up short. An armed guard on the command post? A restricted area? What the hell is going on? he wondered.

"Uh, I'm Major Colyer, CO of the 66th Squadron I don't know anything about this 'green' badge, but I have business inside."

"I recognize the major, but I'll have to ask someone to escort you. I'm sorry, but I can't admit you without proper identification." He pressed a button alongside the closed door.

A captain Ross recognized as a command post duty officer responded. "Hi, Smitty," Ross said. "I'd like to see the duty controller. What's with the moat and drawbridge act?"

"Oh, hi, Major. C'mon in. ADC just went on yellow alert. The colonel is in a meeting, but he should be able to see you in a minute."

"We're on a *yellow* alert?" Ross asked as the door closed behind him.

"Right. Things are still kinda confused, but the North Koreans just invaded South Korea early this morning. All hell's breaking loose. I just finished talking to your ops officer—your squadron is on fifteen-minute standby, leaves canceled—the whole bit."

"Jesus Christ, I'd better get down there." Ross turned to leave, but hesitated as he saw General Truesdale and Colonel Sebastian emerge from the meeting room.

"Oh, Major Colyer," Truesdale said. "Guess you just landed. Have you gotten the word yet?"

"Yes, sir. I'm on my way back to the squadron. Can you tell me what's up? It's hard to figure why we're going all the way to yellow just because of a border clash five thousand miles away."

"There'll be a briefing for all unit commanders tomorrow morning, Colyer," Sebastian interjected. "In the meantime, just get your planes and crews up to top readiness." He turned to Truesdale. "We're lucky to have Major Colyer if we're going to war, General," he said with a smirk. "He's the one who wanted to shoot down a civilian passenger plane because we didn't have a flight plan for it. Did you run across another one today, Major?"

Ross forced a stiff smile. "No, sir. But I did have an experience that bothers me. I came straight here to report it."

"Oh?"

"Yes, sir. Our flight was returning from a practice scramble. About fifty miles west, we were cleared to three thousand feet for approach. I had a temporary loss of VOR signal and called Flashlight for verification of our position. The GCI controller said that we'd dropped below their radar coverage."

"Yes, we know that happens. You see, radar works on the line-of-sight principle. The higher you can locate a Ground Controlled Intercept set, the farther it'll reach. Flashlight is on Squaw Mountain, about seven thousand feet elevation. The dish can't be depressed for a return below about three or four thousand feet. I trust you didn't have a problem?"

"No, sir, it was just a temporary loss of signal. But sir . . . ?"

"Yes?"

"It occurred to me: What if I had been flying a TU-4 with an A-bomb on board? I could have flown right over the center of Seattle without a shot ever being fired at me."

Sebastian laughed. "Now you sound like those nervous Nellies in Colorado Springs. There's a crowd there that preaches the same thing. Colyer, the chances of a plane the size of a B-29 getting that close, flying at low altitude, are zero to none."

"How about a B-24?" Ross asked softly.

"A what? A B-24? Well, the Reds don't have any, but we'll include them."

"Colonel, I flew on the low-level raid over Ploesti. We took a hundred and seventy B-24s two thousand miles and dropped at an altitude of fifty feet. They were waiting for us, and we got the shit shot out of us—but we still put thirty percent of our bombs on target. It takes only one A-bomb."

"Another time; another situation." Sebastian waved a hand in airy dismissal. "You persist in refighting that war. It could never happen here. Now, General, if you'll excuse me, I'll get that briefing for tomorrow put together."

Truesdale grunted permission. A thoughtful expression on his face, he said, "How about stepping inside the conference room with me for a minute, Major. I'd like to hear some more about this low-level threat you perceive."

Ross tossed his gear onto his bunk and picked up a scrawled note. "Major Colyer: Your wife called and asks you to call back tonight. She says it's urgent. That if she isn't at the hotel, to try the TV station." Ross glanced at his watch. Time for a shower, a change, and a quick bite at the club. He shook his head—urgent—she'd heard about the Korean incident. Well, he had bigger problems right now than what to tell the squadron wives back at Hanson.

It was past seven o'clock when Ross paid his check and strolled to the club's public phone booth. Janet answered before the second ring. "Hi, honey, this is Ross. How's your vacation coming? I got your message. What's so urgent?"

"Oh, Ross. God, it's always good to hear from you. A few days away from the base has been a lifesaver, and the TV film turned out simply great—Craig and the people at the station have nothing but good things to say about it. But Ross, this business in Korea. Is it going to affect you?"

Ross laughed. "You probably know more about what's going on over there than I do. We're getting a briefing tomorrow morning, but I don't see any signs of packing up and moving out. Why?"

"Well, I called General Cipolla this afternoon—don't get mad, now— he *told* me to call him anytime I had a problem. The girls at Hanson—I also talked to Betsy Curtiss. She says they're pretty worked up."

"What did the general say?"

"Well, he said in effect that it was unlikely the squadron would be brought back to Hanson in a strictly training status anytime soon."

"And?"

"What do you think?"

"Far be it from me to contradict the general. Janet, you're talking in circles. What's really bothering you?"

"I miss you, damnit. If the dependents should be sent back to their homes of record, would you want me to come to Seattle and live off base?"

Ross chewed his lower lip and stared at the pay phone's dial. He mentally replayed his conversation with General Truesdale that afternoon. "I can't really answer that until I attend this briefing tomorrow morning— not that I wouldn't *want* to have you here—but, you know. It may be bad timing, until we see how this Korean thing goes."

Janet's indrawn breath was audible above the long-distance circuit's background static. "Ross, remember what you said back at Hanson about taking Craig Montgomery's job offer?"

"Yeah, and I meant it."

"And I meant it when I said I'd stay with the squadron wives as long as you thought it was important. If all the wives are sent home, would you still be agreeable to me taking a job with the station?"

"Full time?"

"That was the offer."

"Doing what?"

"If this Korean incident becomes serious, if we are drawn into it, I'd like to cover the situation—from over there."

"Oh, for Christ's sake, Janet—no, wait a minute. Forget I said that. Was this Montgomery's idea?"

"No. I wanted to talk it over with you before I suggested it. I believe he'd approve it, however."

"This is important to you, isn't it?"

"Not as important as having a good marriage; raising our family; being with you for more than three months at a time; sharing our life. But if we can't have that, then I need something to—oh, hell, I'm saying this all wrong, aren't I?"

"Not at all. I can't say no. *If* the girls at Hanson are sent home, I'll not ask that you come to Seattle. We're here on TDY—it would be Dayton and Wright Field all over. I don't like the idea of your going to a possible war zone, but if it's gonna be, it's gonna be."

"Your time is up, caller," a nasal voice interrupted. "Please deposit one dollar, twenty-five cents for another three minutes."

"Thank you, operator. Let me know what you decide, Janet, okay?"

"I will. I love you very, very much, Ross Colyer." Ross was left listening to a dial tone.

2134 Hours, 25 June 1950
San Francisco

Craig eyed the scattering of used coffee cups and remains of sandwiches littering the conference table. "Almost midnight—time to sum up and go home, troops," he announced to the six weary members of the news section. "And for Christ's sake, will someone get a janitor in here so we can use this table for something besides eating and drinking? JoJo, what do you have for the six A.M. slot?"

The red-eyed middle-aged reporter flipped pages of a spiral-bound notebook. "Well," he drawled, "the navy has put a gag order on everyone at fleet headquarters regarding Korea. I did overhear a conversation to the effect that the president's sending the Seventh Fleet to Taiwan, however."

"What the hell does that have to do with the price of eggs in Korea, JoJo?" an exasperated voice inquired.

"Damned if I know," JoJo confessed. "But it made my nose twitch. Why—in the middle of a panic like this border skirmish—would the navy be in such a rush to deploy a task force to a spot damn near fifteen hundred miles away from the fighting?"

Janet regarded the veteran reporter with new interest. "You know, Craig, I came away from INS with a similar reaction. This doesn't appear to be just an exchange between some border guards who got bored and started shooting for the hell of it. Their Tokyo bureau is sending estimates of maybe ten thousand NKPA troops along that little stretch of border. Supposedly their 'counterattack' is now almost thirty miles deep inside South Korea. MacArthur has all U.S. forces on full alert."

Craig rubbed unshaven jowls and assumed a reflective expression. "Well, it looks as if we may have a big story on our hands. Keep digging. Don has wire dispatches a foot deep he can read for the early morning spot. Maybe we can get a break before the evening news. Let's get some sleep now. Oh, Janet—could you stay for a moment?"

Janet said her good nights and moved to let the cleaning crew finish. "I won't keep you long," Montgomery said. "It's just that I feel so damn frustrated. I'm a businessman, and I'm convinced television will be big, really big business. We have a great program director, but this live news aspect is new to all of us. I can't get a handle on how to organize it. Do you have any new ideas?"

"Craig, you have the right instincts. There's an old adage among writers: Show, don't tell." Janet opened her notebook. "Today, for example. We can't use what JoJo and I spent a half day to get. When Don repeats what we saw and were told, it's secondhand rumor. But if we'd had a photographer along to record those conversations, the implications would be clear. Now, Don is handsome and has a beautiful speaking style, but for him to read all those dispatches—well, it'll be boring.

"This, to me, is what's so exciting about TV news—the viewer is right on the spot *seeing* the action. People would rather see news themselves than have it read to them."

"A good point, Janet. I agree. This incident convinces me that I need a department head to do nothing but oversee the gathering and presenting of news. Remember that talk we had back at Hanson?"

"About full-time employment?"

"Right. Will you take on the job?"

"Oh, Craig. I'd love to, but I know my limitations. You need someone with contacts, a respected name in the news business. Besides, it wouldn't be fair to you if I accepted a job with long-term career implications. I have a husband to think of. I can't guarantee I'll be here indefinitely."

"I admire your honesty, Janet. Speaking of Ross, have you been able to get his reaction to this Korean business?"

"I talked to him briefly, earlier this evening." Janet selected her words carefully. "Somehow I don't think this Korean affair is a big surprise to him."

"Oh?"

"Sorry, Craig. Nothing I could use."

"I understand. Well, I guess I'd better start looking for a top-notch news director. Any suggestions?"

A faint smile tugged at Janet's lips. "You know, I just may have someone for you. The man I talked with at INS today, Clay Henderson—he gave me my first job and he's a super guy. I got the impression that he's less than happy with his position. When I told him what I'm doing, he said he envies me, that he feels stale. Also, Clay is at a dead end unless he goes to New York and joins what he calls 'that bunch of has-beens' there. This challenge would be right down his alley. But he'd be expensive."

"The man sounds perfect." Craig retrieved a crumpled napkin and rubbed at a spot of ketchup on the tabletop. "Okay, this is no time to pinch pennies. I'll call him tomorow."

"You won't regret it, *if* he agrees. Craig, I feel rotten about asking for a favor after I've turned down your job offer, but may I?"

"Of course."

"I love this work—it's in my blood. I promised Ross to stay at Hanson as long as any of the other wives did so, but I'd love to be able to do more features for you." She took a deep breath. "In fact, I have an idea. . . ."

30 June 1950
Kweilin, China

Yuri shifted position on the crude wooden bench and tried to maintain an observant expression. One hundred plus bodies packed inside the corrugated-iron hangar, already radiating heat from the noonday sun, brought both temperature and humidity to steam-bath level. Major Lin, apparently minus sweat glands, his diminutive figure clad in a freshly pressed uniform, waved his arms in outraged gestulation as he hurled words at his captive audience.

Why are the Russians at this hastily called assembly? Yuri wondered. He glanced at his fellow instructors flanking him; all looked blankly miserable. Blank because other than two of them, they couldn't understand a word being said. Despite his misery, Yuri permitted himself a chuckle that evoked an icy glare from Major Malozenov, seated alongside. Yuri sobered immediately and concentrated on taking mental notes. It would be his lot to explain later what the agitated political officer was telling the group of Chinese officers and NCOs.

"Fewer than twenty-four hours ago, the imperialistic American gangsters loosed their puppet mad dogs in South Korea, led by the traitor Syngman Rhee, against their peace-loving neighbors north of the thirty-eighth parallel. Launching a savage attack under the concealing cloak of darkness, the butchers killed, raped, and looted at will before defensive forces of the People's Democratic Republic of Korea could be mobilized."

Yuri blinked. What is this? he asked himself. That incident was reported three days ago on Radio Taiwan. Why is Lin telling them otherwise? He glanced sideways at the dour-expressioned Malozenov. Does he know? He gets his information from Moscow. Should I tell him that I listen to shortwave broadcasts other than Radio Peking?

"But the people's glorious leader, Kim Il Sung, was not caught napping." Spittle flew from between Lin's lips as he became even more incensed. "With brilliant foresight, he had foreseen the perfidious American intent: to destabilize all of Asia. Set neighbor against neighbor, incite armed conflict, then smugly place their power at the disposal of the illegal aggressors. Brave soldiers responded to his call and even today have driven the cowardly attackers deep into South Korea."

"Why is he telling us all about Korea?" Yuri whispered to Malozenov. "What does this have to do with the invasion of Taiwan?"

The major's scowl deepened. With his sketchy understanding of Chinese, he could grasp only the gist of the commissar's comments. He didn't reply.

"The power-mad members of that group of lackeys who gather at the United Nations have meekly agreed that the American Seventh Fleet should be sent off our shores to, 'keep the peace.'" Lin sneered. "Their scheme will fail, however. Despite Western aid to Rhee's corrupt government, the gallant army of the People's Democratic Republic will quell the dissidents and unite that country's loyal citizens.

"Closer to home, yet another example of Western treachery has been exposed. Units of the Chinese People's Army stationed around Canton have been stricken with an epidemic of schistosomiasis. A training exercise these troops were to take part in has been canceled as a result. Investigators from our political administration have discovered conclusive evidence that the microbes were induced into the army's food and water by foreign saboteurs."

Oh-ho, Yuri thought. The invasion has been called off. I see now why Lin had the Russian contingent attend his meeting. They know that we know about the planned invasion. This is their way of telling us they've changed their minds without losing face.

I wonder what's in store for us? Will we continue to train pilots for a battle that may never be fought? Is the chance to distinguish myself in battle to be lost? *If* it ever was intended that the instructors would participate in the invasion. Malozenov had dismissed his question with a curt, "Do not indulge in idle speculation, Yuri Pavel." His thoughts turned to Marya's last letter, folded in his breast pocket. She'd written, ". . . The bread ration was increased again this week, and we seldom have to line up for milk and cheese. . . ." Good news. Papa's situation remained unchanged.

A change in Major Lin's strident harangue prompted a flash of insight. The American fleet off our shores is actually standing by off the island of Taiwan, Yuri realized. The epidemic of schistosomiasis within the invasion task force is a lie. The Chinese are afraid to attack! We may be here indefinitely.

He sighed. Would he ever see his beloved MiG-15s again?

18

Janet pressed her face to the Boeing Stratocruiser's porthole-size window, searching for a glimpse of Mount Fuji on the haze-shrouded horizon. Do they never wash these things? she wondered. She leaned back in her seat and chuckled. The blowsy blonde seated beside her roused and regarded Janet with a vacuous stare.

"Sorry. I thought the window was dirty, but it's just that my eyes are half glued shut from lack of sleep," Janet said.

"Yeah, it's been a bitch, hasn't it?" the blonde—she'd introduced herself as Eva—mumbled. She peered at her watch. "I lost it all back at Wake Island when we crossed that international date line. Is this yesterday or tomorrow?"

"I'm not sure I really care," Janet replied. "I'll just take someone's word for it when we get on the ground."

"That damned Clyde better be there to meet me. And he'd better have a place for us to live lined up—one with a soft bed and hot shower." Eva crossed her legs clad in rumpled, red slacks and returned to the near-comatose state of insulation she'd occupied for the past twenty-four hours.

Janet closed her own eyes and thought back over the past three weeks. Hectic? Wild? Confused? She searched her mental thesaurus for an appropriate term. It had started the Monday morning Clayton Henderson showed up at Craig's KSTV offices. He hadn't just accepted Craig's offer—he'd pounced.

"I can't believe I'm so damned lucky," he'd announced to Craig and Janet. "To be able to do something I've always dreamed of, and at my age, well . . ." His dark eyes gleamed from normally saturnine features. "I'm ready to start right now; I can clean up things at INS at night. So, what's happening?"

Janet threw her briefcase onto the table and removed a stack of assorted papers and magazines. She selected copies of *Life* and *Look* magazines and tossed them in front of her new boss. "Pictures, Clay. Action, events that happened today right in your living room tonight—with the people involved telling you the story."

"Yeah," Henderson breathed. "With one of the really nifty portable movie cameras coming out, it can be done. I like it."

"Another reporter and I spent a half day doing interviews last week." Janet paced excitedly as she talked. "When the pieces aired it was just Don Simpson—and he's a great announcer—*reading* our notes. Hell, people would rather *see* news themselves, not have someone else read it to them. Newsreels at the theaters, great picture mags, like these, are fine to look at, but the news is stale."

"Gotcha. I know an ace photog who'll walk through fire to get in on this. And two stories are breaking right now that are tailor-made for this medium. I'm a word editor, Craig, but with Janet to help me with the picture angle, we'll knock 'em dead."

"Well, Clay"—Montgomery cleared his throat—"I know you're going to give KSTV a great news department. But Janet thinks she has a first-rate leadoff project."

"Yeah? What's your thinking, Janet?"

"Korea."

"That little skirmish? It'll be outta the news in two weeks, and it's damn near five thousand miles away."

"On the five-thousand-miles business, you're right. The two-weeks bit—we picked up enough to make us think otherwise, Clay."

Henderson regarded Janet with a shrewd squint. "Your husband, Ross. He's an air force officer, right?"

"Ross would never divulge classified information—even to me. I wouldn't touch it if he did, you know that."

"Ah, so," Clay murmured. "Seventh Fleet headed for the Far East—the guys down at the Press Club may have blown one. What sort of footage did you have in mind?"

"Features. Interviews with GIs, air crews, Japanese civilians, and the like. *If,* as I believe, the United States gets drawn into supporting the troops we have stationed in South Korea, we'll be leading the pack."

Clay nodded. "Good thinking. How do you plan to get the film back here? The military can't get involved with a commercial enterprise. The mail? Forget it: The Postal Department will be drowned overnight. The fighting will be over before you get your first can of film."

"We have a plan for that, too," Montgomery interjected. "The air force already has a contract airlift into Japan set up with Northwest Airlines and Canadian Pacific Airlines. The army and air force public information departments will jump at a chance to get their stories on the air; getting permission to toss a bag of movie film on board one of those civilian airplanes will be a cinch. They make one refueling stop between Tokyo and Seattle—we can have stuff on the air within twenty-four hours after it leaves Japan."

"I'll bet you'd even consider sharing that film with other stations—for a price, naturally," Clay said gleefully.

"I may not be an expert in the news-gathering game, Clay, but I'm sure as hell a businessman."

Clay slapped his knee. "Okay, let's get going. First we need to get a reporter assigned. I can get him accredited with the DOD public information office. He'll need a passport, shots brought up to date, and a contact in Tokyo to get him settled in. Who you got in mind, Craig? This JoJo I met?"

"I thought I'd go, Clay," Janet interjected.

"What? Oh, come now, Janet. You're good, very good, but an overseas assignment in what may become a war zone? I cut my teeth in that business in World War II. It's a tough life."

"And I'm a woman."

"Now, Janet, damnit, I didn't say that. I saw your work as a reporter on that Jewish Relief Foundation affair in INS's D.C. bureau."

"But you thought it." Janet chuckled and added a copy of the *New York Herald Tribune* to the stack in front of Henderson. "A woman named Maggie Higgins is already over there, sending back copy."

Montgomery leaned back in his chair and chuckled. "Why is it I get this feeling you're waging a losing battle, Clay?"

Janet snapped from her reverie as a tinny voice from the overhead loudspeaker announced, "We'll be landing at Tokyo's Narita International Airport in about twenty minutes, folks. Please have your passports and shot records ready. Your baggage can be claimed at the customs

counter. Thank you for flying—" Janet shut the voice out and started collecting her personal belongings. Eva roused and did likewise.

"Well, I sure hope your Clyde is here to meet you," Janet said. "We
didn't get to talk much during the flight, but I hope you enjoy your visit."

"It's no damn visit. We're gonna hafta *live* here, for God knows how
long."

"Really? Is your husband in the service?"

"Not in uniform. He's with the Agriculture Department. They sent him
on loan to teach the Japs how to raise hogs. Clyde knows all there is to
know about raising hogs—he's even got a degree in it. Except the Japs
don't call 'em hogs. They're pigs over here, Clyde informs me."

"Oh? Well . . ."

"He tells me we'll be living in some little village the hell-an'-gone up
north while he fools around with this project he's on. Ya see, fuel is
scarce as hen's teeth over here. He's gonna show them how to make
gas—meth something or other—out of pig manure. You can burn it, he
says, instead of expensive stuff."

"So I'm gonna be up there in the deep boondocks, don't understand
a word of this crazy language, living in some kind of a house made out
of paper, eating God knows what, while Clyde tries to make gas out of
pigshit. Oh, it's gonna be a scream, I'll tell you."

Janet smothered a laugh and laid a hand on the indignant woman's arm.
"Eva, somehow I think you're going to make out just fine. I hope to run
across you someday. Somehow, somewhere, we'll find a place that makes
a dry martini, and I want to hear all about Clyde's project."

Janet joined the serpentine line of weary, glassy-eyed travelers shuffling into the cavernous echo chamber that was Tokyo's major civilian
airport. Her last-minute exchange with Eva had cheered her immensely,
and she actually smiled at the officious little man who examined her
passport and wished her, "Have most happy time in Japan, missy."

The immigration clerk examined her shot record and recorded the fact
that Janet was an accredited reporter. After curt directions to customs,
Janet wandered toward a bank of signs that gave directions in four languages. A neatly dressed young Oriental stood to one side holding a placard with COLYER scrawled in grease pencil.

"Is it Janet Colyer you're looking for?" she inquired.

"Yes, ma'am. I am Eijo Tonekawa, from the Tokyo International News Bureau. Mister Henderson, formerly with our San Francisco Bureau, wired and requested that we meet you and guide you safely to a hostel. I am lucky to be that person."

Janet thought that the nattily attired Japanese looked less than sincere about the "lucky" part. She smiled and extended her hand. "I'm pleased to meet you. Shall I call you Eijo, or Mr. Tonekawa?"

"I believe the American way is to address persons they know well by given name, as 'Eijo.' The Japanese way is to address male persons by surname with the suffix "san" until very good friends."

"I see. I would like to call you Eijo-san. Not that I don't hope we become 'very good friends.' Now if you can direct me to the customs counter . . ."

Tonekawa bowed and said, "Not necessary, Mrs. Colyer. It is arranged that official visitors not have baggage inspected. INS has vouched for you. Your bags will be delivered to the hotel you select. Do you have reservations? I will direct the porter."

"Not really. Clay—Mr. Henderson—suggested that I follow the local office's suggestion."

"Very well. Foreign correspondents mostly reside at the Tokyo Palace. A fine, newly built hotel."

"Oh? Are there a lot of them? Foreign correspondents, that is."

"Almost one hundred, I believe."

"Oh, dear. I'd thought to find a smaller, more private place to live and work. Can you recommend one?

Tonekawa regarded her at length, then asked, "I gather madam does not speak Japanese fluently?"

"You're quite right. I hope to learn some, but I'll also be asking you to find an interpreter."

"Ah, so. Some American visitors find the Lotus Flower to their liking. The facility is not large, but is Japanese in decor and menu. The Ozawa family own the establishment and speak English. They will make you comfortable."

"I like the sound of that. Shall we call a taxi?"

"Not necessary. I drive you in INS automobile."

Janet gawked like a schoolgirl at the county fair as Tonekawa tooled the little sedan through throngs of chattering pedestrians and bicycles.

Now and then a sign written in English caught her attention, but in general the indecipherable Japanese symbols made her very much aware she was in an alien world.

Half of a city block standing empty among the press of surrounding buildings was a mute reminder of the firebombings of 1945. "Did this part of the city suffer during the bombings?"

Tonekawa didn't divert his attention from threading his way through the swirling traffic. "Yes."

That was a prize gaffe, Colyer, she admonished herself. Watch your tongue. Aloud she asked, "What is your job with INS?"

"I have honor of being deputy bureau chief."

Janet blinked. They sent their number two man to meet her? Either she underestimated the significance of being identified as a foreign journalist, or Clay Henderson still carried a lot of weight with INS.

Without warning, Tonekawa wheeled the car through a narrow entryway and followed a cobblestoned alley to a recessed doorway framed by brightly enameled posts. "The Lotus Flower," he announced. "Not impressive, but with all amenities. Your bags will be delivered very soon now. The—I believe you call them streetcars—run on the street outside. A taxi can be summoned by telephone." Her escort moved to the left passenger door and bowed as Janet stepped to the freshly swept and scrubbed walkway. The grounds, still minus the carefully trimmed trees she knew must have existed five years ago, appeared to have been shaped with exacting care. I'm going to love this place, she thought.

Tonekawa bowed and said, "I will introduce you to the Madam Ozawa then, a thousand apologies, I must return to my office. I'm sure you can understand that we are extremely busy just now."

"I certainly can. I just wish there was some way to show my appreciation for your help. I'd still be floundering around that airport. Can I buy you dinner sometime—is there a Madam Eijo?"

Tonekawa's eyes twinkled. "There is no Madam Eijo, and I will treasure your kind invitation. Now, please, it is custom to remove shoes here and don a pair of the slippers you see. Your shoes will be cleaned and polished in your absence."

A young, kimono-clad girl extended a cheerful greeting from behind an ornately carved table that served as a reception desk. "You honor this humble house, Mrs. Colyer. Tonekawa-san has telephoned us of your coming. Your room is waiting and luggage will arrive shortly. If you will be so good as to sign the register?"

Janet gave Tonekawa a look of pleased surprise. "You certainly work fast. I didn't even notice you making all these arrangements—a thousand thank-you's. Now, before you leave, I have one more favor to ask. The interpreter I mentioned. Can you recommend one? And, oh, yes. I'll need one who speaks both Japanese and Korean."

"Korean, madam?"

"Yes. I plan to go there to gather pictures and material for our broadcasts. My photographer will arrive the day after tomorrow. I want to leave as soon as possible."

Tonekawa drew a deep, hissing breath. "Such would not be wise, Mrs. Colyer. There is fierce fighting. Also, while you can ask at the American military headquarters, I doubt permission will be granted for you to visit Korea as a journalist."

"I'll deal with that aspect. Can you find me an interpreter?"

Tonekawa's features reflected disapproval, but he said, "I will arrange it immediately after I return to my office. Call me tomorrow morning—I will provide instructions for meeting."

Thirty minutes later, Janet collapsed on what she suspected was the only Western-style bed the Lotus Flower owned. Glimpses into other rooms as Susie—the cheerful receptionist—guided her to a sparsely furnished cubicle had revealed rolled-up tatami mats. Sliding a bamboo and paper panel to one side, Janet discovered a delightfully manicured enclosed garden. She'd deferred exploration, however, and explained to Susie that she would sleep until the evening meal.

What a truly fascinating place, Janet thought as she felt her eyes closing. Tonekawa. How about that? The *deputy bureau chief* placing himself at her disposal—a funny man. Ever so polite, but she sensed resentment. He'd thanked her profusely for the dinner invitation—but he hadn't accepted it. He was distinctly put out to discover her plans to go to Korea.

And Madam Ozawa—what a dragon she was. She appeared to be a hundred years old, with a face like a faded prune. Even her daughter, Susie, seemed afraid of her. Wonder if there's a Papa Ozawa? Is he the one who keeps these grounds so immaculate? Ross—God, I wish you were here. Wonder when you'll get to Japan and where you'll be stationed? Hope you get my letter. A delicious gray oblivion prevented further introspection.

13 July 1950
McChord Field

Ross tossed his briefcase onto the table alongside an envelope bearing Janet's handwriting. Scraps of conversation drifted along the hall as the BOQ filled with crews, pausing after work to change before the club bar opened at five. Should he shower and change, then read the letter while sipping a drink? Or should he—could he—wait?

Janet had been much on his mind since their conversation about taking a job at the TV station. He could be entering a little apartment in town now, stooping to receive her welcoming kiss instead of coming home to a sterile BOQ room. She'd have come to Seattle. It was in her voice. All he had to do was ask. It wouldn't have been fair. Wright Field—D.C.—she'd tried to conceal her restless frustration there, but it showed. Ironically, their best times had been at that sorry base in the desert that all the others hated.

He removed the bottle of scotch from a dresser drawer, sloshed three fingers into a water glass, scooped up the letter, then stretched out on his bunk and started reading.

Dearest Ross,

I'll either be in Tokyo, or en route when you receive this. Why didn't I call? I couldn't. Twice I dialed your BOQ, then hung up before the phone was answered. I knew I'd get cold feet the moment I heard your voice and turn down this opportunity. Yes, I took the job.

I hope you understand how much this work means to me, and deep in my heart I believe you do. WHY, I ask myself, must all of our major decisions be so heart-wrenching? My solemn promise: After this fling, I'll become the dutiful, loving homemaker you so richly deserve.

I had a farewell dinner with the wives at Hanson when I went back to clear quarters. All of them have orders and probably are gone by now. The household goods are in storage, and I put our wills, powers of attorney, and such in the safe deposit box in Reno. That was a bad day, parting with everything we share. We haven't accumulated much, but it's ours, and very precious. I had dinner that evening with the Cipollas. I believe Maria understood my situation, but I'm not so sure about the general. He told me to give you his best wishes, but nothing about your TDY ending anytime soon.

So, my darling, once more we go separate ways, but already I'm counting the days.

All my love,
Janet

Ross reread the letter, then folded it and threw it toward the far wall. Damnit! he raged inwardly. Janet's words "WHY, I ask myself, must all of our major decisions be so heart-wrenching?" hit home. "I don't blame you for going, and don't feel guilty," he muttered to the empty room. I think you really wanted me to insist that you join me here, he added silently. And I couldn't, after what General Truesdale told me—not with a clear conscience.

Ross had spent more than an hour with the wing commander that day in the briefing room. "Ross, you made a shrewd observation—regarding the possibility of a low-level sneak attack. Here's the situation: Two factions are working at cross-purposes in the Pentagon. The Strategics and the Tacticals, I'll call them.

"The Strategics advocate an intercontinental bomber force and an intercontinental ballistic missile—both carrying A-bombs. With such a formidable strike capability, they say, the Russians won't dare launch a preemptive strike. The Tacticals point out that both systems are still on the drawing board. In the meantime, the Reds *do* have the ability to hit our industrial complex. If they do, then we won't have the *means* to build this formidable deterring force."

When Ross only nodded without speaking, the general went on. "Unfortunately, advocates of these conflicting policies aren't all in the Pentagon. We're even divided, to some extent, inside our own wing.

Colonel Sebastian, for example, is a B-47 man. He was assigned because ADC headquarters feels that we need a broad base of technical knowledge to devise a defense against bomber attack. Need I say more?"

"It's a struggle for funding, I'd guess."

"And you'd be one-hundred percent right. It's scary from where I sit. I'm charged with defending the Northwest's industrial complex, and I've got a big gap in my defenses. Now, I was impressed with your reaction to that intercept the other day. You have the right instincts. I'd like to enlist you in a scheme that will undoubtedly put my ass in a sling, and very possibly yours. Interested?"

Ross grinned. "I'm all ears."

"This Korean business isn't just an isolated border incident, Ross. I can't fully bring you into the picture—the briefing I attended was Top Secret–Need to Know. But South Korea *didn't* invade her neighbor. It was the other way around, orchestrated by none other than Joseph Stalin. Is it a diversion to draw our forces to the Far East and set us up for a surprise attack? That's my concern.

"Anyway, that little war is going to spread, and we'll be in it up to our necks. I'd say your days on TDY with the Air Defense Command are numbered—low numbers. That puts you in a perfect position to carry out this little demonstration. You're already outside the ADC administrative structure, and, I have a hunch, will soon be even farther. What I have in mind is going to scare the shit out some people, and fur will fly. Still game?"

"I'm still listening, sir."

That conversation had taken place the day he'd called Janet. Ross regarded his empty glass. Should he have another? Or go to the club for a quick meal, then come back and work on that flight plan? General Truesdale's background briefing had been sobering—had accounted for Ross's reluctance to ask Janet to come to Seattle, in fact. He returned the scotch bottle to its drawer and headed for the shower. Tomorrow would require a clear head.

Major Cook was waiting in base operations when Ross walked in the following morning. "Hi, Ross," the grizzled, middle-aged command pilot called. "I got our flight plan to Winnipeg figured, weather checked, and rarin' to go. I can't wait to hear what that old fox has up his sleeve, but it's bound to be something to tell my grandkids about. Like I told you the other day, that guy saved my ass once in France and kept the bastards from turning me out to pasture after the war. I'm just tickled he sent you to me for help."

Ross grinned. "I don't think you'll be disappointed." He picked up the flight plan. "Okay, I'm listed as pilot in command and you're the instructor pilot. Good. Remember, you're on board to monitor my flying technique—I decide when and where we go. Right?"

"That's what the man said. But after that checkride, I'd trust you with a B-25 anywhere. How long did you say it's been since you flew one?"

"Six–seven years, but I had a real iron-ass IP. Ready? I'll give you the scoop after we're airborne."

15 July 1950
Winnipeg, Canada
"Okay, here's our return flight plan," Ross told Cook the following morning; they were leaning over the flight-planning desk in Winnipeg's municipal terminal. "See, I've saved you the trouble of filling out the route. Let's go to the Met office, figure in the winds, and you'll watch me sign it."

Major Cook's weathered features were stretched in an ear-to-ear grin. "Gotcha. And I can swear later that I had to go to the men's room and didn't dream that you forgot to file it."

"Winnipeg Tower, this is Air Force Four-Three-Seven-Three-Two, on the transient ramp. Request taxi and take off for a four-hour local, over." Ross lowered the hand-held mike and watched Cook fumble to replace his headset.

"Roger, Four-Three-Seven-Three-Two, Winnipeg Tower here. You're cleared to taxi. Active runway is two-one, altimeter is three-zero-decimal zero five, winds from two-two-zero at seven knots, over."

Ross acknowledged and added power to the idling Pratt & Whitneys. "You got your headset fixed?" he asked. "I copied the clearance—we're cleared as filed."

"You know, I feel kinda shitty about ducking the violation you're gonna get hit with," Cook said. "Besides, this is gonna be fun, and I hate to be left out. Not to mention I'll look like a real dumb-ass—sitting here in the right seat and letting some guy take off without a flight plan; fly all the way to Seattle, crossing an international border in the meantime; violating ADIZ. She-ee-it."

Ross stopped short of the active and said, "Well, if the general's right, there ain't gonna be any violations filed. If he's wrong—well, I'm apt to be unavailable for a board of inquiry, if what I'm hearing is right. Now get to work. Get us a takeoff clearance and keep me five hundred feet above terrain."

The Seattle skyline loomed on the horizon, and Ross pulled up to a thousand feet. "There she is. We did it." The exuberance both of them had displayed during the eleven-hundred mile race above the treetops faded. Their feat was no longer a boyish prank. The United States' vaunted air defense shield had been penetrated.

The B-25's VFR landing went unnoticed, and Ross parked in front of the base flight hangar without incident. An hour later he faced a furious Colonel Sebastian. "I came straight to your office, sir. I'm sure you'll want my report classified—I can vouch for Major Cook."

"You've violated enough air force and civil air regs to warrant a general court-martial, Colyer. I'm placing you under arrest—confined to quarters. I'll see that this Major Cook is similarly charged. And there'll be no written report." Sebastian's voice trembled; his features alternated between an apoplectic purple and ashen white.

"I'm sorry you feel that way, Colonel. I've already prepared a hand-written draft of the report to General Truesdale—for your signature, naturally."

"What?!"

"Yes, sir. After we talked that day, I could see you were disturbed by that dead spot in our radar coverage. I was afraid that the test couldn't be kept absolutely secret, so I took a couple days' leave, borrowed a B-25 from base flight, and made the trip on my own. If I could do it, someone else will do it by accident—just hope it isn't a TU-4. I believe General Truesdale has a right to know. I'm sure you'll have some recommendations for corrective action to include."

Sebastian stared at Ross through narrowed eyes. Several moments passed. Finally he asked, "Does Cook plan to submit a report as well?"

"I doubt it, sir. He's sorta unhappy with me. You see, I tricked him—showed him the flight plan but didn't file it."

"Do you have that draft with you?"

"Yes, sir. I finished while I was waiting to see you."

The colonel held out his hand. "This will be marked Top Secret. You are not to discuss this incident with *anyone,* do you understand? Now, I'm sure the general will want to hand-carry it to General Stovall at ADC headquarters. I'm sure there'll be strong repercussions, but I'll cover for you—keep your name out of it. I don't think you'll have to worry about facing charges."

"Thank you, sir." Ross stood and saluted.

"Colyer."

Ross interrupted his exit. "Yes, sir?"

"I don't like you. You think you're pretty damned smart. Don't ever make the mistake of requesting assignment to an outfit I command."

Ross departed without responding.

17 July 1950
McChord Field

"Ross, Cappy Cipolla here."

"Good morning, sir. It's good to hear from you. How are you and Maria?"

"Fine, fine. Can you be down here at Nellis first thing tomorrow morning?"

"I believe so, sir. I can use the T-bird."

"Okay, I'll look for you. Bring clothes for two or three days. We got lots to talk about, and you may be in for a change of scenery."

"May I make a guess?"

"You may not. And Ross—it seems I'm always asking this—what the hell have you been up to?"

"I'm sorry, sir. I don't understand."

"I have a letter from General Truesdale up there. He says circumstances prevent him from recommending you for a commendation, but you're one of the finest officers he's had the privilege of serving with. He ends by telling me that I'm a damned fool if I don't know it. I'll want chapter and verse when you get here—the *whole* story, understand?"

19

30 July 1950
Imperial Palace, Peking, China
Major Zhu Wong struggled to keep his diminutive body stiffly erect as the big green sedan lurched through and around potholes marring the Road to Heavenly Peace. That he might be thrown rudely against the porcine body of Gen. Hae Chun, slumped to his left, was his greatest fear. The general, eyes closed, his broad, pockmarked features in repose, appeared to be asleep. Wong knew otherwise. To be summoned before the Chinese People's Army hierarchy was not an experience to induce total peace of mind. Content of the papers, stuffed inside the shiny leather briefcase Wong clutched in his lap, would not be well received by the body of hard-faced leaders, he knew.

Sure enough, the piggish eyes flew open as a truck, laden with construction debris, nearly sideswiped the general's most cherished possession. He had seized the vehicle, still crated, on a Shanghai dock during the last days of the civil war. The big four-door automobile, made in America by Chevrolet, ran on real gasoline. When most vehicles in Peking today spluttered along on wood fuel burned from a device projecting over the rear fender, the general's car made big face.

"Take care, you awkward fool," Hae Chun barked at his driver. "One scratch, one dent, and you will join your cousins over there." He waggled sausagelike fingers toward where a horde of straw-hatted coolies—alongside ragged political prisoners and war criminals—labored in the late summer heat. With hoes, shovels, and buckets suspended from shoulder yokes, the swarm of humanity was engaged in restoring one of the artificial lakes, drained during the Japanese occupation, to its former pristine beauty.

Dust swirled through open windows from the dry lakebed. Major Zhu fastidiously wiped it from the briefcase he guarded and said, "We approach the Zhong Nan Hai, Comrade General. Shall I direct the driver to the Hall of Longevity?"

"Where else?" General Hae growled. "Would you have me deliver my presentation from the Porch for Awaiting the Moon?"

The bland-faced aide sensed an answer was best left unsaid. He removed his cap and mopped perspiration from his smoothly shaven pate, watching the Park of Beautiful Bounty's collection of gardens and curly-roofed pavilions emerge from the dust eddies. A guard waved the familiar sedan through gates leading to the Communist regime's nerve center.

Major Zhu glanced at his watch as the general made his ponderous exit from the backseat. It was seven minutes past the time for General Hae's appointment. They had deliberately dawdled. The old man knew his timing, Zhu conceded—it was his subtle way of demonstrating his favored status with the supreme commander.

Zhu followed three steps to the rear as Hae crossed the courtyard. Weeds grew knee high between cracks in broken flagstones. Some of the elegantly carved panels glowed with fresh varnish, but in general the badly deteriorated buildings were in need of paint. Restoration following neglect during the civil war was in full swing, however.

White-gloved sentries guarded temporary administrative offices in buildings with such exotic names as the Porch of Secret Repose, the Studio of Simple Meditation, and the Tower for Listening to Wild Geese.

Inside the Hall of Longevity, evidence of elaborate redecoration clashed with its shabby exterior. Silver-gray carpeting stretched from wall to wall. Leather-upholstered armchairs, blue-enameled spittoons, and gleaming low tables attested to the importance of the men gathered at a polished-teakwood conference table. The guard commander, dressed in a high-necked jacket and polished holster belt, led them through the forty or fifty lesser staff officers seated a discreet distance from the center of power.

Marshal Xu Dong was in fit of rage. Screaming at General "One-ear" Zing Wu, his chief planner, he finished his tirade with, "And I say you're wrong!" As Hae waddled to a seat near the head of the table, the supreme commander of the Chinese People's Army turned and clapped him on the shoulder. "Old Chun, tell him he is wrong," the marshall cried.

General Hae feigned deep thought. Major Zhu knew his chief didn't have the slightest idea what the argument was about, but to plead ignorance would lose face. General Hae glanced an inquiry at General Ye, district commander from the southern province of Guangdong. The sleek officer, with brilliantined hair and toothbrush mustache, resembled the American movie version of a Chinese gangster. He flashed a gleaming smile in recognition of Hae's dilemma and said, "I agree that it will take at least four months to move a force to be reckoned with against Taiwan."

"Ha," Marshal Xu snorted. "We perhaps are now recruiting turtles into the army?"

Hae sighed and swung his head from side to side like a weary bull. "The situation is more grave than a matter of weeks, Marshal. I performed the study you directed." He motioned to Zhu, who sprang to an easel and produced a figure-filled chart. The general continued. "To be blunt, the overall condition of the People's Army is such that no invasion of Taiwan can be launched within a year with reasonable expectation of victory."

Hisses of indrawn breath greeted Hae's audacious pronouncement. Xu Dong leaped to his feet. "What? I directed a study of ways and means to best meet the Revolutionary Council's objective to stamp out that viper's nest across the Formosa Strait. Your findings are unacceptable."

Hae abjectly bowed his head. "A thousand apologies, Comrade Marshal, but to mislead you would be equally unacceptable. May I proceed?"

"You may." Xu had obvious problems controlling his fury.

Hae Chun continued. "Of the five million men we have under arms, fewer than half can be considered combat ready." Marshal Xu bent a furious glare toward each of his field commanders, receiving an impassive reaction from each. They knew the truth, but lacked the courage to provide the volatile marshal with unpleasant facts, Major Zhu knew.

"The reason rests with recruiting methods during the civil war," Hae intoned dispassionately. "In our haste to enlist anyone willing to bear arms, little attention was paid to ideological commitment or professional aptitude. Worse, two million prisoners had to be absorbed into the People's Army—the alternative being to allow them to roam free, causing trouble.

"My unpleasant discussions with the finance minister points in one direction only: We are a fat man in urgent need of a diet. Demobilization of perhaps one third of our army, Comrade Marshal, must be considered."

Xu Dong pounded the table to silence the ensuing uproar. "General Hae speaks sour words, comrades, but hear him out. He is not a fool. It is written, 'When you have faults, do not fear to abandon them.'"

"But Comrade Marshal," an agitated voice cried, "what of Tibet? I have an army poised to retake that territory, which is rightfully ours." Another protest stated, "The South. Bandits terrorize the farms and villages." "And plans to subdue the criminals who fled to Taiwan," General Yu-kwei stated flatly. Named to head the invasion, the aristocratic-featured officer pinned Hae with an icy glare and added, "You dare to suggest that bone is to stay in our throat?"

"I deal in facts," General Hae rumbled. "You have neither the arms nor the logistical support for ambitious operations. Thus the sudden epidemic of 'schistosomiasis' suffered by your invasion force. In your zeal, all of you, you will attack a tiger with your bare hands, cross a river without a boat. The figures you flaunt: two million rifles captured, a quarter million machine guns, fifty-five thousand artillery pieces, six hundred twenty-two tanks, five hundred-sixty-one armored cars, plus items abandoned by the Japanese.

"Study the chart. More than half of our arms are either worn out or rendered useless by shortage of spare parts. The one hundred thirty-two aircraft and one hundred twenty-two naval vessels are hopelessly obsolete. With our peasants paying taxes of twenty-one percent already, additional funds within the near future are out of the question."

Marshal Xu Dong lit a cigarette and spoke into the stunned silence. "The Revolutionary Council will not look with favor on a recommendation to abandon the attack on Taiwan. Even with your pessimistic analysis, Comrade Hae, you must concede enough resources exist to overwhelm the meager defense we will encounter."

"Possibly," Hae replied phlegmatically. "The council realistically considers the American Seventh Fleet to constitute more than a 'meager' defense. But overhasty action may be ill-advised in view of a even more ominous cloud building in the east, however."

Xu Dong's eyes glittered dangerously. "Elaborate."

"Korea," Hae stated simply. "Our comrades of the North Korean People's Army confront the overwhelming technical superiority of the United States. If the South Koreans—with support of the Americans—

emerge victorious, China faces a Western-oriented society across a river less than a mile wide. Compare that with the one hundred miles of water separating Taiwan from our mainland."

"Oh, really, Chun, you prattle of matters already decided," General Yu-kwei responded scornfully. "The NKPA occupies all of Korea except a tiny pocket of resistance on the tip of the peninsula. The enemy is pinned to the ocean and faces annihilation."

"A tiger pinned within a bamboo thicket is still a tiger, General," Hae cautioned. "The NKPA is operating from supply lines stretched danger-ously thin and exposed to a vastly superior American air force. If the fox, MacArthur, breaks out of that pen, they will roll unchecked all the way to the Yalu."

"What are you suggesting, Comrade Hae?" Xu Dong asked softly.

"I suggest nothing, Comrade Marshal. But it occurs to me the chairman may consider intervention if our Korean comrades are forced to retreat." The beefy general's words touched off a cacophony of shouted protest.

"Impossible. If we have not the resources to recover our own territo-ries—I thought we were discussing economies?"

"Leave the Korean situation to the Russians. They are the ones respon-sible for actions of their puppet, Kim Il Sung."

"China face the Americans in open warfare? You would have Peking suffer the fate of Hiroshima?"

Xu Dong ignored the outburst, staring thoughtfully into space and smoking his cigarette during it all. Finally he slapped the table with his open palm, silencing the babble. "This meeting is adjourned," he said. "We will meet again in ten days' time. In the meantime I will meet with the Revolutionary Council and privately with Chairman Mao. Comrade Hae, you will stay behind. All others are dismissed."

31 July 1950
Misawa, Japan
Ross leaned against the front fender of General Cipolla's waxed and pol-ished jeep and gnawed his lower lip. The breeze blowing off the bay was chilly—a reminder of the northern latitude—and Ross wore his leather A-2 jacket zipped to the top. Beside him, Doug Curtiss, similarly attired, stood with crossed arms and a glum expression.

"So that's how things stand, boys," Cipolla said. "While you were on the high seas, the Commies went through Seoul like they were on their way to happy hour. With Kimpo down the drain, there's no place in Korea for the 14th Wing to roost. Misawa was the only base with F-80 overhaul facilities that had room—the '80 group here went to Itazuke—and FEAF decided to divert you here." The general leaned back in his seat, propped his feet on the dash, and stripped cellophane from a fresh cigar.

"Goddamnit, sir, they can't own *all* the bases in the South." Ross stood and paced the quay's moisture-glazed macadam. "We may as well stop unloading and go home." He nodded toward where a crane lowered an F-80—minus outer wing panels, and its gleaming surface dulled with anticorrosion paint—onto a waiting flatbed.

"There were only three bases south of the thirty-eighth that could support jet fighters to begin with. Pusan had five thousand feet of hard surface, but it's been chewed all to hell by overloaded transports. Suwon is saturated. Now, you ain't gonna believe what's happening." Cipolla chuckled. "We're switching F-80 units back to Mustangs. There's another ship right behind this one with F-51s on board."

"You mean we're just going to park these birds and fly prop jobs?"

"Not the 66th. Besides you and Curtiss, only one other of your pilots ever checked out in the airplane. Two squadrons of the 14th will stay here at Misawa and pull air defense alert. The third squadron, probably the 17th, will draw on the other two for '51-qualified pilots and go to Korea with the birds being shipped."

"Sorta makes you feel like poor relations showing up unexpectedly at Aunt Helen's formal dinner party," Doug observed. "Air defense. Against what? The navy? North Korea sure as hell doesn't have anything in the air to worry about this far away."

"I know how you must feel. I'm sorta disgusted myself." Cipolla relit his dead cigar. "But I remember reading somewhere that 'War, like any other activity, has the ability to expand so as to require every available pair of hands.' I want you to get your airplanes restored to operational status, your crews sharpened up—this little fracas is a long way from being over."

"Yes, sir."

"You want to take a crack at converting the 66th back to Mustangs, Ross? Take it to Korea? The decision hasn't been made as to which unit will go."

Ross looked at Doug, a question in his eyes. Doug shrugged. "The pay's all the same, I guess."

"Damnit, sir," Ross said, "they can't win a war going backwards. We have a good outfit and a good airplane. I'm going to take the girl home I brought to this party."

"I kinda thought you might feel that way. Now listen to this. The F-80 group that was here moved to Itazuke because it's the only Jap base within striking distance of South Korea. Even from there they only have about fifteen minutes loitering time over the target. Before they pulled out, a couple of lieutenants had modified a tip tank to hold two hundred sixty-five gallons—increases endurance by about forty minutes."

Ross and Doug moved closer to the driverless jeep. "I thought that might get your attention," Cipolla continued. "Now, how much of that crazy stunt you two pulled back at Hanson was sheer guesswork, and how much was based on some semblance of engineering research? Don't bullshit me. . . ."

"General, we had original prints from Lockheed to work with." Doug Curtiss's voice crackled with conviction. "I talked with their tech rep at Nellis. That wing will support an eighteen-thousand-pound takeoff weight—and still have a substantial safety factor. I'll fly the first one myself."

Cipolla grunted. "You may have a chance to do just that. This airplane has had everyone afraid of it from the very beginning. While Air Materiel Command refuses to approve the modification, some brave soul—who'll remain nameless—authorized local manufacture for a limited number of the tanks. About one sortie in four flying out of Itazuke will use them.

"Everyone is holding their breath, waiting for a wing to fall off." The general paused to utter a nasty chuckle. "Wait till I suggest we hang another two-thousand-pound bomb load on that wing. Hell, they don't even have bomb shackles installed."

"We can do that right here at Misawa, sir," Doug said. "That tech rep confirmed my figures on the station where the shackle should go. We already removed the outer wing for shipping—it'll be a cinch. And they won't interfere with the rocket pods."

"Wait a minute. Are you saying you plan on adding bombs *and* rocket tubes?"

"And it'll still gross out below eighteen thousand, sir."

"What kind of takeoff roll we talking about?"

"We didn't get that far with our testing, General," Ross interjected. "But we think we'll need seven thousand feet of hard-surfaced runway to be safe."

"We'll never see that in Korea," Cipolla mused aloud.

"How about JATO bottles, sir." Doug said.

"J—what?"

"Jet Assisted Take Off—they've been attaching them to B-47s. You drop 'em immediately after you're airborne."

"I'll look into it. I have a hunch things are going to get hectic. We may need to drag out every trick in the book, plus cooking up a few new ones of our own. Now, you start getting your outfit glued back together, Ross. Put bomb shackles on at least two planes. Go over to the navy base— they're bound to have some they'll let you have—sell you, more than likely. Take some booze with you. Doug, you catch a hop to Itazuke. Talk to a squadron maintenance officer—no one any higher—and tell him your conclusions. Urge him to keep cranking out those new tanks."

Ross and Doug watched Cipolla's jeep disappear, then turned to each other, wearing wide grins. "We're in business after all," Ross said. "Let's go get some chow. I want to stop by and check for mail again. I'm sure Janet got the APO address right—she *is* a reporter, for Christ's sake. If I don't have anything by Friday, I'm gonna find the local Military Amateur Radio station and make an overseas telephone call."

4 August 1950
Misawa

"You're right at seventeen thousand pounds, Ross." Doug slapped the thousand pound bomb, filled with sand, slung beneath the F-80's wing. "I don't think your rotation and liftoff speed will be much higher than a hundred and thirty, but figure on a good five thousand feet for a takeoff run. I've rigged this push-button bomb release—scrounged it from the dispensary. It's wired through your gun switch, so you'll have hot guns when you drop. Whatever you do, though, don't use up your ammo before you release the bombs and burn off about half the fuel in those bigger tip tanks. Your center of gravity is pretty close to the aft limits."

Ross clambered onto the wing and looked down at Doug's upturned, anxious face. "We just may make a bit of history today, my friend—one way or another. Get some good pictures."

"I'll do that. Okay, I'll be right behind you. Start engines in five minutes, right?

Ross saw his crew chief pull the power cord as the rpm and tailpipe temperature gauges stabilized. He pressed the mike button: Dolly Two, Dolly One here. Ready to go?"

"Ready to taxi, One."

"Roger. Misawa Tower, Dolly flight ready for taxi and takeoff, over."

"Dolly One, cleared to runway zero-three. Altimeter setting is two-niner-decimal-eight-two, wind from zero-eight-zero—fourteen knots. Hold for release, over."

Ross followed the before-takeoff checklist's familiar routine, grinning when he saw Doug's improvised bomb release secured to the upper dash. You'd better work, gadget, he thought. I'd hate to think about landing with both of those still out there—or worse, only one. Even full of inert ballast, they would still put one helluva strain on the wings. He flipped the toggle switches for both tip tanks and verified they were feeding.

Acknowledging the tower's clearance for takeoff, Ross waved to Doug parked off his right wing and rolled onto the runway. A quick reading of the instrument panel was passed to Doug, standard procedure for test flights. "Canopy, closed and locked. Arming switch, SAFE—bomb selector, ALL. Fuselage tank bypass, OFF. Instrument pressure, four inches. Hydraulic pressure, one thousand pounds. Generator, ON, oil pressure in the green."

"Clear to roll, Dolly One," Doug verified.

Ross fixed his gaze on the three-thousand-foot marker. He and Doug had estimated that as refusal point. Acceleration, never spectacular, seemed even slower; he kept one eye on the airspeed indicator and the other on runway markers. Eighty knots at the two thousand foot marker—looking good, he thought. Oh, oh. Tailpipe temperature creeping up—watch that. One hundred knots—refusal point coming up—what the hell! Ross felt the plane start a lazy oscillation that no amount of rudder and aileron could dampen. The three-thousand-foot marker flashed past.

"Dolly One aborting on the runway," he snapped into his mike. Okay, baby, he muttered to himself, let's slow down now—pop the dive brake—throttle around the horn to OFF. Drop the tip tanks? Doug will have a fit, they're the only ones we have—wait a while yet, she should get stopped on the runway. C'mon, brakes, not too much, though, don't blow a tire at this point. End of runway coming up—ain't gonna make it—it's gonna be close. Nope, there goes the nose wheel over the lip, but it didn't fold. Hey, we're stopped!

Ross accepted a cup of coffee from an anxious-faced ops clerk with a grateful nod. "It was weird. Not violent, but there wasn't a damned thing I could do to stop it." Ross kicked at his helmet lying on the concrete floor. "Shit. The guys in the 49th didn't report any problem like that—it's the same tank, and not too different from the one we experimented with at Hanson."

Doug hiked his butt onto the operations counter and munched on a doughnut. "Gotta be the bombs. Do you suppose they're screwing up the air flow?"

"Hey, we carried that same kind underneath a Mustang. No, it's something else. Maybe, however, it *is* the extra weight. Say the tank shape is unstable. It's controllable until you add the inertia of two thousand pounds rocking back and forth."

"That could be." Doug slid to the floor and crossed to the coffeepot. "I'm gonna try adding a tab—sort of a little horizontal stabilizer—on the tapered rear end of that tank. Could be that the extra length is causing a burble back there."

"Okay, we can try again without the bombs, then with maybe five-hundred-pounders," Ross said. "But we got another problem with that over-temp. She was pulling well over seven hundred, and I wasn't even close to liftoff speed."

"Not enough air flow. It's taking too long at max power to accelerate to flying speed. Next time we'll wait for a twenty-five-knot head wind, I'll bet that'll hold it down. But water injection is the real answer. I saw a bulletin before we left Hanson. There's a mod kit for the A-5 version of the J-33. I'll talk to the maintenance squadron commander—see if they have the things on order. Well, I got work to do." He paused at the door. "Damn fine job of keeping that bird in one piece, guy."

* * *

Ross ducked to clear the Nissen hut's low doorway. "Evening, Major," the MARS operator greeted him. "Gonna try again tonight?"

"Yeah, Sergeant. One more time, if you will. If there's still no answer, I have another number for you."

"Okay, sir. Propagation's real good tonight. I was just working an op in Kearney, Nebraska. If Gloria, in Seattle, is down, we'll go back and do a patch through him. Long-distance toll to 'Frisco will be a bit more, though."

"No problem." The shirt-sleeved NCO turned to his already warm shortwave set and started twirling knobs. Ross selected a spot on the sagging, lumpy sofa and picked up a six-month-old copy of *Collier's*. Damnit, he seethed as he listened to the radio operator trying to raise his counterpart in Seattle, where *is* that woman? She's been over here for three weeks. For that matter, where is my mail?

The mail clerk hadn't seemed unduly upset that the troops who'd arrived on the *Bataan* were still without mail. "Happens a lot, sir. One of these days you'll get enough to read for a week."

"I'm working Gloria, Major," he heard the sergeant call out. "And we got an answer, sir. Gloria's confirming that they'll accept a collect call. You wanna come around here? Remember, this is a radio, not a telephone—gotta wait till the other party stops transmitting before you talk."

"Hello, this is Ross Colyer calling. Who is this, over?"

"Major Colyer, what a surprise. This is Clay Henderson. Where on earth are you?"

"I'm calling from Japan, Clay—MARS radio with a telephone patch. You have to end each transmission with 'over', by the way."

"How about that? Okay, what can I do for you, over?"

"Janet. I can't get in touch with her. She doesn't know I'm over here. She'll be sending my letters to McChord, and they'll forward to the APO. It'll take weeks for them to catch up. Can you give me a phone number and address, over?"

"Sure. She's living in some Japanese hotel in Tokyo, but we contact her through the INS bureau there. I told her you'd shipped out, but she's touring the bases. It's hard to say exactly where she is right now. But if she does call in, where can she contact you, over?"

"Damn. I can't tell you. The only thing we can divulge is our APO address. Just tell her I'm over here, and I'll keep trying your INS bureau, over."

"Okay. Sorry I can't be of more help. She's doing a great job, by the way. She's already sent us one thirty-minute feature, and it's outstanding work. You can be proud of her, over."

"Yeah, thanks. I'll tell her that—if and when I ever run her to earth. Thanks again. Over and out."

Ross thanked the cheerful radio op and trudged out the door, torn between anger and concern. Okay, tomorrow I go to the Red Cross, he thought. And what the hell went wrong this morning? Should I have opted to take a Mustang squadron? What a screwed-up war.

20

4 August 1950
Headquarters, 87th Bomb Wing, Iwakuni, Japan
Janet's face lit up as she accepted a cup of coffee. "Ooh—real coffee. The place where I'm staying in Tokyo serves only tea. Good tea, but I'm an eight-cup-a-day java person when I'm working."

Brigadier General Mike Starr lounged on a leather-upholstered sofa, a lazy smile on his face. "My secretary said you wanted an interview, but she wasn't clear on either why, or exactly who you represent."

"First, I want to thank you for even seeing me on short notice," Janet said. "I know you must be extremely busy. I'm with television station KSTV in San Francisco. We plan a different news program format. Thirty-minute broadcasts interviewing people actually involved in the— we don't call it a war. We hope to make it a regular Sunday night feature. As to why, well, my husband is air force. I just feel more comfortable talking with someone in a blue uniform."

Starr's sandy eyebrows arched. "An ambitious undertaking—and a most ingenious idea. Sort of a newsreel in your own living room. But why start your series with me? General MacArthur would jump at the chance to get his face on a television screen."

"My boss was a reporter in Europe during the war there. He is a firm believer in Ernie Pyle's philosophy: Talk with the guys in the trenches. Readers don't believe what the headquarters brass says anyway. The 87th Bomb Wing is the only combat unit I can get to—for now."

The slender BG massaged his reddish-brown crew cut. Janet noticed the hand's covering of hair and freckles was marred with what could be a burn scar. She thought of Ross; his hand carried a similar disfiguration. "Where is your husband just now?" Starr asked.

"He's commander of the 66th Fighter Squadron. It's a TAC unit on TDY to an Air Defense Wing in McChord, Washington."

"I see. You don't by chance have a pro-air force slant in mind for your series?" The words were accompanied by a wide grin.

"Please, General Starr. I plan to cover all angles."

"I'm sure you do. I apologize. Very well, what would you like to discuss?"

"Then you'll agree to appear on film? I have a photographer waiting outside, but we can schedule the interview at your convenience."

"Do I have a choice? I don't care for one of those snotty 'General Starr declined to be interviewed' comments."

"I would never do that, General."

"Just making a joke—may I call you Janet?" At Janet's nod he continued, "As it happens, you called at a good time. I need a break; this business in Korea has everyone working day and night. How about joining me for lunch? Not at the club; I can't get a minute's peace there. I'll have something sent in from the mess. You can tell me what you're after, and I'll tell you how much of it can be discussed on the air, okay? Then we'll talk on camera this very afternoon."

Janet selected a ham and cheese sandwich and chewed while she reviewed her notebook. She swallowed and said, "I'd like to fly a mission with one of your crews, General."

"Out of the question. Next item."

"Sir, my boss flew on bombing missions as a reporter in Europe."

"A different war—different rules. There's no room for noncombatants on my airplanes."

"I'll pass on that one for the time being, but I intend to pursue the request—all the way to General MacArthur's headquarters, if necessary."

"Be my guest."

"May I interview one of your crews, on the ground?"

"No problem. I'll have Major Fenton, our PIO, arrange it."

"Thank you. Can we talk about your personal views of the conflict? What happened? How long do you think it will last? That type of thing?"

"Janet, you seem a levelheaded type." Starr refilled their coffee cups. "You're an air force wife. But you're out of your element here—just now, anyway. I think you could benefit from some off-the-record background before we deal with those questions. Agree?"

"I've never liked off-the-record comments, General Starr, and I detect a patronizing note. Please, I'm not presuming on my husband's affili-

ation. I'm an accredited war correspondent. I'm not cleared for classified material, but if you can't answer a question for any other reason,
why not say so?"

"Why not indeed?" Starr rose and transferred empty dishes to an end
table. "Mostly because I'd like to stay around for retirement. Tell you
what. Let's pretend that I'm at the club talking to your husband—one
unit commander to another. Consider how he might treat what I'm about
to say. If you think he'd spread it around, then go ahead."

"But I have no idea what it is you're going to tell me. Besides, you
could always deny anything you say; there's only the two of us here."

"You have your ethics, I have mine. I don't deny anything I say or do."

Janet pointedly closed her notebook and laid it aside. "As you asked
earlier: Do I have a choice?"

"I'm beginning to like you, Janet Colyer. You talk straight from the
shoulder. Okay, those personal opinions you asked for. I'm terribly afraid
we're into something we can't win. We've committed the unpardonable:
We underestimated the enemy and overestimated our own strength. Plus,
the political aspects greatly outweigh any military objective. I must confess to sitting back and watching this all happen, telling myself there
wasn't anything I could do about it anyway.

"Our Japanese Army of Occupation is largely made up of men who
never knew the harsh discipline of World War II. Those who do remember it have read the Doolittle Board findings. Without a war to fight,
we've been on an extended furlough. Imagine a soldier paying a quarter
to have his shoes shined, his bunk made, and his rifle and equipment
made inspection ready by some kid who also offers the companionship
of his sister for a box of rations. Our bases seem to have more servants
than masters."

"General, isn't this similar to what happened in 1941? I lived with my
parents on the base at Hickam: It was party time. But when we had to,
we got tough in a hurry."

"We also lost a helluva bunch of men in the process. Surely we should
have learned something. Just as an aside, I hope the irony of 'where were
all our leaders on that Sunday morning the North Koreans attacked?'
doesn't escape you. But when our troops got hustled to Korea, they were
hardly prepared to survive a training bivouac, much less fight."

"Was the air force in any better shape?"

"Somewhat. Most of our crews are rotated in and out of the States on shorter tours. They didn't have time to get sloppy. Besides, we've kept up a wartime posture because we have a boss who's preparing for a war with Russia."

"I beg your pardon?"

"That's right. But let's get on with the current situation. The North Korean soldier is a tough, well-trained cookie. What he lacks in sophisticated equipment, he makes up through dedication, physical conditioning, and unquestioning obedience to orders. I heard one GI say, 'Them North Korean trucks all got ten toes.' They're driving General Walker nuts. He tries to make a stand, but before he can get a defense perimeter set up, enemy troops he thought were twenty miles away are knocking at his back door."

"What about the air war? That's really why I asked to interview you."

"There isn't any air 'war.' The few, mostly Russian-built planes they had were obsolete models and were wiped out by our fighters during the first couple of weeks. They don't need air power, and we can't use ours."

"Can't?"

"Okay, I knew it would come down to this." Starr crossed to the stack of luncheon dishes and shook the empty coffeepot. "Damn," he muttered. "About our vaunted, combat-ready air force. The targets we need to take out are off-limits. The ones we are permitted to destroy, we can't find."

"I'm confused."

"We don't have maps, Janet. Don't look shocked. Nobody ever thought that we might be fighting in Korea. We got pilots—and planners—using maps ripped out of some kid's schoolbook, written in Korean. Some poor bastard crouched in a foxhole gets on the horn and says, 'About ten thousand of them sons of bitches are ten miles away, and headed our way with tanks. Take 'em out for Christ's sake!'

"So the guy on our end says, 'Right away. Where are they?'"

"'Well,' this GI says, 'Go south from Seoul about twenty miles. They're in a valley with a good-size river, and there's a town named Blitsamupf or something like that, real close.'

"Don't laugh, I'm serious. But it gets worse. Our guy calls Far East Air Forces command post. 'Got a target. Ten thousand enemy troops and tanks. Request clearance to launch the F-51s.'

"'Exactly where is this target?' the duty officer asks. The GI tells him, 'South of Seoul about twenty miles, close to some town named Blegsdmppz, I think.' After a while, the duty officer comes back, 'Roger, we've relayed the strike request to Supreme Allied Headquarters. Stand by.'

"Well, I won't go any farther," General Starr made a resigned gesture, "you get the idea. By the time MacArthur's headquarters confirms that we have no friendlies within fifty miles, and no civilians, horses, dogs, and the like are endangered, it's dark. The Mustangs can't find a target, and the poor bastard's company was overrun at about sixteen hundred hours."

"Unbelievable. But what's this about some of your targets being 'off-limits'?"

"Just that. It's this way. General MacArthur isn't fond of the air force—calls us glory-hoggers. He's never really gotten over the press claiming it was the A-bomb that ended World War II. So we have these hundred or so bombers out here. They can carry upward of twenty thousand pounds of bombs, hit targets day or night, any kind of weather—even deliver the big one, if need be.

"Now, the North Korean troops are being supplied from the north—*way* north in some cases, but that's another story. The factories, the railroad yards, the power-generating dams, everything you need to supply an army is sitting up there—naked. We have radar navigation, we have target photos taken by our RB-29s out of Okinawa, so one might think, 'I say, chaps, let's take out all those fat targets and starve the expedition armies, whose supply line is already stretched to the breaking point.'

"'No way,' Mac says. 'The air force's role is close support of our ground attack. Instead of sending a dozen '51s to strafe that convoy, send three Superforts.' It's like hunting mice with a .45 automatic. You don't hit many, but sure make a lotta noise and leave a bunch of neat holes in the ground.

"Okay." Starr's impassioned discourse ceased with a short laugh. "I sort of got carried away, but you asked my opinion."

Janet retrieved her notebook and made some notes. "All right, General, let's go outside and let me throw you some marshmallows. I can be a hypocritical bitch when the occasion demands. Your supply of questions to ask when I get to Korea is worth sacrificing a few principles."

"Korea?"

"Yes."

Starr crossed to the telephone. "Dotty?" he barked. "Find Major Fenton and send him in." He returned to stand in front of Janet. "You'll never make it. The PDRK troops are pouring down the eastern coast like the proverbial stuff through a tin horn. They'll be across the Han River by week's end. Another column moving down the center route is headed for a hookup. When that happens, Korea's southeast corner is going to resemble the Alamo. There's no chance that General Walker is going to admit any more reporters right now."

"Wanna bet?" Janet cocked an eyebrow, her chin outthrust.

Starr's reply was cut short by three sharp raps on the door behind him. "Come in."

A not unhandsome figure, with colorless features and black hair combed straight back, entered and saluted. "Yes, sir. You asked to see me?"

"Yeah. Web, meet Janet Colyer. She's from a 'Frisco TV station. Janet, this is Web Fenton, our public information officer. He'll help you line up any interviews you want."

Janet reached up to accept the major's outstretched hand. "I'm certainly glad to meet you, Major Fenton. I promise not to be a pest."

"Helping lovely damsels in distress in my favorite vocation, Miss Colyer." He held her hand a bit longer than necessary.

Oh great, Janet thought. Just what I need, a Lothario in blue. Okay buster, let's dance. "Mrs. Colyer, Major. But call me Janet, please." Her eyelashes didn't *quite* flutter. "This damsel needs oodles of background. A drink at the club after five, perhaps?"

5 August 1950
Supreme Allied Headquarters, Tokyo, Japan

Janet unfolded the half-page telegram and handed it to the middle-aged captain sitting across from her. "Captain Cox, read this, please. This film-interview series I'm doing is hot. I have to get cleared for Korea."

The captain accepted the yellow missive with a weary sigh and started reading. Janet watched his eyes—she knew the contents by heart:

UR ITEMS 101-102 SMASH HITS STOP SWITCHBOARD
JAMMED AND SUBSIDIARY REQUESTS MOUNT STOP
CREW INTERVIEW TOPS COMMA LAY OFF BRASS STOP
NEED TWO PER WEEK SOME WITH ACTION AH LA HIG-
GINS STOP WHEN KOREA QUESTION MARK

HENDERSON

* * *

"Miz Colyer—Janet—we got maybe fifty reporters hanging around wanting the same thing." He waved a limp hand to indicate the crowded public information nerve center. "General Walker is adamant—General MacArthur agrees. No more correspondents until the situation stabilizes over there. The ROK troops—along with ours—are fighting for their very lives. Can't you understand that? They don't *need* someone else to worry about."

"I resent the attitude that correspondents are a 'liability', Captain. We take care of our own needs and run no more risks than those poor refugees. Don't those damned generals realize they need the world's public support? How else will they get it without letting the people back home know what the hell's going on?"

"I shall relay your concerns to General MacArthur the very instant I have the opportunity, Janet. Now, I have a million—"

"Okay, okay. I'll get out of your hair—for today at least. But I have a personal favor to ask if you could take a few minutes."

"Shoot."

"My editor tells me that my husband left the States three weeks ago by ship. He called Mr. Henderson from here, asking for a way to contact me. You see, I only have his Stateside address, and they only have an APO number—God knows when he'll get the letters I've sent him. You have a line to the navy, I know. Could you find out where that ship docked?"

"You're getting close to asking for classified information, Janet."

"It's my husband, Captain Cox."

"I'll try, but don't be surprised if I get read off. What's the ship's name?"

"I wasn't told, but it's a good bet it was carrying the 66th's F-80s."

"Great." He dialed the desk phone. "Ollie, you owe me one, remember?" Cox grinned. "The hell you don't. You keep a book on favors that Price Waterhouse would envy. Look, there's a baby flattop inbound with a load of air force F-80s deckloaded. Has she docked, and if so, where?"

Cox cradled the receiver on his shoulder and lit a cigarette while he waited. "You understand all about favors, I guess," he told Janet. "This damn place would go out of business without 'em. If I produce, you owe *me* one, right?"

Janet nodded.

"Yeah, Ollie, I'm still here. That right? Gotcha, and thanks—now you only owe me eight." He hung up and said, "The *Bataan*. The movement reports show her tied up at Pusan. Been there almost a week."

Janet stood. "Oh, thanks a million, Captain. I'll surely hear from him any day now. If he contacts this office would you *please* get word to me?"

"Now, that would be another favor, wouldn't it?"

"It would be that—a big one."

"Okay, this is my day to be bighearted. Two for one—you can pay me back for both by just staying the hell away from this office until we get your Korean clearance."

Janet laughed. "Done. I'm staying at the Lotus Flower; you have the telephone number."

"You're staying where?"

"The Lotus Flower. In Europe I guess you'd call it a *pension*. Eijo Tonekawa, over at the INS office, found it for me."

"Janet, gal, listen to me. That place just missed getting placed on the off limits list. What in the *hell* was Tonekawa thinking of?"

"Why—why, you must be thinking of some other place. This one is clean, neat, the food is good—relatively speaking, of course—and the people who run it are friendly."

"I don't think so. Neat, clean, good food—I won't argue. But friendly, them folks ain't."

"I don't understand."

Cox's brow furrowed. After a moment he said, "Is the name something like Ogana?"

"Ozawa."

"Yeah. Well, they owned a big hotel before the war. It was in a part of town wiped out during the firebombing. They filed a claim for compensation, and it was turned down. Then—do you have the run of the place?"

"I suppose so, it isn't a large building."

"You ever see a little shrine, grotto, or a religious-looking place?"

"Yes, there's a little rock enclosure in the corner of the garden like that."

"Check it out. Sure as hell you're going to see a picture of a young man wearing a flier's uniform. Their son—he was a *kamikaze* pilot. They hate Westerners, Americans especially. Two–three years ago a couple of GIs visiting Tokyo damn near got beat to death there. I'd suggest you get the hell outta there—today."

"Why on earth would Tonekawa send me there? He's as pro-West as they come. Works for the INS."

"*That*, m'dear, I intend to find out myself. Maybe the guy isn't as pro-Western as he appears. So, good luck on running your husband to earth. I'll get in touch as soon as your clearance comes through—or I get a message from Hubby. I'd suggest you move to the Tokyo Palace with the rest of the horde. You'll at least be safe there."

"I will. And thanks again. It looks like I owe you another favor now, in addition to making myself scarce."

Cox replied with a good-humored chortle and dismissive wave. "Anytime, Janet—I kid around a lot. It's the only way I stay sane."

8 August 1950
Iwakuni Officers' Club

"Thanks so much for the dinner invitation, Web. Really, I just dropped in to tell you and General Starr that the film we shot made a big hit with my boss." She accepted her martini from a petite, kimono-clad waitress and continued, "I'm on my way to Itazuke to do a similar thing with the fighter group there."

Major Webon Fenton raised his glass. "Well, the guys will be glad to hear that they're movie stars now—as will General Starr. He sends his regrets that he couldn't join us for dinner. It's been a bad week for him."

"Oh?"

"Off the record now, Janet, okay?"

"You know how I feel about that phrase, but go ahead."

"I also know you'll sell your soul for an exclusive interview." Fenton's pinched features formed the best effort he could muster in the way of a wide smile. "Anyway, MacArthur is hell bent on using the Superforts like fighter-bombers. We lost one to ground fire, missed two bridges, and bombed hell out of one of our own convoys this week."

"Oh, m'God. Web, can't you get me on one of those low-level sorties? I can show how futile it is."

"No, for two reasons. One: The general isn't going to let *any* reporter ride along on a combat mission. Two: MacArthur would kick you out of the theater the minute he saw any footage showing failure."

"I suppose you're right, damnit. But—" Conversation halted as they placed food orders. "But, I must confess to stopping over to ask yet another favor," Janet continued.

"You couldn't have come to a more willing source. What can I do?"

"Web, I *must* get to Korea. My editor is doing handsprings over this idea. The PIO at headquarters in Tokyo is firm: No more correspondents until the 'situation stabilizes.' By the time that happens, the reporters already there, Maggie Higgins included, will all have Pulitzers."

"I'm sympathetic, but you're talking about something out of my league."

Janet covered one of Fenton's hands with both of her own. "Web, there's a steady stream of transports, some out of here, going to Korean airfields every day. Find me a pilot who'll smuggle me on board. I can pay—my editor won't turn a hair at, say, five hundred dollars."

"You're crazy. Even if I could find a money-hungry pilot, a woman would never even get past the loading dock."

"What if I cut my hair short and wore fatigues?"

Fenton's eyes were drawn to where Janet's soft, warm hands covered his own. He licked his lips. "It'd never work, never in hell. You'd be caught within twenty-four hours. Everyone involved would be court-martialed."

Janet withdrew her hands and waited while the waitress slid plates of aromatic seafood before them. "Ummm, this is delicious. Could I have a glass of white wine?"

"Sure," Major Fenton responded, showing relief that the conversation topic had shifted. He was premature.

"I've thought the thing out, Web. I have everything I need to be inside Korea legally—passport, visa, accreditation as a war correspondent. I'll operate out of off-base housing. With the confusion in Pusan refugees are creating, I'll be invisible."

"Pusan?"

"Yes, all the dispatches say that Pusan will be held at all costs. Didn't I mention that's where I wanted to go? Anyway, there's another reason to go there. My husband is over here. He doesn't have any way to contact me."

"And?"

"Well, I just found out that his ship is bound for Pusan. If I have any problems—okay, I'll have him to turn to."

Fenton's normally lean features tightened even further. "Your husband is in Pusan—with a shipload of F-80s? You're sure of that?"

"That's according to the official navy report. Web, if *you* could make one of those transport runs—you wouldn't have to know your load-masters—I'd be taking my photographer, naturally."

"I'm no longer on flying status, Janet. I—I had a break in service after '45. To get back on active duty I had to accept nonflying status."

"Oh, I didn't realize that. I just saw the wings on your uniform and assumed, you know. . . . Ross had a break in service, too. He got my father-in-law, Senator Templeton, mad at him. He got it worked out, however, and came back with a regular commission."

Fenton toyed with his food, a thoughtful look on his face. At last he said, "Janet, will you excuse me while I make a couple of phone calls? I just may be able to help."

"Take all night," Janet replied fervently.

Fenton wore an enigmatic smile when he returned. He pushed the plate with his unfinished meal alongside Janet's long-ago-emptied one. "Horse-trading time, Janet. How badly do you want to get to the combat zone?"

"The PIO in Tokyo told me that getting things done in this war depended on favors. I can give as well as take, Web."

Major Fenton shot a quick glance at her.

Think what you like, Major, Janet thought. If you want to read some-thing into that statement, well . . . She slowly closed and reopened her eyes, and waited.

Fenton suddenly had trouble expressing himself. "Okay, uh, here's a possibility. I just talked with General Starr at his command post. He's most anxious that the American people know that it's the army's fault that the B-29s aren't doing their job. If you'll accept a temporary job as an official public relations technician for the 87th Wing, well, I can escort you to Taegu. The 51's are flying close support out of there. You can interview their crews—I assure you that they make jokes about the FB-29s. You include that in your dispatches, and I'll see that you get to Pusan to see your husband."

Janet's impassive expression didn't change. "Where and when?"

21

10 August 1950
Taegu City, South Korea

A new trickle of rainwater penetrated the thatched roof and found Janet's bared neck as she leaned over her cup of lukewarm chicken soup. "Damn!" she snarled. "Does it rain in this wretched place *all* the time?" She shifted her camp stool to the left in search of a dry spot on the rickety packing crate-cum-table.

"We're hurtin' for something to send out if it keeps up," her photographer, Skip O'Connor, grumbled. He shoved the half-finished container of K rations to one side with a grimace of distaste and fished a limp cigarette from its damp pack.

Janet watched him place it between stained, crooked teeth and glowered at the slightly built Irishman. His Continental affectations, like holding his cigarette between his teeth instead of his lips, were getting on her nerves.

"We're going to the airfield at Pohang tomorrow, come hell, high water, or a plague," she grated. "Another '51 outfit is pulling back to Japan—they'll be gone as soon as this weather clears. They were on a sortie to Ch'ongiu two days ago when the B-29s really screwed up. Six bombers managed to hit one train, blew up half the city's residential area, and shot down a navy Hellcat. The only reason we're here is to get stories like this for General Starr. I want to get some of those fighter pilots' stories on film before it's too late."

O'Connor glanced at his watch, worn face-up on the inside of his wrist—another habit that irritated Janet. "Almost noon. Will you want to do that scene with the refugee kids, if it stops raining?"

"I suppose. They're partially under a roof, at least. I have to have *something* to send out tonight. Yeah, we'll do it, even if it's still raining."

"Janet, I keep trying to tell you"—O'Connor ground the cigarette butt beneath his boot. "this portable, sixteen-millimeter camera is one of a kind over here. Mr. Henderson wrangled it from the factory before it ever reached the stores.

"But it isn't sealed against moisture, and if it gets ruined, well, we're back to using those bulky thirty-five-millimeter newsreel jobs—with two and a half minutes per big reel. A fifteen-minute segment runs seven reels, right? It's tough enough to get a pilot to hand-carry only one of these little sixteen-millimeter cans outta here. I hate to take chances with it."

"That's your problem, Skip, one you're being well paid for. I'll meet you at the orphanage by two. Then we're going to the airfield early tomorrow; count on it."

"If I can get transportation. Damnit, can't you see they're fixing to pull out of this place? Half the light trucks and jeeps went with Partridge's advance headquarters staff to Pusan. If you ask me, we should be goin' with 'em. That noise you hear up north ain't no thunderstorm."

"Requisition a six-by-six if you have to. As for Pusan, the only stories there are about behind-the-lines headquarters types. Let Maggie Higgins do those. *We* talk with combat troops. Anyway, Major Fenton will be back from Pusan tonight. He'll have an up-to-date briefing on the ground war. Maybe we can drive closer to the action and get some GI's version of a B-29 raid."

O'Connor shrugged, tucked the crumpled cigarette pack in his sock top, and ducked into the persistent drizzle. Janet searched her musette bag for a fresh pack of her own, lit one, and stared out into her dismal, dripping surroundings.

What a sorry damn country, she thought. Whatever possessed me to leave Japan? Living like one of the thousands of refugees pouring down from the north, in a rundown—hovel—was the best term she could come up with. Being the only female, besides the nurses, she was given separate, private quarters. Hah! Big deal. The men lived in communal tents with dry floors and a mess hall next door. That goddamn army major was just hoping he could make things so tough for her, she'd up and leave.

Janet chattered gaily with Skip and their driver next morning as their six-by-six truck lumbered through warm sunlight, bound for Pohang.

Web Fenton's assurance that he'd dispatched a hand-carried message to Ross on board the *Bataan* cheered her immensely.

She'd ignored the major's suggestion that perhaps they should move south to Pusan. "Janet, they had a near thing at Masan a few days ago. Damned PDRK troops came pouring in out of nowhere. Caught a regimental headquarters unit flatfooted. They got pushed back, but there was one helluva firefight. If they *had* overrun Masan, they'd be knocking at Pusan's back door tonight."

"Web, we aren't going to get high-grade news sitting in some headquarters command post. I know you're my 'escort' and General Starr holds you responsible for my safety, but I'm not a helpless child. And my father taught me how to use this forty-five I carry, when I was about twelve years old." She smiled. The good major was sleeping in, she supposed, blissfully unaware that she'd gone to Pohang without his permission.

The driver, a fuzzy-cheeked corporal, slowed suddenly and muttered, "Oh, oh. Roadblock ahead." He let the truck coast to a stop in response to an MP's arm signals.

"Priority traffic southbound, folks. Afraid you'll have to pull off here and wait 'till it clears the road."

"Well, thank goodness we got an early start, Skip, Janet said. She reached for the thermos. "I'm ready for a coffee stop anyway. Thanks to Skip's thieving manners, we have cinnamon rolls from the mess hall, too."

The trio sprawled in shade cast by a jumble of boulders and watched a column of bulldozers, earth-movers, and dump trucks rumble past. "*That's* priority traffic?" Janet asked one of the MPs who had joined the impromptu coffee break.

"Construction equipment from Pohang airfield. Guess the brass decided that the Commies are getting too close. These guys were up there extending the runway. Tell ya, we gonna have to quit runnin' and make a stand somewhere."

"Corporal, I'm Janet Colyer—station KSTV News in San Francisco. Could you tell our listeners a little bit about what it's like up there at Pohang? You'll be on television in a week or so."

"You're kidding. *Television?* Back home?"

"Where's home?"

"Chicago."

"Hopefully, someday soon. It'll show on our San Francisco station first, however. Skip, will you get the camera? We may as well do something productive while we're stuck here." She turned to the grinning MP as O'Connor scrambled down the muddy slope to the parked six-by-six.

"All right, Corporal. Why don't we stand over here where that string of construction equipment passes across the background. . . . "Janet paused as a rumbling sound, faint at first, then building to a whistle, rent the air.

"Jesus Christ, that's incoming!" the MP yelled. "Get the hell under cover—ma'am!"

The blast threw Janet to the ground. She saw the driver crawl toward her, his mouth working—she realized the detonation had left her totally deaf. Dazed, she felt the young GI dragging her behind a boulder. A quick glimpse toward the road revealed a gaping crater. The six-by-six lay on its side, twisted frame enveloped in orange flames tipped with black smoke.

"Skip!" she felt, rather than heard herself scream. The driver, crouched beside her, grabbed an arm as she started to scramble toward the fiercely burning vehicle.

"Nothing you can do, ma'am!" she heard the MP shout into her ear. Enough hearing returned to detect that chilling, shrieking whistle once again. She plastered herself into the red mud behind the boulder. This time she saw a bulldozer tossed end over end, its driver flung aside like a discarded, broken doll. The roadside swarmed with fleeing figures.

Then their driver was tugging her arm again. "Behind us . . . on top of the hill . . . goddamned tank—ma'am. We gotta go, incoming or no incoming. He'll nail us with MG fire."

Both men took an arm and hustled Janet into the shallow crater left by the first shell. The depression was still giving off curls of steam and smoke; the biting tang of burned cordite made her cough.

"Where the *hell* did those bastards come from?" the MP asked no one in particular. "They're headed for the airfield, that's for certain. Oh, Christ, our defense perimeter is *north* of Pohang—they'll slaughter those poor bastards."

A swirling breeze partially cleared their bowl-shaped shelter of its acrid fumes. They were replaced by a sickeningly sweet stench. Janet peeked over the rim, seeking its source. She screamed—a rising, piercing wail. Not fifty feet away lay what was unquestionably a human figure, guttering flames consuming the blackened remains. "Skip—oh, my God, *no!*" She slumped to her former prone position, scalding tears forming ocher-colored rivulets on her mud-smeared features.

The shaken MP patted Janet's shoulder, a clumsy effort to comfort her. "Helluva thing for a lady to see, ma'am. Don't look again."

Janet sat upright, only to be shoved rudely below the shell hole's concealing lip. "I'm not a goddamned *lady,*" she blazed. "I'm a reporter—a professional. Don't ever call me that name again."

"Okay, ma'am. Okay, okay. But it looks like help's on the way."

Janet heard it then. Even she could recognize the distinctive snarl of Rolls-Royce, V-12 inline engines. A pair of F-51s streaked overhead. She saw them move to an in-trail formation and enter a shallow turn. They loomed larger, passing above the crouching trio headed toward the tank.

The urge to watch was overpowering. Three heads, two wearing helmets and one displaying a close-cut mop of red hair, emerged from the shell crater. Janet saw two oblong shapes tumble from their shackles beneath the Mustangs' wings. "Napalm, by God," she heard the MP mutter in awestruck tones.

Reddish-orange flames blossomed from the first bomb's impact well short of its target. Janet watched a river of fire race toward the now frantically fleeing tank. It was no contest. In less than a minute the Russian-made T-52 was engulfed. _? in 1950? T34_

"Burn, damn you, burn." Janet was surprised to discover the vehement words were hers. The driver gave her a startled look. Only then did she realize that her teeth were bared in a feral snarl.

Janet tumbled from the ambulance and shook off friendly hands. "I'm all right," she snapped. "All I want to do is get home and take a hot bath."

"You really oughta go by the dispensary for a checkup, ma'am," the white-smocked medic said. "That was a pretty rough scene up there, they tell me. You may have an injury you won't know about until the shock wears off."

"I'm not in shock, and I damn well know when I'm hurt. Now let me pass."

The NCO shrugged and stepped aside. Janet almost collided with Major Fenton. He blocked her way, arms crossed, his face a white mask.

"Oh, Web." Janet wailed. "Am I ever glad to see you. It was—was, well, horrible. Skip O'Connor is—he's dead, Web. He was in the truck when it was hit by artillery fire."

"I know. What the *hell* did you think you were doing?"

"I'm sorry, Web. I should have told you, but I simply had to talk with those fighter pilots up there. I knew you'd try to talk me out of it."

"Try, hell. I'd have tied you to a tree if necessary. If you'd bothered to attend the five-o'clock press briefing yesterday, you'd have known that Pohang is right in the PDRK's main line of attack. All hell broke loose up there, and it's doubtful that we can hold the place. Even if you had reached the base, you sure as hell wouldn't have found idle pilots to interview."

"I was doing an interview at the orphanage yesterday. I had—"

"You had your head up and locked. As a result, you almost got yourself killed—plus a driver. Unfortunately, O'Connor wasn't so lucky. You gonna write a letter to his wife and kids? Tell them how it happened? Huh? I oughta belt you one, you stubborn—"

"*Web*," Janet whispered. "What an awful thing to say. I feel terrible about Skip, but I didn't—"

"Oh, hell. I know you didn't deliberately place your party in danger. I'm sorry, and I take it all back. I—I was just blowing off steam. Now, that place of yours doesn't have a decent bath. I'm going to take you over to the nurses' area—they at least have a decent shower setup. Then I'm going to get a strong drink and some food inside you and keep you in sight until we leave for Pusan."

"Pusan?"

"We'll talk about it later. C'mon."

Janet, perspiring in the hut's damp heat despite stripping to bra and panties, paced and chain-smoked cigarettes. What a mess, she thought. Skip dead—*am* I responsible? Nothing to show for the trip over here but one roll of film interviewing refugees, and one with that pompous army brigadier what's-his-name. Now, I'm helpless. No photographer—not even a camera; that sixteen-millimeter is irreplaceable. Web is furious with me. I suppose he'll tell me tomorrow that he's taking me to Pusan and dumping me—can't say I blame him. She stubbed out her cigarette and walked toward the lumpy-mattressed bed.

Three sharp knocks at the flimsy door interrupted her. "Who is it?"
"It's me."

Janet recognized Web Fenton's rasping voice. "Just a minute." She drew on a thin, cotton robe and crossed to the door.

Fenton barely glanced at her as he walked in with a sleeping bag over his shoulder. "What's this?" Janet asked peevishly. "I was just going to bed."

"Don't let me stop you. I told you I was going to keep an eye on you until we get to Pusan. We'll catch the eight-o'clock shuttle, by the way. You packed?"

"As a matter of fact, I am. Do you plan to spend the night *here?*"

"That's the general idea."

"Well, you can just get another idea. Good night, Major Fenton."

"I'm in no mood to argue.Go on and get some sleep. I'll stretch out here on the floor."

Janet flounced behind the partition that pretended to create a bedroom and threw herself onto the unyielding bunk. Jaws clenched, she lay rigid. Of all the goddamned nerve! She heard the rustle of clothing and a Zippo lighter click. Suddenly she wished she'd thought to bring her own pack of cigarettes. Well, damned if I'll go back out there to get them.

If only Ross were here, she thought. It seems like ages since he held me—since we made love. God, how I miss him. Who else can I tell how scared I was up there today? War—close up—is a lot different than I'd imagined. Well, once in Pusan . . .

Sleep eluded her. After several minutes of tossing restlessly on the sweat-dampened mattress cover, she swung feet over the bed's edge and reached for her robe.

Janet could see the gleam of Fenton's bare torso in the glow of his lighted cigarette. "It's too hot to sleep," she said. "I think I'll step outside and have a cigarette."

"I wouldn't. There're furry critters, not to mention the crawly kind, that prowl for food after dark."

"Oh." Janet fell silent as a sudden torrent of rain lashed the thatched roof.

"As if that isn't enough," the barely visible Fenton observed. "do you happen to have a drink in the house?"

"A flask of not-very-good scotch in my musette bag."

"Maybe a drink would help us get to sleep."

"It's worth a try." Janet retrieved the liquor and fumbled in the dark for glasses. "No ice, however."

"That's okay."

Janet stooped to hand Fenton's glass to him, then curled her feet beneath her and sat alongside the sleeping bag. Cupping the already warm drink in both hands she asked, "Web, about what you said this morning, am I to blame for Skip O'Connor getting—killed?"

"Aw, I was just shooting off my mouth. If it's anyone's fault it's some guys called Kim Il Sung, Joe Stalin, Mao Tse-tung, maybe even one called MacArthur. Forget I said it."

"I can't. It's one of the reasons I couldn't sleep. And what will I do now? I'm out of a job, I guess. Not only will General Starr fire me, maybe my boss in San Francisco as well."

"You'll survive, Janet, I'll bet next month's pay on it. Your boss in 'Frisco isn't going to fire you—this angle you're using is too good. He can maybe send you another photog, or you can pick up a freelance from Tokyo. Okay, right now, you're full of remorse and feeling guilty. It'll pass. Although you won't admit it, you've been in mild shock all afternoon."

"I dunno, Web. I've had down times before, but this one is different somehow. I'll talk it over with Ross when I get to Pusan, but I know he'll insist I go back home."

Fenton drank deeply and didn't speak for several moments.

"Ross isn't in Pusan, Janet."

"This damn rain—I can hardly hear you. It sounded like you said that Ross isn't in Pusan."

"I did."

"I don't understand, Web. I thought you said—"

"A message just after evening chow. The guy I sent to deliver the note to Ross says the *Bataan* never got to Pusan. They were diverted to Japan—he isn't sure where. I was going to wait until morning to tell you."

"What? Oh, no. Then what—what . . . ?

"What are you going to do? I'm going to take you back to Tokyo. Your husband isn't here, and I think you've seen enough war—enough to last you a lifetime."

"You can't order me around like one of your clerks! I'm here legally, and I intend to finish the job I came over to do."

"Sorry. You're fired, as of now. Without the status of an air force civilian employee, you're *not* here legally. C'mon, Janet. You manipulated me, lady. You had no thoughts of following through on those come-hither looks and suggestive remarks. You used me to get to where you thought your husband would be—and I fell for it. So it's Pusan tomorrow, and Tokyo on the first available. Believe it."

Janet jumped to her feet and moved to the door. She became tangled in the sleeping bag and almost fell. Fenton reached to steady her. "Don't touch me, you bastard. I'd rather fall and break my neck. Out, this very minute."

Fenton took only enough time to scoop up his clothing and fled into the downpour.

17 August 1950
San Francisco
Craig Montgomery looked up and nodded a greeting as his news department chief entered the big corner office. Henderson waited until his boss initialed a paper and tossed it into the OUT basket. "Morning, Craig. Have a good weekend?"

Montgomery made a wry grimace. "Grandkids. That daughter of mine spawns them, then drops by with a 'Jim and I are going to the cabin this weekend, Dad—ya mind?'"

Clay chuckled. "Ah, the joys of bachelorhood. Janet included this with the last film." He tossed a handscrawled note on the desk. "Thought you might want to read it."

"Sure." Clay took a seat and concentrated on trimming his fingernails as Montgomery read the one-page missive.

> *Dear Clay,*
> *Re my cable of 8/11/50. I'm still trying to get over Skip O'Connor's death. I've started a half-dozen letters to his wife. How do you tell someone that her husband, the father of her kids, got killed following your orders? What's going to happen to them? Don't all life insurance policies have war clauses? Would you get in touch with her and let me know?*

As you can see, I'm in Tokyo. For how long I can't say—a lot of grim rumors floating. The air force yanked my employee status, they said they could no longer guarantee my safety. Anyway, my stuff may not be real regular for a while. I lined up a photographer—of sorts—and sent you about ten minutes I did with an old Korean woman before I left Pusan—she walked all the way from Seoul.

Getting anyone in uniform to talk on camera is tough. They are all either under a gag order or too busy. Getting back to Korea for on-the-spot pieces with the fighting troops is out of the question for now.

Do you plan to send a replacement for Skip? The local talent isn't all that good, and, as you'll see, they all use thirty-five millimeter cameras. Can you possible rush me another sixteen? I didn't realize how much easier they are to use.

Gotta run,
Janet

Montgomery refolded the letter and tapped his desk with it. "So, whatcha think?"

"I think we have a shook-up reporter on our hands. Also an older, more experienced one. I'd guess that's the first time she ever saw a man killed—especially one she was close to."

"She seems determined to keep going."

"To an extent. Notice she doesn't sound anxious to get back to Korea. Her stories will lose their punch."

"You want to pull her out?"

"Good question. I have the same feeling about her as she's having about O'Connor. There's a good—a damn good—chance that we can't hold Pusan. What if I can arrange for her to go back to Korea and she gets killed?

"As for her reporting, she's tougher than she realizes she can be. We'll get nothing but human interest stories for awhile, but MacArthur is either going to break out of that box he's in, or buy the farm. Either way, there's going to be some red-hot material. She'll bounce back. I say send her the camera and wait to see what Mac does."

"And if Pusan does fall? And she's captured?"

"You asking me to play God, Craig?" Henderson's lean features became even more skull-like. "Don't."

"Okay, I know this was a tough decision for you. We'll let it play out. So, with that one behind you, I'll drop another on you. The program format is getting some high-level interest. The NBC is making polite inquiries."

"Well, well. I'm not surprised, you know. The vultures gather whenever there's fresh kill. What kind of inquiries?"

"Like are yours and Janet's contracts for sale?"

"What! And what contracts are they talking about?"

"Now, Clay, I told you once I was a businessman, not a newsman." Craig smirked. "You wouldn't want them to think we ran a casual operation where our top guns worked as free agents, would you?"

"Well, I'll be damned. What will you do?"

"It's up to you and Janet. I won't deny that the station won't participate in the sale proceeds, but, after all, you *are* both free agents."

"Okay, I can't speak for her; I suggest you write her with the offer. But for me, I don't want anything to do with another international news-gathering operation, INS was enough. I've never been happier in my life than while putting this project together."

"That makes me feel good, Clay, but think it over. I won't hold you to anything you just said—and why don't *you* write Janet? Speaking of which, she doesn't even mention Ross in that letter. Did they ever get linked up?"

"I noticed that as well, and it concerns me. I have a strong hunch they haven't. All hell could break loose when he finds she's getting shot at. I'll stay on top of the situation."

Henderson turned at the door. "By the way, why don't you suggest to your daughter that she have a long talk with her gynecologist? It would maybe improve your Monday morning disposition."

22

18 August 1950
Itazuke Air Base

Ross leaned against the F-80's wing and patted the ugly, olive-drab nose of a five-hundred-pound bomb slung on improvised shackles. "It'll work, sir," he told the beetle-browed colonel. "We made a dozen flights out of Misawa carrying full, two-hundred-sixty-five-gallon tip tanks with bombs. We had a lateral control problem with the thousand-pounders, but Captain Curtiss added a stabilizing fin on the rear of the tip tank and cured that. This pair of five-hundreds don't seem to make a dime's worth of difference in performance. 'Course, you don't do acrobatics with all this hung underneath."

The dozen officers facing Ross gave polite chuckles. The dark-visaged colonel gave a smartly uniformed lieutenant colonel standing beside him a sharp look. The man cleared his throat and said, "I'm Colonel McKenzie, Air Materiel Command, Major Colyer. As I told Colonel Axelrod, our engineers believe you're overstressing the wing by just adding larger tip tanks. We've already had two incidents of main-spar failure."

"Yes, sir. I know about those. I also know that neither airplane was recovered and examined. Many things cause cracked wing spars, and we advocate frequent inspections when adding this much weight. But our maintenance officer had access to original design blueprints and talked with a Lockheed engineer. We both flew operational suitability tests on this plane at Wright Field. It's our consensus that a gross weight of eighteen thousand pounds at take off is well within design limits."

McKenzie's face flushed. "We stand by our recommendation, Colonel Axelrod. You have a supplement to the *Pilot's Operating Handbook* to that effect."

"I know that," the colonel growled. "I also know that my wing has a combat mission to perform. If General Cipolla wants to send me a couple of volunteers and a pair of airplanes that can do a job we can't do now, I'll listen.

This shift to a strictly interdiction mission for the '80s puts us in a bind. With a fifteen-minute time-over-target limitation and nothing but fifty-calibers to work with you're not gonna do a lot of interdicting. You hang four five-inch HVARs, and you don't even have fifteen minutes."

"So have at it, you two." He nodded to Ross and a major wearing a flight suit bearing the 36th Wing's shoulder patch. "Bring me back some scalps." The colonel turned and walked toward the hangar with his entourage trailing behind.

"You all set?" the angular-featured major inquired.

Ross nodded. He'd only met Major Krantz at briefing that morning, but liked him immediately. "Anytime you are. Any last-minute words of wisdom?"

"Naw, we just have to fly our sorties by instinct. Keep on my wing and get a feel for the terrain and the tactical control situation. When—*if*—we find a target, we'll separate and decide whether to use your bombs or my rockets first."

Ross actually relaxed as Krantz leveled the two ship formation at thirty thousand feet above the Sea of Japan. Back in combat. Even the choppy surface below and the horizon blurred by hazy mist looked familiar. Old fighter-pilot instincts returned: Keep your head moving; your job is to protect your leader's rear; keep track of exactly how much fuel is remaining. This is what it's all about—being a better pilot and having a better airplane than the other guy.

A rugged coastline emerged through the thin, scattered clouds below. Ross heard Krantz's "Mellow, this is Hot Dog Eleven. Flight of two hot pipes on station. We're heavy, over."

"Roger, Hot Dog. A slow day on the freeway. All the action is in the Baker-Queen area. A lot of activity reported last night along the Han River south of Andong, but a recce up there an hour ago came up empty. You might wander up there and try to shake something loose, over."

"Roger, Mellow. Break. You copy, Hot Dog Two?"

"Copy, One. What now?"

"Okay, they hole up during daylight. We'll drop down to about eight and take a shifty along the river. Their main supply route follows the valley. Be on the lookout for clumps of hay—they like to hide stores beneath the stuff—a bridge that looks broken but isn't. A 'village' that's really a bunch of parked trucks camouflaged. They're good at hiding stuff. Watch your fuel totalizer, we're thirty minutes from home—in a clean configuration—as of now."

Ten minutes of fruitless searching later, Krantz announced, "Okay, let's cross this ridge to the east, maybe slip up on an unsuspecting soul. One of their POWs said they hate the jets because they can't hear us coming—whoa. Tally ho, I do believe. Ten o'clock—see that road that goes right down to the river and stops?"

"Yeah, I got it."

"All right, I'm gonna do a two-seventy degree turn and come back upstream. Look real close, I think I can see ripples where the road ends. Those rascals have done gone and replaced that underwater bridge we took out not two weeks ago. Either the river is running low, or they didn't get it deep enough. The new bridge floor can't be more'n a foot under the surface."

Damn, Ross thought. Either I'm getting old, or this guy has eyes like a hungry hawk. I don't see a damn thing. You got some sharpening up to do, old boy. His self-admonishment was interrupted by Krantz.

"Oh, hey. This *is* our day—pay dirt. Forget that bridge. See those twin railroad tunnel entrances?"

"Got 'em."

"The one on our right, the one that looks closed by boulders?"

"Right."

"Them ain't boulders, my friend. They're broken crates covered with burlap. I was up here two days ago, and it was open. They got a big, beautiful train hid in that tunnel. Now, just how good are you with those beauties you've lugged all the way up here?"

"Good question. Without a bombsight, I'll just have to eyeball a release point."

"Now's the time to try it out. Boy, are they ever going to be surprised. The B-26s can't get into a box like this and skip something *into* the tunnel. Okay, I'll fly top cover while you make your run. Can you drop one at a time?"

"I dunno. We've never tried it. I'm not sure this is the time or place to experiment."

"Right you are. Sling 'em both. I'll run to the north end and try at least to break the track up with my HVARs."

Ross peeled off and lost altitude to what he judged to be five thousand feet above the valley floor. The briefing officer's words returned: "I've been thinking about something you mentioned earlier, Colyer. You say a forty-five-degree angle at about three-fifty knots is your best delivery profile. Where you'll be hunting, most targets—convoys, rail lines, troop concentrations—will be in valleys. If you parallel the ridgelines, you're gonna be below the tops when you pull up. These guys like to park thirty-seven-millimeter stuff on those peaks, so keep an eye out."

This ain't gonna work, Colyer, he told himself. Allowing for pull-up room, a forty-five-degree dive will put your release point a good thousand yards from that cliff face. You're not gonna hit shit from that distance. Okay, your tip tanks are almost empty; drop 'em and you can plus the three-fifty red line by maybe a hundred knots. Get on the deck, raise the nose about ten degrees to give the bombs an arc, squeeze 'em off, then suck the stick in your gut and pray you clear the ridgeline. AA guns? Worry about that when the time comes.

The bulky tip tanks separated cleanly. Ross nosed over and watched his airspeed build—four hundred, four-twenty. At four-fifty he leveled at fewer than five hundred feet. Green and dun terrain flashed past. A quick glance sideways revealed a puzzling landscape—almost like stair steps up the steep slope passing off his wing. Rice paddies—I'll be damned, they terrace the things all the way up.

He returned full attention to the bomb run. The twin tunnel entrances took shape, enlarging rapidly like a pair of malevolent eyes. Now? A little closer, closer—close enough. Ross squeezed the bomb release, sucked the stick back, and pointed the nose skyward.

G forces tugged at his cheeks; his shoulders sagged as if a hundred-pound weight had been added. The horizon blurred in a gray mist—don't black out, he told himself. Ease off—there, clear sky, you're past the crest.

A quick glance at his airspeed—you're well above stall speed. Level and roll right—get back and see your strike results. Krantz's voice eliminated that need.

"Good shooting, guy. Not perfect, but it'll do. They ain't gonna come out *this* end anytime soon. Okay, join up and let's go seal the other end."

Ross rolled onto a north heading and searched the horizon. He spotted his lead ship in a diving turn. He's getting in position for his run, Ross thought. Okay, I'll stay at altitude and cover him. He saw the distant aircraft drop below the ridgeline and moved to keep it in view. Smoke spurted from beneath the wings—four matchstick-size objects streaked toward an unseen target.

Banking his airplane in an effort to observe the rockets' impact point, Ross saw red, golf-ball-like tracers spurt from two locations atop the ridge. "Break left, One!" he yelled into his mike. "Ground fire from your three o'clock!"

Krantz's ship entered a sharp climbing turn—too late. Ross saw at least a half-dozen tracers impact. A piece of metal flashed briefly in the sunlight. Gray smoke trickled from beneath one wing. The stricken craft wavered, then steadied on a south course. "One, this is Two. You okay?" He waited a full minute and repeated his call. "Hot Dog One, this is Two. Do you read me, over?"

Damn, he's lost his radio, Ross muttered. Now what? He added power and moved alongside the crippled fighter. He could see Krantz turn to face him and clap hands over his ears. Okay—no radio. We're going due south—our return course to base is southeast. I'll take over lead. He patted his helmet and held up one finger, then pointed to his left.

Krantz shook his head while pointing his finger at Ross, then toward the coast. He then pointed to himself and made a swooping motion, palm down.

Ross frowned. He wants me to break off and head for home, that I get. But that other—okay, he's telling me that he doesn't think he can make it back. He'll head south and try to land at a friendly base. Where? Guess I'd better get on the radio. "Mellow, this is Hot Dog Two with a mayday."

"Go ahead, Hot Dog Two."

"Hot Dog One has mechanical problems. I'm assuming lead. Request vector to nearest landing strip, over."

"Understand, Hot Dog Two. What is your position?"

Ross frantically searched the strip map strapped to his knee-mounted clipboard. "Uh, sector Love-Twelve, Mellow."

"Transmit in the clear, Two. No enemy aircraft in area."

"Roger, we're following the Han River south, about twenty miles south of Andong."

"Understand. Fighting around both Pohang and Taegu. Pusan definitely unsuitable for your aircraft."

"Roger. Uh, I'm down to minimum fuel, Mellow. Could you call in another flight to cover Hot Dog One?"

"I'm not in contact with other aircraft, Two. Try your emergency frequency."

Ross blinked and shook his head in disbelief. A ground control who couldn't call in other airplanes. He punched "D" channel and called, "This is Hot Dog Two with a mayday for any aircraft in the Andong-Taegu area. Come in, please."

"Hot Dog Two, this is Lazy Dog. What is the nature of your emergency?"

"F-80 with damage, no radio, needs escort to nearest landing strip, over."

"This is a ground control station, Hot Dog Two. I'll attempt to relay your message. What is your location?"

Ross squeezed his mike button. About to scream, "You dumb ass-holes . . ." he saw a finger of flame emerge from around Krantz's tailpipe. He breathed a sigh of relief as he saw the plane's canopy fly off. The ejection seat followed almost immediately. They were over enemy territory, however—he felt an icy tingle course his spine.

"Lazy Dog, this is Hot Dog Two. The pilot just ejected. Are any friendlies in the area north of Taegu along the Han River, over?"

"Uh, negative, Two. We have an artillery-spotting plane somewhere in that sector. I'll attempt to contact him."

"Do that." Ross hoped the electronic transmission would retain his sarcasm. "I'll stay in the area and cap him as long as I can."

And just how damn long will that be? he wondered. A glance at his fuel totalizer wasn't reassuring. Thirty minutes from home and just about that much fuel remaining. Well, to hell with it. He'd watch Krantz land and at least see if he walked away. The guy had been through escape and evasion school, and he wasn't far from the wildly shifting battle lines.

The white chute canopy drifted lower, then Ross saw it collapse. Not a bad spot, he mused, in a small clearing near a forested slope. From a low orbit, he observed Krantz stand and wave his arms. He exhaled a sigh, then immediately sucked in another lungful of air. A plume of dust trailed a racing vehicle—a huddle of men visible in its bed.

Damn, five minutes and they'll have him, Ross thought. Well, I don't need to haul all this fifty-caliber ammo home anyway. He checked his gun switches—ARMED & ON. He stood the '80 on one wing and rolled out on a heading that would give him a shallow deflection shot. Squeezing the trigger in short bursts, he watched tracers walk the road toward the now crazily weaving truck. It stopped, and figures spilled from the sides—the six converging streams of .50-caliber slugs arrived in time to catch most of them. The truck belched flames and disintegrated.

Swooping upward in a tight Immleman, Ross returned to the site to rake the flight of two soldiers toward the tree line. Both stumbled and lay still. Fuel. Good Christ, he was down to fewer than two hundred gallons. He waggled his wings as he passed above Krantz and clawed for altitude.

At thirty thousand feet, he leveled and took stock. Any way he could figure, Ross came up with dry tanks somewhere over the Sea of Japan. Try for one of the '51 strips at Taegu or Pusan? It would have to be a belly landing. Oh, well, hadn't he flown the dead-engine profiles at Wright Field? It got tricky there at the end, but an empty plane at thirty thousand had a no-wind gliding distance of a hundred miles. He slowed to two hundred thirty indicated and tuned in the Itazuke ADF.

Ross leaned on the debriefing table and glared at the discomfited intelligence officer. "Colonel, we had a better aircraft control and warning network in China, using peasants. I couldn't believe what I was hearing—a ground controller saying that he *couldn't talk to other airplanes?*"

"I'll ask you not to shout, Major Colyer," the red-faced lieutenant colonel responded in frosty tones. "We've only been engaged over there for about eight weeks. Trained operators and equipment are being rushed to the front as fast as they can be found."

"I'll agree you have a valid gripe, Colyer," Colonel Axelrod said from where he lounged against the doorway. "But don't take it out on Sid here. The idea of a joint operations command just didn't get off the ground. The army feels that the air force's only role is to support their ground troops. All their forward elements act as observers, not controllers. The navy—well—it goes its own way.

"Take the Superforts, for example. Supreme Headquarters insists they are better utilized dropping bombs against advancing North Korean units than taking out strategic targets upstream in the supply chain—hence an interdiction role for the F-80."

"Then, we're just now getting maps for example, and reliable radios," the intelligence officer added. "The mosquito observation planes are doing a great job, but again they direct strikes against army targets. As far as I know the only common VHF frequency over here is the international emergency channel.

"Now, you did one helluva job saving Major Krantz. I have every belief that he'll walk out. It took guts to cap him after you were already below your fuel reserve. I'm impressed, not only with that sixty-mile, engine-out final approach, but with the way your bomb drop went as well. We'll get to work jury-rigging the gunsight to use as a bombsight and I think we're gonna have some surprises for the PDRK troops. I'm sending a letter back to Misawa with you, thanking General Cipolla for his cooperation and your help. So, I'll see you in Seoul, Major—Kim-boy has about run his string out."

30 August 1950
Kweilin

Yuri Pavel switched off the shortwave radio and mopped sweat from his face and naked chest. The little cubicle housing the bulky receiver was stifling. He glanced at his watch. In less than an hour he was expected to give his weekly report on Radio Peking's latest announcements. Should he temper today's hysterical outpouring with what he firmly believed was the truth?

> The mad dog American war machine, not content with crouching over the prostrate Chinese island of Taiwan, has poked a bloody forepaw into Chinese sovereign territory! Early this morning, American warplanes crossed into Manchuria and dropped bombs on defenseless Chinese villages. Hundreds of innocent civilians have been slaughtered. Doctors and nurses rushed to the scene work unceasingly to save the horribly mutilated women and children. Even as I speak, Comrade Chou En-lai lodges a strong protest at United Nations headquarters and urges that the United States punish the pilots, then undertake to compensate the severe loss of life and property.

Yuri had promptly changed frequency to that of Radio Taiwan. He only listened to this station wearing earphones. Secretly, he suspected that the broadcast was actually a stepchild of the forbidden Voice of America.

The news was usually contradictory to that issued by Radio Peking, but over the weeks, he'd found their statements invariably to be verified by later events.

This time, like the Chinese account of South Korea attacking the PDRK, Radio Taiwan had announced the incident two days earlier. Further, Peking's gleeful proclamation that the weak, cowardly forces of the traitor Syngman Rhee were trapped in the port city of Pusan and slated for humiliating defeat was offset by Western statements that Kim's drive had been blunted and the defensive perimeter was holding.

Yuri fled the ovenlike confines of his room, moving to the cooler porch outside their hostel. What was one to believe? he wondered. Official government announcements must be factual—else why make them? But why add such wild, inflammatory embellishments? Announcers in the Western world related events in unemotional terms—and provided both good and bad news. He sighed and returned to his room to don a uniform tunic. He'd report the air attack, but refrain from drawing political implications. Time would tell.

Major Malozenov resolved Yuri's misgivings with his opening statement: "The political discussion usually held at this time is postponed," the worried-looking political officer announced. "Certain international developments have caused the high command to reassess our mission. The instructor detachment will relocate to bases located in the Chinese province of Manchuria. You will turn over all training records to the Chinese operations officer and prepare for immediate departure. Do not discuss the move with any Chinese national. Lieutenant Pavel, you will remain behind. Everyone else is dismissed."

Malozenov paced the room as he spoke. "You do not seem overly concerned with this news, Yuri Sergeievich."

"I will follow all orders without comment, Comrade Major. That isn't to say I'm not curious."

"Since I'm in the dark regarding the reason for this sudden move myself, I can do little to satisfy your curiosity, Lieutenant," Malozenov responded peevishly. "In fact, I thought perhaps *you* could cast some light on the matter—something you may have overheard while listening to Radio Taiwan."

Yuri hoped the stab of fear he felt wasn't reflected in his expression. "Radio Taiwan, Comrade Major?"

"I'm not a complete idiot, Yuri Sergeievich. You spend more hours monitoring shortwave broadcasts than you do reading political doctrine."

"As a matter of fact, Comrade Major, I was prepared to divulge some important news I acquired only hours before I came to the meeting."

"Yes?"

"American warplanes crossed into Manchuria from bases in Korea last night and bombed several villages."

"And?"

Something in Malozenov's expression told Yuri that the major wasn't surprised. Had he underestimated the man? From where and how did he obtain his information? "I sometimes listen to the Western propaganda station on Taiwan to learn how they distort the truth. I was puzzled to learn that they had reported the American incursion into Chinese territory two days ago. They claim it was only one plane and it resulted from a navigational error. They submitted an apology to the CPR."

"And what conclusion were you prepared to present to the discussion group?"

"No conclusion, Comrade Major. Other than to offer it as an example of American arrogance—they broadcast their intentions before they act. Or perhaps they intend to mislead the Communist countries with false candor. And I can't help but speculate that the American attack in Manchuria and our sudden reassignment there are somehow connected."

"I caution you, Lieutenant Pavel, do not take me for a fool. You are not what you pretend to be. You are highly educated and a dedicated Party member. Before I left Moscow, I was cautioned by the political administration's chief of staff to watch you. Now I will tell you why I'm doubly suspicious of what you may be up to. First, I will ask what the three X's in the space reserved for Assignment Limitations on your master military record mean."

Yuri didn't need to force a blank look; he blinked. "I don't know what you're talking about, Comrade Major. I've never seen my master record."

"I'll accept *that,* but you must know that you have special assignment restrictions."

"No, Comrade Major, I don't know."

"I have difficulty believing you. I was briefed on each of the twelve instructor pilots I would be responsible for. Three of you—Androzov, Shtykov, and yourself—have such entries. They were placed there by the army, and no explanation is obtainable—even from the army high command. Each of you is a graduate of Chinese-language school, and each is a qualified jet pilot.

"A coincidence, you ask? Possibly, but the orders I have for this move place you three in a different category: You will report to the diplomatic mission in Mukden. The others will proceed to the Russian advisor to the CPA training detachment at Antung Air Field."

"I assure you, I am at a loss to explain the entry on my records, Comrade Major. Upon my oath as an officer and loyal member of the Party, I have no undercover mission."

"Hmmph. Well, your speculation regarding the sudden relocation has a basis. The Chinese People's Republic has purchased one hundred fifty MiG-15 jet fighters from us. They are at present en route to bases in Manchuria."

23

5 September 1950
Hall for Consummation of the Martial Arts, Peking
Their heads bowed, floppy peaked caps pulled low, members of the general staff fought their way through a gale-force dust storm toward the new meeting place designated by Marshal Xu Dong. The barren Peking plain, denuded of trees during the war by a populace desperate for firewood, provided an endless supply of the billowing brown clouds. Inside the smaller, less opulently appointed building, Major Zhu waged a losing battle to keep surfaces clear of gritty dust that poured through every crack and crevice.

Xu Dong assumed his place at the head of the table. One glance at his somber demeanor, and the conferees resigned themselves to a painful session. There was no need for the grim-faced marshal to call the meeting to order. Without preamble, he waved an imperious hand in General Hae's direction.

The oxlike general levered his bulk to a standing position. Mopping his face with a handkerchief already stained the color of ocher by dust and sweat, he said, "We have recent intelligence from Korea, comrades. A People's Liberation Army officer, in place as an observer, provides sobering information. It is true that the North Korean People's Army has driven remnants of the South Korean and American forces into a pocket around the port city of Pusan.

"The feat results from a series of brilliant maneuvers, tenacity of disciplined troops, and unparalleled courage. The apparent victory is not without a price, however—a shocking price. The NKPA forces suffered forty percent casualties during the drive—fifty thousand in the final push."

Hae waited for the buzz of worried comments to die, then continued. The destruction of guns, tanks, fuel, and ammunition by American airpower mounts—losses in transit exceed those resulting from combat.

According to our source, an early victory depends upon driving the enemy into the sea within a matter of days. The final thrust is planned and will be launched within the coming week."

"Forty percent casualties?" a shocked voice inquired. "What if this last effort fails?"

"The Revolutionary Council is most concerned that failure of this coup de grâce will evolve into a prolonged war of attrition," Xu Dong responded. "The Americans, with uncontested control of the air lanes and sea lanes, will tilt the balance of power. I have orders to lay plans for intervention if South Korean forces counterattack and advance north of the thirty-eighth parallel."

"What?" General Yu-kwei sprang to his feet, his normally composed features contorted, flying spittle punctuating his speech. "If, as old Chun maintains, our forces are so pathetically weak, we will pit them against the Americans? On foreign soil? To defend an inferior race of people?"

"You tread dangerously close to insubordination, Comrade General," Xu Dong snapped.

"One thousand pardons, Comrade Marshal," Yu-kwei replied in more conciliatory tones. "It's just that I—I am confused by this decision. I hear nothing but praise for the gallant NKPA. Are we not their equal? They enjoy unlimited supplies of arms from Russia. What role is China to play in this intervention?"

Hae looked at Xu Dong, who nodded permission for the sweating general to respond. "I will tell you that thanks to Soviet support the NKPA is better equipped, better organized, and better trained in the methods of modern warfare than our own PLA." Ignoring the threat of angry protests, he pressed on. "Our strength lies in numbers. The entire NKPA consists of fewer men than one of our field armies. Now, the agenda today is one of planning the best use of our strength. And bear in mind, we do not plan for victory in Korea—we plan for China's very survival."

One-ear Zing Wu, chief of planning, broke the subdued silence. "How much time do we have?"

Hae shrugged. "Much depends on the outcome of the battle for Pusan. A confrontation could come in as few as ninety days or as long as several months. Even if the NKPA succeeds in taking this last stronghold, however, do not fall into complacency. The American commander,

MacArthur, is cunning. He has a disturbing habit of doing the unexpected."

Zing Wu nodded. "What of the recent shipment from Russia of the new MiG jet fighters? Our stated purpose to the Soviets was to use them solely as defense against bombers attacking Chinese territory. Are they to assume a role if 'intervention' becomes necessary?"

Xu Dong's eyes narrowed. "Consider every contingency—rule out nothing," he replied carefully. "What has to be done will be done. Even now, the chairman flies to Moscow to consult with the Kremlin leaders. The possibility you speak of will undoubtedly be a topic.

"General Yu-kwei, you will immediately deploy your invasion army to Manchuria. There you will be consolidated with General Li-jong's northern army. General Hae will assume overall command of the intervention force."

Hac's beefy figure became a focus for all eyes. Some, he noted, projected congratulations; others glittered with ill-concealed jealousy. He sighed and longed for retirement in his comfortable home overlooking the Yangtse River.

Marshal Xu continued. "The Revolutionary Council has named Comrade Jai Quing senior political commissar to oversee 'ideological correctness' within the intervention force. A stern man—one with the ear of Chairman Mao." He stopped short of adding: a word of caution.

His voice harsh, the Marshal added, "I am rescinding any orders you have regarding demobilization of the inept and unreliable. Organize these persons into attack battalions and ship them north. In the event intervention becomes necessary, they will be in the van of an initial confrontation.

10 September 1950
Mukden (Shenyang), Manchuria

Yuri paused at the curb and surveyed his destination across two opposing streams of humanity. Low-lying thunderclouds sealed the city beneath a stifling blanket. Sweating men, wearing conical straw hats and ragged, dirty singlets, propelled rickshas with reckless abandon through the throng. Gangs of coolies, bare shoulders glistening under bamboo shoulder poles, ignored the chattering, singsong, almost festive background of food vendors, astrologers, conjurers, and assorted hawkers. A somber note added by a round pillbox, its concrete sides beginning to chip and crumble, went unnoticed. Erected in the exact center of a street intersection by the Nationalist government as defense against Mao's ragtag rebel troops, it was now a place for youngsters to perch and shout insults at passersby.

The Shenyang arsenal had seen better days, only slightly better preserved than the pillbox, Yuri observed. A sloe-eyed Chinese girl he'd met on the train had provided the old building's lurid history. There had been other, far more interesting interludes during the long hours of darkness, but now he did his best to recall her detailed account of the famous landmark.

"It was built during the dynasty of Mu? Tsu?—I think," the girl Tusuan Pi-wu explained. "The warlords of that era expanded it to protect their cannon and ammunition in addition to making it a garrison for troops. The Japanese added many hectares of workshops filled with machine tools during their occupation. They produced artillery pieces, even tanks and airplanes. When your army drove them out in 1945, your engineers moved all the captured arms-making equipment west."

"Soviet soldiers were not well liked," she'd told him candidly. "It is said that more were killed by drunken driving than during the few weeks they fought the Japanese. But you are honored to be given a place to live in such venerable surroundings, even if in a sorry state of disrepair."

"You know a great deal of the city's history," Yuri observed. "Do you live in Mukden—Shenyang?" he corrected himself to use the new name coined by the Communists.

"I did before the revolution, but during the great war I lived in Chungking. Now"—she wrinkled her button nose—"that city is dull. No money, no places of pleasure, no one has fun times."

"What will you do in Shenyang?"

"I'm dance entertainer girl. Many soldiers are coming to Shenyang." She rolled her eyes. "They will have much money to spend on girls. You will come to see me dance? I use name Jade Butterfly for purposes of exotic performing." She brushed his crotch with a featherlike touch, reminding Yuri that it would be several hours before the ancient coach's lights were extinguished for the night.

"I'll be there on your opening night," Yuri replied laughingly. "But tell me, how does a dance hall girl obtain a permit to travel such a distance?"

"O-o-h, the questions you do ask. I have a patron, a very important person. He arranges for me to be near him," Pi-wu replied roguishly.

"He must be a very important person indeed. An officer? A member of government?"

"A political commissar—very highly placed. You will see his name, Jai Quing, many times in newspaper."

Yuri shouldered his duffel and picked his way through the swirl of traffic. So, many soldiers are coming? he mused. It must be so if the dance hall girls know—they're always the first to arrive. He stepped aside as a crew of blue-smocked laborers dragged a miscellany of rubbish through the citadel's heavy portals. He spotted rusted Japanese bayonets, moldy canvas leggings, and empty ammunition and ration boxes. Another carton was nearly filled with empty vodka bottles. A microcosm of war, he thought—the flotsam left behind by three displaced armies in the confusion of flight.

Following the jabbering workmen back across a weed-choked moat, inside the formidable protective walls. Standing in the cavernous entry hall, Yuri searched for some sign of official presence. It *was* to this address he'd been directed to report. He extracted his orders and double-checked. "Is someone here from the Soviet embassy?" he inquired of a scurrying figure wearing Western-type jacket and trousers.

The man paused and eyed Yuri's uniform. "Soviet embassy? I'm afraid you're in the wrong part of the city. This building is being refurbished to house the Chinese People's Army's Fourth Army Headquarters. A temporary office exists on the next level, however; you could perhaps inquire there. Excuse me, but you addressed me in Chinese—you wear a Soviet uniform."

"Yes, I just assumed—"

"Of course, you're bilingual. Understandable, but actually, I'm Korean. Colonel Kim Joungwan, Democratic People's Republic of Korea—I'm attached to the Chinese Army. Come, I'll introduce you to the CPA duty officer."

The duty officer, following Chairman Mao Tse-tung's early custom of not wearing rank insignia, regarded Yuri with suspicious eyes. After examining his orders—written in both Russian and Chinese—with exacting care, he barked, "Your billets are not ready for occupancy now, much work remains to be done."

"But the orders say . . ." Yuri fell silent as the duty officer's pinched features took on an angry flush. "I will seek an explanation at the Soviet embassy," he finished lamely.

"Perhaps I can help, Lieutenant," Colonel Kim interjected. "Please come with me. We have a small contingent of Korean Army personnel in a nearby hotel. I can offer you food and lodging until you can clarify your situation."

Yuri suffered though a meal of rice, salty fish, and the favorite Korean dish of fermented cabbage, *kimchee,* with forced enthusiasm. The several glasses of rice wine required to assuage his offended taste buds, plus a tiny cup of Chinese triple-distilled wine, left him slightly muzzy, however. He accepted the proffered pack of cigarettes—American Camels, he noted with surprise—and said, "I'm most grateful for your hospitality, Comrade Colonel."

"Ah, yes. We allies must watch out for each other in this foreign land."

"Allies?"

"Oh, yes. The Korean people would be in dire straits today, but for Soviet aid. But tell me, if you're permitted, what brings you to this part of the world? I notice you wear the aviator's badge."

"I'm not certain, Comrade Colonel. I was an instructor pilot, attached to the Chinese Air Force in Kweilin, when the orders came."

"I see. What type aircraft?"

"The YAK-9 at Kweilin, but I was formerly assigned to jet fighters—the MiG-15. I am hopeful that I will be similarly assigned to train Chinese pilots to fly the new fighters."

Kim regarded his guest through a cloud of cigarette smoke. "Chinese pilots? To fly the MiG-15?"

"It is my understanding that they have purchased a number of them."

"I see. It's surprising that you were permitted to see inside the arsenal. The Chinese are most secretive regarding the 'new headquarters' being established here. For what purpose? people ask. The CPA Fourth Army is headquartered at Changchun. Anyway, I would have thought that you would join General Lobov's Russian air regiment at Anshan. They are equipped with the jet fighters."

It was Yuri's turn to express surprise. "A *Russian* air regiment? Flying MiGs?"

"Oh, yes. A number of our own pilots train there."

"For what purpose is all this? Is there a chance the Americans would be so foolish as to cross into Chinese or Soviet territory with their big bombers? I understand your PDRK armies have them contained on the southern tip of your country."

"One must never underestimate the animal cunning of the American general, MacArthur. We have liberated virtually all of South Korea, but the Americans control both air lanes and sea lanes. Their ability to resupply the garrison holding Pusan is unlimited. Our own supply lines grow dangerously extended."

The diminutive colonel stubbed out his cigarette and stood. "I wish you a good night's rest and hope you resolve the confusion regarding your orders, Lieutenant Pavel. Feel free to use this facility as long as you need to. Now, I must excuse myself. There is much work to do this evening."

Yuri accepted a cup of tea and sat pondering his conversation with Colonel Kim. As his mind cleared of its alcohol-induced euphoria, he wondered if perhaps he'd talked too freely. The Korean had seemed surprised, and a trifle piqued, at hearing of a shipment of Russian jets to China. Was it something the Koreans weren't supposed to know?

But Russian jets in Manchuria? An entire air regiment? That news crowded all other thoughts aside. Had Major Malozenov known? Yuri frowned and wished for the shortwave radio set he'd surrendered before leaving Kweilin.

Yuri's sallow-complexioned interrogator's expression never varied. For two days he'd led the discomfited young officer through a multipage document he kept concealed inside a file folder. Yuri knew, however, that it was one of the many background questionnaires he'd completed in the past. Probing questions followed each other in a monotonous procession. "When you attended the academy at Armavir, did you associate with one Boris Kutznev?" "When your father returned from Berlin, did he appear worried? Happy? Angry?" "Do you recall the names of any frequent guests at his quarters in Moscow?"

Did all the questions regarding his father indicate the general's case was being reviewed? What other purpose could this grueling inquiry serve? But then, others in the restored barracks into which he'd moved told of similar sessions. In addition to Lieutenants Androzov and Shtykov from Kweilin, a total of twenty MiG-qualified pilots had been assigned billets in the old arsenal. It was midafternoon when the impassive man—who'd never introduced himself—closed the file and stood. "That will be all, Lieutenant Pavel. You may return to duty."

Duty? What duty? Yuri wondered. He returned to the cubicle he called home and found a note on his bed that read, "Report to Meeting Room 4 at 0800 hours, 15 September." He considered resting on his cot for the remainder of the afternoon. He was under no restrictions, so why not see if one of the others would join him in a tour of the old city?"

Lieutenant Androzov was most willing to escape the musty, depressing confines of the old arsenal. Neither mentioned the closed-door sessions with a political officer—it was distinctly unwise to discuss these secret conversations. "Amazing what these people have done in only five days, isn't it?" Androzov said as they strolled through scrubbed, painted, and waxed hallways.

"When it comes to applying sheer numbers to a problem, they have no equal," Yuri agreed. "I understand a big Chinese general, Hae Chun, moved his staff in yesterday. No wonder they were in such a rush to get the place in order."

A uniformed, armed sentry—a recent addition, Yuri noted—waved them onto the street. They paused. The scene bore little resemblance to the one Yuri recalled from only two days previous. The throng of bicyclists and pedestrians was augmented by perhaps two hundred soldiers wearing the shapeless, unornamented uniform of the CPA.

The two Russians looked at each other and shrugged. "The general arrived with a sizable escort," Androzov commented.

Yuri shook his head and grinned. "Never underestimate a woman's ability to acquire secrets. A dance hall girl told me to expect this a week ago. I wonder what the crowd is listening to over there." He nodded toward where a silent throng gathered around one of the frequent, street-lamp-mounted loudspeakers was uttering raucous imprecations.

"American imperialists try to scare us with war. Honestly speaking, we can never be scared by such a threat. We, with four hundred fifty million people, are ready to deal a deadly blow to anyone who should dare to invade our territory. The masses of the Chinese people are determined to fight for peace, and are ready to take up arms at any time against whoever disturbs the peace and whichever imperialist provocateurs dare to violate the territorial integrity of China. Officers and men of the People's Liberation Army say to the warmongers, 'We have weapons in our hands; we love peace and do not fear war.'"

"What on earth is that all about?" Androzov muttered. "The Americans are nowhere near this place. Other than the plane that strayed across the Yalu two weeks ago, the war, what's left of it, is in Korea. Are these fools *daring* the Americans to start bombing Chinese targets?"

Yuri stroked his chin. "There is a great deal more going on beneath the surface here than we know, my friend. I'm willing to bet that these troops were in Canton this time last month, ready to invade Taiwan. Now, why would they rush them up here? And the matter of MiG fighters. Why should we suddenly decide to sell the CPA more than a hundred, when not all of our own units have been so equipped?

"We've spent enough time in China to know this crowd *never* does anything without purpose—and they're masters at concealing that purpose. Oh, well, we have a free afternoon. Let's see if we can find an establishment featuring a dancer named Jade Butterfly."

Yuri confronted twin rows of wooden benches almost filled with his fellow pilots when he entered Meeting Room 4 the next morning. An armed guard, one who wore a Soviet uniform and was checking identity papers at the door, didn't go unnoticed. He selected an end seat and listened to the subdued murmurs around him. "It must be that we're to get our assignments" came from behind him. "More probable, we're going to have an all-day political discussion," said another. "We haven't had one since we arrived."

The group sprang to attention as two men, wearing the uniform and shoulder tabs of Soviet Army colonels, strode into the room. One wore flashes of the political administration, Yuri noticed; the other was from the air force. The latter seated himself behind the small table facing them, while the political officer, a stern-faced individual with a Stalin-style mustache, took up a crossed-arms stance and barked, "You may take your seats."

He bent a piercing gaze at each of the seated pilots and said, "You are a select group whose political reliability has been reconfirmed during the past two days. You are about to be given a most important mission—one of utmost importance to the Communist Party and the Motherland. One that will never be discussed with any person not present here this morning. Failure to observe that order, or any other you will receive at this meeting, will result in an immediate trial before a Party tribunal on charges of treason."

He paused, while the assemblage had time to digest the gravity of his admonition, then continued. "From here you will proceed to Antung Airfield and assume duties of senior instructor pilots. You will provide oversight of other Soviet instructor pilots teaching Chinese pilots to fly the MiG-15 fighter plane."

Yuri's inner glow was quickly extinguished. "There is one difference in your status. Other pilots will instruct the technique to *fly* the airplane. You will instruct fighter tactics, but in no case will you teach Chinese pilots the most advanced maneuvers used today by Soviet air forces. Colonel Zagoria," he waved a casual hand toward the seated air force colonel, "will direct you in that duty. He is your detachment commander."

Yuri exchanged a puzzled glance with the man seated to his right. The exchange didn't go unnoticed by the political officer.

"Generalissimo Stalin, exercising great foresight, decreed from the start that the slumbering giant that is China never be allowed to attain military parity with the Soviet Union. Each of you is a product of that wisdom. 'Select our finest pilots,' he ordered. 'Ensure each is loyal to the Party, then teach them to live among the Chinese. The day will come when the knowledge they acquire will serve our own army in good stead.' That day is at hand, and the career paths you have followed were preordained by Comrade Stalin himself even before the Great Patriotic War was decided."

Yuri's mind reeled. *His* air force career, language school, all part of a plan conceived years earlier? Did Papa know? Marshal Yokolov? He forced himself to concentrate on the political colonel's next words.

"The Soviet Union's overall task is to deny the so-called United Nations—actually, the imperialistic United States—a toehold on the Asian continent. This must be done without arousing that country's armed forces. This is not the time nor the place for a confrontation.

"The Politburo planners have elected to involve the Chinese military in driving the United Nations' forces from all of Korea. Outstanding performance by the North Korean People's Army notwithstanding, total victory can only be realized through superior airpower. Such will serve both to secure a Communist government for that nation and further to bleed strength from an already weak Chinese nation. Remember, China and Russia have long and deep-seated ideological differences. The man you train today, could well be your enemy tomorrow. President Kim Il Sung has avowed total allegiance to the Soviet Union in return for substantial military aid already provided. Once the peninsula is secured, Soviet borders will be secure."

As Yuri grappled with the enormity of what he was hearing, the political officer turned toward where an anxious-faced major peered through the partially opened door.

"I'm terribly sorry, Comrade Colonel. But a dispatch, just arrived, is marked for your immediate attention."

The political officer scowled, but accepted the slim envelope and ripped it open. Yuri watched his expression change from annoyance, to anger, then to a speculative blankness. He returned the one-page document to its envelope and handed it to the thus far silent air force colonel.

The political officer then made eye contact with each of the seated pilots and announced, "The Americans have successfully carried out an amphibious landing at the western-coast port city of Inchon—fewer than eighty kilometers south of the thirty-eighth parallel. General Hae Chun has confided to me that his orders are to intercede if U.N. forces advance north of that line. The wolf is loose, comrades. Prepare to slay it."

24

20 September 1950
Misawa

"Ross, this is downright embarrassing for me, but General Stratemeyer passed the word for me to have an unofficial chat with you." General Cipolla scowled and stared out the window.

"Yes, sir?"

"About Janet. I always figure a man's wife is free to do pretty much as she pleases, as long as she doesn't interfere with the mission. Well, it seems that FEAF feels she's doing just that."

"Janet? Interfering with the FEAF mission? I'm sorry, sir, but I'm totally in the dark."

"Actually, the rumble goes even higher than FEAF—all the way to General MacArthur's headquarters. She's stepping on some big toes, Ross. I wonder if you could have a talk with her. Ask her maybe to put a more positive twist to her interviews. This isn't an order, you understand—just a suggestion that she may be causing some morale problems."

"General, this is all foreign to me, I assure you. I can't imagine how Janet is interfering with the conduct of the war. Of course, I haven't been in touch with her since I got over here. When we got diverted, the APO mail got totally screwed up. None of my stateside mail has caught up with me. I even tried to get in touch with her through the MARS ham radio net and the Red Cross."

Cipolla blinked, started to speak, then shook his head. "Let's see if I get this right. You haven't seen or even talked with Janet since you left the States?"

"That's right, sir. Is she in some kind of trouble?"

"Wh-o-o-o-boy. This is one for the books." Cipolla stood and walked to the window, idly scratching a buttock while he contemplated the approaching dusk. "I guess then you had no way of knowing that Janet was in Korea sending filmed news interviews back to the States."

"*What?*"

"I can understand your reaction. Don't ask me how it all happened, but she's here—you can make book on that— and she's making waves with some of the stuff she's sending home. Tell you what: I'm going to break a few rules—hell it *is* after five o'clock—and break out a bottle of scotch. I think we're both gonna need it."

Ross blundered through early darkness, not realizing that he was walk-ing in the wrong direction until he stepped off the board-walkway into cold mud. He cursed under his breath and reversed course. What the *hell* possessed that woman? He allowed himself a chuckle. You always knew that red hair covered the mind of an inveterate busybody, he thought. That business with INS and the Senator Templeton caper—running off to Seattle by herself to work in a defense plant during the war—yeah. If he wasn't so goddamn mad at her for not getting word to him, he'd applaud. But hell, she wasn't to blame.

Ace Aldershot looked up from the tattered magazine he was reading as Ross entered their Nissen hut. "Hey, where you been? You missed evening chow."

"I drank my evening meal, Ace, old buddy. I may get that bottle out of my footlocker and continue to get blind drunk."

Ace tossed the magazine aside and swung his feet to the floor. "What the hell has happened now?"

"Oh, nothing much. I just discovered that Janet is, or was, in Korea—doing film interviews for that San Francisco TV station. She's telling the truth about the B-29's sorry performance, and shit has hit fans all the way up to Big Mac himself."

Ace sat, slack-jawed, unable to speak.

"I ask you, Ace, what other wife would think there was anything un-usual about barging into a combat zone and throwing darts at the generals while her husband sat blissfully ignorant, doing nothing?"

"Good God," Ace was finally able to say. "That job she was going to take with the TV station—is that . . . ?"

"Right on target, my friend. Give that man the big, stuffed teddy bear."

"Well, I don't know what she's saying, but why not just pull her permit, accreditation, or whatever?"

"Oh, you're a scream, Ace. You come up with some real knee-slappers. Get a load of this: General Stratemeyer builds a little fire every night and dances around it, laughing like hell all the while. *He* has been fighting MacArthur tooth and nail to do exactly what Janet is inducing troops in the field to say: Get the B-29s the hell up where they belong and stop screwing around trying to drop bombs on platoon-size targets.

"Okay, he's convinced MacArthur's hatchet men that the media carry too much clout to risk getting them pissed off. So who ends up holding the baby? Ol' Ross. Like: Look, old man, you wear the pants in your family. *You* tell your wife to go home and bake apple pies."

"Jesus. What a mess. What're you gonna do?"

"Well, on the way home I thought of a lot of things I'd *like* to do. But they put husbands in jail for doing any of them. I decided to kill that Craig Montgomery guy. But you know what? I'll bet he's an innocent bystander. Instinct tells me *Janet* is the one who dreamed up this crazy business, of going into a war zone. Me telling her to knock it off is like telling a kid not to put beans up his nose."

"Well, at least you know where she is." Ace scratched his jaw. "How are you going to contact her?"

"Ace, you've missed your calling. You should have been the straight man in one of those old traveling minstrel shows. Janet *was* in Pusan. That was before we pulled off that end run to Inchon. No one seems to know *where* the hell she is now.

"I don't understand. How can she get permission to go roaming around Korea—anyplace she decides to visit? What does she use for transportation?"

"Janet could give Houdini lessons in charming his way through locked doors. Now, I know what you're going to ask next, and I'll save you the effort. Yes, I did ask General Cipolla for leave, so I could hitchhike a ride to Korea and find her. His answer is the reason I'm not already halfway through that bottle of Red Label.

"We're shipping out. The F-80 outfit at Itazuke will move to Taegu as soon as the Eighth Army declares it secure. We'll replace them and fly missions out of Itazuke until Kimpo is ready for use by jets. We're finally in business."

22 September 1950
Antung Airfield, Manchuria

Yuri stepped from the wheezing bus and hugged his chest against the piercing, foggy chill. His twenty fellow pilots straggled into a group and surveyed their surroundings. Trucks, fuel transporters, and the occasional utility vehicle raced through and around a swarm of green-coverall-clad pedestrians and bicyclists. A half-dozen aircraft hangars sprawled in the background, and beyond that at least two hectares of olive-green tents. The noise was deafening.

What caught, and held, the new arrivals' attention, however, was the profusion of gleaming, factory-new MiG-15 aircraft. Parked nose to tail on taxiways, perimeter circuits, and all of the hard-surfaced parking ramp, they left little room for aircraft to taxi to and from the single runway. Well over a hundred, Yuri judged.

A staff car drew to a halt, and Colonel Zagoria stepped out to greet them. He waved toward a covered truck coming to a stop behind him. "Load your baggage and find seats. You'll be taken to your living area, then an orderly will direct you to where you will receive your initial briefing. You will change into the clothing you'll find on your bunks. Your Soviet Air Force uniforms will be packed and stored for the duration of your stay here."

An hour later, Yuri and the senior instructors' group followed their orderly, wearing the ill-fitting, padded uniform of the Chinese People's Army—clothing identical to their own—into a large tent. Colonel Zagoria, still wearing his Soviet uniform, waited for them to take seats on crude benches, impatiently drumming his fingers on the tabletop beside him.

"Your duties commence immediately," the detachment commander ordered. "The surprise landing by the Americans at Inchon makes it necessary to accelerate the training curriculum. You will provide basic flight training until the first class solos, then shift to teaching combat tactics. Upon return to your tent, you will find printed instructions as to exactly which maneuvers are approved.

"You will wear the uniform you were issued while on duty. Visits into the city are authorized. Western-style civilian clothing will be worn on those occasions. Speak Russian only within the confines of the living area. Now, before you go to meet your first class, are there questions?"

A man behind Yuri stood and asked, "Comrade Colonel, so many airplanes, are *we* to train enough pilots to fly them all?"

"No. Our regiment will fly only forty. Another forty will be flown by pilots already combat-trained. The others will be later moved to another base."

"Chinese pilots, already combat-trained in the MiG?"

"No." Zagoria paused. "You will know eventually, so I'll tell you now. The regiment housed at the field's north end are Russian volunteers."

Yuri and Lieutenant Androzov sat on their bunks after the evening meal and studied each other. How much could he discuss freely with his tent-mate? Yuri wondered. So much had happened today, he had trouble sorting it out, but it was rumored that one of every four officers was an undercover informant for the political administration. "Kozlov, I swear on my oath as an officer, I am not an informer," he finally blurted. "Are you?"

The other man chuckled. "No, Yuri Sergeievich, I'm not. And I believe you. It's a relief, isn't it?"

"Then what do you think of today's store of surprises?"

"First, I think ten sorties to qualify a student is a joke. You and I required *three hundred* to become pilots Third class."

"I agree," Yuri responded. "And after those who don't kill themselves just learning to take off and land complete ten sorties, *we* are to teach them combat tactics? Tactics we,"—he waved the mimeographed pamphlet of approved maneuvers—"abandoned even during the Great Patriotic War. Elements of five, flying line abreast. It's suicide."

"Thank goodness it won't be us leading them to certain slaughter."

"Think again, Kozlov. I believe such is *exactly* the plan."

"But—but, Russia is not at war with Korea—nor is the United Nations."

"What of the 'volunteers' who occupy the north end of the field?—volunteers in the same sense that we are, I wager. Remember the words of that political officer in Shenyang that Russia's purpose is to deny Korea to the West without inciting the Americans to a declared war? Ah, yes.

When Mao decides to commit his armies to halt the inevitable U.N. advance, they will be 'volunteers' as well. We are not here to defend China's borders, nor our own. Count on it."

Androzov glumly contemplated the high-topped, red-leather boots issued to Chinese pilots. "At any rate, the American planes we may confront are inferior machines, flown by rich, indolent playboys. Our superior airplanes will provide the advantage we need."

"Don't count on that either, my friend. My father was stationed in Berlin during our blockade—*attempted* blockade of the city. He states that the American pilots are first-rate, and their airplanes are anything but inferior. No one is telling the truth, Kozlov. Not the Chinese, not our own leaders, not, I suspect, the Americans. We are on the brink of a serious war—one where the enemy has the advantage."

Yuri stood. "I'm going to the canteen we saw earlier today. A glass of vodka is in order. Will you join me?"

Androzov stood and laughed. "Of course. Tomorrow promises to be an interesting day. I will solo all my students before you do so, Yuri, or I buy the drinks. And who knows? Perhaps we'll see some of the others from Kweilin at the canteen."

"I hope so. I miss them—I even wish that Major Malozenov was our political officer instead of that cold-fish colonel. I wonder if the major's on base."

Androzev paused in the door to give Yuri a direct look. "You don't know? That's right—you left the day before the rest of us. Major Malozenov was placed on a train under armed guard the following day. It was rumored that he was charged with trying to defect."

"*What?*"

"Yes." Kozlov's gaze sharpened. "I even entertained the thought for a time that it had been you who informed on him."

Yuri, unable to speak, could only shake his head in denial and the pair strolled without conversing toward the edge of the Russian billets where the canteen tent stood. Yuri's mind reeled. The major a defector? Could it be? How could anyone know? Was the man trying to sound Yuri out that last night? The talk of listening to Radio Taiwan?

A wave of laughing, high-spirited conversation interrupted Yuri's thoughts. He stopped to examine its source—a double file of uniformed figures extending out of sight beyond a canopy of pole-mounted yellow lights. The serpentine shuffled toward a long string of railroad cars parked on a spur track leading onto the airfield.

"There, Kozlov, are some of your Chinese volunteers," he said softly. "That train is headed east, across the Yalu bridge. Chairman Mao doesn't wait for events to warrant intervention. Those young men will be in camouflaged positions by sunup, waiting for an unsuspecting enemy. How soon, do you think, before we join them?"

6 October 1950
Kimpo Airfield, South Korea

"Kimpo Tower, this is Bozo One with a flight of four, requesting landing, over." Ross, flying Bozo Two and tucked in position off General Cipolla's right wing, grinned as he heard what amounted to a victory speech. About damn time, he thought. How we ever allowed those little brown bastards to chase us practically all the way back home, I'll never know. Well, Sung, old buddy, the big dogs have arrived on the block. Head for your porch.

Inside a hangar, still riddled with shell holes, Ross lounged against a drum of motor oil while General Cipolla gathered the thirty-plus, just-landed pilots in a semicircle facing him. "Okay, gents, we're here to fight a war. It's what we've trained to do; now let's do it right. You saw the condition this field is in when you landed. Remember, a bird lost in an accident is just as big a loss as one shot down in combat.

"We're already on the ready board and will fly our first mission tomorrow morning. Intelligence briefing is at sixteen hundred hours. Now, get your gear stowed and a bite to eat. Mission briefing is set for oh-five-thirty, so don't plan on heading into town to celebrate—not that there's much town left to see, they tell me.

"Next on the agenda, however, is a meeting with the PIO gang. They're waiting next door with a roomful of correspondents. Remember your security classifications, and remember to act like professional combat pilots, not some bunch of barnstormers at the county fair." A wide grin removed the sting from his last words.

Ross followed the chattering group of pilots into what appeared to have been a barracks attached to the hangar. A bank of photographers greeted them with a dancing array of flashbulbs. A major wearing class A blues waved his arms and shouted for their attention. "Gentlemen"—he added, "and lady," prompted scattered chuckles and heads to swivel. "General Cipolla will have a few remarks, then his aircrews will be open for questions."

Ross turned a deaf ear as Cipolla started his canned remarks. "The F-80s have returned to Kimpo, folks. This time to stay. We mean business. . . ."

Whom to schedule first? Ross wondered. He and Ace had discussed the best lineup before departing Itazuke, but decided to make a last-minute decision after observing the flight to Kimpo. As his eyes recovered from the blinding-white flashbulbs, he idly scanned the assembly of correspondents. He recognized one he'd met in Japan, a slightly built man with thick, rimless glasses, and . . . His knees turned to jelly; he looked in vain for a chair.

There was no mistaking that profile, and that red hair, cut short and tucked beneath a stained GI fatigue hat. Janet! he started to shout. No, he thought. Christ, you can't do that—you'll disrupt the whole press conference. I have to get her attention, get the hell out of this room. He cast a wild glance toward all exits. There, just behind her—he ducked and slipped out by the same door they'd used to enter.

Ross raced around the sprawling hangar, dodging scattered parts of wrecked airplanes and assorted junk. He reached a door that transmitted muffled voices of the press conference. He eased it open and spotted Janet standing fewer than ten feet away. Tiptoeing to a position just behind her, he tapped her shoulder and whispered, "Dr. Livingstone-Colyer, I presume?"

Janet's shriek brought proceedings to a confused halt. "Oh, my God," she cried through laughter mixed with tears, "Guys, this is my *husband!*"

The PIO major finally gave up trying to restore any semblance of decorum. The correspondents, cynical veterans all, recognized that the reunion's human interest aspect eclipsed any dry recapitulation of the order of battle, the logistical situation, and hollow promises to "Have these boys home by Christmas."

Janet refused to release her arms from around Ross's neck. Her comments were smothered monosyllables from lips buried against his chest. "No, I didn't know. . . ." "Yes, I did know he was over here someplace. . . ." At last she stood back and dabbed streaming eyes. "You could have told me, you big lug."

Ross steered her to where General Cipolla leaned against a table, his face wreathed in a bemused smile. "Uh, General—sir, I think you know my wife," Ross mumbled.

"Oh, yes. Yes, I know your beautiful bride—I was at your wedding, remember?"

"Oh, yeah, that's right," Ross said with a shaky laugh.

"Janet, my dear, I guess it would be a rhetorical question to ask, 'How are you?'" Cipolla asked.

"Oh, General, I'm the happiest woman alive just now. And I'm—I've been . . ." She waved vaguely in the direction of where the grinning crew of reporters stood.

"Yes, yes, I know what you've been doing. Yes—I'm not totally uninformed, you know. Now, Ross, can Ace Aldershot put up four crews tomorrow morning that won't be an embarrassment to the wing?"

"Oh, yes, sir. We talked about that—"

"I know. But *you* won't be flying lead, as you had penciled into the schedule. You see, I'm putting you on DNIF for twenty-four hours, understand? I don't want to see you until noon tomorrow. But consider what I just said. You're on *Duty* Not Involving Flying. You know what that duty is."

Ross blinked. "Yes, sir, I understand. And thanks, General."

"Don't thank me yet. I suspect you'd rather be flying a combat sortie before you finish this mission. Now go; maybe we can still salvage a press conference here."

Janet clung to Ross's arm and chattered nonstop as the jeep the PIO major produced jounced across a pontoon bridge spanning the Han River and down the still-unrestored road into Seoul. Ross strongly suspected that the quick conversation he'd witnessed between Cipolla and the PIO officer had resulted in the major's reluctant offer of a scarce vehicle.

"The hotel wasn't touched during the fighting and isn't really all that bad," Janet said. "There's running water—you can't drink it, but most of the time it's warm enough to take a shower in. Most of the correspondents stay there—there's even a bar. Not well stocked, but well patronized." She uttered a giddy laugh.

Ross tossed his lightly packed B-4 bag to the floor of the shabby but neatly maintained room and enfolded Janet in a tight embrace. She disengaged herself and said, "My treat." She crossed to the dresser and removed a brown, one-liter bottle. "Genuine, fourteen-year-old, single malt scotch whisky. A treasure produced by my Australian photographer. You get to break the seal."

Ross obliged and sloshed two fingers into each of the glasses Janet produced. Janet clinked her glass to his. Gazing deep into Ross's eyes, she murmured, "To us. Nobody else, nothing else in the world, just us." As Ross savored the rich, full-bodied liquor, Janet set her glass on the dresser and reached for the full-length front zipper to his flight suit.

Ross roused from fitful sleep to discover that darkness had fallen. He reached for Janet and found her side of the bed empty—the faint sound of water splashing came from the closet-size bathroom. He shook his head to clear sleep cobwebs and swung his feet to the floor just as Janet emerged from the dimly lighted cubicle.

"Hi, darling," she called softly. "Did I wake you?"

"Naw. I must have been more pooped than I thought. What did I sleep, three–four hours?"

"Close to four." Janet wrapped a towel, toga style, around her and perched beside Ross. "Are you hungry?"

"Starved. Where's the local Stork Club?"

"Dreamer," Janet replied laughingly. "We've missed evening chow at Kimpo, but Mama Kum still operates a dining room downstairs. The menu usually features, and is limited to, rice, dried fish, and that horrible *kimchee*. But the good news is that she has a Chinese cook who does something with Spam that makes it taste like Mongolian barbecue. I can take him a can from my emergency rations, a can of peaches, and we'll have a romantic dinner by candlelight. The alternative is to stay here and eat K rations that I also have stashed."

Ross stood and stretched. "Not much of a decision. But I have yet to find any way to keep Spam from tasting like Spam. I'll get dressed."

Mama Kum bustled about the dining room, empty now but for Ross and Janet, darting annoyed looks in their direction. Janet laughed. "I do believe Mama wants to close up."

"No nightclubs open I guess?"

"None that *I* would care to visit."

"Okay then. How do I leave a tip for that cook? By damn, he *did* do something to that Spam—it tasted just like goat simmered in Tabasco sauce."

"You're spoiled. We poor scribes have to live off the land. Boy, am I ever collecting recipes—putting them in a file marked 'Never Use, Nohow, No Way.'"

Ross let Janet precede him into the room, then closed and locked the door behind them. He accepted the drink Janet poured for him and stretched out on the lumpy mattress. "Okay, we got as far as you going to work for Clay Henderson and coming up with the idea to make a movie version of the Sunday Supplement. Maybe someday my mail will catch up with me and I can read all this, but in the meantime, I'll listen."

Janet took up a cross-legged sitting position on the foot end of the bed. After sipping her drink, she said, "So when I got to Tokyo, I got the runaround. No permits were being issued for Korea until the situation 'stabilized'—meaning of course, until we stop running. So when someone told me about the B-29 outfit at Iwakuni, I decided to try for an interview with the division commander and maybe a crew.

"Well, this BG, Starr, made me do something I swore never to agree to: I let him talk off the record. He unloaded. The Superforts were being used for low-level ground support by MacArthur's headquarters. The results were embarrassing. I got some reasonably good stuff there and decided to go south to Itazuke. They were supposed to have F-80s there and I thought, just *maybe* . . . you know."

"But I wasn't there."

"No. But on the way down from Tokyo, I stopped off to stay overnight at Iwakuni again. I ran across his PIO, Major Fenton, and talked him into smuggling me and my photographer on board a transport for Taegu.

"You *what?*"

"Well, it wasn't all that illegal, actually. I had my passport and visa, I was accredited as a correspondent—I just couldn't get a permit to board a military plane, and all the civilian flights had been canceled."

"Legal, hell—I just can't believe what I'm hearing."

"I—sort of talked him into getting me hired temporarily by General

Starr as a public information technician. This made everything official and let me use army facilities in Korea. In return I would do interviews with people who knew damn well the '29s were being misused and not afraid to say so. Major Fenton went along as my supervisor."

"So *that's* . . ." Ross breathed. "Okay, go ahead."

"Well, I did something dumb at Taegu."

"You waited all that time to do something dumb? Up till then you'd been real smart—is that what you're telling me?"

"Don't be sarcastic. It isn't easy telling you this."

Janet recited the disastrous events leading to Skip O'Connor's death, and why Fenton forced her to return to Japan. She fell silent and waited as Ross contemplated his empty glass.

"Okay," he said finally. "Before I wring your neck, I want to hear how you got permission to come back here."

"Oh, please, you're angry with me, and I'd so like to have our reunion without that. Can't that part wait until morning? Look." She scrambled from the bed and removed a scrap of red cloth from the dresser drawer. "I was damned if I would go to bed with you tonight wearing GI long johns. Don't laugh; there's no heat in this place, you know. Anyway, while you were sleeping I dashed around the corner to this little boutique that survived the fighting." She held up a scarlet silk nightgown of daring cut and scanty proportions.

Ross's glowering countenance dissolved. After erupting with laughter, he said, "You always did know the quickest way to my heart, Redhead." He spread his arms, adding, "Come to bed. Your war stories can wait."

Janet added the contents of the packet of instant coffee to boiling water provided by Mama Kum and watched it dissolve. "I suppose you still insist on hearing how I happen to be here."

"Yes, that—and we have some other matters to discuss."

"Oh? Well, I was thinking. While you still have the jeep, why don't we drive to a little park I found. It's on the way to Kimpo."

"Done. I don't have to report in until noon, but I am anxious to see how our first sortie went. I'll go back to the room and get my things, then meet you back down here in a few minutes."

"Ross . . ."

"Yes."

"Must you take all of your things? You'll be able to stay here most nights, won't you?"

"That's one of the things we need to discuss. In a nutshell—no. There're a lot of reasons, but the main one is that we're fighting a war that doesn't run by the clock. I need to be with the squadron twenty-four hours a day."

"I—I guess you must. I'll wait here for you."

The little secluded park, actually more of a garden, had been bypassed by the war's ravaging instruments of destruction. Ross and Janet crossed to where a handhewn bench faced the small lake from beneath a giant sycamore tree. Ignoring the chill, they lit cigarettes and Janet gazed toward the horizon.

"I really didn't want to come back, you know."

"Then why did you?"

"I don't know. I really don't know. Maybe I'm learning about myself for the first time. I'm not the brave, hard-bitten woman reporter doing a man's job the others describe. I was terrified that day at Taegu.

"In a way, that makes what I have to say next somewhat easier." He gave a hollow chuckle.

"What's that?"

"You have to go home, Janet. Preferably the States, but at least back to Japan."

"I don't understand. Because of Web Fenton?"

"No. Do you recall Cipolla reminding me I would be on *duty* not involving flying?"

"I did wonder about that."

"It was my duty to tell you that you are *persona non grata* over here. Tell you in a way that would save a public backlash if you were kicked out."

Janet sat erect, dislodging Ross's arm. "Who says I have to leave?"

"In your own inimitable way, you've managed to piss off the king—the great General MacArthur himself—with your B-29 features."

"I don't believe it. Why—he can't *do* this. It wasn't me offering those opinions. And every word is true, you know that."

"I seem to recall another redhead saying something like that: Mary, Queen of Scots, just before they lopped off her head."

"Well, that arrogant, pompous bastard isn't going to lop off *this* head. Wait until I pass this on to Clay and to CBC. They'll crucify him."

Ross chuckled. "Where is the contrite, frightened little lamb of five minutes ago? Let me finish." Janet returned to his one-armed embrace and remained silent, her cheeks flaming nevertheless.

"I've been designated to convince you to go home. An implied order, and what the general meant yesterday by my still being on duty. Squadron commanders are not irreplaceable, Janet, and no explanation for reassignment is normally given."

"That's outrageous! Punish *you* because they have a quarrel with *me?* What will you do—if I refuse to go home voluntarily?"

"First, I'll ask nicely: Will you?"

"Until you told me about the despicable position they've put you in, I'd have maybe said yes. Now, no. I didn't mention it because I was undecided, but I received a cablegram yesterday from Clay—he wants me to be in Pyongyang when it falls. They were ecstatic with the Seoul segment.

"I wasn't sure because, I must admit, I was scared stiff at Seoul. I just wasn't sure I wanted to go through that again. It's one thing to go to my grave feeling guilty about Skip O'Connor, but quite another to carry knowledge that I chickened out when the going got tough—when *you* put your life on the line with every sortie. I'm going. When I come back, I'll ask to go back to Japan. I'll even ease up on scorching the B-29s."

Ross drew her to his chest and kissed her soundly. "Go," he said. "And don't worry about what they can do to me—I still carry the paper from the guys who bought Allied Air. I love you very much, Redhead."

General Cipolla talked while scanning a stack of paperwork. "Well, how'd it go?"

"Great. I can't thank you enough. How did the mission go?"

"Not so great. All but six ships brought their ordnance home. Forward air control didn't have anything, so they blundered around looking for targets of opportunity. Ace will fill you in. I asked you how things went, and you said 'great.' I assume that means that Janet is catching the next plane out?"

"Not the next one, sir. Maybe a few days from now. CBC wants her to cover the fall of Pyongyang."

Cipolla glared. "Don't be a smart-ass, Colyer. You know what I mean."

"Yes, sir. She claims that she did nothing more than provide a forum for others to express an opinion, and that supreme headquarters has no basis for ejecting her from the theater."

"And?"

"I got the distinct impression that she's ready to take on, not only the air force, but the army and the United Nations as well, to prove her point."

The general leaned back and rubbed his jaw. Suddenly he chuckled, a mirthless sound that grew to a full, belly-shaking laugh. Wiping his eyes, he said, "You know, I love that red-haired wife of yours. Guts? I ask you. Christ, what a general she'd have made. So what do you plan to do— other than sit around reading *The Short but Interesting Air Force Career of Ross Colyer?*"

"I'll deal with whatever they hand out, General."

"Okay. I'll take my lumps right along with you; so, I have a hunch, will General Stratemeyer. I'm pretty goddamned proud of both of you—don't tell Janet that just yet, though. Now get your ass back to work. We got a small war on our hands."

25

14 October 1950
Antung Airfield

Yuri stood in the shabby teahouse's recessed doorway and watched the little group of Chinese officers huddled on the railway platform across the street. The group looked miserable, standing there in a cold wind whipping in off the Yalu. Swirling air currents carried tendrils of black smoke from burning buildings on the Korean side, buildings hit by unseen planes from above the overcast only this morning. Low clouds promised rain or, even more likely, snow, Yuri thought. "Why don't they go inside the station house?" he asked the ancient, almond-eyed owner of the teahouse.

"Very important general. Tough. Chinese officers very tough, no mind cold. He comes to see soldiers go."

"Go?"

"Yes. Time has come for Chinese to chase big-nose Americans out of Korea."

"Won't their bombers attack Antung if China sends soldiers to fight them in Korea? Will China make war with the entire United Nations just to help Korea?"

"Already they drop bombs inside China—here, in Antung. Their airplanes killed many only days ago. We are not afraid. We are many, very strong."

"Where did the bombs hit?" Yuri asked. "I was here that day the radio says they killed women and children. I saw and heard nothing."

The old man threw Yuri a suspicious glance. "The speaker for the 'Hate America' campaign says so. The speaker on the radio says so. Antung is large city, you were in wrong place to see and hear. Why do you ask questions? You are not Chinese—you speak well, but you are a foreigner."

"Yes, I'm from Russia."

"You are from airfield? Soldier?" the man's features, covered by yellow parchmentlike skin, expressed interest.

"Yes, I'm a pilot—here to teach Chinese pilots to fly the jet fighters."

"Ah, so." The proprietors hostility vanished. "Have more tea—no pay. I have very excellent tea leaves only my wife and I enjoy."

While he waited, Yuri saw a red- and gold-decorated locomotive, further adorned with flags and banners, chuff into view. Travel-stained coaches halted at the platform with a screeching of steel brake shoes, the locomotive expelling hissing plumes of steam. A choking pall of soft-coal smoke was added to the stench from smoldering rubble from across the river.

A flood of men wearing padded khaki uniforms poured from the doors. Lugging backpacks and rifles, they laughed and jostled while a screaming NCO tried to form them into a semblance of a formation. He finally abandoned the task and wheeled to salute the general and his staff.

The beaming teahouse owner reappeared with steaming cups of tea. They sipped the fragrant brew and watched the lines of armed soldiers snake eastward away from the station, marching on planks laid across the railroad ties. The general walked alongside for a ways, slapping shoulders and shouting encouragement.

"Are they going to walk across?" Yuri asked. "Why don't they take the train?"

The old man scowled. "Plenty big bombs fall on Korea side. Bridge will not hold heavy train. Big general soon chase bandits away and repair bridge."

"I'm sure he will," Yuri mused. To himself, he added: I wonder what he intends to use to chase the bombers with? Russian MiGs, perhaps? The last transmission I heard from Taiwan told of virtually complete destruction of the NKPA's Air Force.

Aloud, he said, "If I'm not mistaken, the general's name is Hae Chun, and he is scheduled to inspect our air regiments this afternoon."

The teahouse owner bared stained, snaggle teeth in a smile. "Airplane fliers from Russia will bring much honor to China—make plenty big face."

* * *

Yuri shuffled two steps forward as the line of Russian instructor pilots filed past Gen. Hae Chun. Curious, Yuri thought. The unnumbered regiment of Russian volunteers isn't represented at the old boy's reception. Neither, come to think of it, did he inspect their parked airplanes this afternoon. The last of the Chinese officers bowed and moved on; then it was Colonel Zagoria's turn. Yuri cocked an ear to hear what was said.

"Honorable Colonel Zagoria, commander of Russian volunteers to provide pilot instruction," a major—introduced that afternoon as Zhu Wong—chanted.

Yuri turned to make eye contact with Lieutenant Androzov behind him. A wry smile signaled that his friend had also caught the word "volunteer." Yuri turned to try to overhear what else was said. A tall Chinese man, standing two paces behind and to Gen. Hae Chuns's left, caught his attention. The man was dressed in a brown, unadorned singlet—the nondress uniform of the CPA—and appeared aloof to what transpired in the receiving line.

Wrong, Yuri thought; this guy misses nothing. The black, sleepy-looking eyes beneath hooded lids moved constantly. He affected a wispy mustache and goatee, but not a single hair marred the glistening, shaven pate. "Political officer" was written all over him.

Yuri passed his name and rank to Major Zhu and bowed toward the general. "The Chinese People's Army is honored by your presence, Lieutenant Pavel," the old general rumbled. "Do our pilots show progress in the fine new jet fighters?"

"Yes, Comrade General. They are a fine group of young men and they learn quickly. After possibly three hundred practice sorties, you will have a formidable, combat-ready jet fighter force."

From the corner of an eye, Yuri saw Colonel Zagoria flinch. At the same time he saw the skull-like features of the political officer turn toward him. "And how many, as you call them, 'sorties' have they flown to date?" General Hae asked.

"Most have ten, Comrade General, but not all."

Major Zhu fidgeted and coughed, urging Yuri to move on. He did so and strolled to a table along the far wall laden with food and drink. Colonel Zagoria materialized at his elbow before he could finish pouring a glass of wine. "Watch what you say to these men," he hissed. "We cannot possibly provide that much training, and you know it. That civilian is a political commissar from their revolutionary council. His name is Jai Quing, and he's important."

"I'm sorry, Comrade Colonel. I didn't know the Chinese were expecting a corps of skilled combat pilots in one month's time."

The colonel didn't respond, just glared and stalked away. Yuri moved down the table selecting delicacies the name and contents of which he had no idea. Reaching the end of the table, he looked up to confront Gen. Hae Chun, and the civilian, Jai Quing.

"Comrade Lieutenant," Gen. Hae said. "I have the impression that you believe our pilots need much more training than is planned. Is that correct?"

"I'm not aware of how extensive the course is to be, Comrade General. I only know that I flew three hundred sorties before I was certified."

"Ah, so. But if the situation were urgent, they could give a good accounting of themselves much sooner. Am I wrong?"

"Brave men always give a good accounting of themselves in battle, Comrade General. The outcome, however, would depend much upon relative merits of the airplanes and skill of the pilots."

"Is not the MiG-15 a plane superior to any in existence today?" Jai Quing spoke the first words Yuri had heard him utter, a rasping voice, barely above a whisper.

"Without question."

"Well, then, are not our dedicated young pilots the equal of, say, the decadent, cowardly Americans?"

Yuri bowed acknowledgement. "It is as your Chairman Mao said, however: 'Never enter battle overestimating your own strength and underestimating the enemy's.'"

What passed for a smile crossed Jai Quing's gaunt features—it had a cruel aspect, however, that rendered it devoid of humor. "Well spoken, but I detect a certain reservation regarding committing our air force to battle."

Yuri glanced around frantically, seeking a diversion to extricate himself from what he sensed was developing into a confrontation. No opportunity presented itself; Colonel Zagoria seemed to be making a point of avoiding eye contact, in fact.

He squared his shoulders and said, "My father confronted Americans when he was stationed in Berlin. He cautioned me against thinking they were soft and politically unmotivated. Their aircraft are well made. My concern regarding imminent hostilities is for the safety of our own airplanes. They make tempting targets, parked wingtip to wingtip and nose to tail."

"The Americans would never attack a force with such formidable potential for retaliation," the political commissar scoffed. "I'm assured that your General Lubov's airplanes can launch in fifteen minutes' time."

Gen. Hae Chun stroked his chin and looked thoughtful.

"Possibly," Yuri responded. "*If* our pilots can see the bombers. Each morning, an American B-29 flies the length of the Yalu. It takes pictures. Their intelligence officers know exactly where to look for a fat target. The B-29 can bomb through clouds our fighters can't penetrate. I know this because I've examined our own TU-4; much of it's gear was adapted from American design."

"You would move them to bases farther from the border, then?" Gen. Hae Chun asked.

"I would."

"Impossible." Jai Quing's hoarse voice carried an edge now. "The provincial governor insists that the planes be located in a manner to impress visiting officials with a display of our invincibility."

Yuri was spared a rejoinder by one of the Chinese generals, who, a bit inebriated, inserted himself into the little group. Yuri fled, pausing only long enough to tell Androzov, "I'm leaving early—no matter what the colonel will say tomorrow."

7 November 1950
Kimpo Airfield

"The RF-80 reports at least fifteen YAKs parked in revetments." The intelligence officer tapped his pointer on the city of Siniuju. "It's right on the Yalu, across from all those lovely MiGs parked at Antung. You know the rules, don't even give them a second look. Major Colyer, the floor is all yours."

Ross left the space heater's comfort zone and strode across the briefing room to a huge wall map. "Okay, we'll attack in three flights of two from east to west. My lead element will take the first pass with two five-hundred-pounders each. Bozo Two and Bozo Three flights will follow with their spread of HVARs. Break immediately, because you'll be damn nearly on top of the river after release. I'll orbit north of the target and come back in for a strafing pass; the rest of you follow in trail. We won't be all that fat for fuel, so I'll ask for a reading. Anyone without enough go juice will form on Ace in Bozo Two and head for home. Any questions?

"How about AA?"

"The '51s worked that area over pretty well last week. Expect some small-caliber stuff from the south side of the river. North, around the field at Antung, they have lots of it—thirty-seven- and forty-millimeter. Just don't get within reach. Okay, saddle up."

Ross crawled aboard the six-by-six crew transport and regarded the dripping overcast with a critical eye. If they came home on fumes and this stuff was still hanging around. . . . He grinned as a pair of tractors crept past, towing a B-26 with a folded nose gear, and jabbed Ace with an elbow. "Ya know who was flying that bird last night?"

"Who doesn't? The B-26 jocks were telling anyone who would listen at chow this morning. Their CO, Ol' Blood and Guts Benny himself. Less than a week ago he was threatening—threatening, hell, he was guaranteeing—a court-martial for any pilot pranging one of 'his' airplanes. So he comes in high and hot, rolls onto that PSP overrun, brakes won't hold, and he drops the nose wheel in a ditch. Serves the posturing little prick right."

Ross ran preflight checks, fired up, and led his five loaded charges toward the takeoff point. The damned field was feeling like Grand Central Station, he groused. B-26s, F-51s, F-82s, plus their three squadrons of Shooting Stars had every nook and cranny filled. Takeoffs and landings were controlled like L.A. Municipal. Good thing the NKPA was almost out of airplanes—one bomber could really raise hell around here.

Bozo Flight broke into clear air and formed up. Ross made a perfunctory check with the AT-6—providing air control for the zone north of Pyongyang—just to advise that they would be operating through his area. Impulsively he added, "What's the situation at Ping-Pong today, Whiskey Five?"

"Quiet. No action so far. The last gooks pulled out about noon yesterday."

Ross relaxed. Janet had promised to return to Seoul after Pyongyang was secured. He would hold her to that promise to go straight on to Tokyo, he vowed. He glanced at his howgozit—time to head out over water and let down to attack altitude. "Tee time in ten minutes, Bozo Flight," he advised.

At three thousand feet over the Yellow Sea, Ross skirted the ungainly aircraft carrier—always on station there and with itchy trigger fingers—and checked his armament switches. The coastline loomed out of the haze, and he searched for his landfall checkpoint. Spotting the little bay shaped like a cup and saucer, he turned to his run-in heading.

Habit made him reach for the target folder and extract yesterday's aerial photograph—the old check and double-check rule. Okay, there was the main runway, the perimeter taxiway—what the hell? The revetments, with cross-shaped shadows revealing parked airplanes within the U-shaped earthen embankments, were just as he remembered them from the briefing. No one had noticed, however, the *goddamned revetments'* open end faced northeast! The off-limits Yalu River lay not a hundred yards away.

Ross squeezed his mike button. "Bozo Two, Bozo Three, abort plan A—no room, repeat no room, to place your ordnance in open end. We will make run on west-to-east axis. My aiming point is still maintenance hangar complex. Two and Three elements, try for oblique shot into open end of revetments. Strafing runs will be on same headings, but increase your dive angle. Watch that damned river! Acknowledge."

"Gotcha, this is Two."

"Gotcha, Three here."

Ross rolled to a heading that paralleled the shoreline and searched for the telltale, ruler-straight lines of a runway. Damn! How could everyone have missed this? he admonished himself. How the hell could *I* have failed to check it?

There, through lightly falling snow, he caught the unmistakable geometric shapes of buildings. A dusting of snow emphasized the paved runway.

Three thousand feet on the altimeter—buildings disappearing beneath the nose—slight drift to the right—correct five degrees and set up a forty-five-degree dive—tracers from ground fire arced from his left: Caught you asleep, didn't we? You're too late, flashed through his mind.

Target in the gun sight—airspeed building—now! He squeezed the trigger and sucked the stick back. Roll right—level at three thousand and reverse the turn. He swiveled his head to see his wingman pitch up after release. Orange-centered clouds erupted from the hangar complex.

"Bull's-eye, One; this is Two. We're aborting. Three, suggest you do likewise."

"What's the problem, Two?"

"Guess you didn't have time to look, but them revetments is empty—as in nobody home today. Wanna work over the built-up area, or look for a target of opportunity?"

If he'd had a free hand, he would have pounded something in frustration. Damn. As Ross fumed, Bozo Three called, "One, cast your gaze across yon river. Am I seeing things, or is Antung empty as well?"

Ross turned toward the border and peered through the thin layer of scattered clouds. There was no mistake: Empty parking ramps and taxiways gave the field a deserted, abandoned look. What the hell was going on? "Give me fuel readings, Two–Three," he snapped.

"Two's setting on a good hour."

"Three: likewise."

"Roger. Let's go hunting. I'll see if the Mosquito guy down by Sugar Nan has something." Ross punched channel C and called, "Whiskey Five, Bozo Flight here. We've aborted the primary and available. Six birds with full loads and an hour's go juice."

"Good morning there, Bozo. It happens I do have something. Sector How-Tare. Troops report heavy opposition, they're pinned down by artillery-supported infantry. I've called in two flights of Corsairs from the flattop—keep an eye out for them."

"Roger, Whiskey Five. Bozo Flight will be on the scene in about ten minutes. What frequency can we use to work the marines? over."

"Uh—unless you have one-twenty-seven-decimal-eight installed, you'll have to coordinate through me, Bozo One."

Ross clamped his lips. Damnit, would anyone *ever* get this tactical control mess straightened out? The cloud cover beneath them commenced to break up, and the six-ship formation arrived over sector How-Tare at ten thousand feet in the clear.

The source of the army's trouble wasn't hard to spot. Ross's F-80s entered a shallow orbit above a juncture of two valleys. A road that followed the southeastern leg of the V carried a dozen or so vehicles and a

clot of troops scattered on either side. Around the turn, concealed from
the advancing U.N. troops, the northeastern valley contained a phalanx
of what Ross guessed to be as many as one thousand troops.

"Whiskey Five, Bozo One here. Advise the army to *get the hell outta
that valley.* It's a trap—they're outnumbered about ten to one. Tell the
Corsairs that we'll be making firing passes on a southeast-to-northwest
axis. Break, break. Bozo Two, you take over lead and expend rockets on
the main body. Three, you follow. I'll come behind and strafe. Avoid the
intersection; that's where the friendlies are mixing it up with the gooks."

Ross pitched up into a wide turn. Swooping into position behind Bozo
Three, he heard his wingman call, "Bogies, lead. Our eleven o'clock
high."

The Corsairs, Ross thought—they didn't waste any time. He scanned
cobalt-blue skies expecting to see the distinctive gull-winged silhouettes.
He caught movement and frowned. The distant airplanes had straight
wings and inline engines. "Bandits, Bozo Flight! Ten o'clock high and
closing. Unload and rally at angels twenty."

Ross added full throttle and zoomed for altitude. I can't believe it, he
muttered to himself. I didn't think the gooks had a dozen fighters left in
flyable condition. And why would they risk them all at one time? Oh,
well, as soon as Two and Three climb into position, they'd have the
slower YAKs at an altitude disadvantage. It would be a real turkey-shoot.

Standing his '80 on one wing, he tried to reacquire the enemy formation. He picked them up immediately, directly beneath his orbit. Two V
elements of three, cruising along straight and level like dowagers out for
a Sunday stroll, he thought. Christ, they act like they don't even know
we're around!

"Break left, lead!" Ross heard his wingman yell. "Bandits four o'clock
level!"

What the hell? Ross thought as he shoved the stick into the left forward
corner. Tracers—not the orange pinpoints indicating machine-gun fire,
but big, golfball-size ones—streaked past. Cannon fire. At twenty thousand feet? He racked the swiftly accelerating fighter into a tight, descending spiral. Make the bastard overshoot me so I can get a look at him.

"He's on your tail, lead. It's a friggin' *jet.* Swept wing—you got a goddamn MiG on your ass. Hang tight. I'm behind him; on the way."

Ross tightened his turn and felt G forces cram him deeper into the

bucket seat. Bless your heart, Kramer, he thought. Those simulated dog-
fights back at Hanson—you remembered to pitch up and right into a barrel roll as I broke down and left. Now close in and hose him good. But
can the kid catch up? We've conjectured enough on just how fast the MiG
is. I guess we'll find out.

Ross stood at the briefing blackboard, marks from his oxygen mask
visible in his sweat-grimed cheeks, and drew swift lines with the chalk.
"He was a loner and flew the basic pursuit curve from four o'clock.
Kramer deserves a medal; he was doing his job and picked the MiG up
before the bastard got us dead to rights. His break up and right was perfect, and we had the gook pilot boxed. We found out one thing: We can
outdive the MiG at lower altitude. This guy was no green bean. When he
got the picture, he broke off, climbed away from us, and headed north."

General Cipolla slouched in the briefing room's only chair, his feet
resting on the bench back in front of him. He spat out a shred of his cigar
butt and said, "Well, shit. It was a MiG—you're both dead certain?"

"No question, sir," Ross and Kramer replied in unison.

"A loner. It doesn't make sense," the general mused. "Suckered you
into his sights with that YAK formation—that was cute. But why? Just to
see how good that fancy bent-wing fighter is?"

"A couple of things suggest themselves to me," the intelligence officer
interjected. "Number one: A force of the size Colyer saw in that valley
had to contain damned nearly as many men as the NKPA has left in the
west. Then, Eighth Army reports being stopped in their tracks at two
other places today. Question: Are these new troops Korean or Chinese?
We've seen the troop build up in Manchuria—and the NPKA sure as hell
doesn't have MiGs. I have no idea how the Chinks could get so many
men this far south without us knowing, but . . .

"Secondly, why did the Chicoms pull their fighters out of Antung? Just
where the hell are they right now?"

8 November 1950
CPA Regional Headquarters, Shenyang
Major Zhu Wong sat on the edge of his chair, every nerve alert despite
the lateness of the hour. It was past midnight, but much depended on the
news they would receive yet tonight. His boss, Gen. Hae Chun, had gam-

bled heavily today, and Comrade Jai Quing sat in the background like a vulture, ready to tear at the remains if the dice came up wrong.

The words had become heated before the general gave the attack order. "To wait longer is to see the North Korean People's Army reduced to shreds," General Hae insisted. "The march south must be made. You will have China walk alone? While the Americans grow stronger and stronger?"

"A slug does not grow stronger with age. Winter is our best weapon now. The pampered, well-fed Americans will sit in their warm quarters during the Korean mountain blizzards. Their shoddy machines will sit frozen and silent. No, let our ally Russia first commit herself to the ideological struggle— provide the trucks, tanks, and rifles China needs so desperately. The fleet of fighter planes at Antung will be our bulwark. Nothing can cross the Yalu with them in place."

"Ideology will not prevail over sophisticated machines in all cases, Commissar," Hae Chun snapped. "Japan learned that bitter lesson during the last war. Time and strategic position are not on our side. Use our superior numbers now, before the American factories can flood the country with planes, guns, and tanks.

"The Soviet lieutenant spoke honestly when he said our pilots are not ready for meeting the better-trained American Air Force. No, the revolutionary council—Chairman Mao himself—charged me with striking at my discretion. I say the time is now."

"And the American big bombers?" Jai Quing had asked slyly. "Will innocent thousands perish in fireballs if the gangster Truman decides to retaliate by declaring war on China and using the atomic bomb?"

"That issue has been decided. If it happens, the opinion prevails that China's millions can survive. The 'bulwark' of jet fighter planes you mentioned are something else, however. They are most vulnerable, again as the Soviet lieutenant pointed out. I am ordering them dispersed prior to committing our troops openly to battle."

"The provincial governor specifically stated—"

"Will the provincial governor explain to the chairman why all of our fine, new airplanes lie in smoking ruins?"

That exchange had transpired before daylight this morning. General Hae Chun, weakened by the fever and chills of a deep cold, told Zhu to issue the attack order, and returned to his sickbed. Jai Quing sat by the message center all day, his features cold and impassive. The general was behind his desk again when the Soviet general Lubov triumphantly relayed word that one of his pilots had encountered six of the vaunted American jets and escaped unscathed.

Jai Quing's eyes had glittered with satisfaction as he read the dispatch. The general's reminder—"Notice he used the word 'escaped'; wars are not won by soldiers who escape without inflicting losses on the enemy"—was not well received.

Major Zhu sighed. If Gen. Hae Chun's view prevailed this day, he should shoot the recalcitrant political officer, and cite treasonous activity as justification. No voice would be raised in protest; the major felt certain of that.

26

5 December 1950
Kimpo Airfield

Kyle Wilson popped dive brakes and let his Sabrejet drift in trail behind Major Yocum for the landing approach. A quick glance at the ground provided a sobering reminder that he was, at last, in a war zone. Blackened shells of buildings, entire city blocks devoid of any sign of population— the city of Seoul looked dead and alone.

"Dagger One on the break, Tower." Lead's transmission prompted Kyle to return his attention to landing. As he spaced himself behind lead and started counting down for pitchout, the view from his cockpit was even more depressing. At traffic pattern altitude their F-86s were brushing the bases of somber, gray clouds. Even a combat novice could recognize the symmetrical pockmarks on and around the field as unfilled shell craters.

Don't let the fact that this is probably the sorriest runway you've ever landed on throw you, Kyle thought as he scanned the cockpit in a last-minute before-landing check. Five thousand feet of uneven hard surface with a PSP overrun. "Go easy with the binders on that PSP," he recalled the briefing officer at Itazuke warning them.

He couldn't suppress a cocky grin beneath his oxygen mask, however, as he felt the main gear impact "on the numbers." Hope Major Colyer was watching that, he thought as his rollout quickly diminished to taxi speed before reaching the stretch of pierced steel planking.

It wasn't until Kyle was outside his cockpit and adjusted to the feeling of being on terra firma that the pace of activity on the field registered. Behind him, a flight of F-80s lumbered into the murk, each with four one-thousand-pound bombs slung beneath its wings. Across the field, bellowing radial engines shattered the cold, damp atmosphere as ground crews ran max-power checks. Wheeled vehicles wove through parked airplanes with reckless abandon.

Despite the feverish tempo, he noticed that every face wore a grim expression. The only touch of irrepressible GI humor was a sign some wag had erected at the Sabrejets' cramped parking area. It read, WELCOME TO KIMPO SABRE PILOTS. Beneath a big arrow the painter had added, THIS WAY TO SEE THE MIGS—200 MILES.

A six-by-six dropped the Sabre pilots and their gear in front of the two-story operations building with a glass-enclosed control tower perched on top. Just about the only glass visible, Kyle noticed. In the ops building itself, only two windows facing the runway boasted a transparent barrier against the elements. A half-dozen others displayed smoke-blackened borders.

Inside, the chilly operations room was a similar profusion of loudly talking, sober-faced men. Kyle searched for Major Colyer's familiar visage and rangy figure, then hardly recognized his friend. Ross was walking toward him, but the smile of welcome seemed forced.

Kyle's first thought was: My God, the major's been out on an all-night bender. Ross's flight suit was wrinkled and soiled, his face drawn and grimy; strands of blond hair extending below the sweat stained flight cap didn't appear to have been trimmed for weeks.

"Kyle," Ross said flatly as he extended his hand, "I'm sure glad to see you. But any celebration will have to wait. How the hell are you?"

"Kinda confused, sir. Someone went and pushed the panic button back home. Eight days ago we got pulled out on twenty-four hours' notice and put on a Northwest Airlines charter. God only knows how they got airplanes in place this fast, but here we are—ready to make the world safe for democracy. I figure we can get the job done and be home for Christmas."

Ross chuckled. "Same old Kyle. Look, I have about two hours before briefing for my second sortie today. Why don't you stow your gear someplace and come to the mess tent with me? I'll see your CO and assure him that I'll get you to the right billets."

Kyle wasn't hungry, but picked at his plate of American hot dogs and beans while Ross talked between bites. "How did Terri take your sudden departure?"

"Ah, she's a solid citizen. Mom wanted Terri to come to D.C. and stay with her and Dad. But Terri decided to take an apartment in Seattle. She'll find a job—if this business drags into winter."

"I think you can count on that," Ross said grimly. "How are your folks?"

"Great. I'm almost embarrassed to tell you Mom's latest stunt."

"I gotta know," Ross replied laughingly. "*Nothing* she does will ever surprise me."

"Well, a friend of hers got a letter from her son—he's in a B-26 squadron somewhere over here. He was complaining about the cold, wet tents they live in—said he's sleeping in his flying suit and wool socks. So his mom sent him—of all the dumb things—an electric blanket. Mom told me just before I left that she's shipping me one. Can you imagine? In a war zone, getting shot at every day, and sleeping beneath an electric blanket? Where, I ask you, am I supposed to plug it in?"

Ross chewed and swallowed, then said, "If you don't get a higher offer, I'll give you a hundred bucks for it. You're gonna have what is probably the most valuable possession on base. The engineers always run lights to the billeting areas, by the way."

Ignoring Kyle's dumbfounded expression, Ross continued. "I don't know how much of a briefing you've had, but you're getting here at what I believe the eggheads call an auspicious moment."

"Yeah, I hear the Chinks are into the act in a big way."

"Very big, as in steamroller. North Korea looks like a big anthill—the bastards are *everywhere*. We've all been flying two to three sorties a day; you kill maybe a thousand and go home. You go back the next day and there're *two* thousand shooting at you, and during the night they've gotten ten miles closer."

"How about those MiG-15s? That's what I'm interested in. The brass tells us they're the reason for the rush-rush to get us over here."

"They're up north—no problem finding them. They're sitting in plain sight only five miles across the Yalu. And they're as safe as if they were in church. You *don't* cross that river. They wait until you're up there—running low on fuel—then swarm across, take a quick shot, and dash for home."

"Are they as good as we've been told?"

"Probably better. The airplane is fast, maneuverable, and has a ceiling of around fifty thousand feet. They carry cannons. They're chewing up our F-80's unless we can outsmart one now and then. They don't seem to carry enough fuel to come more than about a hundred miles south, but the targets we simply gotta take out are all within that range.

"The B-29s are their meat. The Superforts can't bomb at night from high altitude and hit anything, so they stroll in during daylight at about eight thou and get the holy shit shot out of them. Their central fire control system can't even track a MiG at full deflection, plus they're down in the gooks' ack-ack range."

"I'd guess that we'll be flying escort then."

"You guess right. But don't be surprised if you're alerted for an oh-five-thirty interdiction sortie when you get back to your quarters."

"Really?"

"Really. The only reason I'm waiting around before flying my second sortie is to see if I still have a target. We're going all out to hold Pyongyang. When I was up there on an armed recce this morning, the bomb line was right on the north side of the city. There's a good chance the army has pulled south by now, in which case we'll have to wait until they get out of the city and dug in again."

"It's that bad then?"

"It's that bad. There's already talk that we may get chased out of here."

"Je-e-sus. Where the hell will we go?"

"All the way to Japan. There won't be a field left in Korea that'll handle a jet."

Kyle whistled. "I guess we'd best get saddled up then. Christ, I can't wait to get a crack at a MiG. We haven't even had anything to practice dogfighting with that can make it interesting."

Ross pushed his tray aside and sipped coffee. "Don't get cocky. That airplane is good. The pilots—well, you never know. Some are as good as any of ours—the one I tangled with was no tenderfoot. Then you'll find one who flies like it was his first solo. Just use your head."

"I gotcha. Anyway, what do you hear from Janet?"

"Janet's up there—in Pyongyang, according to the last note I had from her."

"She's *what?* Up there where—"

"Where the Chicoms are cranking their meat grinder—yeah. Damnit, I tried to send her back to Japan—weeks ago. She's in hot water with

MacArthur's headquarters, she's . . . Ah, hell. I'm sure she's okay, but I wish she'd get her butt back down here—so I could kick it." Ross's harried expression belied his flippant demeanor.

"Surely there was enough time for—" Kyle looked up as a weary-looking noncom stopped at their table.

"Major Colyer?"

"Yeah, I'm Colyer."

"I'm an air evac medic, sir. May I may have a word with you?"

"Of course. Sit down. She's all right, isn't she?" Kyle saw blood drain from Ross's face.

"In a manner of speaking, sir. A bit of frostbite is all. I rode with her in a chopper to the dispensary here just now. They're putting her on an air medevac flight leaving very shortly now for Tachikawa. She asked me to try to get word to you."

"Oh, my God." Ross sprang to his feet. "Look, Kyle, I gotta run—see if I can catch her before they load that plane. Then I have a sortie to fly. I'll look you up tonight. Oh, and thanks for chasing me down, Sergeant."

8 December 1950
Antung Airfield

Yuri sat wooden-faced while Colonel Zagoria outlined the day's mission. General Lobov and four of his volunteer pilots occupied a rear bench. "I will lead the formation of five, five-ship elements," the colonel said. "You four instructor pilots will lead elements two, three, four, and five. This will be your students' first entry into a war zone, so brief them carefully. Under no circumstances will a student pilot leave the formation, except to return home with an emergency. Neither will we engage the enemy. Our task is to draw the Americans into an attack.

"The American Shooting Star pilots are aggressive.They are certain to react when our large formation approaches their bombers. General Lobov's experienced volunteer pilots will orbit in the sun at thirteen thousand meters. *They,* not us, will strike from above. Brief your Chinese students to watch carefully; this is only a training flight for them. Let them observe the Americans' tactics. Report now to the ready rooms and select your crews. Standby-aircraft time is thirteen hundred hours. That is all."

Yuri struggled to control his frustration as the contingent of instructors filed from the room. Who had planned this bit of idiocy? The way to train a fighter pilot was to put him on the wing of an experienced one. To send twenty novices into enemy territory was asking for disaster.

What if one—only one—enemy plane penetrated the formation? Chaos would result; single planes would be all over the sky. Fat targets, if they managed to avoid midair collisions, that is.

"You have the look of a troubled man, Yuri Sergeievich." Yuri turned to discover Colonel Zagoria walking alongside. "Are you not proud to be one of the first to engage the enemy?"

"I would be proud to be among the first to *engage* the Americans, Comrade Colonel. What we're doing today could hardly be called that."

"A modest beginning. Later, after our charges become adjusted, we will attack the bomber formations. With General Lobov's pilots flying top cover, of course."

"Colonel, ten, twenty, even fifty sorties will not prepare our student pilots for confronting hostile fire. The young pilots in my section are eager and trying hard, but few will survive their first brush with the American fighter cover—even with piston-engined Mustangs."

"A regrettable possibility, Yuri Sergeivich. But recall our meeting in Shenyang. Our mission is *not* to defend the Chinese mainland, remember? Our sole objective is to deny Korea to the Western imperialists. If we must use the abundant supply of Chinese manpower to do so . . ."

"I know," Yuri responded. "The master plan. It seems, Comrade Colonel, that each of us is little more than a pawn in someone else's master plan. Is there no room for individual initiative?"

"Take care, Yuri Sergeievich. You come dangerously close to revisionism."

"I know, Comrade Colonel, and I'm sorry. I realize that everything we're doing is for the good of the Party. It's just that some of these students are no different from our own—bright, anxious to learn. I hate to squander them unnecessarily."

"You're a professional soldier, Lieutenant Pavel. I'm surprised to hear you question orders. Naturally, we strive to keep losses to a minimum, but some losses must be expected during combat. Just make certain you aren't one of them."

"Colonel Zagoria." The mission commander turned as his name was called from behind. Yuri continued toward the ready room, deep in thought. Marya's letter yesterday had praised a film she'd seen the evening before at a Red Banner meeting. So Papa was still well. That was good news, because it appeared that his son's goal of attaining recognition by exemplary performance was not in the immediate future.

15 December 1950
Kimpo Airfield

"We're going to give the gook quarterbacks a different defense lineup today, troops." General Cipolla lounged against the briefing podium, using a dead cigar for a pointer. "The B-29s haven't been able to do more than hit some of the approaches to the pair of bridges across the Yalu at Sinuiju. So we're gonna take the entire 14th Wing up there today and put those damn spans on the south end under water."

Cipolla, a big grin on his face, waited for the mutters of dismay to subside. "I know, I know, we're sticking our head in the lion's mouth. This is where we spring our surprise. Today we're gonna use the B-29s as a diversionary force. *They* will be bait to draw the MiGs out of position instead of the other way around.

"The bombers will cross the coastline on a course for the ammo and chemical plants at Hungnam. The Sabrejets have been escorting them, so the Chicoms will launch a max effort to counter this raid. It's the same principle as suckering a defensive back with a screen pass: a matter of timing. As soon as the main MiG formation is on its way from Antung to the east coast, we're going to hit the railroad bridge at Sinuiju with eight F-80s from Major Colyer's 66th Squadron."

A few chuckles revealed that some of the worried-looking pilots had picked up on the strategy. "You're right. At the exact time Ross is starting his run, the B-29s are going to hightail it north out of the MiGs' range— *china is N of Korea* 'cause the F-86s are going to be flying top cover for our other two squadrons of F-80s coming in ten minutes after Ross. The Reds are going to launch their reserve MiGs, of course, when our first planes show up. This will give the F-86 guys the chance they've been waiting for—hit the Chinese form *their* blind side for a change.

"Meanwhile, the main Chicom force is caught in the middle of Korea and can't reach either of our attacking formations with enough fuel to engage. The only thing they can do is run for home and refuel. Well, it takes twenty minutes, minimum, for them to turn around. By that time the Superforts have come back, hit their targets at Hungnam, and headed home. We, likewise, have wiped out the bridges and most of the MiG reserve force. Neat, huh?"

Ross strolled to the mess hall at Cipolla's invitation for coffee. "Well, whadya think of Operation Snipe Hunt, Ross?"

"I know you played football at the Point, General, but were you ever in an all-star game?" Ross countered.

"Nope, can't say I ever was."

"That's what this mission reminds me of. Three players—the F-80s, F86s, and B-29s—all of them stars in their own right, trying to run a screen pass without ever practicing it."

Cipolla grunted. "The timing."

"Yes, sir. If all the players aren't in their assigned positions at exactly the right time, the ball gets dropped—fumbled—intercepted, even."

"It's tight, and I won't pretend that I don't have a few reservations myself. Keep your options open; you're in the kickoff spot. I didn't include this in my briefing, but an RB-29 will be overhead along the border to see if the gang at Antung takes the bait. If they don't, it's up to you to give me the recall code word. Now, what do you hear from Janet?"

"An ATC pilot brought me a note from her yesterday. She's out of the hospital but has trouble walking. She froze both heels standing in snow doing a goddamned interview with an NKPA officer who wanted to defect."

"I see. The FEAF PIO asked me about her just the other day. I told him they could relax, she was in Tokyo and headed back to the States after that—right?"

"As far as I can determine, but you know Janet, sir."

"I do. I'll believe she's going to give up meekly and leave when I hear she's at home teaching Sunday school. Well, time to fire up, I guess. See you when we all gather at the river, as the song goes."

Kyle closed both eyes for a brief respite from the eyeball-searing sunlight; even dark glasses couldn't provide total protection at forty-five thousand feet. He flexed the fingers of his right hand gripping the stick. They should be seeing action momentarily. The orbiting RB-29 had made a cryptic announcement twenty minutes earlier that Red Riding Hood was in the forest—the signal that Korean radar had detected the bomber stream and MiGs had taken off from Antung, most of them, at least. He glanced behind to see that the four other two-ship elements—loafing behind at a fuel-conserving 220 knots—were still in position. It was now three minutes before Ross's ETA for Sinuiju. That's when the fun would start.

Major Yocum had edged his formation of Sabres westward until Kyle could catch glimpses of the Yalu River through the scattered clouds below. He strained to identify the airfield at Antung, but fluffy white heaps of cumulus kept drifting across the scene.

"Bandits, Dagger Flight." The electrifying words were repeated. "This is Pigeon. Repeat, bandits, many your one o'clock, angels fifty, heading green seven, over."

What the hell! Kyle asked himself. Bandits? Many? Northeast? Headed east by south? He glanced at his map. Where had they come from? Not from Antung, for certain. My God, they were headed for the bombers! When the B-29s changed course north to evade the fighters from Antung, they had turned directly into this new force's path. He glanced at Major Yocum—what would they do? Belatedly he thought to punch channel C for air combat control.

". . . Estimated to be forty in number. Dagger Flight will divert and intercept. That's authenticated by the CG, Dagger Lead," Kyle heard.

"Roger, Whiskey Five," he heard Yocum reply. "Bozo Flight, did you copy?"

"Copy all, Dagger One. Have fun. Sorry you'll miss our party."

Kyle switched back to squadron frequency in time to hear, "Dagger Flight, this is Dagger One. Change course now. Estimate contact in one-zero minutes—many bandits reported at angels fifty." He added power to stay on Yocum's wing. This is crazy, he thought. We're going off and leaving the F-80s on their own—they'll get slaughtered. And ten of us are taking on maybe *forty* MiGs that are at fifty thousand, which we can't even *reach?*

A cluster of black dots ahead and above were barely visible when Major Yocum broke radio silence. "Bandits twelve o'clock high, dagger Flight. Hold until they dive for attack, then follow them down."

27

15 December 1950
35,000 Feet Above Unsan, North Korea
Yuri glanced again at his instrument-panel clock. The Ch'ongch'on River's silver thread shimmered fewer than thirty kilometers ahead. They were at the limit of their radius of action—he watched for Colonel Zagoria's entry into the sweeping turn that would return them to Antung. Where were the American fighters? Surely their radar had detected the huge targets that twenty-five MiGs, flying wingtip to wingtip, would present. For that matter, where were the big bombers? It was perfect weather for them.

He looked left and right at his wingmen and felt a surge of pride. He'd selected his best students for this ill-advised—to his way of thinking—effect to draw the American jets into an ambush, and they had held flawless formation all the way. He searched overhead but failed to locate their top cover. They must be up there—a brief, coded announcement had confirmed that the all-Soviet force as airborne from the group based at Shenyang. The trap was set, but where was the prey?

Yuri saw Zagoria rock his wings, then enter a shallow turn to the left. He took a deep breath—this was the test. Five elements of five ships executing a 180-degree turn while maintaining line abreast formation wasn't a simple maneuver for novice pilots. Sure enough, before the turn was half completed, he caught glimpses of wingmen dropping out of position. He shook his head. The group would be halfway back to Antung before the gaggle of aircraft reformed.

Thirty miles behind the Chinese formation, Kyle strained to keep the distant MiG formation in view through a thin haze of ice crystals. He jerked as he heard Major Yocum break radio silence with a terse,

"Whiskey Five, Dagger One. We have bandits, three o'clock, low. I'm engaging, over."

"Roger, understand, Dagger One. Be advised the target is believed to be a diversion, over."

"Gotcha, Whiskey Five, We'll keep our eyes peeled. Okay, Dagger Flight, let's go get 'em. The formation appears to be pretty ragged—look for stragglers. We'll yo-yo, but watch your fuel."

Kyle saw Yocum's drop tanks separate and punched his own. All right! he enthused silently. This is it—this is the day I get my first MiG, maybe two. He lagged behind to cover his lead's tail, but he'd have his chance to break off and find his own target after the first slashing pass through the still unsuspecting formation. One last double check of his armament selector switches and he watched the enemy planes take shape in his gunsight.

Yocum had selected his target, a lone ship separated from the others by at least five hundred yards. Kyle scanned the main body of fighters; they still seemed blissfully unaware of the Sabres' presence. A dozen heartbeats later he saw tracers from Yocum's plane impact squarely into the MiG's engine compartment. A flash of dirty yellowish flame and debris erupted into their flight path.

Kyle followed Yocum's abrupt pull-up and climbing turn. Leveling above the attack site, Kyle slid away from his lead and searched for a new victim. He blinked as he regarded the confused swirl of enemy and friendly aircraft. From the corner of an eye he saw three smoking, out-of-control fighters tumbling earthward—MiGs, he thought, but couldn't be sure. Yocum rolled into a firing pass on an aimlessly circling single. Kyle, seeing no threat to his leader's rear, searched for a target of his own. He spotted one whose distinctive placement of the horizontal stabilizer labeled it a MiG and turned to center it in his gunsight.

Not yet, he admonished himself. Get close, closer: Don't shoot until you think you're going to ram him, he recalled his gunnery instructor saying. Almost—his eyes widened in disbelief as he saw the MiG's canopy fly off, followed by a tumbling figure. Then he was past. What the hell? The goddamn pilot *ejected* before I could fire a shot.

Kyle was still shaking his head as he racked the Sabre into a screaming

Immelmann to rejoin the fray. Directly ahead he saw the silhoutte of an F-86, its white star unmistakable, locked in a deadly series of gyrations with a tenacious opponent. He saw the Sabre pilot pitch up into a six-G loop. The MiG on his tail executed an even tighter one and loosed a burst of cannon fire. The Sabre staggered slightly and broke straight down.

Without even attempting to make a kill shot, Kyle squeezed off a burst in the general direction of the enemy attacker. The eight .50-caliber tracers, arcing lazily in front of the MiG, succeeded in breaking up the dogfight, but Kyle found himself closing nose-to-nose with his intended quarry at more than a thousand miles per hour.

She-e-e-sch, he muttered under his breath. He broke hard down and to the right. How the hell did he do that?

"Break left, Kyle!" he heard someone yell over his headset. "You got one on your ass."

Kyle reflexively rolled left and sucked the stick toward his gut. The Sabre bucked and groaned as he felt the tubes of his G-suit inflate to counteract the wing-straining maneuver. He immediately recalled Major Colyer's advice: "Don't try to outclimb a MiG." Before his attitude stabilized, he continued his roll into a split-S and streaked straight down.

The surprise change in direction caused the pursuing MiG to overshoot. Kyle slid behind him. Before he could line up a shot, the Chinese jet entered a near-vertical climb. Kyle looked around to see the other MiGs doing likewise, as if in reaction to a recall order. They were headed home, and the F-86s had only enough fuel to do the same.

The tight-lipped two-star general glared at weary pilots slumped on the briefing room's straight-backed benches. "This was *not* one of FEAF's better performances," the DCS OPS snarled. "Intelligence is still trying to piece together what the hell went wrong, but, by God, *I* know a couple of things we can start with. Colonel Bates, maybe you would like to tell us why in the hell your command post diverted Dagger Flight from its briefed mission."

A slim, nattily uniformed man stood. "An OPS IMMEDIATE from the joint United Nations targeting group, sir. I have a copy here." He waved a pink flimsy. "The targets at Hungnam were given a triple-A priority—the B-29s had to take them out at all costs."

The FEAF general's features turned near-apoplectic. "And did you think to consult General Stratemeyer—or myself—before issuing the order?"

"Our standing orders don't require it, sir. Target priorties stand without question."

"We'll see about *that* in the future. Now, whose bright idea was it to switch targets from the MiG formation going after the Superforts to that fucking diversionary force?"

Major Yocum stood. "That was my decision, sir. The enemy formation ahead was virtually out of our range. Even if we could have caught it, we wouldn't have had more than five or ten minutes' time for engagement. I elected to attack the nearer force, where we had an opportunity to inflict major losses—which we did."

"You made that decision all by yourself, did you?"

"Yes, sir. I believe when all kills are confirmed we'll be credited with destroying eight and damaging three out of twenty-five enemy aircraft, sir."

"And you can take great pride in your accomplishment, Major Yocum. You managed to shoot down almost an entire squadron of what we believe were pilot trainees, while somehow losing one of your own. Meanwhile, their big brothers made mincemeat of nine B-29s and kept them from bombing their primary target.

"Perhaps you can engrave that on a plaque and hang it in your office—for that's your next assignment. You've led your last fighter formation while you're in FEAF."

Kyle saw Yocum's features turn to a frozen mask as he sat down. Goddamnit! Kyle wanted to scream. How the hell were we to know it was a diversionary force? Besides, not all those cats were greenhorns. The one that got Parker—and I tangled with—was a pro. He bit back the words, however, as the irate general continued.

"The upshot of this fiasco is that the plan to put both bridges at Sinuiju out of commission was a bust. Its net result: one span of the railroad bridge severely damaged, for the third time. The F-80s ran into intense, and accurate, antiaircraft fire and were hit by MiGs from Antung. We lost ten Shooting Stars. Their wing commander, General Cipolla, was shot down trying to cover a shot-up wingman.

"I've known Cappy Cipolla since we flew together during World War II. A greater guy and a better pilot has yet to come down the pike. Maybe that's why . . . Well, enough said. We lost one of the air force's giants today, men."

Kyle felt as if he'd been kicked in the stomach. This is going to hit Ross hard, he thought.

15 December 1950
Antung Airfield

Yuri stared at the briefing room floor between those stupid red-leather boots the Chinese insisted on their pilots wearing—never mind that they came off when you ejected. He could still see the dazed, stricken looks on his surviving students' faces after landing. It was the first time he could remember that they hadn't gathered around laughing and chattering as they boasted of their flying skills.

The briefing officer's harsh words roused him from his glum introspection. Yuri recognized the political officer who'd briefed them at Shenyang. He looked around for Colonel Zagoria but couldn't see him.

"A terrible blow was struck against the boasting, cowardly, imperialist invaders today. As a result of our cunning planning, their massive fleet of big bombers was cut to ribbons and sent home without inflicting noticeable damage."

"Blind luck," one of General Lobov's pilots had enthused to Yuri on the way to debriefing. "While we were trying to find the decoy formation, we ran straight into nine of their Superforts. Where they came from, or where they were headed, nobody knows, but we caught them by surprise and got three on the first pass. We managed to cripple two more, but those babies make tough targets."

The exuberant political colonel continued. "One of the largest formations of fighter-bombers mounted by the enemy to date was prevented from destroying the twin bridges between here and Sinuiju. Their losses were staggering; our comrades in the volunteer regiment accounted for at least twenty confirmed kills."

"We should have gotten at least half their number," another volunteer pilot had complained to Yuri. "We didn't get airborne in time to hit the first wave that took out one span of the railroad bridge. Then that group kept us from hitting the major formation before they could jettison their bombs and get into a defensive formation. The Shooting Star is slower and isn't as maneuverable as our MiG, but those pilots are nothing to fool around with. They took a beating from our antiaircraft, but I believe we shot down only three."

The briefing officer's tone grew cold as he said, "Unfortunately, our decoy formation missed its rendezvous with the group from Shenyang because of faulty navigation. A roving force of perhaps fifty of a new, faster, but still inferior fighter plane, called the Sabrejet, ambushed the Chinese formation and inflicted grievous losses. The bloodthirsty gangsters even murdered some of our brave airmen who were forced to eject from crippled airplanes.

"Colonel Zagoria has confessed to serious error in straying from the briefed course and has returned to Moscow. You will meet your new commander tomorrow morning."

That isn't true, Yuri wanted to protest. We *were* on the briefed flight path. We *did* make our turn on time and at the right checkpoint. And the idea that they gunned down helpless pilots—I know better. I saw one break off an attack after one or our foolish young pilots ejected rather than fight. And that new, swept-wing fighter we saw is *not* an inferior machine—by no stretch of the imagination.

Lieutenant Androzov took one look at Yuri as his roommate dragged into their billet and said, "I do believe we should go directly to the canteen before the vodka is all gone."

3 January 1951
Kimpo Airfield

Still dazed by General Cipolla's death, Ross stowed the gaily wrapped bottle of champagne, Janet's Christmas gift, in the footlocker destined to be flown to Itazuke by C-47 the next morning. There's been damn little to celebrate recently, he observed to himself.

Even after being assured that a formal ceremony would be held at Arlington, complete with presentation of the Medal of Honor to Maria, the brief memorial service this morning seemed totally inadequate. The "missing man" formation Ross had insisted he lead as a flyover was laden with bombs on its way to try to stem the inexorable Chinese advance. He hoped Cappy would appreciate the irony.

They'd failed. He cocked an ear at the faint rumble of artillery fire. When he led the squadron in the morning, it would be on a ferry flight to Itazuke. Kimpo was being abandoned once again. An angry, frustrated

Kyle had flown out with the F-86 contingent the day before. "Misawa? Air defense?" he'd wailed.

Ross picked up Janet's letter that had accompanied the champagne and scanned her holiday message once more. Following her profession of undying love, she'd added:

> *I'm walking normally at last. The doctor says I'll experience some pain during cold, damp weather for a time. So much for Christmas in Michigan next year! By the way, darling, I asked the medics to give you a can of film. It was an interview I did before I left Pyongyang, and Clay says they never received it. It was a very, very important film. Can you trace it from there?*

Ross scowled and tossed the missive into his B-4 bag—he had other things to worry about. Not one damned word about her going home herself, he noted.

"Major Colyer?" An airman wearing a GI parka and overshoes asked through the open door.

"Yeah."

"General Eubanks would like to see you in his office right after chow, sir."

"Okay, thank you. Any idea what's up?"

"No, sir. General Cipolla's replacement is on base, however. Maybe he wants you to meet him."

Ross grunted. How would it be, working for someone besides the shrewd, acid-tongued Italian? he wondered. He slipped into his fleece-lined bomber jacket and headed for the mess hall to have lunch with Doug. The maintenance officer would be staying behind to the last, over-seeing the shipment of spare parts.

General Eubanks returned Ross's salute and waved him to an inverted packing crate. Ross eyed the full colonel already ensconced in the office's only other chair and nodded a greeting. Outside, airmen were busily assembling crates of records for evacuation.

"Excuse the mess, but we're bugging out at sixteen hundred. Ross, meet Colonel Tom Wadley. Tom's replacing Cappy as CO of the 14th."

Ross crossed the near-empty office and shook hands. "My condolences, Major Colyer. I understand that you and the general went back a few years."

"Yes, sir. I feel like I've lost a family member." A tinge of bitterness was impossible to conceal.

Eubanks chuckled. "Go ahead and say it, Ross. Your reaction to Snipe Hunt is no secret."

"I guess maybe I talked out of turn at debriefing, sir. It won't happen again. But it was hard to take, especially after General Cipolla himself expressed concern about the intricate timing the mission entailed."

"Oh, I agree with what you said. It's the reason I asked you over here at the last moment. Since the entire Fifth Air Force is being scrambled, it seems a good time to make some badly needed changes."

"Sir?"

"First, your maintenance officer, Captain Curtiss, will be reassigned to FEAF headquarters as chief of jet engine maintenance. It'll mean a promotion, by the way."

"He's one of the best, sir. But I'll sure miss him."

"Oh, I don't think you'll miss him too badly. You see, you won't be CO of the 66th any longer."

"I beg your pardon, sir?"

"No; you're going to have a chance to fix the thing you've been complaining about—forward air control. General Stratemeyer wants you to come back to Tokyo headquarters and put together some kind of joint communications–operations center—command post—the thing doesn't even have a name yet. Anyway, what maybe caused us to lose Cappy shouldn't happen. Can you do it?"

"I—I'll do my best, sir. But—"

"There's your squadron; there's a war on; they can't get along without you—I know all about that. I've been down that road myself, and it's always a surprise to go back to the old outfit a few months later and find that they're doing just fine, thank you. Now"—the general fumbled in his desk drawer—"you'll need these." He tossed a pair of silver oak leaves onto his desk. "Pin 'em on tomorrow morning."

Ross shook his head. "This is . . . well, I don't know what to say. I had no idea—"

"Getting promoted out of the cockpit is always a shock, Ross. But it's inevitable, and you'll get used to it. Now, who do you suggest as your replacement?"

"Uh—Ace Aldershot, sir. He's up to date on everything that goes on."

"I thought maybe you'd say that, and I agree. If I can find someone with a typewriter that isn't packed away, we'll cut orders yet this afternoon. He'll take the squadron to Itazuke while you take the Gooney Bird to Tokyo.

"Good luck, Colyer. Sorry there's no time for the usual hoopla that goes along with this kind of thing; that'll have to wait until after we chase those yellow-skinned sons of bitches back north of the Yalu. Okay, anything you want to say?"

"Yes, sir. My wife sent me a bottle of champagne for Christmas. I haven't had a reason to open it until now. I'd like very much for you to drop by my hut before you leave and join me in a last toast to General Cipolla. I'll have Doug and Ace there as well."

"It'll be an honor and a privilege, Colonel Colyer."

6 January 1951
Tokyo
"Ross?" Janet asked breathlessly. "Ross? Is it really you? Where are you calling from?"

"I'm at Tachikawa. I just landed—"

"*Tachikawa?* You mean it? Oh, m'God. I have to sit down. No, I'm not going to sit down—I'm on my way. Where should I meet you?"

Ross laughed. "Make it the officers' club. I haven't even had time to get a BOQ room."

"Have one by the time I get there."

Ross woke to see Janet, barely visible in the early dawn light, propped on one elbow while she traced the lines in his face with a feather-soft touch. As his eyes flickered, she leaned over and kissed him lightly. "Good morning, you handsome devil. God, how I've missed waking up beside you."

"With any luck, it may get to be habit-forming. I assume I'll be based here until I get whatever it is I'm supposed to organize put together. It's going to take some getting used to, but maybe a tour behind a desk won't be as bad as I've always thought.

"Speaking of which, we'd better look for a place to live, that is if you plan to keep on working." Ross chuckled. "The billeting officer let me get away with having a woman in my BOQ room for one night, but we'll have to move on today."

"Ross, I'd like you to see the place I'm living. I'm sure the *mamasan* can give us a double room with a Western bed."

"A *Western* bed? What the hell kind of place are you in?"

"A Japanese hotel—more of a pension. It's a funny story. When I first arrived, a Japanese employee at INS recommended it. Then I was told by an American that the family hated all Americans—they lost a son in the war. Some GIs who stayed there had even been beaten up. I moved, of course, but when I came back, I started asking more. Eijo, the Japanese who took me there, explained that the family didn't *hate* me; they were worried that I'd feel their place was inferior. I went back, and I love it."

"Okay, I'll take a look, but what's this business about a bed?"

"You want to try a tatami mat and a wooden block for a pillow? Come on, lazybones. Let's get some breakfast. I'm starved."

Ross pushed his plate aside and poured more coffee. "Okay, you've talked all around your job. What are you up to?"

"Well, all the networks started doing the same thing we're doing, so it isn't new and different anymore. And working for a big outfit can get frustrating. At least one cablegram every day; WE'D THINK IT NEAT IF . . . WHY NOT FOLLOW UP ON . . . NEED MORE ON. . . . In short, I gave Clay my resignation."

"What? I thought—"

"That I'd found my lifetime work? It took that ride out of Pyongyang to bring me down to earth. I was in the way over there, Ross. That chopper would have been bringing out a wounded GI, but for me. Then I still think of Skip O'Connor. . . . I believe in keeping the public informed, but I'm ready to let someone else do the job."

"I can understand. In a way, I feel I'm getting into the same trap—working for a big corporation instead of a little proprietorship."

"You'll do just great. And as a lieutenant colonel—wow. And I'm just thrilled to pieces about Doug and Ace's promotions. What a party we'll have when we all get together at home again. If only General Cipolla . . . I wrote Maria a long letter, by the way. How awful. You say that it was a screwup?"

"In the worst way. It's what I'm supposed to keep from happening again."

"I'm sure you will. Oh, and Ross, that can of movie film I wrote about. Did you find out what happened to it?"

"Uh, no, 'fraid not. Things were getting a bit hectic then. I'm not surprised it went astray. What was so special about it?"

"It was a great interview. This North Korean officer was taken prisoner and brought to a holding pen outside Pyongyang. He said he wanted to talk to an American reporter, and I lucked out and got to him first. It was a miserable day, and I had to walk through slush and cold mud to get there, then stand around for half a day to get to see him—that's how I got frostbite.

"Anyway, he claimed to be an NKPA pilot who'd crash-landed on a mission to Pyongyang and been captured. He said he took flight training in a MiG-15 inside Manchuria at a Russian airfield."

"That would probably be Antung. We know they have some Russian instructor pilots, but it's a Chinese air force base."

"That's what I suggested. But he said no, it was at a place farther north, an all-Soviet air regiment. The Russians all wore Chinese uniforms—he had to wear one as well—and the airplanes all carried Chinese markings. He insisted that it was a one hundred percent Soviet operation."

"Aw, he was putting you on. What did he want? Money?"

"No, just to get the story in American hands. He was most convincing, Ross."

"I would be, too, if I was freezing my ass in a Korean POW camp. I'd like to see the piece, though, if it ever turns up. And so, I'm sure, would our intelligence people. If true, it confirms suspicions a lot of pilots are expressing. So, what will you do? Be a lady of leisure?"

"No, I can't stay over here as a military dependent. I lucked out and got a job offer. Do you know what the United States Information Service does?"

"Yeah, they go around to foreign capitals setting up places where you can get American reading material."

"Right. Well, I had a visit from the local USIS director while I was still in the hospital. He was interested in my background, and bingo, out of the blue, he asked me if I'd like to work for him. I start next Monday."

28

12 January 1951
Iwakuni Air Base

Brig. Gen. Mike Starr laid the letter he'd just perused on the desktop and nodded. "An overdue move, Colonel Colyer. How may I help you?"

"I just returned from Kimpo, sir, flying F-80s. I know that coordination of air strikes is—well—pretty weak. I've been assigned to FEAF headquarters to form a joint strike–coordinating unit—we'll call it a command post—to smooth out the rough spots. I plan to requisition a member from each of the major strike forces: bombers, fighters, fighter-bombers, the army and marine ground commands, the navy, and foreign units.

"This unit will allocate resources to support missions laid on by the joint target coordinating committee. We'll standardize some procedures, such as communications, and try to select the best and quickest resources to cope with the forward combat situation."

Starr regarded Ross with a bemused smile. "So this memo says. Who is your boss?"

"I report to the deputy commander, FEAF, sir, Lieutenant General Sims. When we get organized, and with a firm mission statement, I plan to set up shop in Korea, probably Fifth Air Force headquarters."

Starr picked the single page up and pretended to examine both sides. "It seems to be in order, but I don't see General MacArthur's signature anyplace."

"No, sir. This is strictly General Stratemeyer's idea."

"I see. How's your wife—I believe her name is Janet—getting along, Ross?"

"I—I beg your pardon, sir?"

Starr chuckled. "That was a dirty trick. I know her. I gave Janet her first interview last fall. I like her, and I like what she's doing."

Ross gulped. "I didn't know that. Anyway, she isn't doing those film interviews. She was evacuated out of Pyongyang with frostbite and decided she'd had enough. She's taken a job with the USIS office in Tokyo.

"Give her my regards." Starr chuckled. "She ruffled some feathers for sure. Now, back to the reason for your visit. Naturally, I'll cooperate with an order signed by my boss, but may I offer an observation?"

"Please do."

"Without MacArthur's personal okay, you're pissing into the wind, Colonel. You've been up there, and seen what's wrong. It's an army show. To put it bluntly, you don't have the horsepower to do a damn thing about it. Neither, I suspect, does General Stratemeyer—not as long as MacArthur's staff is sitting there in Dai Ichi.

"The only thing I agree with him about is the incongruence of permitting that sanctuary north of the Yalu to exist. But that's a political thing, and *he* isn't going to budge the president or the JCS. So in the meantime we're going to continue to *react* to the Chicoms—fight along a World War I–type 'front line'.

"You'll get your staff; no one is going to defy General Stratemeyer openly. But you're going to get officers who are headquarters excess— drunks, misfits, nonproducers, but not bad enough to boot out of the service. In other words, you're going to end up running the show all by yourself."

Ross felt his facial muscles tightening and a flush forming in his cheeks. "I don't plan to let that happen, sir."

"I'll believe it when I see it. Now, I'm going to give you someone who *can* help you—and I'll probably be the only one to take this strike coordinating effort seriously. All I ask is that you do anything you can to get the B-29 back to doing the job it was designed for. Do you follow me?"

"I believe I do, General. I've seen them trying to knock out gun emplacements with thousand-pound bombs dropped from three thousand feet, while the strategic targets in the northwest go unscathed."

"Exactly. I'm going to attach a Major Blevens to your staff. Ken is— was—an aircraft commander. He's DNIF just now, awaiting a physical evaluation board. His ship took a twenty-millimeter round in the cockpit, and he came home with a shattered left elbow. He'll never be restored to flying status and will be lucky to stay on active duty. He's bitter.

"I have him doing busywork. He knows it and resents not having a responsible job. I also know he's spending more time at the club bar than I like to see. Now, I know you don't need any more challenges, but consider this: Can we salvage a damn fine officer?"

"I sweat six months of DNIF after an injury, General. I damn near cried when the flight surgeon gave me a clean bill of health. I'll do my damndest."

"Good. He'll report to you in Tokyo on Monday."

1 March 1951
Joint Strike Force Command Post, Taegu, South Korea
Ross picked his way through a sea of mud toward the shell-scarred Quonset hut housing the JSF command post. Behind him, a half dozen trucks and bulldozers moved toward a crippled B-29 blocking the field's only serviceable runway. Lieutenant Commander Duke Ormsby looked up as Ross entered and regarded him from behind the makeshift radio console. He held a foot-long message from the radio-teletype printer. "A bad one," he advised.

"Any word on why the bombers missed the rendezvous with the fighters?" Ross asked.

"Yeah. They ran into a hundred-and-twenty-mile headwind. They were twenty minutes behind flight plan when they got to Pyongyang. The F-80 escort had only enough fuel to stay with them for about ten minutes. They ran into MiGs during the bomb run at Kogunyong. The Chicoms had a field day.

"The B-29s went into a defensive formation, so they missed the bridge. They fought off the MiGs until the bastards ran out of fuel and broke off, but the ten Superforts that couldn't make it home limped into here. That pretty well sums up the story."

"Damn." Ross slipped off muddy overshoes and flopped into his chair. "Maybe General Starr will finally admit that his goddamn Superforts aren't so super when they get hit by jet fighters. Anyway, I feel like we're spinning our wheels here. We've managed to improve communications; we can react to the army requests for ground support without screwing around all day; we've even gotten to the point where we can talk to the navy—thanks to you." He threw the red-haired Ormsby a weak grin. "But we've got no assets that can put a stopper in the bottle up north."

"A real no-win situation," Ormsby agreed. "So long as the Chicoms can pour supplies and reinforcements in from Manchuria, the grunts can't take back an airfield close enough for us to provide Sabres for escort. Until we can do that, the B-29s can't bomb the bridges and main supply route."

"You know—" Ross fell silent as Major Blevens opened the door. While Blevens was still removing overshoes and jacket, Ross asked, "You learn anything new at debriefing?"

"Just that your coordinated strike was a goddamned disaster, Colonel Master Coordinator."

Ross's jaw muscles formed white knots. "Duke, could you take a break for a few minutes?"

"Sure, Ross. I'll leave this TWX on your desk."

"Ken," Ross said as soon as the door closed behind Commander Ormsby, "we've been sparring around long enough. I know that you objected to working for me, and you lost. Our personal animosity is interfering with our job. It's time for us to decide what to do about it."

"How's it interfering? I'm pulling my weight."

"Like hell you are. I talked to the AC of that B-29 sitting on its belly out there. He said the RB-29 weather ship reported that freak band of hundred-and-twenty-mile-an-hour wind at oh-nine-hundred this morning. *You* talked to the 87th's command post before the mission took off. Did they say anything about it? Think carefully, because I intend to check it out."

"So what if they did mention it? That wind, like you say, is a freak. It may not even exist a hundred miles away. The navigators are always having to find ways around it."

"Cut the crap, Ken. If you did know, and you didn't tell me, I can only conclude that you deliberately sabotaged the mission to make me look bad. It was my responsibility—*our* responsibility—to see that the rendezvous came off exactly on time."

"Hey, I hope you aren't planning to hang this fiasco on me."

"Only if I find out you deliberately withheld information. And if I do, by God, we're talking court-martial, Ken."

"Oh, for Christ's sake, Colonel Colyer—talk about letting personalities screw up *my* thinking. Use your head. I have about as much riding on this assignment as you do. General Starr wants this idea to work in the worst way. Why the hell would I do anything to throw sand in the gears? Those '29 crews are my buddies."

"One reason that comes to mind is that you can't see the worth of any job other than flying missions. This is a game to you. You resent my pulling you away from a place where everyone felt sorry for you—babied you—and I'm making you do a day's work."

Blevens's face turned purple, then white. "You're just goddamned lucky your leaf is silver and mine's brown, Colyer. It took a hit that left me a cripple to take me out of combat. What's your explanation?"

"Oh, hell, this isn't getting us anywhwere." Ross stood, crossed to the coffeepot, and grunted when he found it empty. "We're both going to be job-hunting if we can't figure a way to get General Starr's bombers over those bridges and marshaling yards this side of the Yalu."

"The only answer is to send them at night. The MiGs can't fly then, and that's when the trains run," Blevens responded sullenly.

"Granted. But the Superfort's airborne radar isn't accurate enough to hit a bridge, and if they miss and drop inside Manchuria—turn out the lights."

"There's a way to do it."

"Oh?"

"Yeah. Contrary to your opinion, I do take this job seriously. I talked to the navigator and radar operator on one of the crews that landed here today. One of them mentioned that when we were in the States, they used a ground radar to grade practice bomb drops. They picked up the airplane's release signal, then calculated its impact point. All you have to do is reverse things and let the ground operator tell the bombardier when to drop to hit a predetermined set of coordinates."

"Good God! It's as simple as that?"

"There's a catch, of course. You have to get that bomb-scoring unit within about twenty miles of the target, and your charts have to be dead accurate."

Ross considered the dilemma while he searched for the supply of coffee. "We could maybe put the BSU radar on one of the carriers and get it close enough. I'll talk to Ormsby."

"Good thinking," Blevens said grudgingly. "But if you do it, don't forget to tell General Starr it was my idea, okay?"

"I will, because it's the truth. Shake on it?"

"Don't get carried away, Colyer. I'll work with you because it's to my best interest—but that doesn't include shaking hands." He slipped into his jacket and pulled on the muddy overshoes. He paused at the door and said, "I won't forget that crack about being a crybaby."

6 March 1951
Suwon Airfield (Seoul), South Korea

Ross huddled in a chilly drizzle, arms clasped across his chest, and surveyed the dismal expanse of debris half buried in soupy mud. "God, this is worse than Kimpo ever thought of being," he observed.

The F-86 commander, Major Guthrie, standing beside him, shrugged deeper into his leather flying jacket. "Nellis Air Force Base it ain't," he agreed. The runway is solid enough, but we have to land, turn around, and taxi back to the parking area before another plane can take off or land." He waved toward where fully two hundred Korean women and old men were digging drainage channels. It'll take 'em a good week to clear us a taxiway."

"Well, at least we can show the gooks a few Sabres again; that should give 'em some sleepless nights. Can you put as many as eight in the air and recover them with this setup, Major?"

"Two flights of four, twenty minutes apart—yeah, we can do that."

"Great. Now, as to why I'm up here. I'm in charge of the Joint Strike Force command post at Taegu. We'll be coordinating your escort missions for the B-29s. It's essential that we know what you can and can't do."

"I'm glad that someone is thinking along those lines. We're hurtin' just now, but I know the whole interdiction plan is bogged down—we'll bust our balls."

"I know you will. We'll do everything we can for you, but we've got a problem. Fifth Air Force promised to attach an F-86 pilot to the command post—someone who knows the airplane's performance and keep us from laying something impossible on you. So far they haven't come through. Can you spare us a pilot? It'll be on a rotating basis, of course."

"Colonel, I'm up here with ten birds and twelve pilots—one of which is me. I'm promised four replacements in a couple of weeks. Maybe then."

"I see. Well, I'd hoped you could spare Lieutenant Wilson—I know him."

"Oh?"

"Family friend—and we both flew the F-80 at Wright Field doing suitability tests."

Major Guthrie scratched his jaw. "I don't know just how to put this—seeing you're trying to do what we've been screaming for. Kyle is junior to half the squadron, but off the record, he's the best pilot I have. I'd rather not lose him, but I suspect you have the clout to take him if you really want to."

"No way. I just came from commanding a squadron. You pick who you want to send when you're able." Ross paused. "Guthrie, have you heard anything about Soviets flying those MiGs instead of Chinese?"

"Probably the same rumors you hear, Colonel. A couple of the guys insist they've gotten close enough to recognize Caucasian features. A pilot swears that he's heard radio transmissions where the pilot got excited and lapsed from Chinese into Russian. I dunno, but considering China's recent acquisition of jets, they have some pilots who sure as hell learned combat tactics in a hurry."

"I guess this all gets passed along during mission debriefing?"

"Yeah, but nothing ever seems to come of it."

"Okay. Thanks for your offer of help later. I'll wander over to the billeting area and look for Kyle, then head back to Taegu. Good hunting."

Ross stood in the ready room's entry and grinned at the familiar scene. Six men wearing flight suits and ferocious scowls huddled around a rickety table draped with a GI blanket. A heap of multicolored banknotes filled the center. The room was rank with the smell of wet clothing, fumes from the charcoal space heater, and cigarette smoke.

A rumpled lieutenant tossed an oversized bill into the pot. "I call."

"Whoa. What the hell is that thing?" the man across from him asked.

"Five pounds, Australian. Exchange rate is three-point-seven to one."

"Bullshit." Ross recognized Kyle's voice. "I'll swear you guys will try to get away with anything. Yen from three countries, pounds, American and Canadian dollars, you seem to think you have collectors' items. If you want three-seventy for that paper, go to Sydney. It's worth two bucks in this game."

Ross's chuckle came ahead of the ensuing argument. Kyle turned. "Colonel Colyer. Hey, it's good to see you. Congratulations on the promotion. What are you doing in these parts? Deal me out of the next hand, guys." He folded his cards and stood.

"Let's take a seat over here, away from this bunch of thieves. We're on fifteen-minute standby, so can't leave—not that there's any better place in this mudhole."

Ross sank into a sagging rattan chair. "How's it going?"

"Grim. It's good to be back where the action is, but I'll be lucky to get in one sortie per day. Weather, this crumby field—you know. Hey, I haven't talked with you since General Cipolla went down. That was a really bad show."

"It was that. I—I don't even like to talk about it. It led to my new job, however. I'm putting together a joint task force command post down at Taegu. Maybe keep that sort of screwup from happening again. That's why I'm up here, trying to talk your CO out of an '86 pilot."

"To work in a command post? Any luck?"

"Not immediately. He's expecting some replacements in shortly—maybe then."

"Don't look at me, Colonel, please. Not that it isn't something we need, it's just that—well, damnit, I have my mind set on getting that ace rating. Major Guthrie's hinted that I may be made an element lead when those new guys get here. I'm looking forward to that; I'm not getting any kills flying wing."

"How about that?" Ross stood. "Well, I gotta get back. And Kyle, don't be too anxious to get those five kills—do everything by the book, okay? Those MiGs are damn good machines, and some of their pilots are real tigers."

"Don't I know it. My face is still red from letting the first one I tangled with get on my tail. The only good thing about our time in Japan was to let us practice some real nifty moves. They're in for a surprise. Say hi to Janet for me, and good luck on your new job."

Ross trudged back to where the T-6 he'd borrowed waited. Colonel Ted is gonna be proud of his son, he thought.

30 March 1951
Headquarters, Far East Air Forces, Japan

"I'm disappointed, Colonel Colyer." General Sims carefully squared

Ross's report with his blotter and pen set, then removed his reading glasses.

"It was a difficult report for me to write, sir. I'm far from being pleased with our Joint Task Force results myself. But the F-86 nutcracker operation that went awry can't be written off as just being unfortunate—it is another example of uncoordinated mission execution. I believe the situation calls for a change in our mission."

"So I see." Sims flicked the report with his forefinger. "Please elaborate."

Ross drew a deep breath and glanced at Brigadier General Starr, seated at Sim's left. "Interservice and interdepartmental rivalry must first be resolved. The field commanders didn't accept the concept. As a result, the command post has never been fully manned with experienced officers. The army provided a lieutenant, recently arrived in Korea, who was recalled to his unit after only two weeks. The marines have yet to assign a member, and the F-86 squadron commander at Suwon can't give me a pilot without reducing his combat readiness. General Starr and the navy are the only commanders to cooperate fully."

"Have you read this report, Mike?"

"No, sir, but Colonel Colyer discussed his recommendation with me at length."

"And?"

"I agree with him. Other than neutralizing that setup north of the river—"

"Mike." Sims pointed his pencil at the bomber commander. "Your views on that matter are well known—have become tiresome, in fact. That's enough. I don't want to hear more; neither, I might add, does General Stratemeyer."

"Yes, sir. But the idea of pairing SHORAN and bomb-scoring radar is well worth looking into. We'll never get close enough to the source of their MSR in daylight with that bunch of MiGs parked only—"

"Mike. I'll not warn you again."

"Yes, sir. However, if we can establish a circular error of less than one hundred yards dropping from above twenty thousand at night, we'll do damage—serious damage—with minimum losses."

"Do we have all the right hardware?"

"Both the SHORAN and bomb-scoring units are in the theater. It's only a matter of putting them together and giving them some training."

"And you believe, Colyer, your man Blevens, and this navy officer, Ormsby, can do it?"

"I have the utmost faith in that crew."

"Very well. I'll brief the CG and let you know within twenty-four hours."

2 April 1951
Iwakuni Air Base, Japan

Brigadier General Mike Starr stood at the briefing podium, grinning from ear to ear. "To quote the Monday morning quarterbacks, 'We smeared 'em last night, coach.'"

Lieutenant General Sims, seated in the front row and flanked by his entourage of headquarters experts, acknowledged the quip with a glacial smile.

"I hated to cut short some of the crew's sleep who flew the mission, but I want them to give you a firsthand briefing. Major Wilks, you have the floor."

A haggard-looking officer who, despite his immaculately pressed class A uniform, didn't seem quite with it, accepted the rubber-tipped pointer and said, General Sims, General Starr, gentlemen, I was aircraft commander on *Daisy's Delight* last night on a mission to disrupt a major enemy troop concentration here"—he tapped the wall map—"north of Hongchon, which posed a threat to the Ninth Corps' advance.

"We employed the recently developed tactic 'Phantom', which couples the use of SHORAN vectors to an MPQ radar site, which in turn provides direction all the way to bomb release. We made radio contact with 'Vaudeville' at twenty-three-eighteen hours and received a heading for 'Island', the MPQ site that would take over for the bomb run. We flew the entire mission at eighteen thousand feet above an overcast, and with strong and variable crosswinds.

"Our ordnance consisted of forty five-hundred-pound general-purpose bombs wrapped with heavy wire and equipped with proximity fuses. A bomb so configured is designed to detonate before impact and create a burst of fifteen thousand fragments covering an area one hundred fifty feet in diameter.

"The mission was flown as briefed, with bombs away at zero-zero-one-two. Communications were excellent, there were no mechanical or electronic malfunctions, and no enemy defensive action was encountered. Are there any questions?"

General Starr stood and spoke into the silence that followed the major's unemotional account. "We hurt 'em—badly, General. An early morning recce by an RF-80 counted at least four hundred casualties, and the army reports that an advance patrol encountered no opposition. We've finally hit on the Superfort's ace serve."

General Sims stood and faced the assemblage. "Tear 'em a new asshole, Mike. It's about time things started turning our way. Now, I asked the Joint Task Force staff to attend this debriefing because I have some trinkets to pass out. Colonel Colyer?"

Ross stood. "Yes, sir."

"C'mon up here." He gave a disgusted look at Ross's triple row of ribbons and growled, "You already have damn near every decoration in the book, but here's an oak leaf cluster for that Silver Star. Something you did when you were still CO of the 66th Squadron." He ignored Ross's stammered thanks and called, "Major Blevens?"

"Yes, sir."

"Nothing quite so fancy for you. Just an envelope. In it you'll find an approval for your request to remain on active duty. Lieutenant Commander Ormsby?"

"Yes, sir."

"You'll have to wait for some admiral to do the honors, but here's the copy of a letter General Stratemeyer sent the secretary of the navy expressing our thanks for the job you've turned in on the Joint Strike Force command post."

The general's dour facade cracked, replaced by a broad smile. "Now, I suppose I should spout some words about the finest traditions, how you've bestowed honor and all that, but I'll simply say, you three were given a damn tough job, one nobody thought you could do, and by God you did it. That's what professional soldiers are supposed to do. A damn fine show, gentlemen. Major Wilks, give my congratulations to your crew as well. Now, carry on."

A crowd of happy, backslapping officers gathered in General Sims's wake to congratulate Colyer, Blevens, and Ormsby. Ken Blevens took advantage of a quiet eddy in the confusion to say, "I owe you, Ross. I don't know why you gave me the credit you did, and I don't care. I doubt that we'll ever be friends, but you shoot square." He gave a twisted smile. "Maybe, if we're lucky, our paths won't cross again."

Ross pondered Blevens's somewhat obscure farewell message as he made his way to where General Starr was pouring a cup of coffee. "General?" Ross asked.

"Yes."

"We proved last night that we can do pinpoint bombing at night and in lousy weather. Isn't it time we went back to those dams along the Yalu and took out some hydroelectric installations?"

"You're reading my mind."

"Do I have the general's permission to fly as an observer on the first mission?"

"For what purpose? You know my policy regarding noncombatants on missions."

"Yes, sir. My purpose is to conduct a study of crew morale: Does it improve when they don't encounter flak or fighters?"

Starr uttered a rumbling laugh. "You gotta do better than that, Ross. You've earned the ride, but I'd like to know the real reason."

"Sir, as I see it, my days of flying combat are close to being over. I've seen it happen over and over—a temporary assignment to a staff job just seems to lead to another, and another, and another. Call this my swan song."

"You're either a psychic or have a pipeline to the Pentagon." Starr scratched his chin. "It so happens that General Sims was talking about a new job for you just this morning."

"Anyway, FEAF has laid on a mission to Sinuiju. There's a major chemical factory there that's still running full blast. It'll be a real test. The MPI is the power plant and electrical substation located fewer than a hundred yards from the Yalu. Antung's regiment of MiGs is just across from the target, by the way. We'll have every fighter we can get off the ground flying cover, and a neat diversion planned. You'll have a ringside seat to see our first big coordinated effort firsthand."

29

Lieutenant Androzov had left a note saying he would be in the canteen when Yuri returned. Mail had been delivered during his absence, however, and his heart surged as he recognized the distinctive handwriting on a heavy, square envelope. Marya. He broke the seal and scanned the contents. A single sentence halfway down the page leaped out at him: ". . . I was feeling depressed today and couldn't resist buying a bright blue babushka I found in the market. . . ."

A cold fist closed around Yuri's heart. Old Marshal Yokolov's words returned from that day on the Black Sea:

> *If she writes of such things as attending the ballet, youth rallies, and the like, you'll know that things are well. If she injects a note of sadness, disappointment, or unhappiness, be aware that problems are surfacing for your father. If a two-month period passes without a letter, or if the words 'bright blue babushka' are included, prepare for the worst.*

It couldn't be, Yuri thought wildly. Both of the powerful political commissars had assured him. . . . Marya had to be mistaken. Papa was innocent of any treasonous activity.

A red mist of rage blurred his vision. *Lies*—they'd lied to him. Always lies, the radio broadcasts to the people, the untruths in *Pravda*. Giesele had warned him—or tried to. Papa would go to prison—Siberia. Or face a firing squad. Perhaps one or the other had already happened.

The handsome young pilot sank to his bed. His mind cleared, became cold—his thinking crystal clear. They would pay for this treachery; each and every one who had connived to bring down his father. He longed to storm into Colonel Zagoria's office and demand the truth. In the same breath, he realized the futility of such a move. No, his only chance lay in a personal plea to Comrade Stalin. He simply *had* to do something so outstanding that he'd be awarded one of the nation's highest awards for bravery.

4 April 1951
Suwon Airfield

"Okay, we're going to try the old trap play again today." Major Guthrie tapped an area bordered with red grease pencil south of the Yalu River. "The Reds got cocky yesterday and chased a couple of stragglers south damn near to Pyongyang. That, my friends, is very close to being the limit of their radius of action. So today I'll be in Dagger One with a flight of six on an armed recce toward Ch'osan. We'll be flying screen for nine B-29s headed for Sinuiju. The boys at Antung won't be able to resist coming after this kind of target, so twenty minutes later, we're slipping eight Sabres north along the coast.

"Dagger One will try to sucker the MiGs south while the Superforts are coming in from the east. Our second section of '86s will then slip inland between the MiGs and the Yalu. I'll draw the Reds to a lower altitude, so they'll be low on fuel when we're ready to put on the squeeze—plus they won't have enough left to engage the bombers. With them caught between Dagger One and Dagger Two, the bombers should sail in, drop, and get the hell out with little opposition. Remember, hot pursuit across the river is okay, but don't blunder into their ack-ack around Antung. Let's have a time-hack now and get to it."

Kyle paced impatiently beside his waiting Sabrejet. Guthrie had scheduled him to lead Dagger Four element today, after admonishing him, "Stay with the game plan, Wilson. We'll be mixing it up with Ruskies, you can bet, and they don't give you second chances."

What a low blow, Kyle complained to himself. Now, with the best setup for killing MiGs I've had so far—no bombers to escort—I draw the squadron's hangar queen for an airplane and a rookie wingman. Stay with the game plan, hell; I'll be lucky just to get up there and back. He saw his crew chief approach, and climbed into the cockpit.

As the coastline disappeared behind the four two-ship elements, Kyle ran through a quick cockpit check: guns, armed; oxygen, okay; fuel flow, okay. He saw that his plane was falling behind the formation and nudged the throttle. What a dog—the word was that someone had warped her in a high-G pullout, and she wouldn't stay trimmed. Oh, well. He stretched cramped shoulders and took a quick glance at his wingman—Tinkerbell, his buddies had dubbed him. Guy seems to be doing all right. God, I hope I can get at least one today.

As usual, the flight maintained radio silence. Bored, Kyle punched channel C—see what's happening around Pyongyang, just passing off their right wing. His headset remained mute. Funny, he thought, things should be going hot and heavy there. He quickly checked channels A and B. Not even a whisper of static. Damnit! he fumed, that's all I need. A dead radio equaled automatic abort. Tomorrow I'll be back to flying wing on escort missions. Never in hell can I get five kills that way. Well, I may as well give Tinkerbell a hand signal and peel off. Maybe not. What if I let *him* fly lead and handle the radio traffic? He immediately rejected the scheme. Shit! He took a frustrated swipe at the offending radio-selector panel. ". . . Roger, Whiskey Five, scratch one . . ." came through loud and clear.

Kyle felt his spirits lift. Hey! It's working. How about that? he enthused to himself. Just a sticky relay somewhere. A nagging voice from his subconscious whispered, What if it quits again? Right when you need it most? Naw. He rejected the disturbing thought and turned his attention to the rapidly approaching turn inland.

4 April 1951
Antung Airfield

Brassy notes of a bugle call sent Yuri and the three Chinese pilots standing alert, with him scrambling for flight gear. Damn bugle calls, Yuri grumbled to himself. The Chinese were obsessed with them. Why couldn't they install a Klaxon in the ready room? Pulling on helmet and gloves while he trotted to the ready line, he watched the Chinese tumble into cockpits. More of the same, he supposed as his crew chief boosted him onto the wing. Lead his flight to the area where intruding bombers were reported, then watch the volunteer pilots engage.

"Number One Flight starting to taxi, Control," he said while completing his cockpit check. His actions were reflexive; he'd barely slept last night. He stared at the fuel gauge, unable to remember what it should read.

"I understand, Number One Leader." The controller's voice penetrated his jumbled thoughts. "Climb to ten thousand meters on a heading of one-four-zero. Expect intercept of two intruders near sector Twelve-One."

"Number One proceeding as directed. Follow standing orders?"

"Dragon Flight will not deploy, Number One. You are ordered to engage and destroy the intruders."

Yuri suppressed a shout. At last! He was to lead an attack on the enemy bombers. He sobered. What if the unidentified planes were the dangerous Sabrejets? No, they never arrived ahead of an attacking force. Concern was immediately replaced by savage exultation. To bring down one of the vaunted swept-wing fighters would guarantee praise from high levels.

His thoughts turned to his wingmen. All three had in excess of one hundred sorties. They hold good formation; we'll see how they perform during an attack. He pressed his mike button. "Did you receive instructions, Number One Flight?"

"Number Two, understand."

"Number Three, understand."

"Number Four, understand."

Yuri allowed himself a pleased grin and concentrated on getting his flight airborne. He tensed as he heard, "Dragon Group is scrambling, Number One Flight. Many targets crossing coastline in Sector Eleven. Continue on your assigned mission."

A frown crossed Yuri's features. This was unusual. Two separate air battles under way at the same time? Sector Eleven was on the eastern coast. Why would only two American planes be on the western side? He shrugged. Don't question things—start searching for the intruders, who shouldn't be more than thirty kilometers ahead.

From forty thousand feet, Kyle studied the tops of fleecy-white cumulus towering to nearly twenty-five thousand, he judged. Not good. With their blinding rate of climb, MiGs could be on the eight-ship formation before they realized it. He observed the formation slowing to loitering speed. Now what?

As if in answer to his silent question, Kyle heard, "Dagger Flight from Dagger One. Whiskey Control reports two enemy formations aloft. The main force is headed away from area of intended engagement. Daggers Two, Three, and Five, attempt intercept in Sector Oboe-Victor. Dagger Four, maintain station. I'm at angels thirty, holding at point Able, over."

Kyle wanted to yell approval. He was on his own. God help the MiG that even stuck it's head out of those clouds below. He pumped a clenched fist at Tinkerbell, who responded with an identical gesture.

Halfway around his first orbit, Kyle heard, "Dagger Four, Dagger One here. I have contact—bandits my ten o'clock, I'm withdrawing on heading one-eight-zero."

Yuri, flying a winding course between the soaring cloud columns, found himself in the clear and commenced a maximum-effort climb to his assigned altitude of ten thousand meters. Passing through nine thousand, however, he saw two black specks on the horizon. Contact! As he watched, the planes changed direction and headed directly away from him. He paused in the act of adding power—instinct caused him to search all quadrants above him before starting pursuit. A cold fist clutched his heart. There, swept-back wings and tail clearly in silhouette, a pair of the dreaded Sabrejets were turning toward him.

A trap! His previous uneasy feeling vindicated, Yuri responded to standing orders: Do not, under any circumstances, lead the Chinese pilots into a dogfight with the Sabrejets. He started to make a tight turn and set course for home when he realized the attackers were between him and Antung. He squeezed his mike button. "Number One Flight, disperse. Make your way home through the cloud cover individually."

Yuri saw his wingmen break away and set up random courses toward the mass of clouds. Good. Now for his own situation. He glanced at his fuel gauge—enough for evasive maneuvers and more. Somehow he had to cross the line guarded by the two fighters streaking toward him, however. He added max power and pulled his plane's nose straight up.

Kyle watched the MiGs disperse and swore under his breath. Damn. They could have gotten at least two, maybe three on one pass. Okay, so they want to play hide-and-seek. We have the angle and altitude on them. He punched off his drop tanks. Wait, that damn leader is *climbing*. Too late Kyle realized that he'd lost the advantage. The Chinese MiG, already above him, could outclimb his out-of-rig Sabre. By the time he caught up, he'd no longer be between the scattered formation and the Yalu. With a sinking feeling, Kyle realized that he'd acted too soon, Guthrie had briefed them to lay back and let Dagger One close the nutcracker.

Look for the others who'd scattered? Kyle wondered. No, damnit. If the intelligence types were right, this was a formation of Chinese pilots led by a Russian. He clenched his jaws and added one hundred percent power. Ivan was not going to have an easy trip home. He squeezed the mike button—may as well get the bad news over with. "Dagger One, this is Dagger Four. Enemy formation has sighted us and scattered. I'm in pursuit on westerly heading."

"Pursuit, Dagger Four?"

"Roger, he's using the cloud cover."

Tinkerbell had remained tucked into position throughout, Kyle noted with satisfaction. He called, "When we get closer, spread and try to box him, Tink. Do your best to get between him and the river, over." He watched the MiG close the angle of convergence and cursed his sluggish ship. At forty-five thousand he ceased trying to climb and concentrated on keeping his quarry from turning southwest. The bastard has to come down sometime, he thought.

The strategy was working, Kyle noted with grim satisfaction. The guy can maybe get over the border into northern Manchuria and punch out, but he sure as hell isn't gonna be putting his feet underneath the mess table at home base tonight. Tink's doing his job—his ship's maybe ten knots faster than this dog I'm flying, and I do believe he's gaining.

Five long minutes passed without appreciable change in their relative positions. Okay, you bastard, you must be starting to sweat fuel up there. Decision time, and Tink's in position to cut you off at the pass.

His eyes widened as he heard his wingman call, "One of the others just popped out of a cloud below me. I've got him dead to rights. I'm starting a firing pass."

"No!" Kyle screamed. "Knock it off—get the hell back here. . . ." He let his voice trail off. Gunsmoke and a cloud of spent cartridges streamed from the nose of Tinkerbell's ship. The MiG flipped onto its back, with flames and smoke streaming from the left wing root. Kyle didn't even respond to Tink's exultant "Got 'im!"

The second Sabrejet's diversion didn't escape Yuri's notice. Did he now have enough room to squeeze past the one remaining pursuer? His fuel gauge was slipping into the emergency reserve band. His mind cleared. He'd let habit control his tactics: Never, never take a chance of being shot down over Korea, Colonel Zagoria had pounded into his Russian instructors.

I'll never have another opportunity like this, Yuri decided—one on one, and with an altitude advantage. Papa would never forgive me for evading combat. He rolled left until he was headed directly at the American Sabrejet.

Kyle blinked. The son of a bitch was attacking! What . . . ? Why the sudden change of tactics? Had the pilot decided he couldn't reach sanctuary and elected to slug it out? Well, all right—this is what I've been waiting for. We practiced this situation in Japan—you don't attack a Sabrejet head-on, ol' buddy. He looked around in vain for Tinkerbell. His wingman was nowhere to be seen. Rule one: Don't engage solo, keep your tail covered. To hell with that. Kyle whipped into a one-eighty turn—let the guy think he had a pigeon.

The MiG was closing swiftly from Kyle's rear. It would be within maximum range of its 20mm cannon soon. Kyle retarded the throttle, popped speed brakes, and hauled the nose up. He held his breath. Would the MiG pilot be alert enough to get off a burst before he overran his quarry? This trick was sure to place a fleeing airplane in a position to become pursuer, but it depended upon catching the other pilot by surprise.

Kyle's answer was a half-dozen tracers zipping past his left wing. Damn! This guy was good. He completed the maneuver; rolling into a split-S—sure enough he was now above and behind the MiG. He sucked in the speed brakes and added power.

Yuri mentally loosed a string of Russian oaths. The sudden reversal of roles was a bigger blow to his pride than a threat. The American fighter was no match for his faster more maneuverable MiG, and he would pit his flying skill against anyone. The sagging fuel indicator was a factor to consider, however. His determination to score a kill was a consuming flame—nothing would keep him from returning home victorious.

The heavier Sabrejet now had the advantage. A steep spiral would rectify that—Yuri stood the MiG on one wing to turn inside the slower, heavier plane. As the G forces built, he glanced at the fuel gauge—it wasn't reassuring; he'd have to make this a quick kill.

* * *

Kyle's lips split in a pleased smile. You blew it fella, he thought. You should have climbed. The Sabre's flying tail plus the speed I can develop in a dive will keep me inside the turn. You best start praying to whatever it is you Russians believe takes care of your soul, 'cause your ass is mine. He keyed his mike in another fruitless effort to summon Tinkerbell.

Too late, Yuri discovered he was losing ground in the screaming spiral. It was time to reverse his turn and head for the Yalu. As he was about to start his escape, a wave of frustrated anger stayed his hand. No! I can't admit defeat, he raged inwardly. I have the better airplane; I am the better pilot. I *will* destroy this pampered, arrogant capitalist. I *won't* return home in defeat. This can well be the only chance I have to save Papa from certain death. He lowered the MiG's nose and applied more back pressure to the already shuddering control stick.

Already beyond its designed tolerance to speed-induced stress, the nimble fighter faltered. Yuri felt it try to pitch up; a noticeable yaw served to counteract the pilot's effort to extract yet a tighter turning radius. Despair overwhelmed Yuri as he saw tracer rounds creep closer. His last thoughts were a realization that he was about to die—to die for false masters. Liars, corrupt, power-hungry leaders . . . a hail of armor-piercing .50-caliber slugs turned his cockpit into a shrieking, flaming coffin.

Kyle swept past the disintegrating MiG and rolled into a climbing turn. What the hell possessed that guy? he wondered. He was home free; then, despite his earlier display of flying skill, he did everything wrong. He saw the smoking ruin impact into snow-dusted terrain and shrugged. Now, where the hell is Tinkerbell? He tried his dead radio one more time, then headed south.

The nerve-jarring blare of a warning horn interrupted Kyle's letdown as combat-stimulated adrenaline subsided. A glance at the instrument panel revealed the angry, red orb of an engine fire-warning light. What the hell! Engine oil pressure hit the bottom peg.

He spent precious seconds replaying the dogfight—that burst of tracers; he'd thought they missed; the bastard had scored a lucky hit. The J-47 engine's reassuring background noise ceased abruptly. Okay, Wilson, you've got a dead bird. What now? He searched the ground below for a landmark. He guessed that the dogfight had carried them east. How

far south would he have to glide to reach the gulf coast? The altimeter
was just starting to unwind from twenty thousand feet. Surely he could
get over water—maybe those navy air rescue types would even be waiting for him. . . .

Kyle realized that the fire-warning horn was still bleating its message.
A glance ino the rearview mirror revealed he was trailing a plume of
black smoke—a tongue of red flame sent a chill up his spine. "Screw that
idea," he muttered half aloud. "You're in for a nylon approach—right into
the middle of gookland."

The parachute's opening shock came as a surprise, even though Kyle
was prepared for it. He realized that seat separation had come exactly as
advertised—that was good. He tried to get his bearings by looking down
between his feet. The gyrating horizon revealed he was swinging like a
big pendulum. Pulling on alternate risers dampened the sickening
motion, but he could see nothing but low mountains in all directions.

A chill penetrated his flight suit and leather jacket, confirming his
guess that he was still at about twelve to fourteen thousand feet. Too soon
to start looking for a place to land, he thought. Damn, he hadn't been able
to get off a mayday because of the friggin' radio. And Tinkerbell—the
guy who was supposed to cap him after he touched down—was nowhere
in sight. Kyle suddenly felt very much alone and abandoned.

Details took shape with startling swiftness. he was directly over a
broad valley bisected by a good-size stream that paralleled a highway and
twin railroad tracks. Scraps of lectures on escape and evasion returned:
"If you come down north of the thirty-eighth parallel, avoid major roads
and built-up areas; you're not apt to find friendly natives."

Ant-size shapes scurried along the road. It appeared that he'd land right
among them. A snow-topped ridge beckoned. It appeared to be without
habitation on the other side. Kyle started hauling on his risers, trying to
sideslip across its peak. The figures below were pointing and gesticulating wildly. He saw a pinpoint of light: The bastards were shooting at him!
Now, that, by God, was the final straw. He fingered his holstered .45
automatic, longing to teach these goddamned bandits not to shoot at a
helpless man.

The ridgeline approached with discouraging swiftness. He *had* to cross
it. He was drifting across terraced farm plots now; they'd have a network
of paths to reach him in minutes. After he decided that he would impact

short of the peak, an upslope breeze slowed his rate of descent. He wanted to shout when his feet actually brushed the tops of scattered pine trees, and the ground fell away beneath him.

Other than a clutch of straw-thatched huts huddled at the base of a ravine slashing the mountain's far slope, this valley appeared deserted. Kyle tried to select a good landing spot but gave up—it all looked uniformly covered with rocks and scrub forest. At least he was below the snow line here.

He landed harder than he'd anticipated. Trying to break his impact with the roll they'd showed him in class, he felt a numbing blow to his shoulder. That trick don't work when there are boulders around, he thought.

Kyle hit the parachute harness's quick release and stood to take stock. He had maybe an hour before that bunch in the other valley came pouring down this slope. Run? Hide? The outlook wasn't bright for either course. He gathered up the chute canopy and wadded it into a manageable ball while he thought. Those huts looked deserted . . . no way, that'll be the first place they search. There was no snow this far down; at least they couldn't track him if he ran—but where to run? Where would they be least apt to look for him? For one thing, they wouldn't expect him to head back for the other side.

Thirty minutes later, Kyle was scrambling up a rocky, dry streambed, leaving no trace of his passage. Fifteen more minutes, he decided, and he'd worm his way under the snow-covered bushes alongside and use the white parachute canopy as camouflage. He'd sleep rough tonight, but the memory of that asshole shooting at him left little room for optimism. Something told him these folks hadn't heard about the Geneva Convention.

30

Damn, but it's cold in here, Kyle grumbled to himself. Did someone let the fire go out? He fumbled for his blanket. Realization jerked him wide awake as his fingers encountered cold, slick fabric—his parachute. In dim, filtered light he could tell that he was curled into a ball and tangled in its voluminous folds. He dashed a gloved hand across eyes still gummed with sleep and took stock of his surroundings.

Sitting up provided a sharp reminder of his situation. His head brushed the overhanging bush and loosed a cascade of snow. That added discomfort went almost unnoticed, however, as arm movement drove a lance of pain deep into his shoulder. Sore and aching in every muscle, Kyle retrieved the inflated Mae West life jacket he'd used as a pillow. Seating himself on it, he clutched the 'chute canopy around his shivering torso. So now what? he wondered.

Things hadn't looked quite so bleak last night. Huddled beneath the parachute, he listened to a determined search party examine every square foot of the surrounding mountainside. They'd apparently misjudged his landing point, however. By the time it was too dark to see clearly, they hadn't reached his hidey-hole.

The dozen or so men would be back this morning, he knew. They probably were en route even now—with reinforcements. During the surge of relief at evading capture, he'd decided that walking to the coastline was highly possible.

An inventory of the emergency bailout kit revealed a wealth of treasures, the most valuable of which was an oiled silk map and compass. Tracing the exact route he'd covered during the dogfight at five hundred mph wasn't possible, but he felt sure he knew his location within about a ten mile radius. Walking ten miles per day, he should reach the Yellow

Sea within five days. The concentrated emergency rations, supplemented by edibles he could find along the way, would be enough.

"Stay along the mountain ridgelines," Kyle recalled one of his E & E instructors saying. "The Koreans farm every square foot of tillable land. Most roads and villages are located in the valleys. Travel at night." Okay, he'd just hole up until dark—oops, not here. This place would resemble Grand Central Station any minute now. Slip up this streambed, stay out of sight somewhere on high ground, then strike out tonight. Best he get going.

It was then he saw the child. Scrambling on hands and knees to gather the 'chute canopy into a bundle, he found himself confronting a pair of black eyes set into a rosy-cheeked face, round as a miniature brown moon. "You little fart, what're you doing here?" Kyle barked.

The kid—Kyle couldn't tell if it was a boy or a girl—was squatting just outside the sheltering bush's overhang. The child started to stand at Kyle's startled outburst, then settled back down, darting glances in all directions and dark lashes blinking rapidly. "Hey, I'm sorry I yelled at you," Kyle said less harshly. "I don't suppose you speak English?"

The smooth features didn't change. "That figures." Kyle mused. "Now, we got us a problem. I have to get the hell outta here. You know where I am, and worse, you'll see the direction I go when I leave. You're gonna tell Mama and Daddy; they're going to tell the cops; and I'm dead. Why don't you just go home—right now?" He crawled from under the bush.

The child scampered backward as Kyle emerged from his lair, but stopped a scant dozen feet away. Instinct told Kyle the kid was a boy eight to ten years old. He was scared, it was clear, but curiosity kept him from fleeing—sort of like an exploratory kitten. "Shoo." Kyle flapped both hands. "Go home, hear me? Get."

When there was no reaction, Kyle stooped to gather up his belongings. He dare not hang around here any longer—kid or no kid. The last item he picked up was his .45 automatic; he'd slept with it close at hand. When he turned with the gun dangling from his hand, he saw the boy's eyes grow wide. With a sound resembling "Garrah," the youngster pelted down the slope. He disappeared quickly into what Kyle noticed for the first time was gently falling snow.

"Shit!" he exclaimed aloud, adding under his breath, There goes my running start. He folded his scattered belongings into the chute, reluctantly discarding his hard helmet, parachute harness, and life vest. They could come in handy later, but he had to travel light—and fast.

Rocks, worn smooth by centuries of floodwaters, wore a coating of just enough snow to make footing in the streambed treacherous. Kyle halted after a half hour to catch his breath. Keep it up, he mouthed to the silent white curtain. At least cover the rocks I've stepped on—maybe slow the bastards by a few hours. Peering ahead, he could see his route would soon become a narrow, brush-lined defile. There would be no choice but to leave it or attempt repeating last night's device of crawling under the brushy cover for concealment and shelter against the increasing snowfall.

Voices wafting upward through the opaque screen behind him hastened his decision. Leave the little gully, strike overland, and pray the snow covered his trail. Damned kid, he muttered savagely. What the *hell* were you doing out that time of the morning?

Sensing that he was close to the ridgeline, Kyle lengthened his stride. The footing underneath, mostly a carpet of pine needles, was a welcome change. He took time to check his map. If this was the mountain range he believed it to be, it ran southeast for about five miles before joining a converging valley. That would get him well away from the most intensive search efforts. Dare he ignore the warning to travel only at night? It was tempting. Falling snow provided perfect cover, and the thin stand of pines offered nothing in the way of a hiding place.

To hell with it; he'd keep moving. Taking more time, he cut two panels from his chute and wrapped them toga-style around his head and shoulders. In addition to keeping his flying suit from becoming saturated, it was great camouflage. Kyle checked the compass and strode into the silent forest.

I'll bet the squadron has put up a search effort, he mused as he trudged. Helluva lot of good it will do in this stuff. Wonder where Tinkerbell disappeared to? Not that he could have done much—he'd have only had enough fuel for a ten-to-fifteen-minute stay in the area. But, more important, Air Rescue would have gotten a fix on him. He was too far north for the army choppers to reach him, but those operating off the carrier would be on alert.

Kyle felt his energy start to flag and stopped beneath a tree to munch one of the dry, tasteless food bars in his escape kit. After washing it down with a few handfuls of snow, carefully warmed and melted in his mouth before swallowing, he felt considerably refreshed when he struck out again. Even the throb in his bruised shoulder was less of a handicap. This is going to be easier than I thought, he told himself. This damned parachute canopy is harder to carry than an armful of snot, but it'll be a lifesaver—at least I can keep warm and dry with it. He hummed a few bars of "Off we go, into the wild blue yonder . . ."

Kyle stopped so abruptly he almost lost his footing. What the hell . . . ? he wondered. Preoccupied, he'd failed to notice the snow was thinning and he'd been walking downhill. Now he stood on the verge of a wide, paved highway, the comforting cover of pines behind him. He trotted back to the tree line and scanned the map. No way. The route he'd sketched in his mind showed nothing like this. He squinted into the clearing air. A broad valley stretched out of sight before him. A road of this size should be prominently displayed. His heart sank. He'd misjudged his landing site—had been following the wrong crest and was now completely lost.

The growl of a vehicle laboring up the road in low gear sent a chill over him that was totally unrelated to the inclement weather. Crouched behind a tree, he watched a gray-green, stakebed truck loom into view. Perhaps two dozen men clung to its waist-high panels. They were dressed in nondescript combinations of black pantaloons and padded jackets. Identical black caps, with earflaps tied on top, gave them a faintly military air. Some sort of home guard, Kyle guessed, called out to search for the downed pilot.

The truck halted and a half dozen leaped to the ground. Brandishing short-barreled, automatic weapons, they exchanged laughing banter with their comrades as they took up positions roughly twenty yards apart along the road. They were cordoning off the area, Kyle realized. About to bolt for the deeper reaches of forest, he froze. He'd be clearly visible. Even if he eluded them, his tracks would leave a trail a blind pig could follow.

Crouching lower, Kyle instinctively drew his pistol from its shoulder holster—by God, he wouldn't give up without a fight. Numerous heated arguments about carrying sidearms on missions flashed before him. "Land in the middle of a bunch of gook civilians and wave a pistol, you're gonna get killed. They won't even bother to ask your name, rank, and serial number," one school claimed. "Yeah," the opposing group would respond, "but what if there's only one guy between you and freedom? You're in this rice paddy and the chopper's overhead. Bam. You take him out and let the guys buy drinks for you in the club that night."

The air force left the matter optional, and Kyle had elected to fly armed. Brave words—usually spoken after a few drinks—rang in his ears with hollow bravado. Shoot one and dash across the road? To where? He felt paralyzed with indecision. Three shrill whistle blasts resolved his dilemma. The line of men moved toward where he hunkered behind the inadequate bulk of a medium-size pine. The smoky, noisy Kimpo officers' club bar suddenly seemed light-years away.

Kyle's instinctive huddling beneath the parachute canopy almost saved him. The man approaching his tree was a quarrelsome type and yelled imprecations to his neighbor as he walked. Only at the last moment did he notice footprints leading to a suspicious white lump in the snow. All hell broke loose as the guardsman uttered a startled yelp.

Something prodded Kyle—it felt alarmingly like a rifle barrel. He shrugged off the parachute canopy and rose to his feet, hands spread palms-out. Whistles blew and men came running from both flanks of the search line. Everyone talked at once. It seemed to Kyle that he was the first Westerner they'd encountered. No one approached his six-foot, one-inch presence—none of his captors stood as high as his shoulder. They formed a circle, jabbering and gesticulating with their weapons.

Finally it dawned on Kyle: The object of concern was his .45 pistol, prominently displayed in its shoulder holster. No one wanted to get close enough to take it; neither were they anxious to order him to remove the gun and surrender it. Well, damned if he'd make it easy for them. He scowled and moved his right hand toward his left armpit. A chorus of screams and words that sounded very much like threats halted his bluff. At least six automatic rifles were pointed directly at him.

Behind him, Kyle heard the truck return. A bouncy little man wearing a blue armband strutted toward the excited guardsmen—an officer or NCO, Kyle decided. After a rapid exchange, the new arrival pointed toward the man who'd discovered Kyle—he heard the name Pak used several times. Pak, obviously not happy with his orders, approached gingerly, then snatched the pistol and retreated swiftly.

Things went downhill for Kyle after that. The grinning, boastful Pak virtually assumed charge. A length of cord was produced, and Kyle's arms were lashed behind him at the elbows. He stifled a scream as they twisted his injured shoulder. Escorted by twenty jubilant captors—Pak in front and waving the blue-steel .45—Kyle was led down the hill.

Kyle could smell the village even before they turned the last corner. Fermenting cabbage—*kimchee* in the making—wood smoke, and rancid cooking fat competed with the open sewer system for dominance. Curious villagers had doubled the escorting party's size by the time the procession reached the first buildings.

Their destination, the local police station, was situated in the village's geographic center. The imposing building, surrounded by an eight-foot-high rock wall and entered through a massive wooden gate, was apparently the seat of all government. A block short of the station, Pak, as if to show off his prestigious status as captor, strode in front of Kyle. Walking backward, he jabbed a forefinger in his prisoner's chest and asked, "American?"

Kyle nodded.

Pak pointed to the cloth pilot wings stitched to Kyle's flying suit *"Pi-yang-gi?"*

Kyle recognized the Korean name for airplane and nodded again.

A suddenly incensed Pak turned and yelled a long diatribe at his audience. The carnival atmosphere ceased as if a door had been slammed. Laughingly uttered sallies were replaced by sullen mutters. Before Kyle could figure out this strange turn of events, he was steered into the walled compound.

The village magistrate, police chief, mayor—Kyle guessed the man served in a number of official capacities—was of middle age with a plump face beneath a balding pate. He wore blue army breeches with black boots, but a white, open-collar civilian shirt. He shooed all but four of the guardsmen outside, and Kyle found himself in official custody.

The fact that Kyle spoke no Korean, and none of the arresting party spoke English, seemed to bother the man not at all. He barked brisk orders, and the process of incarceration began. Slashing the cord binding Kyles elbows he shoved a printed form toward the prisoner and held out a pen. Kyle's negative headshake elicited yet another stream of orders. Rough hand marched the prisoner to a table and the—what could only be called robbery—began.

Kyle's watch was deposited on the chief's desk. His Zippo lighter apparently went up for bid. Searching the several zippered pockets of his flight suit became a community project. Even the chief came around to examine this ingenious arrangement, shaking his head in disbelief when he saw pockets placed below the knees. Examining contents of the plastic box containing Kyle's escape kit required a full hour of mystified oohs and aahs.

Indignant rage turned to despair as Kyle watched his personal effects being distributed among his gleeful captors. The thought of eventual escape had never been far from his mind—but without a map, the compass . . . The final straw, however, was the boots. Stripped of anything resembling a trophy, Kyle saw Pak point to his highly polished flight boots. Serious-faced discussion followed.

"No, damnit!" Kyle broke his self-imposed silence. "You can't leave . . ." He fell silent as he realized the bank of astonished faces understood not a word. He crouched and wrapped both arms around the suddenly priceless footgear.

Pak shrugged and looked at the others, who also shrugged in total incomprehension. Pak grasped Kyle's shoulder and casually tipped him backward. To add insult to injury, Kyle found himself staring down the bore of his own .45.

Cursing and struggling, Kyle submitted to being inserted into the facility reserved for prisoners requiring maximum security. He'd barely noticed the structure of bamboo poles that occupied one corner of the multipurpose office. A cage, about eight feet in length, was constructed as a vertical L. A compartment measuring four feet square and perhaps five feet high was joined to another barely three feet high. The prisoner could lie flat, or sit with head and shoulders in the higher portion. Kyle's nose told him a recent occupant must have been the town drunk.

It was dark outside the room's single window when Kyle roused from exhausted sleep. A solitary guard slouched on a bench, automatic rifle across his lap. A croaked "water" brought nothing more than a blank look. Then the guard grinned and rubbed his belly. "Yeah," Kyle responded. "Water, and something to eat."

The guard sauntered to a doorway and yelled something. Five minutes later a wrinkled ancient entered bearing a bowl. She sat it outside Kyle's cage and scuttled back through the doorway. The bowl contained rice that was covered with what appeared to be green slime. Kyle yelled louder this time, "Water!" He immediately had second thoughts as he recalled the open ditch outside with its trickle of pungent sewage.

His spirits at low ebb, Kyle dipped two fingers into the revolting-looking mess and tasted it. He almost threw up. Looking like he remembered the stuff that formed on farm ponds in August, it tasted worse. Wilson, you're in for deep trouble. You're going to die of dehydration, starvation, and probably dysentery. He heard the door leading to the courtyard open and looked up with weary disinterest.

Two figures wearing blue NKPA uniforms, entered. One, a man, wore the badge of a senior enlisted man. The other, a girl of indeterminate age, wore officer's tabs. The guard stood, as close to attention as Kyle had seen to this time. The girl strode to the cage and made a quick assessment. "You're an officer," she said in crisp English.

Kyle sagged with relief. "My god, someone who speaks English, at last."

Ignoring Kyle, she turned to the guard and snapped two short sentences in Korean. The man hurried to the cage and fumbled with its lock. Moments later Kyle crawled to freedom.

Barely able to stand, Kyle took a closer look at his savior. She was attractive, with a full figure barely disguised by her uniform. Straight black hair, cut in square bangs, showed beneath her cap. Exposing even, white teeth, she said, "I will see that you have appropriate accommodations. These ignorant villagers didn't know you were an officer." Her cool aloofness didn't change, however.

"I'll be glad to get out of that contraption, thank you. Also I need a drink, badly. But I'd rather have something like coffee or tea than water if I could."

"You fear the stomach illness. Yes, you foreigners have delicate constitutions. I'll order tea. Is that your evening meal?" She nodded at the barely touched bowl.

Yeah. I'm hungry, but . . . just what *is* that stuff on top?"

"Grass soup. A delicacy this early in the spring. The cook was doing you a favor."

"Oh. I'm grateful, but I can do without it. What's to happen to me next? Is that why you're here?"

The girl motioned for the guard to vacate his bench and indicated Kyle was to sit alongside her. "Yes, I've been ordered to conduct a preliminary interrogation. Where you'll be taken from here depends on how cooperative you are."

"I see. My name is Kyle Wilson, lieutenant, United States Air Force. My serial number is—"

The girl held up a restraining hand. "Please, we know your name from your identity tags. You are a pilot, right?"

"All that I'm required to give you is my name, rank, and serial number."

Full red lips turned down at the corners. "Don't act the fool," the girl said scornfully. You are not, as yet, a prisoner of war."

"Then just what the . . ." Kyle stopped short of swearing. "What am I if not a POW?"

"A foreign national accused of murder."

"What?"

"Exactly. I'd repeat my question, but it's academic since you wear the badge of an aviator. What's important is: Do you fly bombers or fighters?"

"Okay, I'm a pilot. What difference does it make what I fly?"

"A great deal. You see, American bombs hit the next village only a month ago. Several innocent people were killed; many were related to the people living here. If you are a bomber pilot, then the people insist you be tried for murder—the outcome is a foregone conclusion. They will shoot you," she said offhandedly.

"I don't believe it! They can't hold me responsible for something I didn't do. Why, that's against international law."

"As I believe I told you earlier, the villagers here are most provincial in their thinking. They know little of international law, and frankly, will ignore it if they choose to. The empty plane that crashed near here was a fighter plane; an F-86 Sabrejet. If you confirm that it's the plane you flew, then the army will assume custody and you'll be taken to a prisoner-of-war camp."

Kyle gaped in disbelief. "Okay, I'm a fighter pilot."

"Good. We leave immediately. Sergeant Han and I will be your escort."

"Immediately? Yet tonight? This is crazy."

"The roads are unsafe during the daytime." One corner of her mouth twitched. "It would be poetic justice, however, if you were to be killed by your own bombers."

Kyle glared. "What is your name, by the way? You can't be just 'girl' to me if we're to travel together."

"My name is immaterial. You will travel as a prisoner, without special treatment. I doubt that we will have opportunity to carry on casual conversation." She stood. "We will go now."

"Very well. I'll call you Suzie. And just a minute. If we're going on a trip, I at least want my boots back."

Suzie glanced at Kyle's sock-clad feet. "I doubt if that's possible. Leather shoes are highly prized. The man who discovered you claimed them as his reward."

"Damnit, those are *mine*. He stole them from me at gunpoint. And I can't go running around without shoes—it's still winter."

"Prisoners' personal items become the property of the court—to be disposed of as the magistrate sees fit. As for 'running around', as you put it, you won't be. You'll be issued shoes at the camp. Come quickly now."

Despite Kyle's dazed confusion, he had enough presence of mind to snatch one of the compressed food bars from his escape kit lying on the floor alongside the chief's desk. Unable to determine what the rock-hard, evil-looking object was, the man had discarded it. Kyle had a hunch that it might soon be his major source of nourishment.

Outside, Suzie indicated a vehicle parked in the courtyard. "You will ride in the front," she said.

With deep resentment Kyle regarded the familiar shape of an American jeep. Someone had slapped a brush coat of bright blue paint on it; otherwise it appeared to be in the same condition as when some hapless GI abandoned it.

Sergeant Han clambered into the rear; Suzie slid under the wheel. Kyle couldn't bring himself to ask how the jeep was acquired and gazed at the night sky, now nearly clear of clouds. When Suzie swung onto the main road, he identified Polaris—the only heavenly body other than the moon he was sure of. They were headed northwest, he observed. The crews had been briefed to avoid bombing or strafing in the vicinity of Pyoktong, he recalled—that's where the POW camps were located and lay in the country's northwestern corner.

Relief to be out of that bamboo cage soon dispelled the depression that had been building all day. "Where did you learn to speak such good English?" he asked Suzie.

The girl concentrated on driving by the faint glow of slitted blackout headlights without replying. Finally she said, "I attended university in Tokyo; foreign languages were my specialty. And don't try to befriend me—I despise all Americans."

"Oh, hey, now. *All* Americans? What happened? Bad boyfriend experience at the university?"

"The prisoner is not allowed to speak!" Suzie rattled off a short burst of Korean. "I've instructed Sergeant Han to take measures to keep the captive silent."

Kyle felt the sharp jab of Han's rifle barrel in his back and fell silent. He couldn't resist a smug inner smile, however. That thrust about an American boyfriend had hit home. Snotty little bitch.

31

6 April 1951
20,000 Feet—Abeam Pyongyang
"It's gonna be close!" Major Wilks yelled above the B-29's engine and slipstream noise. Ross, crouched between the pilot's and copilot's seats, nodded. "The RB-29 recce ship reports a broken deck over the coast," the major continued. "That fits with the forecast to clear by sunup, but we'll only have enough daylight VFR to get in and out before the target area closes down again."

"How about the Yalu valley?" Ross asked. "Morning fog—I hope?"

Wilks grinned. "Now, that would be icing on the cake, wouldn't it? A clear target and the MiGs grounded. I should be so lucky. Anyway, you can bet a few are gonna find a way to get airborne. That complex at Sinuiju is critical for them; they're not about to roll over and play dead." He paused to listen to his headset. "Radar says IP in forty minutes."

Ross gazed at the tumbled cloudtops stretching out of sight in all directions. "I've spent so much time cramped up in a fighter cockpit that I'd forgotten how nice it is to have some room to move around in—someone to talk with. And all that lovely reserve fuel."

Wilks grunted. "And don't forget how helpless it feels to sit here on a bomb run with the Chicoms throwing everything they have at you. But, no, you know about that—you did your bit in bombers."

Yeah, I'm just disappointed that I can't see this SHORAN/RSU system work."

"FEAF just ain't convinced. They get all trembly at the thought of throwing a stray bomb into Manchuria. It's strictly visual drops only within thirty miles of the border."

"IP in five minutes, Ross," Wilks advised. "I'll have to ask you to strap in for the bomb run. There she is, however." He pointed to their two-o'clock position where twin bridge spans and a sprawl of industrial buildings poked through the early morning mist. "It's funny—"

"Bandits, eleven o'clock high," the central-fire control officer broke in. I count no more than twenty. Keep an eye on 'em, guys. Our little friends have seen 'em however."

Intercom chatter ceased. Anxious eyes searched the clear but hazy sky. Only the bombardier and, Ross knew, the radar operators in the plane's rear compartment concentrated on placing the nine Superforts on their bomb run. He chaffed at being confined in his out-of-the-way seat, but General Starr had balked at even letting him man one of the gun barbettes.

"Bogey at four o'clock!" Ross heard through his headset. "Nail him Gus. Watch that one just above him—he broke through our fighter screen." Ross heard and felt the shuddering concussion of machine guns; a shape flitted across his limited line of vision. "He broke off, but here comes his buddy."

"Bombardier to crew," Ross heard. "We're on the bomb run. I have control, pilot, bomb bay doors coming open. Three minutes to bombs away." Ross could barely contain himself—just to sit here and do *nothing*.

After what seemed an eternity, Ross felt the plane lurch. The bombardier's calm "Bombs away" was anticlimactic. Relief was short-lived as the bombardier continued, "Hung bomb, pilot. I have a red light. Shall I attempt a manual release now?"

"No," Wilks snapped. "Let me break formation first. Are the fighters still after us?"

"CFC to pilot. The F-86s are keeping 'em busy, but we're a long ways from being in the clear."

"Roger. Pilot to bombardier. I'm proceeding to rally the formation. I'll have to close the bomb bay doors until we're able to go single. What's it look like?"

"The panel shows the shackle tripped, but I still have a red light."

"Okay. Pilot to crew, I'm going to depressurize in case we have to enter the bomb bay. Check your oxygen hookups and report in."

"Bomb bay doors coming closed," the bombardier echoed.

Ross tensed. The thousand-pound bomb wouldn't be armed until it hit the slipstream and the fuse's little propeller spun free. Its safety device would likely be deactivated by the tripped shackle, however. He was considering the consequences when he heard a rumbling vibration from behind him.

"The son of a bitch broke loose, pilot!" he heard the bombardier yell. "I think it went right through the friggin' closed doors!"

The silence of collectively held breaths was broken by Wilks's calm announcement. "From the reaction I felt on the controls, I believe it dropped free. Rex, check through the porthole to make sure, but I have a hunch someone down below is gonna get a nasty surprise."

6 April 1951
50 Miles Southwest of Sinuiju
Suzie had pulled off the road just before dawn. "We will stay here today," she announced.

The all-night ride in an open jeep had left Kyle out on his feet. His eyes closed in spite of determined effort to stay awake. He was so cold, he'd lost all feeling—his unshod feet especially. Suzie and Sergeant Han had seemed oblivious to his discomfort. Don't fall asleep—you *can't* fall asleep, he repeated to himself. If you don't escape soon, you'll never manage it; this is the best opportunity you'll ever have.

Kyle roused from his stupor. They were in a small village, parked behind a thatched roof cottage. The odor of stagnant mud, fish, and a salty tang in the air told him they were near water—probably the Yellow Sea's coastline.

Sergeant Han hammered on the door until an elderly couple, their faces resembling wrinkled walnuts in the jeep's headlamps, appeared. Blinking sleep from their eyes, they didn't seem overly surprised or upset that their home was being invaded at such an hour, Kyle thought. The place was probably used frequently by official visitors seeking a daytime sanctuary.

Kyle brushed off Han's attempt to help him from the jeep. His shoulder was a constant source of excruciating pain; the jolting ride had seemed to inflame the swollen joint further. He hobbled on unfeeling feet inside, where the woman had lighted a paraffin lamp and was breathing life into a charcoal brazier. Sergeant Han thwarted Kyle's attempt to slump onto a bench near the fire. He found himself shoved to the floor in a far corner.

The room's relative warmth was like a sedative. Kyle barely saw the food placed before him, just knew that it was hot and aromatic. Rice, a surprisingly good soup, and, of course, *kimchee.* He devoured every morsel and couldn't keep from drinking copious amounts of water; so it's loaded with germs, he thought—that's the least of my worries.

Suzie hadn't spoken to him. As soon as the meal was finished, she and Han had a brief conversation. Through eyes reduced to slits, Kyle saw them look at him and shrug. Apparently he wasn't considered to be in shape to escape. Suzie stretched out on the bench and was sound asleep in seconds. Han, with an apparent endless store of energy, sat with his back propped against the outer door, the ever-present rifle cradled in his lap. The Korean man and wife disappeared into an adjoining room. Silence descended as gray light penetrated the paper windowpanes.

Feigning sleep without dropping off was the most difficult task Kyle could recall undertaking. His gaze remained riveted on the rifle. Han *couldn't* stay awake indefinitely. Despite valiant effort, the exhausted pilot couldn't form an escape plan, however. Grab the gun, put Han and Suzie out of commission, race to the jeep—he hadn't seen any effort to disable it, and it didn't require an ignition key—then . . . beyond that point, he drew a blank.

Kyle saw the outer door propel Sergeant Han halfway across the room before he heard a sound. The detonation, when it reached him, was an ear-shattering concussion. He could feel a rush of air suck his lungs empty. Events seemed to slow down, noise was a physical thing, but remote. He regarded Han's broken, twisted body without seeing anything out of the ordinary. The paraffin lamp lay shattered; a tongue of orange flame followed a trail of spilled fuel across the floor.

Suzie's scream was cut off by a cascade of ceiling beams and thatch that formed a shoulder-high mound of debris. Awareness returned to Kyle with a rush. That was one helluvan explosion, he thought. A regular bomb—bomb! Could it be an air raid? There hadn't been any kind of warning sirens, but . . . his mind sprang into high gear. Escape. Han's rifle—he'd seen it still beneath the guard's lifeless form just before the roof caved in. He started tearing at the rubble with bare hands.

Suddenly Kyle could feel heat coming from his left side. At first it felt good, then uncomfortable. Smoke burned his eyes and nose. A quick glance established that the broken lamp had ignited tinder-dry thatch. A fire of blowtorch intensity was engulfing the room. Kyle covered his face with his forearm and backed away.

A series of hoarse, animal-like cries from behind him interrupted his bitter frustration at not being able to recover the rifle that he associated with escape. He turned. The door leading into the adjoining room hung drunkenly from one hinge. The cries came from inside. Kyle kicked the broken door aside and stepped over a heap of more ceiling beams and thatch.

Fire hadn't yet reached this room, but by its rosy glow Kyle could see the old man struggling to pull a jumble of wood and straw away from one corner. In a near-hysterical state, the man was incapable of concerted effort. My God, Kyle realized, his wife is under there—he could see half of one withered arm protruding from the wreckage.

The explosion had demolished half of the far wall. Cool, dark openness beckoned. Freedom lay ten steps away. Already a cacophony of confused voices and pounding feet filled the night. He could be blocks away before any sort of order was restored.

About to leap toward the opening, he glanced at the tableau barely visible in the fire's angry glow. The old man turned. Tears coursed in rivulets down wrinkled cheeks, his keening lament plainly audible above the crackling blaze next door. Kyle took in the situation with one swift glance. The woman was pinned by a six-inch peeled log that lay propped against the remaining wall. Lifting it six inches would free her. He sprang to the old man's side.

Yelling instructions he knew the man couldn't comprehend, he motioned to pull the inert woman free when he moved the log. He crouched until he had the roof beam across his back, then started to straighten. The massive timber didn't yield. Kyle took a deep breath and tried again. Pain shot through his injured shoulder like a white-hot stiletto. About to collapse, he felt movement. An inch. Another massive heave and the hundred-year-old timber yielded a noticeable distance. From the tail of his eye, he saw the woman's frail body slide free.

Trembling in every muscle, Kyle's first inclination was to lie prone and recover. Survival instinct intervened, however. This place is gonna go up like a goddamned skyrocket, he thought. Struggling to his feet, he slipped his good arm beneath the unconscious woman. With the old man's help he half carried, half dragged her through the wall's gaping breach.

The courtyard was a confused swirl of activity. Kyle turned to try to tell the old man he was leaving. He found himself confronting a steely, unwavering gaze. Total understanding flowed like a tangible current. Kyle didn't protest when directed to help carry the woman away from the scene.

After stumbling four blocks along a dark alley, the man opened a heavy plank door. He seemed to know his way, and shortly an oil lamp cast its feeble glow over an austerely furnished cottage's two-room interior. As Kyle helped lower the wife to a sleeping mat, her eyes flickered open. The old man kissed her wan cheek and, with obvious reluctance to leave, hustled Kyle outside. He wrenched open the door to a crude lean-to and motioned for Kyle to enter.

The roof was barely high enough for Kyle to stand, and the smell of fish emanating from a pile of netting was overpowering. The old man spoke at length, then gathered Kyle into an embrace whose strength belied his advanced years. Kyle sank onto the heap of malodorous, impromptu bedding and passed out. His last thought was: You know, I've heard of ESP, and never believed in it. But so help me God, I understood everything he was saying.

11 April 1951
Tachikawa Base Hospital

"So I hid out in that lean-to for two days. Stink? I'll never eat another fish, so help me." Kyle eased the pillow behind him to a more comfortable position and continued. "My shoulder was killing me, and I paid the price for all that water I drank. But the old woman, and her daughter-in-law, gave me royal treatment. I'm sure I ate half of their available food and they changed hot packs on my shoulder every hour."

Ross leaned against the wall and listened intently. Janet, seated in the room's only chair, muttered, "How wonderfully kind of them."

"That second night, the son came for me—it was his house the old man took me to. In the few words of English he could muster, my dozen words of Korean, and lots of sign language, he told me he was taking me aboard his fishing boat. I was trusting the family completely by then, and went with him gladly. I hid in the boat's bottom with those stinking damn nets again and we sailed about dawn.

"Once we were in open water, he let me come on deck and motioned to the little dory tied onto the stern. He made whirling motions with his hands, and imitated the sound of a helicopter perfectly. He gave me a keg of water and a ball of rice, then pointed me south."

"You mean he just abandoned you out there in the middle of the ocean?" Janet asked.

"Well, not the ocean exactly—the Yellow Sea." Kyle chuckled. "Anyway, he knew that planes off the carrier parked out there swept the area on a regular basis. So I sat there until well past noon. Miserable? My damn shoulder was killing me, nothing to eat but rice and warm water, and a little scrap of sailcloth for shelter. But about the time I was ready to give up, here they came. Two lovely Corsairs, right down on the deck. They circled me, and a few minutes later I heard the Air Rescue choppers. So here I am, hale and hearty.

"There's one other thing, however. Janet, I'm sure Ross knows this, but most of what I've told you is confidential. A funny thing, I was lost from the time I punched out, but I'm not supposed to advertise where I was— which I still don't know for sure—or how I got picked up. It wouldn't be too hard for the NKPA to figure out which people helped me. So keep it in the family, okay?"

"Of course," Janet replied. "God forbid that anything happen to *them*. What wonderful people—to risk their lives to save yours."

"Don't be gushy," Ross observed dryly. "Kyle passed up a chance to escape and damn near got killed saving the wife. The old man knew that and was repaying a debt, that's all. To that time, they were hard-line Commies, you can bet. How did that NKPA lieutenant know to put in there otherwise?"

"Ross!"

"Okay, so he didn't have to. But when you're passing out bouquets, be evenhanded. Were you ever able to talk to the old man again, Kyle?"

"Oddly enough, no. He never showed up again. But after the war, I'm gonna try to look him up. Maybe, as you say, he *was* a hard-line Commie. But he was sure as hell sincere."

"Good morning, folks; Colonel." A white-smocked man with a stethoscope draped around his neck called from the door. "How're we feeling this morning?"

"Fine, Doc," Kyle replied. "Ready to get out of this place, in fact."

"You're lying through your teeth, Wilson." The doctor chuckled. "You *don't* feel fine, and I know it. That shoulder feels like an abscessed tooth. Twenty-four hours without a pain pill and you'll be climbing the wall. That's what I came to talk to you about. You have a severe separation—done when you were straining to lift that beam with an already dislocated joint, no doubt. So we're going to send you back to the States, where you can get some sophisticated surgery. Mrs. Colyer, if you could excuse us a moment, I'll run a quick checkup before I sign Kyle's release."

The perfunctory exam required only a few minutes. "I'm not sure I like the sound of this," Kyle said after the doctor left. "You don't suppose—?"

"That you could have a permanent disability?" Ross finished the question. "Frankly, I don't think you need be overly concerned. I learned to read doctors' faces when I was sweating out a full recovery. Trust me, this guy is leveling with you. At least *he* doesn't see anything that would keep you off flying status.

"But that's the one thing about this business that's so damned frustrating—and something you can't do a thing about. You take your life in your hands on every mission—then bust yourself up doing something totally unrelated to combat.

I went through six months of hell after that accident at Langley. If it hadn't been for Janet . . . Well, looking back, I can see that that ordeal set our marriage—which didn't get off to a very good start—in concrete. War is hard on marriages, Kyle. All I can say is that you have a winner in Terri. Keep that in mind while you're sweating this thing out."

Kyle gave Ross a quizzical glance. "You're in a funny mood this morning. Something bothering you?"

"I have an appointment with General Sims at two o'clock. I'm sure it has to do with reassignment. General officers don't usually do this sort of thing personally. I gotta believe it will involve a decision—one that will require keeping what I've just told you in mind. And, yeah, it bothers me."

2 May 1951
Tokyo

Ross adjusted himself to a more comfortable position as the Boeing Stratocruiser's pilot finished his engine run-up. A pensive look crossed his face as he watched an F-80 take the runway ahead of them. I'm spending a helluva lot more time as a passenger than as a pilot these days, he thought.

Wistfully, he recalled the thrill of takeoff, the excitement of the chase, the satisfaction of knowing you're the best pilot, flying the best airplanes in the world. But then there were those 2:00 A.M. wake-ups—preflighting with a flashlight while crouched against blowing snow; on landing, the deep fatigue induced by tension, g-forces, and bone-numbing cold.

He regarded Janet's head, resting on his shoulder, with a fond look. She'd taken the move better than he'd expected.

"In a way, I think I'm just as happy to become wife of an eight-to-five headquarters officer. I haven't touched my manuscript since I came over here." That's when she said, "By the way, I saw my doctor today."

"Oh?" he'd inquired casually. "Everything okay?"

"More or less. I'm okay, but doc told me the poor rabbit died."

Ross sat in stunned silence for several moments. Then he started shaking with silent laughter.

Janet turned her face toward him. "What's so funny?"

"Mom and Pop Colyer. I can't get over it."

"You'll get used to it. The flight attendant told me our first refueling stop is at a place called Cold Bay, in the Aleutian Islands. A ten-hour flight, which gives us lots of time to talk."

"Oh, great. What about? The modern way to raise babies?"

"Among other things. But you can start by explaining why you turned down command of one of the new B-47 squadrons to take the job of military attaché in Moscow.The officers' wives' club underground is alive and well, Full Colonel Colyer."

Glossary of Acronyms

AA Anti-aircraft [gun]

AC Aircraft Commander

ADC Air Defence Command

ADF Automatic Direction Finder [Radio Navigation Aid]

ADIZ Air Defense Identification Zone [air space surrounding U.S. boundaries inside which approaching aircraft must be positively identified.]

AFIT Air Force Institute of Technology

APO Army Post Office [Discreet address of overseas military personnel]

ATC Air Transport Command

BG Brigadier General

BOQ Bachelor Officer Quarters

BSU Bomb Scoring Unit [Radar]

CBC Continental Broadcasting Company

CBI China-Burma-India [Theater of Operations]

CFC Central Fire Control

CG Commanding General

CIA Central Intelligence Agency

CO Commanding Officer

CPA Chinese People's Army

CPR Chinese People's Republic

CW Continuous Wave [unmodulated radio transmission]

DCS OPS Deputy Chief of Staff Operations

DFC Distinguished Flying Cross

DNIF Duty Not Including Flying [medical reasons]

DOD Department Of Defense

DSC Distinguished Service Cross

ETA Estimated Time of Arrival

FEAF Far East Air Force

GCA Ground Control Approach [radar]

GCI Ground Control Intercept [radar]

GPU Ground Power Unit

HVAR High Velocity Aerial Rocket

IFR Instrument Flight Rules

INS International News Service
IP Used to designate both an Instructor Pilot and Initial Point on bomb run
JAG Judge Advocate General
JATO Jet Assisted Take Off
JCS Joint Chiefs of Staff
JP Justice of the Peace
JSF Joint Strike Force
KGB Soviet Intelligence Bureau
MARS Military Amateur Radio Service
MG Machine Gun
MPI Main Point of Impact [bomb drop]
MPQ Designation of one type navigational radar
MSR Main Supply Route
NCO Noncommissioned Officer
NKPA North Korean People's Army
NKVD Soviet Secret Police
NOTAM Notice To Airman
OD Used to designate both Officer of the Day and Olive Drab uniform color
OSS Office of Strategic Services
PDRK Peoples Democratic Republic of Korea
PIO Public Information Office
PLA People's Liberation Army
PSP Pierced Steel Planking [Temporary Runway]
RAF Royal Air Force [British]
RO Radio Operator
ROK Royal Army of Korea [South] → REPUBLIC OF KOREA
RON Remain Over Night
SHORAN Short Range Air Navigation [Electronic]
TAC Tactical Air Command
TDY Temporary Duty
TPT Tail Pipe Temperature
TWX Electrical message transmission system
UR Unsatisfactory Report
USAFE United States Air Forces Europe
USIS United States Information Service

VFR Visual Flight Rules
VHF Very High Frequency [radio]
VMI Virginia Military Institute
VOR VHF Omni-directional Range on very high radio frequencies [Radio Navigation Aid]
YAK Soviet aircraft manufactures designation [YAK-9]